REBEL SPY

ALSO BY VERONICA ROSSI

Under the Never Sky

Through the Ever Night

Into the Still Blue

★

Riders

Seeker

REBEL SPY

VERONICA ROSSI

DELACORTE PRESS

Text copyright © 2020 by Veronica Rossi
Jacket photo copyright © 2020 by Rekha Garton/Arcangel Images

All rights reserved. Published in the United States by Delacorte Press, an imprint of Random House Children's Books, a division of Penguin Random House LLC, New York.

Delacorte Press is a registered trademark and the colophon is a trademark of Penguin Random House LLC.

Visit us on the Web! GetUnderlined.com

Educators and librarians, for a variety of teaching tools, visit us at RHTeachersLibrarians.com

Library of Congress Cataloging-in-Publication Data
Names: Rossi, Veronica, author.
Title: Rebel spy / Veronica Rossi.
Description: First edition. | New York : Delacorte Press, [2020] | Audience: Ages 12 up | Audience: Grades 7–9 | Summary: In 1776, fifteen-year-old Francisca escapes a dangerous life in the Bahamas by posing as a wealthy shipwreck victim, and soon finds herself a spy for George Washington in New York.
Identifiers: LCCN 2019025641 | ISBN 978-1-5247-7122-5 (hardcover) | ISBN 978-1-5247-7125-6 (library binding) | ISBN 978-1-5247-7123-2 (ebook)
Subjects: CYAC: Impersonation—Fiction. | Spies—Fiction. | Social classes—Fiction. | Love—Fiction. | United States—History—Revolution, 1775–1783–Fiction.
Classification: LCC PZ7.R7216 Reb 2020 | DDC [Fic]—dc23

The text of this book is set in 10.6-point Apolline Std.
Interior design by Stephanie Moss

Printed in the United States of America
10 9 8 7 6 5 4 3 2 1
First Edition

FOR EVERY 355.

During the American Revolution, General George Washington employed a ring of spies in and around New York City, the headquarters for the British war effort in North America. These spies identified themselves in their letters by code numbers. One was known as "355," which stood for "lady."

To date, her true identity remains unknown.

The waves have rolled upon me,
the billows are repeatedly broken over me,
yet I am not sunk down.

—Mercy Otis Warren

PRISONER

★

I'd swum with deadly sharks and stolen from deadlier men.
I'd survived hurricanes, war, and even love—but I didn't
know if I'd survive this.

I pulled myself off the floorboards, my legs shaking as I stood.
The cabin spun around me. I drew a deep breath to steady myself,
smelling pine tar and bilgewater, tensing as the door swung open.

Two redcoats hurried inside. One carried shears; the other,
a length of rope. They were big men, filling the cabin with their
bright regimentals and shocked stares. They obviously hadn't expected to find a young lady in a torn silk gown, bleeding from a
head wound.

"We have orders to cut your hair," said the one with the rope.
He cleared his throat and raised the rope higher. "If you resist, I
shall be forced to use this."

I swallowed thickly. I had an idea what this meant. "I won't
resist." I stepped forward. "Go ahead. Cut it."

The man with the shears hesitated, then gathered my hair in
a clumsy swipe and sliced. My long locks came away in his hand.

1

He blinked at them like he was confused, then tossed them down and carried on hastily, cutting so close at times he nicked my scalp and left my eyes watering.

As my dark curls tumbled to the floor, years of dance assemblies and fine dinners flashed before my eyes. I shut them and imagined I was feeling Mama's gentle hands on me instead of this stranger's. Mama, singing in Spanish as she teased out my tangles with the patience of an entire ocean.

What would she think of this? I'd promised her I'd find a safe, respectable life—and done the exact opposite.

"Why?" whispered the man with the rope. I opened my eyes. The candle on the floor guttered and popped, making his shadow writhe behind him. He licked his lips. "Why are you here? Are you—are you *a spy*?"

"Shut up, Wilcox," said the other one. Then he glanced at me like he wanted to know, too.

"Tell me where I'm being sent and I'll answer." I already thought I knew, but I needed to be sure.

They shared a look.

"Go on, Wilcox," said the one with the shears. "Tell her."

"*You* tell her, Bradley."

Bradley lowered the shears and exhaled, his breath sour with the smell of tobacco. "There's whispers amongst the men you're going to the *Jersey* prison hulk."

My knees nearly crumpled beneath me. *Prison.* I'd guessed right. But even worse—the *Jersey*. Where men were sent to die. Where no women were sent at all. I'd be the first one. The only one.

"Your turn," Bradley said, impatient for my answer.

"No. I'm not a spy," I lied, though I could've told the truth. I'd been caught; the worst had already happened. But I didn't owe these men anything. Certainly not what I valued most. "This is all just a misunderstanding," I added, and in spite of everything, I felt a smile tug at my lips.

Bradley snorted.

Snip went the shears.

When he was done, I ran my hand over my scalp, learning a part of myself for the first time. I felt sharper. Honed. I could feel the air around me the same way I used to feel the ocean when I dove.

The marine with the rope—Wilcox—stepped outside and came back with a bundle of folded clothing.

"You're to change into these." He set the bundle on the berth, then turned away. Bradley went to stand beside him.

I stared at their backs for a moment, letting a wave of fear pass. Hands trembling, I unlaced my gown and petticoats and let them slip off. My stays laced in back, though.

"I need help," I said.

"I'll go get—"

"No." I knew who they'd bring and I couldn't bear to see him again. I went to Bradley, turning my back to him. "Cut the laces."

"Lord forgive me," he muttered. Then he sliced a path up my spine.

The pressure of the stays gave way and my lungs eased fully open. I stepped away and tossed them on the berth, then pulled my shift over my head. As it billowed to my feet, gooseflesh rippled over me and I had the strange realization this was my first time bare in the presence of a man. That it was *two* men and nothing at all how I'd hoped it would be.

I pulled on the shirt and trousers, the ozenbrig material rough as a cat's tongue. Such a part of my past—and now my future. There were leather shoes as well, dirty and worn, but a decent fit.

"I'm ready," I said. Another lie, but a strange calm had befallen me. I felt as quiet inside as winter. I was trapped—but freed from decisions. From calculations and lies. All I could do now was continue.

The men turned.

Bradley shook his head. "There's no being ready for where you're going."

"Miss . . ." Wilcox's brow pinched with distress. "Whatever you may have done to find yourself here, surely it can be *un-done?*"

I thought of Townsend and the intelligence I'd given him. "I hope not."

I'd given up everything for it.

I had given my very life.

CHAPTER 1

WRECKER

★

West End, Grand Bahama Island
August 1776

The last time I ever went wrecking was August of my fifteenth year. I was still just a wild girl then, living in West End, not a thought in my head about war yet, nor about spying. My mind was only on Mama.

She'd passed on to heaven only a week earlier, but in my imagination, she was still breathing. Still singing to herself as she stirred the pepper pot soup. Still telling me stories about her girlhood days in España as she worked a comb through my sea-brined hair.

When Sewel came to fetch me to go wrecking—Sewel was Mama's husband, not my real papa—he found me in the garden pulling weeds and daydreaming of the great castle in Baiona that Mama used to run through barefoot when she was my age.

"Francisca," he said, in the same gravelly voice he used with the goats and the swine.

I set my spade down and shaded my eyes as I looked up. With the afternoon sun over his shoulders, I couldn't see his face—only that he was already swaying. "Yes, sir?"

"Storm's coming in fast, and the currents is swirling round *Valparaíso* wreck." He said it *Val-prizo*. Not how Mama said it, the right way, like our Spanish forebears. "Get your diving trousers on and don't make me wait, else you'll be swimming out there, understand?"

"Yes, sir."

He leaned over and spat tobacco so close to me I could almost taste it. Then he turned down the beach trail, grunting with every step he took on his foot with the missing toes.

I tugged my gardening apron off and hurried home, eagerness and dread tumbling in my stomach. I loved diving wrecks more than anything, but it meant spending time alone with Sewel.

Pushing through the door, I stopped to breathe in the last traces of Mama's scent—a mix of sweet coconut and the sour sweat that had come when she'd taken to bed for good. My gaze went to the empty mattress, then to the dirty pots stacked by the basin and the sand dusting the planks beneath my feet. I'd always taken pride in this house. It was made of salvaged ship's timbers, puzzled together with pine logs I'd helped cut down myself. At night, with whisper of the surf drifting in, it felt like living inside a great conch shell. But since losing Mama, nothing felt the same.

Kneeling before the trunk, I found the trousers and shirt I used for diving and changed into them, leaving my jumper and sweaty shift where they fell. Then I sprinted to the beach, my stride long and smooth without petticoats slowing me.

As I came through the trees, I saw thick clouds bunching on the horizon and whispered a quick prayer they'd stay there. In

West End, two things that never stayed away long enough were hurricanes and hunger.

Sewel had already gotten the wherry past the breakers. Two other boats bobbed out there as well—our usual wrecking crew. Also every inhabitant on our island. Jonah Baines and his boys were pressed together in their little red skiff, three heads of equal height gleaming like polished copper. Moses Wiggins and his daughter Mercy floated closer to shore, Mercy waving when she saw me.

I smiled and waved back as I broke the first waves with my feet. Then I dove, and all I could hear was the ocean's singing, the bubbles and waves as they rose up and blended with my breaths. With every kick and stroke I felt a little stronger. By the time I reached the wherry, I'd shed some of my sadness and felt halfway to being me again.

I grabbed the gunwale to pull myself in.

Sewel's hand came down on my wrist. "Molasses would've got here first, Francisca."

"Yes, sir."

He didn't let go. I knew better than to meet his bleary eyes, so I kicked in place and stared at the red feather on his new round-brim hat. The very day Mama went in the ground, Sewel had sailed for Nassau, returning only that morning. While I'd poured my tears into her pillow, he'd gone hat shopping.

At last he let me go. I climbed aboard and checked that my shirt covered me in the right places, though there wasn't much to cover. Then I squeezed the water from my braids.

Sewel turned to speak to Mr. Baines, making his voice loud

enough so Moses Wiggins could hear as well. Moses and Mercy were runaways and Sewel never spoke to them direct. "Tide's an iron hook today. Best we run past Memory Rock, then veer north."

With that, the men got to raising the sails and setting a course, except Moses, who had no sail and had to row his way out there.

Soon as we got underway, Sewel unstoppered a bottle of rum and leaned back, resting his arm on the tiller. I could see the silvery letter M branded on the brawn of his thumb. It was Mercy who told me what that letter stood for—manslayer—but I knew what it meant long before I learned the word for it.

I turned fore and trailed my fingers through the water. With the waves rippling and my dark braid hanging over my shoulder, I could almost imagine it was Mama's face staring back at me instead of mine. Fathoms below, an angelfish spooked and disappeared into a bed of whip seaweed. Over on the Baines boat, the boys starting singing songs about Captain Teach and the good days of pirating gone by, when earning your daily bread was as easy as taking it from someone else, while Sewel and Mr. Baines called back and forth about the war with the rebellious American colonies.

Wrecking was how we earned our daily bread. We helped ships that had run up on sandbars or reefs as they cruised through the Bahama Channel—sandbars and reefs we knew better than anyone. If the ship couldn't be kedged back to deep water, we hauled away the cargo for a share. In rarer times, when the ship was a total loss and sank, we dove for its sunken spoils, sometimes uncovering them for years after the wreck itself.

I dove for sunken spoils. Sewel never did the diving because of his missing toes, he claimed, which made no sense to me. Fish swam, didn't they?

Sewel had told me once how he'd lost them on a burning merchant ship when a fiery yard fell and smashed half his foot. He'd nearly been killed that day, he'd said, but God looked out for drunks, fools, and sailors. God must've loved Sewel fierce 'cause he was all three.

Like he was peering into my disloyal thoughts, Sewel stretched out his leg and ran his foot against my shin, the thick scars scratching me like bark.

I pulled away, my heart jumping in my chest.

Sewel shook his head at me. Then he tipped the bottle back and drank.

=★=

By the time we got to the *Valparaíso*, the empty bottle rattled round the bottom of the wherry and thunder rumbled in the distance. The tide was so high that only the tip of the old wreck's mainmast stuck out, like a cross staked right in the sea.

"Less go, Francisca," Sewel slurred. He tossed the anchor overboard and spat at the sea to bring us luck. "We en't got much time."

I checked the rope belting my trousers. The sea flashed like pewter, dull and dark. I always felt a little dizzy when I couldn't see to the bottom, not knowing what awaited me down there.

"Get diving." Sewel pulled off his hat and wiped his sweaty forehead. The rum had brought the blood into his eyes. "And best not disappoint. I en't got a drop of patience today, understand?"

Anger rose inside me like smoke. "Yes, sir."

9

Over on the Baines boat, Owen and Daniel Baines shoved each other and laughed as they dove in. Mercy and Moses were already in the water and their tiny boat ran up and down the swells empty. I sucked in a few breaths, readying my lungs, a feeling of strength and daring filling me.

"Sewel, sir?" I said, looking over my shoulder. "I was just wonderin' . . . you gonna have any patience tomorrow?" He lunged across the wherry to grab me, but I leapt into the air—and crashed into freedom.

Kicking hard, I swam to Mercy.

"You ought not provoke him, Frannie," she said as I reached her. "You can't say things like that no more."

Mercy was thirteen—two years younger than me, but ten years smarter. I'd waited years for a friend in West End. When I'd finally gotten one, I'd gotten the *best* one.

"I just did and here I am, still breathing." She didn't laugh, so I said, "He won't remember. He finished a whole bottle of kill-devil on the way here."

"What if he does remember?" Our knees bumped as we treaded water. "You're *his* daughter now, Frannie. His alone."

My throat cinched up like a belt. For weeks I'd been avoiding that very truth, hiding in my memories of Mama instead, but Mercy was right. Sewel loved to torment me, but when I'd lost my patience before, Mama had been there to stand between us. Without her, I had no idea how I'd survive. "Don't worry, Mercy. I en't afraid of that birdbrain," I said, sinking my voice to a drawl, like Sewel's.

Her eyes slid to him. "Birds are smarter than that man. If he was a bird, he'd fly backward."

I grinned. "Probably barking, too."

We clasped our hands together and drew three deep breaths. Then we let go and dove.

I kicked down, plunging fathom by fathom, the hush of the sea seeping into my mind and my muscles. By the time I touched the slippery wood ribs of the *Valparaíso*, the boats were just blurry shadows on the surface. With the pestering drag of the tide, I knew I wouldn't have much time for searching, but there was no use moaning about it. I ran my hand along the hull, kicking to the seabed; then I rummaged through the sand for whatever felt solid, and pushed off.

I knew as I kicked up I had nothing good. Bits of coral and shells, only. Most of the *Valparaíso*'s treasures were long gone, but a big storm like this might uncover overlooked finds, like shoe buckles or spoons or even coins. *Tesoros del tiempo*, Mama had called them. Treasures brought by time.

"Well?" Sewel said as I broke the surface. He'd moved over to Mr. Baines's boat, and they were sharing a fresh bottle.

"Nothing, sir." I held up my empty hands to show him, then dove before he could holler at me.

A few more searches turned up a rusted hammer, a few nails. Everything slick with the grit and spit of the sea. Nothing worth an egg.

I moved on and began to search the ship itself, swimming through its hatches and twisting through the hold as I peered into silty crates and reached inside murky hogsheads. Soon my mind opened and spun into daydreams, turning the nail that grabbed at my shirttails into a cutpurse, the eel peering from inside a barrel into a demon. Every inch of this ship had told me a story at one time or another, from the ballast bricks, which had surely once made castles, to the rope tied to the prow, which drifted like a string in search of its missing kite.

Mama used to say that some daydreamers built castles in the sky, but I built my *castillos en el mar*. I knew of no better place to open my mind than fathoms below.

After an hour or so, Mercy and I met behind her papa's boat. My eyes burned from the salt and my legs and arms felt heavy as bricks.

"I found plenty of sand." I waited for her to say she'd found plenty of salt water. Mercy and I never found nothing.

"We have to get out, Frannie. Look."

I blinked my pickled eyes and followed her gaze to the black clouds. "You think it's a hurricane?"

"Not the storm. *Look*." She pointed just beyond the *Valparaíso*, where the sea's surface rippled.

My breath caught as a great fin sliced up.

Shark. Biggest one I'd ever seen. Long as the wherry and near as wide.

We'd swum near sharks plenty of times, but never one this excited, pushing so high at times I could see its gills.

"Mercy, come on," Moses said, reaching down to help her into the boat.

I didn't waste a second; I swam for the wherry, fear turning me into an arrow. In seconds, I reached it and heaved myself aboard, landing with a thud.

Sewel snored away like a beast, his big body slumped into the curve of the wherry's stern. Trembling with tiredness and fear, I hauled up the anchor and set it inside the well. The shark still circled nearby, and every rumble of thunder shook the air in my lungs. I grabbed the lines to raise the sail, more than ready to get home.

"Did I say it was time to leave?"

My every muscle tensed. I let go of the line and turned. "No, sir."

Sewel pulled out of his slump. "Sit."

I found myself sinking onto the thwart and grabbing the wood beneath me to keep steady.

He picked his hat up from the well where it'd fallen, and took his time brushing the water and sand away before setting it back on his head. "It's past time we discuss how things are gonna be now, with your mama gone." He rubbed his chin and stared at me, heedless of the lightning bolts slicing across sky. "You are an oddity, Francisca," he said. "An aberration. You have no fortune, nor any beauty. You have no gentleness in your heart, nor a wisp of feminine softness. What you *do* have is a terrible temper and an odious lack of refinement. Added to the disgrace of having a fallen woman for a mother, you got no chance of ever luring an upright man to take you for a wife. So I have decided that *I* will save you. I will make the sacrifice, in your mama's memory, and take you as mine. En't nothing wrong with it, as we en't blood, and I'm nearer in age to you than I was to her, so . . ." He lifted his shoulders. "En't nothing wrong nor unnatural with it."

A warm sickness pushed into my throat and I felt myself falling back. Plunging into a cloud of silence. There was no logic, no sense to his words, but I'd expected this. I'd seen this coming. For months, since Mama had taken to bed, I'd seen hints in his eyes and how they followed me. I'd felt it in his hands, which had

13

found me at any excuse. I'd been dreading this—but I still felt shock. I still couldn't understand it.

"Well? En't you got nothing to say?"

"Yes, sir. I do," I heard myself answer. "I will never be your wife, Sewel. Never."

"Hmm." He nodded slowly. Then his gaze slid over to the shark and the air rushed out of my lungs.

Sewel reached into the bait box for his jackknife. He opened it and looked real slowly at one side of the blade, then turned to the other, pondering that one, the branded *M* shining on his thumb all the while. "You're going back in, Frannie—that en't the question," he said, his voice sweeter sounding than I'd ever heard it. "You brang it upon yourself with your defiance. The only question is whether you want to be bleedin' when you do or not."

I was praying for God's protection as I lowered myself into the water, inch by terrible inch. And crying, too, though crying only ever turned him wickeder. But I hadn't a prayer of holding back my tears.

It took all my strength to let go of the wherry. Every bit of bravery I had. With the clouds reflecting on the sea, I couldn't see the shark till it broke the surface. Here. There. Close—then *much* too close.

"Well, Frannie?" Sewel leaned over the rail, staring down at me with his rum-bleary eyes. "You gonna learn to govern your tongue?"

"Y-y-yes, sir," I stammered as I kicked furiously.

"And?"

"And I'm sorry for back-talking you!"

14

"Lying's a terrible sin. An abomination unto the Lord."

"But I en't lying!" The water shimmered near me. Any moment, teeth would slice into my legs. "I'm sorry!"

"You *are* lying." Sewel's eyes narrowed. "But I am feeling generously today. You are forgiven." He reached down to help me aboard. "See, Francisca? Things can be good between us."

CHAPTER 2

DEEPER WATER

★

Afew days later, we sailed to the *Tumbado* wreck, once again hoping good fortune would find us. Two hours into diving, the only thing that had found me was disappointment.

I rubbed my stinging eyes and sucked on the cut on my thumb that I'd gotten from a broken piece of pottery—the only thing I'd uncovered. The afternoon had brought thunderheads rolling in. Sunlight sliced through them in long beams that roamed over the sea.

Dedos de dios, Mama had called them. God's fingers.

Sewel and Mr. Baines had tied their boats together and were carrying on about a battle in South Carolina colony in which we'd *lost* to the *despicable, cowardly, treasonous rebels.* God help us. I knew I shouldn't risk angering Sewel—I'd begun to think he'd forgotten our conversation, to hope it'd just been the rum talking—but he looked occupied for now, and I saw a chance I couldn't pass up.

I drew a breath and swam for deeper water. Though Sewel had taught me to dive, I always felt it was these clear waters that guided me. Sometimes I heard whispers when I swam, telling me what to do. Voices of the Lucayos who'd lived on Grand Bahama long before we did. They'd been able to dive for a whole hour on a single breath, according to Mercy. We hadn't managed that yet.

With the seabed dropping beneath me, I shored up my lungs once more. Then I swam down, down, down, plunging one fathom at a time, till suddenly, I felt the sea gently wrap round me and there was no rising anymore, no sinking. Just floating, there in the belly of the ocean.

I'd reached it—the seventh fathom. My dreaming depth.

The whole world far away, I stretched out my arms and set my imagination loose.

Sometimes it wandered to Mama's stories and I daydreamed of the castle in Baiona, or of the time she'd seen a tiger in a street market in Cádiz. But today, I went into my own imaginings.

I saw myself as I was—small and square as a boy. Big wide eyes and an "impudent nose," as Sewel called it. My dark hair tied back, but still falling in my face. But instead of my diving garments, I wore a fine blue coat with a ruffled white neck stock and sleeves dripping with lace. I stood at the bow of a grand ship, a spyglass tucked under my arm, as I guided it over every inch of the globe's waters.

For as long as I could hold my breath, I went on adventures and I felt free.

=★=

The clouds opened as I swam back to Mercy. In a matter of moments, the swells rose to six feet and the sea sizzled with a furious rain.

We met behind her papa's boat, where we listened to Sewel and Mr. Baines shouting at each other. Instead of heading for shelter as we ought to have been, they were arguing over whose bright idea it had been to come out this far, exposing us to such foul weather.

"Sewel's never had a bright idea in all his life," I said.

"He's never even had a *dull* idea." Mercy wiped the rain from her eyes. Our knees bumped underwater, talking to each other as we did. "Shame he en't more like my papa."

I'd had the same thought a dozen times myself. In the boat above us, Moses was busy stashing conches in a crate. As we dove for hidden treasures, he dove for dinner, which struck me as wiser. "The real shame is he en't more like yesterday," I said.

Mercy wrinkled her nose. "How's that?"

I grinned. "Gone forever. Never to be seen again."

Mercy laughed, showing all her pretty teeth. Her papa looked down from the boat with a scolding glance that seemed rather mild to me, but Moses never did look mean. He had a face like he was always about to tell you a sad story, even when he smiled.

"C'mon, Mercy. 'Fore the storm trap us out here." He helped her aboard. Then he rowed for West End, his strokes steady as wings in spite of the choppiness of the sea.

"Fran!" Sewel shouted, spotting me in the water. "Get over here!"

I swam over and hoisted myself into the wherry, huddling my shivering body into the curve of the bow.

Sewel shook his head, disappointed at my lack of sturdiness. "Wiggins find anything?"

"No, sir."

"He was diving the wreck and didn't find a thing?"

"Yes, sir."

"Useless." He cast a hateful glance at the retreating boat; then he reefed the sail and weighed anchor, sure and swift, like seafaring was a dance he knew all the steps to.

He was made for the sea, Sewel was. Everything I learned about sailing and wrecking, he'd taught me. For that, I had to be thankful. Mama had told me once that as a boy he'd dreamed of serving in the Royal Navy. I couldn't imagine Sewel as a boy with dreams. But I *could* picture him fighting in a tavern over a spilt drink and killing somebody, which was how he'd earned the M on his thumb. By reciting a Bible verse and getting the brand, he was saved from swinging by a rope round his neck.

"You trying to burst your eyes out your head?" he asked as he took the tiller.

"No, sir," I replied.

"No sir, yes sir, no sir," he piped, shaking his head in disgust. "How about making use of that owl stare and keep track of Baines, if you'd be so kind? I won't have him blamin' me for getting lost out here, top of everything else."

"*Yes, sir,*" I said, and turned to the beating wind.

The Baineses' boat crashed along to our leeward, rising and sinking behind the swells. Moses and Mercy had pulled ahead and were fading into the billows of rain.

"Well?" Sewel hollered behind me. "You see them?"

"Yes, sir. I see them." My real papa was named James Morris and he never hollered. He'd been a simple shoemaker in New Providence, where he and Mama had met. He'd died nine years earlier, when I was six. Sometimes I wished I'd paid closer mind

19

to him, as I only remembered little things about him, like his brown-stained hands and the little gap between his two front teeth that I inherited, but I hadn't known any better back then. I'd always thought he'd be there. After he died, I got wiser and made sure to remember everything Mama did and said. Now all my memories of her twinkled in my mind like stars.

The storm worsened by the minute. Soon, it proved to be what I'd most feared—a hurricane. Gales screamed in my ears. Waves fell upon the wherry like stumbling giants. Bursts of spindrift spit into the air, the droplets like pins against my face. I lost sight of Mercy's boat and prayed she'd made it safe back to West End.

"*Fran!*" Sewel yelled over the howling wind. He tossed a pail at me. "Get bailing!"

I did as he said, bailing water as fast as I could, but every new wave undid my efforts. We were in real danger of being swamped.

"*Sails!* Ho, Baines! *Sails!*"

I looked up, startled by Sewel's shouts, and found him staring into the distance. I squinted, trying to see what he saw, but night had fallen and I could scarce tell the sea apart from the sky. Finally, I spotted it and gasped.

Amid the angry waves, I saw a brig in a terribly wounded state. The poor vessel's mainmast had snapped in half and the top had fallen into the sea. The ship was heeling dreadfully to that side, pulled by the weight of the downed sail.

That wasn't all. It had run up on a reef, one that had grounded dozens of ships before. I could think of no other reason why it'd turned broadside, making itself vulnerable to the surging seas.

I looked at Sewel. He was still staring at the troubled ship.

"Mr. Baines didn't hear you." His boat had kept heading for home.

"Just as well."

I didn't understand. "But we're going to help . . . aren't we?"

"Now, why would we do that?"

My body went cold all the way through.

As we drew closer, I couldn't tear my eyes away. The brig *was* bottoming against the reef. With every wave that passed, its rigging and sails shuddered. Over the storm's howling, I heard the ship's bell tolling desperately. Someone was ringing it hard enough to shake the rafters in heaven.

I turned back to Sewel. "They need help. We could lead them to a safer depth."

He turned to me, his eyes murderous. "It en't right to meddle in others' fates, Francisca."

"But . . ." I gripped the gunwale so tight, the skin on my knuckles burned. There had to be dozens of sailors aboard that ship. I couldn't let them die. Maybe Sewel was a murderer, but not me.

I picked up the oars from the well.

"Put those down."

I slid them into the locks.

"You got one more chance, Francisca. Put those down, or I'll—"

I dug the paddles into the frothing sea and heaved. As I brought the oars forward again, something slammed into my back. The breath drove out of me. I flew forward, cracking my head on the keel. The world flashed white and then went black.

For long seconds I couldn't see. I could only feel Sewel's

hands, wrenching me up. Turning me. As my sight returned, I found myself on my back. Sewel's face hovered above me, rain pouring from his chin and his nose in watery ropes. I'd seen him angry a thousand times before, but never like this.

"Now what?" he said, his breath gasping and ragged. "What are you going to do *now*, Fran?" He leaned down, bringing his face close to mine. I kicked and thrashed, but he held me by the neck and weighed more than a mountain. "That en't gonna do it, Frannie. What about now—what'll you do?" His hand shot under my shirt and squeezed, hard. "*Nothing.* That's what you'll do. You'll *yield* to me, Francisca. Once and for all. You'll learn and you will *obey* me."

He waited for me to speak.

I couldn't. I had gone under. I was ten fathoms below. Far, far away.

He sat back, gripping the gunwale as a wave came, making us spin and tumble.

I stayed where I was, slowly rising back into myself. Pain lanced into my head where it had struck the keel. My body was half-submerged in the slushing well. Every bit of me burned hot and cold at the same time.

Sewel searched for the brig, his head swiveling in panic. "Where is it?" He stepped toward the stern and braced the gunwale as he rose to see farther away, his back turned to me.

I struggled upright. Everything blurred and spun. I had waves of my own now, waves inside me. My eyes fell to the oars. I picked one up and crawled toward Sewel, fighting against the wildly pitching wherry. As we sank into the trough of a wave, where the water smoothed, I saw my chance. I reached back and swung the oar with every bit of strength in me.

The paddle struck Sewel between the shoulder blades with a deep thud. A jolt shot through my arms. Rattled every knuckle in my spine. Sewel flew forward and plunged into the foamy water. He disappeared without a splash, the sea swallowing him whole.

That very instant, I snatched up the other oar and rowed for my life.

Behind me, I heard Sewel roaring in the water, promising to end my life, to destroy me this very night. I kept heaving at the oars, my head pounding. Blood blearing my eyes.

I didn't know what I'd just done. Everything felt broken and twisted like a nightmare.

To my horror, I saw the Baines turning back for Sewel. I had no idea how they'd heard him, nor how they were managing to steer, as my paddles found no grip in the spumy water. The storm tides swept me toward the grounded brig and there was nothing I could do about it.

As I drew closer, the ship's bell tolled louder and I could hear the desperate shouts of the men aboard. Wave after wave struck the brig, smashing it against the reef. Some washed clean over its decks and sent men tumbling into the same salt water I tasted on my tongue.

I didn't know how long I'd been watching when at last the brig surrendered to the surging waves and rolled like a cowardly dog. It finally cleared the reef belly-up, leaving a mess of timber, canvas, and thrashing men in its wake.

Sobs pushed up as I listened to their dying screams. I fought to row toward them, but my efforts were useless and only made my shoulders and thighs burn. As the tides swept me away from the wreck, I slid the useless oars into the well and curled against the curve of the bulwark.

A powerful weariness came over me. I knew I shouldn't sleep—my life was at stake—but my body could no longer hold on.

=★=

"Frannie!"

I woke to the sound of Mercy's shouts. My gut seized, dizziness nearly overtaking me. For a moment, nothing made sense. I didn't understand why Mercy stood on the moonlit beach, waving her arms frantically, nor why I'd been sleeping on the wherry at sea. Then I remembered with a gasp.

Saints . . . what had I done?

Taking the tiller, I steered for shore. The sea was still rough and the wherry had taken water from leaks, but I managed to cruise right into the shallows, where she met me.

"Lord, Frannie!" Mercy wrapped an arm around my waist and helped me out. "You're bleeding so much!"

We stumbled through the water together, my legs shuddering and shaking, my mind still not understanding. This was our beach, the beach where we turned cartwheels through the shallows. Where we danced round bonfires and watched sea turtle hatchlings scurry into the sea, so tiny and brave. But I didn't recognize it now. All manner of items were strewn everywhere. Anchor cables and shattered timber. Shoes, hats, bottles, and jars.

"It's wreckage," Mercy said. "Don't stop, Frannie."

We stumbled up the beach, clearing the reach of the waves. "In heaven's name, what happened?" She took me by the shoulders, the fear plain in her bright eyes.

I opened my mouth to tell her. A sob left me instead.

"Hush now." She drew me down. "Here, sit. Breathe a minute and calm down. Lord, you're cold." She scooted beside me, wrapping an arm over my shoulders.

I breathed and breathed, till I'd shored myself up. Then I told her that Sewel had struck me, and that I'd knocked him overboard. It seemed unreal as I said it, like something I'd imagined.

"About time," Mercy said. "But you ought to have finished him. He's at your house and he's in a fury, Fran. A *murderous* fury."

"I can't go home," I said numbly. The sand was falling away from beneath me. The whole word, sinking.

"Never again, Frannie. If he catches you, he'll kill you."

"Where am I to go?" Everyone I knew lived on this island. I looked at the wherry, so battered after such a rough night. "Even if I had anyplace else, how am I supposed to get there?"

My eyes pulled to a splash of red floating beside it, the color bright even in the darkness. As a wave swept past, I saw a slender arm. The pale curve of a shoulder.

A body.

"Mercy, do you see that?"

"Hush." She tensed beside me. "I hear something."

More than anything, Mercy feared the runaway catchers that came to the island from time to time, but all I heard were the waves throwing themselves against the beach and the wind shaking the palmetto leaves. Finally, I heard someone calling in the distance.

25

"Hallo, there!"

"Is anybody out there?" called another voice.

They were around the bend, the sky around the point brighter with the glow of torches, but their voices carried clear to us on the wind.

"It's only a search party," I said. "Looking for survivors from the wreck." And they wouldn't find any. I looked toward the body floating in the shallows. A warm wave of hope swept over me. Suddenly I found myself walking over to it.

The woman looked younger than I expected. Much younger. Near in age to me. She swayed with the waves, her dark hair waving like a flag about her head. Her eyes were half-closed and her mouth was slightly open, giving her dreamy look. A look like she'd just blown out a candle.

I turned to Mercy, who'd followed me. "Mercy, do you think she looks . . ."

"Yes. Close enough."

"Quick, then. Help me with her gown."

CHAPTER 3

GOD AND TIME

★

"Thank the good Lord," said the big man with the shining buttons as he shook his head in amazement. *"Miss Emmeline—you're alive!"*

Miss Emmeline—that was the dead girl's name. The name of the girl I'd just become.

He handed his torch to one of the men behind him and took a careful step toward me, opening his hands in the air. "Please . . . have no fear. My name is Ruben Jansen. I captain the *Ambrosia* for your father. Your humble servant, madam."

He swept off his hat and bowed.

No man had ever bowed to me before.

Was it possible? Was my hastily thought-out disguise *working?*

Captain Jansen settled his hat and stared at me for long moments. "Miss Emmeline, can you hear me?"

Fresh panic fired through me. I could hear him fine—what I couldn't do was *speak*. I knew how I sounded, gritty and coarse. Two words from my lips and I'd surely give myself away.

I nodded and dropped my gaze to the crimson silk that

poured over me, my heart pounding crazily. The gown was made for a taller, rounder body—a body that now floated not far from where I stood. What if they saw her?

"Her skin's blue as polar ice, Cap'n," said one of the sailors. "She's froze to death." There were a dozen of them, all gawping at me, their torches flickering in the dawn.

"That's a wicked crack on 'er head," said another.

"Unnatural, a lass surviving such a trial. God's had a hand in this."

"Or the devil."

That started them discussing whose hand it was that'd saved Miss Emmeline from a shipwreck no man had survived.

As they carried on, I glanced toward the beach trail. Where was Sewel? If he appeared, my life would truly be over.

The captain took a step closer and crouched on his heels. "Miss Emmeline, we must get you out of the rain," he said gently. One of his eyes was clouded, like milk had been stirred into it. He held his head slightly askance to give the good eye a fuller view. "We must get you to a warm place." He pointed. "Around that bend are boats that will take you to the *Ambrosia*. I shall be with you every step of the way and, on my life, miss, I promise you will be perfectly safe."

This was exactly what I wanted. A way off this island.

I began to walk, my tired legs shuddering beneath the heavy, soaked petticoats. The cut above my eye kept bleeding, blinding me on that side and worsening my dizziness.

Halfway to the bend, my strength gave way. The captain swept me up before I hit the sand. I found myself in the basket of his arms, tensing as needles of fear sank in.

"Please, Miss Coates. Do not be afraid. Allow me to help you."

There was no other way. I nodded.

As he began to walk again, the strangeness of the moment dawned on me. Not since Papa had I been borne up this way, and I felt childish and small. And scared, but less of what lay ahead of me than what lay behind. So I allowed him to keep carrying me across the sand, toward a ship like ones I'd only ever swam through before.

=★=

Half an hour later, I was on the ship's deck, where dozens of men surrounded me.

The sun's first rays lit their stunned faces. Their awed murmurs came to me in pieces—*survivor, girl,* and *impossible.* I swayed in place and listened for *impostor—fraud—deceiver!*

"This way, Miss Emmeline." Captain Jansen removed his hat and gestured toward a hatch. I followed him into a cramped darkness that smelled faintly of urine. "I am afraid it won't approach what you must be used to," he said as he ducked under beams—step and duck, step and duck—stopping before the door at the end. "But these are the finest quarters on the *Ambrosia.* I hope you will find them adequate."

Inside, sunshine cut through a wide bank of stern windows, setting aglow a cabin filled with finery such as I'd only ever imagined. A desk sparkled with brass instruments. A table gleamed with silver and glass. Even the bed tucked into a little alcove glowed with a sheepskin covering.

"You shall have sole use of it as long as necessary," the captain went on. "Izra has already moved my effects, and you shan't be

29

disturbed here, you may be sure. The berths for the crew are in an entirely separate area."

Izra was the young black boy posted by the door, I guessed. He wore a red striped jacket missing some buttons and had clever eyes that held on me.

What did he see? A fine lady?

Or a common girl, pretending to be one?

"Ah, here we are." The captain turned to the bald man who shuffled through the door, setting down a wood trunk. "This is Mr. Withers, the *Ambrosia*'s surgeon."

"Your humble servant, Miss Coates," Mr. Withers said with a small bow. "If you'll allow me to—"

I shot back as he reached for me, knocking against the table. Something slid off and shattered on the floor with a sharp crunch. A silver pocket watch.

"Not to worry, not to worry," the captain rushed to say. "That old watch was already broken. Izra will see to the mess."

Izra was already seeing to it, kneeling to pick up shards of glass.

Mr. Withers's hands were still hanging in the air where my forehead had been. He lowered them. "You've suffered a terrible shock, Miss Coates. And that's a most severe cut on your brow. If you would allow me to—"

I rounded the table and shook my head. He *wasn't* touching me. If I could help it, no man ever would again.

"Perhaps later," Withers said with a thin smile. "In the meantime, I'll prepare a draught of laudanum to help settle you."

I shook my head again. I'd gotten myself off West End, but Sewel was still much too close. I had to stay alert.

"As you wish. I remain at your service." Mr. Withers smiled, but his eyes stayed cold.

The captain reassured me that all was well now, that my only concern ought be resting; then he and Mr. Withers stepped into the passageway, pulling the door half shut behind them.

"She's not said a word," said the captain. "Not a single word since we found her."

"So I gathered," replied Mr. Withers. "I believe the shock's addled her mind and stolen her power of speech."

"'Tis as I feared, then. How long until she recovers?"

"With traumatic muteness, there's no telling. Might be a day, might be never. Only God and time will tell."

"Sweet heaven. . . . *Never?*"

Izra glanced up from where he knelt like he wondered if I'd ever again utter a sound. As he left, I slid the bolt behind him. Checked it and checked it again. Then I stared at my new surroundings.

Along the far wall there was a small door about as high as I was tall, with an empty sea chest in front as if to hide it. I knew from wrecking that sometimes ship's quarters had closets used to hide valuables from thieving crews. This looked like the door to such a cuddy. Pushing the sea chest aside, I checked that bolt, too, and that was as much as I'd trouble with it for now. The cold had settled so deep in me, I wasn't even shaking anymore.

I managed to untie the gown and petticoats and let them drop in a soggy heap. The shift was damp, but I had no other garments to wear. On the desk I found a letter opener and slipped it into my sleeve. A knife would've been better, but wrecking had taught me that even blunt things could cut and I had to be ready for anything.

Pulling the sheepskin blanket off the bed, I climbed atop the long bench that ran beneath the stern windows and curled up close to the glass.

Warm sunlight poured over me, so bright it hid the world in white. Shading my eyes, I squinted at the beach and searched for Sewel's telltale limp. For his new hat with the red feather.

Wherever he was, he would be after me.

I had no idea how long this ship would stay moored here—a day? A week?

Every second gave him more time to find me.

A sudden banging near tore my heart in half. I whirled, looking from the main door to the little cuddy door, but the banging was coming from somewhere deep in the bowels of the ship. Singing drifted in through the window—first a shantyman's lone voice, then dozens calling back. Hope swelled inside me as I finally understood what I heard. The crew was turning the capstan and weighing anchor, readying to set sail.

Saints . . . we were *leaving*.

Soon I felt the ship starting to glide across the sea.

As West End shrank in the distance, a figure appeared at the head of the beach trail. He stood with his thick shoulders curled, his weight born slightly to one side. A spot of red by his hat caught the sunlight.

My eyes blurred.

I'd done it. I'd gotten away from him.

I was safe. For now.

CHAPTER 4

A GIRL ALONE

★

At sea

I woke up gasping at the weight on my chest, fighting desperately to push Sewel away—only to realize it was a nightmare. Shaken, I sat up on the bench and blinked at the fine captain's cabin, telling myself again and again that I was safe. Alone.

Then it hit me . . . I truly was *alone*.

I'd lost Mama. I'd never feel her fingers comb through my hair again, nor hear her whisper *Te quiero tanto, mi vida* in my ear. And I'd lost my home and Mercy, too. I had only myself to count on now.

I brushed the wetness from my cheeks. I was going to have to be enough.

The cabin surrounded me like a beautiful tree, all dark gleaming wood, but outside the sea sparkled, no spot of land anywhere. No wisp of cloud in sight.

My reflection flickered in the window. I leaned closer for a better look—and then wished I hadn't. A terrible bump sat above my right eyebrow, raised and crusted with blood. Beneath it, my eye was so swollen the lids barely parted. It put me in mind of a clam, my eye did. One purplish red in color.

Suddenly I wanted to laugh. Then I wanted to shatter the window. But it didn't matter anymore what Sewel had done 'cause it was over. I had other things to worry about now. I'd tricked my way onto this brig, but I was sure to be found out—if not betrayed by someone who knew the truth, then by my own coarse ways. When it happened, I'd be ready.

I looked up to the rafters, listening to the footsteps that drummed on the deck above me. Going out there was the last thing I wanted to do, but I had to learn where this ship was sailing and anything else that might help me.

I climbed off the bench and stepped back into the damp petticoat, then tugged my hair into a messy braid. Every muscle in my body hurt. My hands wouldn't stop shaking.

Noises came from everywhere. Things creaking. Things thumping. Men's singing muffled through wood. Everything strange, like a nightmare. One that began with a lone girl trapped at sea with a shipful of men.

I smoothed the red silk that spilled over me, adjusting the heavy gown as best I could and brushing off the crusted salt. My gaze fell to my bare feet. At least those were still familiar—sandy, as always.

Ready as I could make myself, I searched the cabin for a drink to slake my terrible thirst. I didn't find one, but I did find the broken pocket watch on the captain's desk. The glass face was gone and neither of the hands moved, but it was silver and would still fetch a good price.

I tucked it into the pocket of my petticoat and added the letter opener, which had slipped from my sleeve as I slept and lay winking at me from the bench. If I was driven off this ship, at least I'd have a way to defend myself and barter for food.

Reaching to unbolt the door, I noticed all the tiny scars and cuts on my hands from meeting nails and splinters and rocks.

Wrecker hands.

Saints . . . I had no idea how I was going to pull off this charade.

=★=

The instant I stepped out into the sunshine, the crew's singing died. Everything stopped like the moment after I dove, when up became down and air became water.

My knees locked. My mind filled with one thought.

They knew.

Someone had discovered me for an impostor.

Now what? Would I be tossed off this ship?

"Captain, Captain!" The little cabin boy, Izra, darted past, his feet slapping the deck, his cries shattering the silence. "She's awake, Captain! Miss Coates is here!"

He tore up the quarterdeck stairs and joined Captain Jansen, who appeared at the top. As they came down to meet me, the men turned back to their tasks, but without singing anymore. My presence had brought a strangeness.

"Good day, Miss Coates," the captain said, folding into a bow. Beside him, the tiny cabin boy scratched off his cap and copied.

I dropped a curtsy, twitchy and quick, too shaky to slow down.

"Heartening to see you about," the captain said. "Very heartening indeed. Will you join me? I have a good place for us to sit just over here."

The good place was by the nested boats amidships, where two crates sat side by side. They were covered with fine Turkish carpets such as I'd only seen in Nassau, left to fade under the sun like nothing special.

I kept ample distance from the captain, sitting so he wouldn't see the blood oozing from my cut. He sent Izra darting off to fetch a drink for me. Thank heaven. Then he gazed across the sea, his breath whistling through his nose. In daylight I could see that his better eye was also a little clouded, as if slowly going blind.

"Beautiful waters, are they not? The sight never tires."

I pretended to observe the beauty as well, but blood was rolling down my cheek like a tear and I had no mama anymore, nor a home, and those seemed more terrible, just then, than the ocean seemed beautiful.

"Allow me to assure you once more that you shall be safe on the *Ambrosia,* and that you may depend upon me as a most devoted guardian. Regarding the matter of your quietude, Mr. Withers tells me there's no cause for concern and that you shall be restored to rights in healing time."

My quietude wasn't going anywhere. I'd heard how the fine ladies in Nassau talked, their voices like perfume floating through the air. I did *not* sound like them. Only trouble was I didn't see how I'd get answers if I couldn't ask any questions. The *Ambrosia* was a British merchant ship sailing north, that much I'd gathered, but I needed to know more.

"Miss Coates, I beg you not to fret about that." I blinked at the captain. Then I realized I'd slipped the watch from my pocket and was running my finger over its tiny hands. "Consider it yours—a gift from me to you. There, see? How easily a mishap becomes a blessing if one only has a bit of faith."

I couldn't believe it. Was this truly the life of a lady? Gifts of silver, falling into your lap?

Izra exploded through a hatch and came running with a pewter cup. He was skinnier than the wind, with dark skin that gleamed in the sunlight. He handed me the cup, flashing a smile full of missing milk teeth. I took it and drank it half down before my throat lit with burning coals. It was watered rum—and not much watered—but I finished it, not about to be choosy. In a blink, the heat seeped into my veins.

"My dear," the captain continued, "in such circumstances 'tis best to speak in plain terms. The *Paladin* was a total loss. Every soul aboard perished. Every life was lost but yours. Your beloved father has passed on to the realm of heaven. I understand he was your sole relation. I met him only once but knew him to be a perfect gentleman and, well, I am sorrier than I can possibly express. Please be assured that it is my most fixed purpose to see to your protection until other arrangements are made."

He blew out a long breath and blinked at the tears in his pearly eyes.

I remained silent, thinking of the real Miss Coates. How Mercy and I had rushed to unpin her gown and tug off her petticoats. We had stripped her to her shift and then pulled her out into water, where she wouldn't be spotted. As we'd done it, I'd prayed for God's forgiveness. Even now, my heart hurt to remember how I'd disrespected her. But I couldn't imagine any other way I'd have survived the night.

The captain cleared his throat. "You must want some time to yourself. Izra will stay close should you need anything." The planks creaked under his weight as he stood. "Perhaps you'll join me this evening for dinner? There is much to consider with regard to your future."

I nodded. I needed information and food. I hoped there'd be troughs of both.

Around me, men swabbed the deck. They scoured pots and pulled hemp from old ropes to make oakum. Never had I *sat* while others worked. Soon the singing began again, but it was only one man this time, up at the helm, singing about a lost true love, his voice so pretty I wanted to cry and cry over it.

A breeze puffed at the sails above me, carrying me away from home. To where? Soon as this voyage was over, I'd have to care for myself, but how? The skills I had wouldn't help me. Wrecking wasn't proper work for girls. I'd only been able to carry on in West End 'cause on an island inhabited by criminals, runaways, and disgraced women, a wayward girl scarcely deserved mention.

Maybe I could knock on doors till I found work as a maid? But who'd bring an orphaned girl into their home—a girl without a single person to vouch for her character?

Dread curled in my bones as the awful truth of my situation sank in.

I knew what happened to a lone woman in this world.

It had been a long while since I'd thought about the time after Papa died of smallpox, but my mind drifted to those dark days now. I remembered Mama crying for days and days. Her heart was broken, she'd told me. It would never be whole again. In time her tears dried up and she took over his shoe shop. I remembered how strong she'd looked hammering nails into soles, sweat rolling down her pretty neck. Papa's customers liked her shoes—she'd made them just like he had. Eventually she'd done one better, burning flowers and patterns into the leather with hot needles and selling buckles she bought from a trader from the Orient. Word had spread of her artful designs and soon merchants from all over the Out Islands came to buy from her—but not a year after Papa's passing, everything had changed again.

A man named Mr. Slade who had his own shoe shop in Nassau accused her of being an immoral and depraved woman. He spread rumors that Mama was having relations with men—some of them enslaved men—and she became a woman of ill fame.

People crossed the road when they saw her. They hissed "filthy strumpet" and "bloody doxy." They threw eggs and rubbish at our shop, sometimes in plain daylight. With a few untruthful words, Mr. Slade had ruined Mama and caused his own business to thrive.

Mama sold the shop and we moved to a room above a tavern. Then the money from the shop ran out, but our hunger didn't, and that was when she started leaving me for long stretches. Day and night, and night and day. I began to suspect she was doing just what she'd been accused of, but I never asked. It didn't matter to me what she did. She was my mama and my everything.

Then Sewel came around and I saw her smiling again. With

him by her side, people still crossed the street—but no one dared speak a backward word to her anymore. With him beside her, she held her head up again.

After they married, we left Nassau to start our life in the Out Islands. Year by year, she laughed less and Sewel drank more, and yelled more, and on bad nights did even worse, but she accepted all of it. He'd claimed her—a fallen woman. And no amount of drunkenness or wickedness mattered, 'cause he was loyal, and that was better than *many* men in the world, Mama said, and certainly better than *no* man.

I was meant to learn from all her hardships. *Live for something more,* she told me, again and again in different ways, but always with that word. *You must have more than I've had. More than my life has given me. More than this.* While we gardened. While we cooked. Even while I slept, I knew she whispered in my ear, sliding her wish for me right into my dreams.

Vivas por algo más, mi hija, she'd say.

Never marry for love, as love doesn't buy bread.

Never marry in haste, as those who rush, stumble.

Never marry low, as poverty is a stain that never washes out.

Instead, I was to find safety. Comfort. Respectability. Things only a good marriage could provide 'cause a woman alone wasn't safe from the words and deeds of evil men. A woman alone had not a thing in this world that couldn't be taken from her if a man wanted it, not even her dignity.

Now here I was. Aboard a strange ship sailing for no place I knew.

A girl alone.

With the sun beginning to dip, I returned to the captain's quarters and found Izra inside.

"Some of your things was recovered before we left, Miss Coates!" he said. He scooped a folded bundle from a basket and set it on the table, where other items had already been spread out. "I'll come back to fetch you for dinner."

He bowed, quick as a sneeze, and sped off, throwing the door shut behind him.

I studied the colorful assortment he'd left me. Most of the items were garments, rumpled and still damp from the sea. A thick cloak of midnight-blue velvet for use in weather such as I'd never known. A gown of sea-green brocade. Petticoats in shades of pink and blue. A shift of white holland. Front-lacing boned stays of pearly silk. A red slipper with a silver buckle. A yellow slipper with a gold buckle. A tangle of ribbons in colors like happy wishes.

In addition to the clothes, there was a leather journal with a cord tied round its bulging pages. I picked it up and brushed my hand over the soft cover, my heart thumping in my chest.

I hadn't thought about *staying* Miss Coates, but . . . *could I?* Miss Coates had true prospects in life. Everything Mama always wanted for me.

I brought the journal to the stern bench and dropped onto the soft sheepskin, which held gentle warmth from the sun. The *Ambrosia* stood in calm waters, barely swaying. Outside, the rising moon was splitting itself in two, one for the sky, another for the sea. The journal pages were wavy and the ink had bled in one corner. Turning to the beginning, I read:

The Reflections and Occasional Musings of Miss Emmeline Cecily Coates, Daughter of Nathaniel Coates and the Late, Beloved Elizabeth Anne Sumner

Miss Coates began her entries the day of her departure from Antigua, on July 29, 1776. *My Grand Adventure Begins!* she declared, sailing from her home on the *Paladin* with the *Ambrosia* in convoy.

How sad. Her grand adventure hadn't lasted long at all.

I read on slowly, pressing dents into the paper in my concentration. Sewel had sold all our books a year ago and I was rusty. Even when we'd had books, I'd seldom read, much preferring the freedom of swimming and dreaming up my own stories, which were always more thrilling. But I kept on and wrestled each word into my understanding.

Emmeline Coates was more given to hoping than dreaming. She hoped she would not be seasick. She hoped her little spaniel, Lionel, would enjoy the sailing voyage north. She hoped she'd like her new home in—

Philadelphia?

I snapped the journal shut. As we were sailing north, I'd already suspected we were bound for the American colonies, but here was proof.

I was heading toward *war*.

Suddenly I wished I'd listened better to Sewel and Mr. Baines's grousing. I knew there'd been taxes levied on the Americans that they didn't want to pay. In a fit, they'd tossed a shipful of good tea into Boston Harbor, and now King George had to set things back to rights. There was more to it, I knew, but politics was the domain of men and not for me to ask.

We were Loyalists; that was all I needed to know, Mama taught me. For men, that meant loyalty to God, king, and country. For women, that meant loyalty to their men.

Even the awful ones.

Swallowing past the ache in my throat, I opened the journal again.

Emmeline Coates was seventeen—two years older than me—and born this month, like me. She'd hoped her father would host a fine assembly to celebrate, with dinner and dancing amongst Philadelphia's finest families. She'd hoped to marry by her twentieth birthday, to a gentleman of sound character and established fortune. He would also be devout, handsome, and fashionable and make a "superb father."

Saints. I thought *I* had an imagination. But it couldn't be any clearer now: Emmeline Coates could give me everything I needed. As her, I'd never have to beg in the streets—or worse. I could have the *something more* Mama wished for me. Comfort and respectability. The fine life of a lady.

That decided it. I was going to become her. I'd already fooled this ship's captain and crew. How much harder would it be to keep going?

A cough yanked me from my thoughts.

I whirled to the cuddy. The journal slipped off my lap and struck the floor with a thud.

For seconds, I didn't dare move. Then I stood and crept toward the little door.

Placing my trembling hands on the wood, I pressed my ear to it.

All I heard were the ship's creaks and whines, but I knew someone was behind the door—I just *knew* it.

Defying good sense, I knocked. Once. Twice.

Then I held my breath and waited.

And waited.

I could hold it a long, long time.

But when I exhaled, still no one had answered.

CHAPTER 5

TO HIDE THE TRUTH

⭐

At sea

"Welcome, Miss Coates." The captain rose from the table and smiled. "I am so pleased you could join me."

As promised, Izra had fetched me for dinner. Unlike my lavish quarters, the musty cabin I'd just entered was cramped and spare, with a table at the center and two berths to one side. A lone moonbeam shone through the porthole, cutting the dimness like a sword.

"I took the liberty of asking Mr. Tom Hackett, the *Ambrosia*'s boatswain, to join us," the captain said, gesturing to the man beside him.

"Good evening, madam," said Mr. Hackett. He was a broad man, thick as a barrel, with scowl lines carved so deep they didn't budge when he smiled. "Your most humble servant." He bowed.

I curtsied, but both Mr. Hackett and the captain kept smiling like they expected more, so I curtsied again, deep and slow, the hem of Miss Coates's gown pooling on the planks and my feet sliding inside her mismatched slippers. The door swung open just as I'd finished.

A young man ducked through it and looked from me to the captain. He was lean as a spar, the very opposite of Mr. Hackett.

"Ah, good. We are all arrived," said Captain Jansen. "Miss Coates, allow me to introduce Mr. Asa Lane, whom I have invited to join us as well. Mr. Lane is the youngest son of a highly respected Rhode Island shipping merchant."

Mister Lane didn't seem right. I didn't put him a day above twenty, and he was bedraggled, his navy coat and waistcoat bagging, his ozenbrig trousers those of a common sailor. Even his hair was untidy, dark pieces slipping from the queue at his nape and falling into his eyes.

"Mr. Lane is a graduate of the prestigious Yale College," the captain went on. "One of the finest in the American colonies."

"Not quite, Captain," said Mr. Lane. "I only attended for a year before I took to sea. And they are the United States now, as last month our Congress declared independence."

The captain coughed in shock, and silence fell like an ax. I fidgeted with the flounces on the sea-green gown I'd changed into as I tried to make sense of his words.

Our Congress? Mr. Lane was an American rebel?

I didn't understand. Why was he on a ship full of Loyalists— his *enemies*?

As the tense silence stretched on, a scarlet flush crept up Mr. Hackett's thick neck.

Finally, Mr. Lane turned to me, resting a hand over his heart. "*Enchanté*, Mademoiselle Coates." He bowed over an extended leg as his free hand swept out to his side. He peered up at me before rising, and more French words poured from his lips, his voice deep and musical. None of it made a drip of sense to my ears.

46

When he finished speaking, I pulled my lips into the most pleasant smile I could manage and dropped yet another curtsy. Then I threw myself into the nearest chair, 'cause surely curtsying wasn't the answer to everything.

My breath raced as I stared at my plate. I knew ladies learned French. I'd heard them before in Nassau, twittering like birds, but it didn't matter that I hadn't answered, I assured myself. My traumatic muteness protected me.

Questions about Mr. Lane continued to dart through my mind as he sat across the table. What had he said in French? Why had he been invited to dinner? I pushed them away; I had more important things to find out.

With everyone seated, a steward by the door came forward to pour wine and serve a lumpy white stew. Never had I been attended to before. I didn't know if I ought to watch the ladling and pouring or pretend it wasn't happening, so I took turns with both.

Once everything was served, I drew a steadying breath and studied the glass and silverware before me. Such a complication of pretty tools. Mr. Lane alone seemed to know what to do with it all. Before I'd settled on which spoon to use, he was eating— and eating in no way I'd ever seen. Every movement smooth and patient.

I did my best to imitate him, keeping my posture upright and forcing myself not to gobble the soupy mixture. The lobscouse stew was oversalted and tough, but I'd have eaten a dead fish in a hot puddle if I'd had to. I was past famished and I needed the strength to keep me alert.

Like true seafarers, the captain and Mr. Hackett discussed the sailing conditions at length as we ate. How the prevailing winds had been that day. How there weren't any now, and what they expected for tomorrow. The *Ambrosia* added her own voice to the conversation, creaking and groaning as the flames of the candles along the table leaned left and right and left and right.

Course, they weren't really swaying. Everything else was.

Little by little, I relaxed. I had worried my coarse manners would draw suspicion, but aside from fumbling my spoon once, I was doing a fine job imitating Mr. Lane's polished ways.

He was a gentleman—of that I was now certain. Never mind his ratty garments. His good breeding was *in* him—in his hands, which sat quiet on the table without tapping. In the way he talked, calm and round, curving the ends of words how I curled the ends of my dives. Most of all in the steady way he had of looking, like he saw only one thing at a time, but saw it whole.

I understood now why the captain had invited him to dinner. Highborn folk only socialized on their own level. Miss Coates would only keep company with such a fine sort as Mr. Lane. I'd need to keep company with that sort myself. Even more, I'd need to *become* that sort.

Tonight I was managing to hide the truth, but I'd have to do better if I meant to fit myself into Miss Coates's life. I'd need to improve my manners, my elegance, my *everything,* wringing the rusticness out of myself like dirty wash water.

With the meal finished and the candles burning low, Izra and the steward cleared away our plates. The captain lit a pipe and sat back in his chair. Mr. Hackett dug through his teeth with grimy fingernails, and Mr. Lane stared at the table linen like it was a beautiful sunset.

Meanwhile, I held perfectly still. The cut on my forehead had started bleeding again, but I was too ashamed to wipe my cheek and call attention to it.

"Izra, would you please find a clean napkin for Miss Coates?" Mr. Lane said.

"He en't for you to command, rebel," Hackett snapped.

"Let it pass, Tom," said the captain. "I have it, Izra." He set his pipe down and rummaged in his coat pocket for a white kerchief, handing it to me. "Miss Coates."

I took it, my face hot with embarrassment. The material in my hand felt soft as a petal and was whiter than anything I'd ever seen. I hated to sully it, but I pressed it to my brow. The pain sharpened and the memory of that night flickered darkly in my mind. Anger at Mr. Lane coiled in my stomach—couldn't he just have ignored it?

Captain Jansen puffed his pipe a few times, then plucked it from his mouth. "Miss Coates, the time has come for us to discuss your future. Please stop me if I overwhelm you."

I nodded, wanting him to get on with it. I'd started to feel a little nauseous.

"Your father was a prudent man. He knew the dangers of sailing in these tense times and took exceeding caution to safeguard his fortune—and your future." He reached into his coat for a letter and set it on the table. The wax seal was broken and the pages fanned open slowly. "This is a copy of his will, which he entrusted to me before we set sail. It describes the conveyance of his estate to you, as well as his plans for your care. Mr. Lane bore witness as I unsealed and read it earlier. He can attest to its authenticity and contents."

Mr. Lane's gaze came to me. "You have my deepest sympathy,

Miss Coates. 'Tis my honor to be at your service in the midst of this grave and life-altering ordeal."

Life-altering?

Saints . . . did he *know*? He looked relaxed, even a little bored. But I saw something else in his eyes. The flash of a quick mind.

"Mr. Hackett has joined us," the captain went on, "to provide you with the comfort of a familiar face in this difficult moment. If you would prefer he leave us, you need only nod."

A thousand pins pierced me suddenly, like I'd leapt into biting-cold water.

A *familiar* face?

I turned to Mr. Hackett. He ran his tongue over his teeth, grinning as he watched me. He'd been waiting for this very moment.

My mind raced back to the long pause after he'd been introduced, when I'd curtsied a second time. Now I realized the captain had been waiting to see if I'd been pleased that Mr. Hackett was there.

Mr. Hackett sat up and leaned on the table. "I know we en't well acquainted, madam, but I sailed for your father some ten years and feel a most *personal* concern for your well-being. We share that special memory, you might recall, when I gave you that starfish in St. John's Harbor? Never seen a brighter smile than yours that day, if I may say so." His grin broadened. *"Miss Coates."*

Raw fear rolled through me. I brought the kerchief down to my lap, curling my trembling fingers around it under the table.

"You may be comforted to know that your father left you a most robust inheritance," the captain continued, having no idea of my terror. Hackett could expose me at any moment. "You shall never go in want, of that you may be sure. I do have some good news of a more sentimental nature. Izra, the box." Izra brought over a small wood trunk that shook the table as he set it down. The captain unlocked it with a key from his coat. "You lost a great deal in the *Paladin*, but your mother's jewels are safe. I was charged with their safekeeping on the *Ambrosia*. They are all right here, my dear."

He opened the lid and turned the trunk toward me. Necklaces, broaches, and bracelets were piled inside, tangled like glittering seaweed. There were smaller velvet boxes as well, surely containing the finest jewels. Mercy and I would've turned cartwheels round the entire island had we ever found such a box wrecking. Now I could scarce give it my attention.

"I shall keep this until we make landfall," Captain Jansen said as he locked the trunk again. "My men are honorable, but better not to tempt them. Now to the matter of your guardianship. You are to be placed under the protection of Dr. Henry Holdridge of New York. Have you any familiarity with the doctor, Miss Coates? He is described in the will as a longtime friend of your father's."

I nodded. My blood roared in my ears and the skin over my knuckles felt ready to split. What a fool I'd been, walking into a life I had no idea about. Why had I *ever* thought this could work?

"I am glad for that," said the captain, "but I must confess, the idea of delivering you to New York in such a troubling time concerns me. York Island is in the hands of the Continental Army, and the situation for those loyal to the Crown has been dangerous for some time. Non-associators, the Americans call us. The hypocrisy astonishes. But I am certain His Majesty will restore order soon."

"I wouldn't depend on it, Captain," said Mr. Lane. "Our forces are strong in New York."

"Forces?" Hackett snorted. "They're farmers with pitchforks."

Lane turned to him. "They are men fighting for their liberty."

"What do you know about fighting, sea dandy?"

Captain Jansen thumped his palm on the table. "*Enough.* Not another word, either of you."

Silence fell, but the air remained thick with their anger. I held as still as I could. I'd been forgotten for now. I did *not* want to be remembered.

The captain popped his pipe back in his mouth and puffed at it anxiously. "Forgive us, Miss Coates. Mr. Lane hails from excellent Tory stock, but he is confused in his allegiance."

Lane regarded him for a moment. "You're correct, sir. My father is a most devoted Loyalist who toasts King George's health every night at dinner. His political stance is but one reason we're estranged. I am *not* confused in my allegiance. I know exactly where I stand, and it is with liberty. With American independence. Not with a tyrant an ocean away who oppresses innocents with fire and sword."

"You rebels and your talky-talky," Hackett said, his eyes dark points of hatred. "'I stand for this' and 'I stand for that.' But it en't nothing more than drivel covering up greed."

"*Tom,*" the captain warned. "Remember yourself."

But Hackett wasn't finished. "This war en't *nothing* to do with rights and freedoms. Sons of Liberty you lot claim to be, but you en't. You're Sons of Profit. You're Sons of I Want Less Taxes So I Can Live in Silk. Stand, rebel. Stand now, if you're so full of noble ideas."

Lane set his napkin aside and unfolded to his full height. He opened his hands. *There. I'm standing,* he seemed to be saying.

Hackett lunged at him—so fast, a blur—but suddenly everything seemed slow, like it was happening underwater. He slammed into Lane and drove him back. The table flew up. Chairs cracked against wood. Plates, cups, and candles spewed into the air. Then panic fired through me, hot and sudden, and time sped up again.

I leapt back, wedging myself between the berths, as Lane and Hackett grappled and swung, the sounds of their blows horrible.

Lane was younger and much taller, but Hackett was a bull. Vicious. He seemed to know exactly what he was doing as he cornered Lane, pushing him up against the bulkhead and jamming an elbow into his throat.

"Livingston!" the captain yelled, struggling to get between them. "Someone—in here *now!*"

Izra came running through the door first, his eyes flaring when he saw the brawl. "Miss Coates!" He dove for my wrist. "Come, Miss Coates! Come!"

As he pulled me out of the cabin, three other men came barreling inside. I rushed past them, seeing rope, batons, knives. Then it was all behind me as Izra and I plunged into the dimness and hurried back to the captain's cabin.

=★=

Hours later, I was still tossing fitfully on the stern bench, unable to sleep. For the tenth time, I patted my petticoats, checking that the letter opener and silver watch were still in my pocket. I had to be ready for anything.

Only hours ago, the *Ambrosia* had felt like my escape. Now it felt like a trap.

I leaned toward the window, peering at the glossy black wake below. Even if I could make the dive from this high, where would I swim? All I could see outside was night.

I balled up the sheepskin and lay down again, the wood bench hard against my shoulder. Nothing in the world felt familiar, within me or without.

I shut my eyes, thinking of Mercy. Pretending you're brave is no different than being brave, she'd told me once. Saints, how I missed her. How I needed her with me now. At last, I felt the edges of a dream curling round my mind—only to be yanked awake by a rapping on the door.

"Miss Coates?" Izra chirped. "The captain's very sorry about dinner. He sent something for you, miss. To show he's exceeding apologetic."

I slid off the bench and opened the door.

Izra stood outside hugging a basket to his chest, his bottom lip wobbling. "Biscuits for you, madam?"

Behind him, holding a ship's lantern against the darkness, stood Tom Hackett.

I lurched back and shut the door. Hackett caught it and pushed it wider. "A word, if you please, Miss Coates." He turned to Izra. "I owe the lady an apology myself, Izra, so you can go." Izra stared up, terrified. "En't nothing to be afeared of, boy. I en't hurting her. Now go on, you little rat. *Go.*"

"Yes, sir." Izra set the basket down and ran off.

Hackett bolted the door behind him and strode right at me. I scurried back, back, back, digging furiously for the letter opener.

My hand found the broken watch instead—but Hackett walked past me. He set the lantern on the table and kept going, stopping before the little door.

"Lane?" He pounded on it. "Say something, Lane, and lemme hear you."

"I'm here," came the reply.

I'd been right earlier—someone was behind that door.

"Yes, you are," said Hackett. "Now listen close and listen good, 'cause you're about to hear some things you're never to speak of. Never, you mark me?"

This was it—my worst fear. Hot saliva rushed into my mouth as I recalled Sewel's strength the night I'd left West End. His weight and bruising hands.

"Hackett." The cuddy door shook on its hinges. "On my soul, Hackett, if you—"

"I'll say it once more, Lane, and once only. Shut your gan and keep it shut. Only way this worsens is if you cause it to." Hackett listened a moment, nodding when he heard silence, then turned back to me. "Well, well. Here we are." His eyes dropped to my hand. "What's that, a letter slicer? We got no need for it. I can't read."

"It's sharp." My disused voice sounded high as a whistle. "Sharper than it looks."

"So am I." He grinned. "And how *surprised* I am to learn you en't mute after all."

Moonlight lit a dark bruise beneath his left eye and showed the swollen bridge of his nose. I remembered how savagely he'd fought. If Lane had barely fended him off, what chance did I have?

"What do you want from me?" I glanced at the cabin door.

"Now, now. Quick as you might be, you en't quick enough. And I'll get to what I want; that you can count on." He moved to the window and crossed his arms, gazing outside. "You know, I thought it a miracle when I first heard it from the hands. Miss Coates—alive!" He shook his head. "Amazing. Just amazing. Then I see her drop on the main deck in the bosun's chair and I says to myself, I says, what the devil? I seen Nathaniel Coates's pretty daughter before and that en't her. I nearly said something, but then I got wondering . . . who is that tiny little peck of salt?" He turned to me. "And why's she pretending to be Miss Coates?"

I swallowed, trying to find my voice again. "I'm not telling you a thing about me." For all I knew, he'd take me back to Sewel.

"No? Well, it don't much matter. I know all I need to know." He came toward me. "You're running from something. You're hiding from it, and you're scared as can be. And you're lying. You're lying to save your tiny little life. En't that right?"

"Stop!" I backed into the bulwark. "Don't come any closer!"

He leered down at me, his teeth snaggled and stained. "You asked me what I want. Well, I'll tell you. What I want's a fee, you might say, for keeping your little secret all the way to New York. Something only Miss Coates can provide."

"You mean . . ." My legs shuddered as it came to me. "You want the *jewels?*"

"Righto."

Relief turned me light as a cloud. "You want me to steal 'em for you?"

"Steal 'em? No, no, no. Lord, girl. Nothing so splashy as that. We go on's what we do. We sail northward, according to plan. You keep being a good Miss Coates till we get to New York, where Jansen'll give you those baubles. Then you give 'em to me and you go your way, still alive, and I go mine a rich man. You seeing how this works?"

I did. I knew just how this worked. *Dive, Frannie. Steal, Frannie.* I had plenty of practice with orders and threats.

Hackett leaned closer. "Well?"

"Yes, you old hellhound! I see!" I cringed at my outburst. If he was anything like Sewel, I'd pay for it.

He scowled. "Old *hellhound?*" He looked up as the ship's bell began to toll the hour. "Time I go, Little Salt." He bowed, swirling a hand mockingly through the air. "Oh—one last thing." He turned at the door. "You keep that mouth shut tight. 'Cause hell, girl, you got a vulgar tongue that en't the least bit ladylike."

CHAPTER 6

FOR THE BLOOD

★

In the morning, I took Miss Coates's journal out to the crates where I'd sat with Captain Jansen, more determined than ever to make myself into her. It wasn't a choice anymore; I needed it for me *and* so I could get the jewels for Hackett.

Opening the journal, I read a swirly love poem Miss Coates had written to her future husband, then pages of her favorite recipes for things like "a superb paste for the skin" and "a secret to keep breath smelling sweet after drink."

I closed it, blowing out a long, frustrated breath that perhaps smelled sweet or perhaps not, but either way I didn't care a whit. I'd reach New York in a week or two, depending on the wind, and I had so much to learn. I knew I didn't talk or eat right. Probably there were a thousand other things I'd need to learn, and this journal wasn't helping one bit. My situation was not looking superb.

The *Ambrosia*'s hands were again scrubbing and climbing and hauling. They were every sort of man, every race and age and shape. They worked perfect together, calling back and forth in

French and Dutch and Spanish. Whenever the watchman spotted sails, they dropped their work and lined up at the gunwale, gazing at the ship that'd been sighted as they waited to know whether it was friend or foe. We'd been lucky to see ships flying English colors so far, but the thing with luck was it always ran out. With every passing wave, I felt closer to war.

As I sat trying not to despair about my future, land appeared in the distance. Endless land that glided by and by and by.

A *continent.*

"Ever been to America, Miss Coates?"

Startled, I spun to find Hackett behind me.

He smirked, the lines in his cheeks going deeper. "I suppose that en't a question you can answer, seeing as you're mute. *And* seeing as you en't even her." He waved at the sea. "Would you look at *all* that sparkle and shine!" He shook his head in amazement. "Beautiful. Just beautiful. The sea's bright as *diamonds* today, en't it?"

He looked terribly pleased with himself at his reminder of what I owed him—as if I could ever forget. In broad daylight the bruise round his eye looked worse, I was glad to see, swollen and purple. Lane had got him good. I wondered what damage Hackett had done back, but I'd yet to see Lane today.

"What's the matter, Little Salt? You hate me or something?"

No one was near enough to hear, so I allowed myself to answer. "Course I hate you, you old buzzard," I hissed, then dropped my gaze.

"You got some pluck, girl." His shadow shook its head on the planks before me. "Fail me and see if *'old buzzard'* don't slice you open gullet to gizzard, then dance a jig on your entrails. Good day

59

to you, madam." He swaggered off, swinging the bosun's club at his side like life was butterflies and honeybees.

I trembled as I watched him go, my gut queasy at his words. He was a blackguard if ever I knew one. Jewels or not, he just might gut me at the end of this either way.

=★=

At sundown, Izra brought my dinner to my cabin in a basket. After the upset of the previous evening, the captain seemed to think I'd prefer privacy, which was more than fine with me.

As Izra set dinner out on the table, he sniffled and hardly looked my way. I knew he felt terrible for letting Hackett in that morning, but I held my tongue. Frannie might apologize to a cabin boy, but Miss Coates surely wouldn't—mute or not.

Soon as he left, I went over to the cuddy and stood before it, trying to shore up my nerve. I had finished Miss Coates's journal entries earlier, and now I had only one hope left: *Lane.*

A little while ago, I'd overheard the hands chattering about him. For speaking against His Majesty King George and inciting Hackett to violence, Lane had been punished with a day of confinement and lost his food ration.

That had given me an idea.

I snatched a knife off the table, shot the bolt back, and swung the door wide.

Lane jumped to his feet and bumped his head on the low ceiling. Then he stood, crouching in the darkness and blinking. His gaze fell to the knife in my hand. "You don't need that. I'm no danger to you."

"Why should I believe you?"

"You shouldn't." He shifted his weight. "But it is the truth."

I didn't know what to make of that. I didn't *fear* him. But I felt breathless and jittery, like when I dove a new wreck.

Though Lane's hair fell loose to his shoulders and the cuddy was dark, I didn't miss the scratches on his neck nor the bloodstains on his collar from his fight with Hackett. His right sleeve had been torn, and I could see the curve of his shoulder. The cuddy itself was cramped and spare, with a porthole against the far side, and a pitcher and folded blanket in a corner. A ladder rose to a hatch, which had to be how he came and went when not being punished for brawling.

Before I lost my nerve, I drew a breath and pushed out the words I'd been practicing. "I heard the hands talking this afternoon about you losing your food ration, for fighting Hackett, and I can help with that. There's dinner enough for us both on that table. I'll share it with you. All you gotta do's answer my questions, as many questions as I have to ask, and don't ask any back. Not one."

His dark eyebrows pulled together like it was the strangest thing he'd ever heard.

Maybe it *was*.

Maybe my vulgar speech offended his genteel ears.

"Very well. I accept your terms."

I blinked. "Well, come on, then." I stepped aside. That had gone easier than I'd expected. "There's a basin over there if you want to wash. And don't worry. No one'll know you're in here. The door's bolted. The main door, meaning."

He entered and swept a slow gaze round the cabin, then crossed to the washbasin. "I'll dirty this," he said over his shoulder.

"It's no trouble. Izra brings fresh water and a clean towel every morning."

As he washed his hands and face, then pulled his dark hair into a knot, I caught myself watching him like he was doing something interesting. I shook my head and set the knife on the table. Then I lit a candle off the ship's lantern, as night had fallen, and sat.

Somewhere above, the *Ambrosia*'s crew danced to a jaunty fiddle, their steps thumping like the beat of a wooden heart. My foot jiggled nervously under the table, making everything shake even more, but I stopped myself as Lane came over.

He settled into the chair across from mine and placed his napkin on his lap, so I did as well. I hadn't thought this far ahead in my planning and I couldn't think at all now. As he poured wine, my only thought was to watch his hands and not his face, 'cause Sewel said I had owl eyes that always stared.

He set the wine down. "I am ready whenever you are."

"What's your name? Your Christian name. I forgot it," I added. Then I felt my face warm for no reason I could understand.

"Asa. Asa Lane."

"How old are you, Asa Lane?"

"Nineteen."

"And why are you on this ship?" I said, in spite of myself. I needed his help, but I couldn't bring myself to just ask for it. I didn't want to appear like a grasping girl trying to rise above her low station—which I was. The clever glint in Asa Lane's eyes only added to my reluctance.

"This was a condition of my release," he replied.

"Your release?"

"Aye. I am a privateersman. I was a marine guard on the schooner *Stalwart*, out of Marblehead, until a few weeks ago. We were cruising to the West Indies, having good success seizing British merchantmen until we grew too brazen and chased after a seventy-four—that's a very large ship."

"I *know*." I sat up, my curiosity instantly sparked. "How many mounted guns on it?"

"Thirty-two."

"*That* must've been a sight. Was your schooner coppered?"

"Nay. And she was sailing sluggish, too."

I shook my head. "Teredo worms, probably." In my mind, I was underwater, running my hands over the whorls of a worm-eaten hull. "You never stood a chance."

His lips tugged up. "You're remarkably familiar with naval affairs, Miss Coates."

I felt the pull of a smile, too. "Well, my father—Nathaniel Coates? He's a shipping merchant. This is his ship—the *Ambrosia*. This table right here's his table." I patted it for good measure.

"Of course." he said, playing along. "I apologize and offer my condolences for your loss."

"Thank you," I said, swallowing past the pinch in my throat. I wasn't mourning Nathaniel Coates, but I *was* mourning. "What happened after the *Stalwart* was seized?" I wanted the entire story now.

"Most of my fellow crewmen were sent to Fort St. Mark—a prison in St. Augustine. Some were sold into bondage. A few were pressed into the Royal Navy. But as I bear the name Lane, and the privilege it accords, fate was kinder to me. My father and uncle pooled wealth and power to apply pressure on the magistrate overseeing my imprisonment—or I should say my *situation*. That was his term, because there was some confusion over whether I was in fact a prisoner.

"To charge me with war crimes, the courts would have needed to recognize America as a sovereign and independent nation. The magistrate chose to view me as an errant British subject instead. But in that view, I couldn't be detained without being charged with a crime. Thanks to that neat riddle, I was pardoned of any wrongdoings and ordered home." He tipped his chin toward the cuddy. "That luxurious little hovel is Old Jansen's idea of 'private quarters,' as provisioned for in my release papers. I shall be holed up in there until I reach Massachusetts, whereupon I'll be officially free again." He smiled—a real smile. "You seem appeased, Miss Coates. I hope I've earned the right to a few bites."

"Yes—eat," I said, feeling like I'd snapped out of a daydream. Never had I been spoken to so openly about the war, but that was only part of it. It was no hardship to look at him, I was realizing. Asa Lane was handsomer than any boy I'd ever seen—by leagues and fathoms, really—and sitting across the table from him, I hadn't a prayer of ignoring it. I couldn't tell whether his eyes were blue or brown. Brown, I thought, 'cause his hair was dark and wavy. But they were beautiful-shaped eyes, whatever their color. Set a little wide and canted at the edges, like under the weight of his lashes. It gave him a solemn look—or a determined one. I couldn't decide.

He picked up his spoon and waited.

"Oh." I picked up mine.

Our dinner was fish and mashed turnips—smash, as we called it in West End. It was overcooked and runny, but I wasn't complaining. In West End, I worked sunup to sundown hoping I'd end up with enough peas and rice to cure my hunger. I had no problem at all with baskets of food showing up at my door.

As we ate, it occurred to me that Lane had kept his word so far, answering my questions and not asking any back. That began to put me at ease.

I could do this. All I had to do was keep on asking questions without overthinking my motives or worrying about looking greedy or covetous. I swallowed a bite. "What would I need to learn if I wanted to become more refined? More ladylike, I mean?"

"Movement," he replied right away, like he'd been waiting for the question. "Your manner is too sharp. You'd need to modify the way you walk, the way you sit, the way you use that spoon."

I sat up straighter. Relaxed my grip on my spoon, holding it more like he held his. "How should I do those things?"

"With elegance and reserve, but also naturally. Gracefully." He glanced toward the stern window. "That music you hear— that is how you ought to move."

The jigging had ended and now the fiddle played a slow, wistful tune. It made me think of seaweed swaying with the tide. I nodded. "I can learn that. What else?"

"Your nose is peeling from the sun. Wear a hat. Keep to the shade. And try to appear a little less hardy. Feign seasickness or heat exhaustion, for instance. Pretend offense when the hands speak coarsely near you. That sort of thing."

They were the same sorts of things Mama had been telling me

for years. As Sewel had turned me into *una niña salvaje,* she'd tried to keep me feminine. "What else?"

"There are rules of propriety." He tipped his head toward the cuddy. "A lady would never, in all her life, have opened that door for me. Her virtue would be her top concern. There's etiquette to consider as well, such as proper table manners."

"I got *plenty* of virtue, Lane," I said, suddenly feeling unvirtuous and more than a little wicked. I shoveled a huge spoonful into my mouth, letting the smash dribble out. "Tabuh murmurs, too," I said through my chewing.

He laughed. It was a different sound from his speaking voice. Husky and loose. "Skip those, then. The real work would be improving your conversation. Reading will strengthen your expression. Words have power. Learn them and that power becomes yours. You'll also need to consider the quality of what you say, which ought to convey modesty, amiability, and elegance."

"Saints . . ." I sat back in my chair, daunted at last. "I'm none of those."

"With respect, Miss Coates, I disagree. I've just discovered you are amiable."

I fussed with the edge of my napkin. Never had I been complimented by anyone but Mama or Mercy. But he hadn't really complimented *me.* "Well, I hate to disappoint you, but I'm not Miss Coates. My name's Frannie. Francisca Tasker. Frannie's fine."

"I'm not disappointed. Not at all. Glad to meet you, Frannie." We fell quiet and sat smiling at each other as the fiddle finished its tune and began a new one. Nothing changed, but suddenly everything felt different. The darkness outside seemed darker.

The creaks of the ship, softer. Even the air inside my lungs felt lighter.

"Frannie, if you can pretend that cut doesn't hurt," he said after a while, "then I think you can pretend anything." I touched the spot above my eye, where his gaze had moved. It felt wet and crusted. Hot and sore. "You really ought to close it with a few stitches. And soon, or it'll scar badly."

"A few *stitches*? It's *skin*."

"Skin can be sewn."

I cringed. "A horrid thought! I could *never* do such a thing."

"I could, for a trade."

"A *trade*? Saints, Asa Lane. You talk like causing pain's a favor."

"I'm good with needle and thread. I was a sailmaker's mate for a time."

"Now I know you're lying. No gentleman would ever do that."

"As it happens, I'm no gentleman."

I frowned. "Then why are you so . . . so . . ." He was educated and mannered, that much was plain, but then again, I'd seen him brawl with Hackett and speak boldly toward the captain. He had tears in his sleeve. Scratches on his neck. And that lean sort of stare. Truth was, I didn't see where Asa Lane fit.

"My father is the gentleman. I'm only his misbegotten son."

"Misbegotten? So you're . . ."

"His bastard. Aye. That's what I am. His 'great mistake,' as he likes to say. The consequence of an affair he had in Paris one year with a young mademoiselle. My mother was only fifteen when she had me. She died soon after I was born, so I was sent to my father's home in Rhode Island. There, he raised me with just enough polish not to shame him any more than I do by existing. I left his home at thirteen and took to the sea, where amongst other things, I've learned to suture gashes." He paused. "I'm no gentleman, Frannie. Nor am I a surgeon. But I do have sure hands."

I'd been trying to understand something about Lane—why he had a separateness about him, like a ship at sea—and now I finally did. He'd never had anyone but himself to depend on. I wanted to know more about him, but he seemed desperate to poke my head with a needle. "I'm not saying yes—I'm *not*—I just want to know . . . what's the trade?"

"I put two points on it. Three, if needed. And in recompense, tomorrow I ask the questions and you answer them."

I laughed. "Tomorrow, you say?" I couldn't seem to stop shaking my head. But I couldn't say no, either. My forehead throbbed. I'd felt like a leaking boat for days. And I'd seen ladies in Nassau with perfect skin; I knew my life as Miss Coates would be easier without a bad scar.

I got up before I could change my mind and went for the sewing kit I'd seen earlier.

Asa chose the finest needle and then tore a strip of material from the sleeve of my gown, tugging a thread loose. "Silk is best," he said. As I watched him lean over the candle and thread the needle deftly, I wondered when this night had gone sideways on me.

"Should I sit or stay standing?" I asked, my voice wobbling. The point looked so sharp.

"Stay standing." He stood and came over.

I found myself staring at his chest; it seemed a better spot than his eyes. "You should do your sleeve next, since you'll already be sewing." Words were spilling out of me. He smelled like ocean and sweat. But a clean sweat, not sour like Sewel.

"Good idea. Tilt your head up."

I had no choice now, so I did. His eyes were blue, but *deep* blue, like the sea just after dusk, and so heavy that he looked downright sleepy, though I knew the truth was the opposite. He handed me a towel. "Hold this here for the blood."

"Why are you helping me?" I blurted out as I pressed the towel under my eyebrow. I couldn't catch my breath.

"I don't know. I'm not sure I should be." He rested a hand on my forehead, lightly pinching my skin, and brought the needle close with the other. "Ready?"

"Yes."

The needle drove in. Tears sprang to my eyes and my heart began to bang a slow beat.

"You all right?"

"Mm-hm." But I wasn't entirely sure. "Why shouldn't you be helping me? You think it's wrong for me to take Miss Coates's life?" I had to keep talking. Anything to take my mind off the pain.

"If your plan is to truly become her, then yes. I do think it's wrong. Dangerous, too."

"Dangerous how?" I knew what *I* worried about. I might never be polished enough to pass. If I was caught in my deception, I imagined I could be sent to a women's asylum. Or perhaps punished severely. But I wanted to know what Lane thought.

"To begin with," he said as he tied off the string, "you're heading directly into war. Captain Jansen was right. Manhattan is the center of conflict. The island is in American hands, but the

British have totally surrounded it. They will lay siege any day. Here we go, Frannie. Once more." The needle bit again, but I breathed through the worst and it passed quickly. "Well done. We're almost there. War aside, you'll be meeting a guardian who might've met the true Miss Coates, and no amount of practice at etiquette or decorum would help you then."

I hadn't given the doctor much thought. Antigua and New York were worlds apart and I hadn't read a single thing about the doctor in Miss Coates's journal entries. But what if Asa was right?

I couldn't let it stop me. Alone, knowing nothing and no one, I was vulnerable. And I had to honor my promise to Mama. I didn't want to spend the rest of my life existing hand to mouth.

"There's risks no matter what I do," I said, "but the only chance I've got at a good life is this—by being her."

He fell silent as he tied the thread again. His fingertips were covered in my blood, but he didn't seem to mind. Right then, I already knew no other conversation in my life would be as strange or memorable. "You're thinking something. I can tell."

The corners of his mouth tugged up. "Aye. 'Tis the problem with having intelligence."

"Well, tell me. What is it?"

"There's a contradiction in your plan. You say becoming Miss Coates is the best chance you have at a good life, but if you become *her*, then you will no longer be *you*."

"That's the idea. I don't want to be me. I've got nothing, Asa. Not anymore."

He stilled, meeting my eyes. "I understand that. But . . . have you truly thought this through?"

"I don't have to think it through." Frustration bubbled up; I just wanted him to agree with me. "I can't go *back*. I won't live the rest of my life married to my own stepfather—a drunk who wants me dead!"

Soon as the words left my mouth, I regretted them. I didn't want Asa's pity, nor his disgust. I stood, my brow throbbing, my breath trapped inside me. Hating Sewel. Even now, he could cause agony in my life.

"All done." Asa set the needle down and washed his hands in the basin. He came back and drew the towel from my forehead. "That's my best work yet."

"Thank you." I swallowed. "It hurt more than I thought it would."

"You bore it with bravery." He set the towel aside. "Astonishing bravery, as a matter of fact." His gaze roamed over my face. "I have many questions, Frannie. Many."

"You do?"

"Aye. I long to hear the story of your life."

My eyes blurred. "You may not like it. There's shipwrecks in it, and sharks, and lots of terrible moments."

"You disappoint me. I'd hoped for more."

"Oh, there's more. There's hurricanes, horrible things said and done—and even a very broken heart."

"Very broken."

"Yes, *very*." With every word, knots loosened inside me. I hadn't realized how much I'd needed to unburden myself. Even this little was helping. "But you can't ask me anything till tomorrow, remember?"

"Ah, right—our trade only begins then." He crossed his arms. "Well, it won't trouble me to wait. Patience has never been—"

71

Outside, the ship's bell began tolling the hour. Asa's mouth lifted with a slow smile, and with every ring his eyes shined brighter.

I counted twelve bells before it fell quiet again.

When it did, I could only shake my head. "It's *midnight*, Asa."

"And so tomorrow becomes today. Now, where to start?"

CHAPTER 7

GRAVITY

★

With a book under my arm and fresh confidence in my heart, I returned to the crates amidships in the morning. Asa had said reading would help me talk more like Miss Coates, so I'd grabbed the thickest tome I could find from the captain's shelf. Settling into my spot, I opened Sir Isaac Newton's book, hoping it would teach me pretty words and high-flying ideas.

Sir Newton's book, I soon discovered, was duller than my elbow's elbow. My mind kept straying from it and running back to last night and all its surprises.

I reached under the brim of the straw hat I'd found in the captain's cabin and ran my fingers over the newly healing cut. It felt a bit itchy but pleasantly tight. All night, Asa and I had shared our stories, one tumbling after the other without stopping, like waves. I'd told him about Sewel, and wrecking, and Mama. He'd told me about his sailing adventures to places like Newfoundland and the Azores, and how he had spent a year with an uncle in Paris when he was ten, learning to value the part of himself that his father loathed most.

Thinking about our night, it seemed a kind of magic had happened. We'd squeezed sunlight from our sad stories and laughed in the darkness. We'd made time itself disappear. It was the best night I'd ever had. Stitches and all.

A soft whistle had me looking up. Asa crouched on the lines above me, a round-brimmed hat throwing a shadow across his smile.

I glanced around. The hands had all moved to the bow and were taking turns peering through a spyglass. "What are you doing up there?" I called up, just loud enough for him to hear.

"Old Jansen needs me. He's saddled with a crew full of landsmen."

I had noticed that myself. As boatswain, Hackett supervised the men working the ship's deck. He was constantly yelling and threatening to punish someone for doing something wrong. With the war, most able sailors had turned to privateering, as the earnings were far better, so merchant ships ended up with inexperienced crews.

"But you told me you were a *marine*," I said. Topmen did the most dangerous work, balancing on ropes halfway in the sky—often in rough seas.

Asa smiled and pretended to wobble on the lines. "Oh no, you're right. I'd better learn this quick. How's your head?"

"Still full of nonsense. You didn't fix anything, Asa."

He laughed. It was my favorite discovery overnight: we could make each other laugh. *Really* laugh, like I did with Mercy, shoulders shaking and everything. "How is Sir Newton treating you? Are you enjoying gravity?" he asked.

"Oh yes! Gravity is so . . . so . . ." I had no idea what gravity was. "So rare."

He shook his head, his grin going even wider. "Rare is you, Frannie. Rare as a comet. Meet me by the prow at the change of watch?"

"Yes—superb."

Asa said something waggish-sounding in French, then climbed the lines like he'd been born to it.

=★=

Ten minutes later, I stood by the prow pretending to read as I waited for him. A few of the hands working nearby glanced over, one or two staring lecherously, which set my heart racing. Even disguised as a highborn lady, I wasn't safe.

Soon Asa strode up with a length of line on his shoulder. He glanced at me as he dropped it on the deck. For a few minutes, as he unwove a frayed line from a clew and replaced it with the new one, he spoke to a man with a grin like a bag of nails who was swabbing the deck nearby.

Last night, as we'd shared our stories, Asa had sewn the tear in his sleeve, and now I found myself remembering the wave of muscle that had peeked from beneath. With the sweat shining on his neck and the easy way he spoke with Bag of Nails, he looked like any other deckhand—no gentleman in him. Mama would have called him a true Son of Neptune. I smiled, thinking of what Mercy would've said about Asa Lane. *Lord, Frannie. For him, I'd suffer.*

Soon the crew was piped in, ending their watch. The men

nearby set their tasks aside to hurry into the shade belowdecks. Finally, Asa joined me at the rail. He took a shilling from his jacket pocket and flipped it into the sea.

I shot forward with a gasp and watched it disappear into the water below.

"That's gravity," he said. "If it were rare, rain would not fall and we'd all be somewhere up in the cosmos. Like you, Comet."

I smiled. Mama had called me Mi Vida, but I liked Comet, too. "Well, I understand it now," I said. I'd never again forget gravity. "But you threw a good coin away!"

"Nay. I invested it in education. Here . . ." He reached into his waistcoat and took out a pamphlet. "Try this instead of Newton. But best keep it hidden. A good Tory girl like Miss Coates would never read such seditious writings."

I reached for it, then hesitated when I saw the cover. Even in my tucked-away corner of the world, I'd heard of *Common Sense*. "Asa, I'm a Tory, too." Sewel preferred calling us "Loyalists," as he thought it got right to the point.

"Take it," Asa said. "I dare you."

"I dare *you*, Asa Lane," I shot back.

"Do you?" His eyes narrowed and his smile hinted at mischief. "What do you dare me to do?"

My heart stumbled inside my chest. "I don't know yet. But I will."

Voices pulled my attention away. A few of the men on the new watch were making their way toward us. Our time for talking was over.

I spotted Hackett amongst them, his walk swaggering and

his chin lifted mulishly. As he looked from me to Asa, fear over-shadowed my good mood. If they fought again, I was afraid it would turn deadly.

Asa's eyes grew hooded. He picked up the old rope, settling it on his shoulder. "See you tonight."

I held my breath till he'd safely passed by Hackett.

=★=

I returned to the crates with the pamphlet slipped inside Sir Newton's book. Careful to keep it hidden from curious eyes, I peered at the cover more closely, running my fingers along Thomas Paine's name. The paper looked worn, softened like old leather. I wondered how often Asa had read it. Had he shared it with other people?

Were any of them girls?

I had seen a copy of *Common Sense* before. Sewel had gotten one from a tobacco trader who came through West End in the spring. He'd brought it on the wherry one day and read it with a rum bottle in the crook of his arm, tearing out each page as he went and tossing it into the sea.

"Why're you doing that?" I'd asked when I could no longer resist my curiosity.

"'Cause it's poison," he'd replied. "'Cause it preaches dis-loyalty and anarchy. Says here I'm as worthy a man as any king." His wiry eyebrows rose up. "Do I look kingly to you, Francisca?"

I held my tongue. With Sewel, few questions had right an-swers. If I'd learned anything from him, it was to choose my words with care so as to avoid stepping into a trap.

"You want to read it, don't you, Frannie? I can see it in your owl eyes. You can read it. All you gotta do's go get those pages. Go on. Go get them."

By then, the papers were spread far and wide on the shifting tide, and I was exhausted from diving all morning. All I wanted to do was get back to West End and find Mercy so we could spend the rest of the day together. "I don't want to read it."

"You sure?"

"Yes, sir."

He'd laughed. "That's good. I wasn't gonna let you anyway."

Now I shivered at the memory. Sewel lived for two things: rum and tormenting me. Had he the means, I knew he'd come after me. He didn't, thank goodness. Sewel was a lazy drunk who'd never leave West End.

I opened the pamphlet—and then tore through it in a breathless fever, reading all forty-some pages without once looking up. Thomas Paine believed all men were born of equal power and no one could be born to preference. The Bible supported this notion, he wrote, which made kings and monarchies ungodly and wrong. But the worst part—or the best?—was how he compared England to a wicked parent.

What had the American colonies done but try to please their mother country? What had they asked for but fair and just treatment? How long, Thomas Paine asked, must America accept the abuses heaped upon it?

Lord, how his words rang bells inside my heart. A horrible tyrant had mistreated me, too. I couldn't count the number of times Sewel had been unfair and unjust toward me.

I was just like America, was the truth.

Only, I couldn't declare independence. All I'd been able to do was run.

═★═

That night, Izra brought another basket of food for me, the captain likely assuming that I preferred to be alone. If only he knew the truth.

As Asa and I shared a dinner of turtle soup, I practiced my table etiquette and told him what I thought of *Common Sense*. When I had finished, he sat back, his eyes shining in the candlelight. He'd spent the day working in the tops, trimming sails and performing repairs while balancing on lines dozens of feet above the deck. Somehow, he looked both tired and enlivened by it.

"Have I just witnessed the birth of a patriot?"

"No." I shook my head. "*Saints,* no."

"Did you not just say that reading that pamphlet felt like discovering your own mind?"

"Yes, but it doesn't change that I'm a Loyalist. I can't allow my ideas to impede with that."

"Interfere. And why not?"

"'Cause I'm loyal." I didn't see why it was so difficult to grasp. "Loyalty means there's no choosing. The whole point is you hold to it no matter what. That's what makes it loyalty."

"And you learned this from?"

"Sewel."

Asa nodded tightly. "Right."

"You knew that."

His shoulders ticked up. "It's nonsense."

"I always thought so too, but—" My throat suddenly tightened and my voice broke. My whole grown life, Sewel had made me feel like *my* thoughts were nonsense and put *his* rotten ideas in my head instead. He'd poisoned me. But I was free of him now, so I didn't understand why I felt like crying.

Asa's gaze held on me, steady as the flame between us. I had no idea what thoughts ran through his mind, but I didn't regret telling him about Sewel. Not even the awful parts. All I felt in his gaze was his strength, passing to me. My own strength rising up, up, up, till I felt it right on my skin.

Then something changed. Suddenly I felt a kind of warm riptide, pulling deep in my core. I picked up my wine and took a bigger sip than I needed. I'd never felt desire before, and the power of it shocked me. Till then, I hadn't thought I *could* feel it. "If what Sewel says is drivel, then what *is* loyalty?"

Asa didn't answer right away. "The reverse of what he says," he replied finally. "Loyalty isn't fealty. Nor is it duty. It can't be demanded or coerced. It must be given freely, like love. One feels it here." He brought a hand to his heart. "As a tyrant who has denied us God-given rights, who has abused, attacked, and killed his own subjects, King George is responsible for the loss of my loyalty—and that of many, many others."

"People have been killed?"

"Aye, at Lexington and Concord. Just to our north, at Sullivan's Island. Those were military actions, but innocents have suffered as well."

I gazed at South Carolina's coastline through the window, trying to imagine a battle, but everything seemed so peaceful, even cheery. For the past hours, boats had brought over supplies from the little town that glowed in the distance. Rather than risk losing the ship's crew to press-gangs, Asa had told me earlier, Captain Jansen had brought the shore's enjoyments to the *Ambrosia*—the "shore's enjoyments" being libations and women, by the sound of things. Laughter, the song of fiddles, and the clomping of dancing feet made a happy noise on the deck above us.

"This war, Asa. Do you truly think it's right?"

"I do, with everything in me. Access to life, liberty, and happiness should be equal to all. We should all have a say in deciding our own fates."

"Well, I never will." I drew a breath, pushing against the tightening in my chest. "Decide my own fate, I mean. Neither will Izra, nor my friend, Mercy. My mama never had much choice. . . . Liberty's not for anyone with a master or a husband."

Asa's gaze fell to the candle between us, which had begun to flicker. "I won't deny the world is unfair. It is. Often horribly. But I believe we can change it for the better. I have to believe that."

"*You* can change it. Not me."

"Why not you?"

"You know why." He watched me, waiting. "I just *said* why, Asa. 'Cause of *this*." I tugged on the sleeve of my gown.

"And you'll allow that to stop you?"

"It's not up to *me*. That's the *point*." I stood and went to the window. He would never understand. He *couldn't*. Even as Miss Coates, I could never go wherever I wished nor do whatever I wanted. I'd never have what he had just 'cause he'd been born a *he*.

A woman's giggle drifted down from the deck above. It sounded forced and a little hysterical. Edged with fear. It only seemed to prove everything on my mind.

I heard the scrape of a chair behind me. Asa came over and

stood before me. Tiny spots of moonlight dashed his nose and bottom lip. "Some help I've been today. Putting treasonous ideas into your mind. Angering you."

"That's not what you were doing."

"Wasn't I?"

I stared into his eyes. He'd made me *think*. "I never thought about changing the world before, Asa. I never even thought I'd *see* any of it."

He tipped his head. "There you are, Miss Tasker. The world."

I looked through the window, at darkness and moonlit clouds. I couldn't actually see the world, but I felt it out there. Waiting for me. All that I'd never thought possible.

"I'd thought to teach you the minuet, but I think I've done enough damage for tonight."

"You haven't."

He smiled. "That's good." We stood a few moments, saying nothing. The space between us drawing me in like the warmth of a fire. Asa cleared his throat and dropped his gaze. "I don't know why I'm still standing here."

"You said we were going to dance." I grabbed his hands, surprising him. Surprising myself, too. But I wasn't going to let him leave. "So let's dance!" I tugged him along as I began to move to the music playing above us. "I already know some country dances."

"Frannie, no—this isn't—I don't know what this is."

"Dancing!" I pulled him in a circle and began to skip. He was right—I had no idea what I was doing. When I danced at beach bonfires with Mercy, we kicked our heels and twirled so fast, we turned the world into a blur. But I was determined not to let him disappear into the cuddy. "Come on, Asa!"

He laughed. Then he wrapped his arms around my waist and swept me in a circle, and we *danced*.

When the music ended, we were both out of breath and sweating. Asa's eyes sparkled with such merriment, I wondered if he'd ever had fun before. And though *I* knew I had, I'd never felt like this. All I wanted was to get closer to him. "I just thought of my dare," I said. "I dare you."

"You dare me?" he echoed. But I could see that he knew exactly what I meant.

"Yes. I dare you."

The longest second in the world passed; then he leaned down and brushed his lips against mine softly, sending heat curling through every part of me. "Frannie . . . ," he whispered by my ear. "Your turn. I dare *you*."

I rose on my toes, threw my arms around his neck, and kissed him. Asa pulled me in tight, his lips parting, his tongue sweeping against mine, and suddenly time disappeared. There was nothing beyond our mouths, gently searching. Our hands, clutching fiercely. And my heart exploding, again and again and again.

We drew apart. I waited for him to say something, but he didn't. I had nothing to say, either. There was no way I could express what I felt. So I stood, wishing he was the sea so I could dive right into him. I wanted to be surrounded by him everywhere and completely. Like water.

=★=

When we started talking again, we didn't stop. We were nowhere close to exhausting our stories. As we sat side by side on the stern bench, with the moonlight dusting our shoulders, he told me about his half brothers, who were serving in Loyalist militia units, and how his political views had only caused more strife between him and his father. Then I told him about how, when the diving was going poorly, Mercy and I sometimes pretended to drink tea deep inside the galleys of sunken wrecks.

"Did you just say you *dive* wrecks?" He brushed the loose hair behind his ear, peering at me. "You actually *dive* them—and you *enjoy* it?"

"Yes! Every new dive is an adventure. It's dangerous, but that's part of why it's thrilling. Sometimes I feel like the thing I'm searching for—a spoon, a Spanish dollar, or whatever—I feel like it's calling to me. Like it *wants* to be found. It's the best feeling."

"I will take your word for it."

I laughed. "You'd like it. The seventh fathom, especially. That's my favorite fathom."

"You have a *favorite* fathom," he said in disbelief. "Hold on— you dive to *seven* fathoms below?"

"Yes, of course. Saints, Asa. Ships don't sink in five feet of water. I dive down to seven fathoms. Ten, twelve, thirteen. Fourteen, when I drop with the anchor or a rock, but I get nosebleeds and headaches, so I don't often do that."

He muttered something in French. "I am astonished. Tell me, Comet. What makes the seventh fathom such a good depth?"

"Well, it's—" I smiled, getting an idea. "Close your eyes. I'll take you there now."

His eyebrows lifted. Then he leaned back against the window and shut his eyes. "Very well. Take me."

My pulse sped at his words and I couldn't resist pausing a moment to study him. He had a keen mind. A mind for midnight thinking, Mercy would've said. As he waited with his eyes closed, I could feel it quietly working.

Before he could catch me looking, I leaned back and closed my eyes. Then I drew a big breath and began. "Imagine you're on a boat that's bobbing under a bright sun. There's not a cloud in the sky above you, not even a wisp, and everywhere you look, clear water's dancing with light. You fill your lungs with air, as much as they'll hold, and then you draw a little more—then you *dive*.

"You break into cool water and the sound of bubbles fills your ears as the heat of the day vanishes from your skin. Then quiet rushes in and your thoughts grow louder, louder, louder, till all you hear is yourself and the deep hum of the sea. If you stretch out like an arrow and kick, the first fathom's over quick.

"Now you're in the second fathom and your body wants to pop up like a cork. Kick with all your might down to the third. The water feels a little colder, and your ears ache like they'll burst. It's best to push the pressure out or it'll only hurt worse as you go deeper.

"The fourth and fifth's just kicking and swimming and letting go of some sunlight behind you. The sixth, you might panic a bit, thinking you need to breathe, but you don't. There's more breath in you than you think, so keep swimming 'cause you're almost there. Then, suddenly, you are.

"In the seventh fathom the sea's no longer wanting to spit

you out. It wraps you up like a blanket, and you can relax and float now 'cause it's got you. It's holding you and you can just stay there, nothing pulling at you. Nothing pushing. Your heart beats real slow and you feel so calm, like you're drifting in a wakeful sleep. Now you can do your best daydreaming, 'cause it feels a little like you already are.

"Right now, in the seventh fathom, there's a castle with towers rising up into a night full of stars. Everything's blue, like twilight, but there's a spot of gold in the highest tower. That's my mama up there, smiling and beautiful. And look, Asa. Do you see it? A comet, shooting across the sky."

"I see it," he said softly. "How long can I stay down here?"

"Only a few seconds, but time's different here. There are moments inside of moments—and every one of them's lasting."

"I feel that." He fell quiet for such a long stretch, I felt myself drifting. I hadn't just taken him to the seventh fathom. I was there myself. "Is this your place, Comet?" he asked at last.

I surfaced just enough to answer him. "Yes . . . it was."

CHAPTER 8

COMET

★

Four days later, the shrill blast of a whistle tore me from the pages of *The Odyssey,* where I'd discovered a world as vivid as my own imagination. I blinked away the images of Sirens and goddesses and spotted Hackett at the quarterdeck, piping urgently on his bosun's whistle. I searched the wide sea around us. It'd been a sluggish day of sailing. With no wind to carry us, the Virginia coastline had appeared stuck on the horizon, but now I saw no land at all. I saw white spots of canvas on the ocean blue.

Sails.

A massive ship appeared to be heading directly at us.

"Ready yourselves!" shouted Livingston, one of the hands, as he pounded past me. "They're flagging us!"

"We are doomed!" yelled another man as he disappeared into a hatch.

Fear lifted the hairs on my arms. I set my book down and hurried to the quarterdeck stairs, desperate for answers. As I weaved past the panicked crew, I looked for Asa's lean figure or the gray knit cap he'd tugged on that morning, but I didn't see him.

I shot up the stairs and ran to the rail, where a gust nearly stole my straw hat. I trapped it and scanned the sea, my heart galloping inside my chest.

Somehow, the war had fallen off the map of my mind. As South Carolina had glided by, I'd filled the blank pages in Miss Coates's journal with the rules of etiquette I learned from Asa, turning it into a commonplace book. Cruising past North Carolina, he'd taught me the figures of the minuet. There'd been other distractions, too. Like Asa's lips, which turned me liquid, and his chest, which was a perfect place for me to rest my head as I plunged us both into my imagination. "Take me back to the seventh fathom," he'd whisper. I was more than happy to oblige.

Hackett preoccupied me as well, always circling like a shark, ready to intimidate me. With all that, I hadn't given a thought— not one—to the possibility of the *Ambrosia* being seized at sea. What would happen to me if it was?

I spotted the approaching ship. I couldn't make out its colors, but it was a heavy vessel. A frigate, I was almost certain, charging after us under a full spread of canvas.

"Miss Coates!" Izra ran up. "The captain suggests you return to your cabin, miss!"

I was already on my way. I had to find Asa.

Inside the cabin, I rushed right to the cuddy and pulled the door open. Empty.

"I'm here, Frannie." I spun as Asa stepped through the main door. "Captain Jansen sent me to see that you're safe."

"What's happening?"

"We've been flagged by the Royal Navy. They will board us

and check the ship's log and cargo." He paused. "And they may press some of the men."

My stomach tightened. I knew the Royal Navy could force men to serve against their will, but it had never mattered to me before. "Will they take you?"

"Nay. My papers protect me."

"*Papers?* That's what you're trusting in?" I had no paper in my life. All I knew about paper was it tore easily, burned easily, and turned into pulp when wet.

"They're orders directly from the British courts mandating my release in Massachusetts. They won't go against their own laws." His mouth pulled up on one side. "Are you worried about me?"

"Yes! Very!" The noises were only growing louder outside. I could feel fear humming in the wood around me.

"There's no need. I promise. You won't be rid of me for a few days yet."

"A few days? That's hardly better." Fear had me by the throat and I was speaking without thinking.

"Frannie . . ." Asa stepped closer, his eyes shining brighter. "What if we stayed together? Beyond New York?"

"*Stay* together?" It made no sense. There were only two ways that could happen—with me either as his wife or as his mistress.

"Be with me, Frannie," he went on. "I know I haven't any fortune to speak of, and that we're young, but I promise to always provide for you, and what I can offer you is me. My name. My mind and body. My heart, which is half yours already. Throw away this plan to become Miss Coates and be with me . . . forever." He paused, drawing a breath. "Marry me, Comet. I dare you."

89

Awe and wonder flooded me, filling me with a glowing warmth. Such beautiful words. For *me*. Was his heart truly half mine?

I wanted to leap into his arms—but suddenly I remembered my promise to Mama.

"Asa, I—" My voice broke. I had to be strong. Mama had prepared me for this. Even now, I could hear her whispering in my ear.

> *Never marry for love, as love doesn't buy bread.*
> *Never marry in haste, as those who rush, stumble.*
> *Never marry low, as poverty is a stain that never*
> *washes out.*

I wouldn't make the mistakes she'd made with Sewel. No matter what I *felt*, I had to choose *right*. "Asa," I tried again. "I'm sorry, but I *can't*."

Pain filled his blue eyes. Clouds over the sea. "Of course." He cleared his throat and looked down. "Forgive me. That was rash, and I . . ." He let go of my hands; I had no idea when he'd taken them. "I have to go. The crew's been ordered to muster."

"Wait, Asa." He stopped at the door. I waited for him to turn back, to look at me. He didn't. "There's things you don't know. Things I've promised." My chest was caving in. I didn't know what to say to make everything right again. Had I broken us?

"You don't have to explain." He glanced over his shoulder. "I'll see you tonight."

After he left, I stood and waited for the hurt to lessen, but I only hurt more.

I *knew* I'd done the right thing. A week ago, he'd been a stranger—how well did I truly know him? Enough to promise I'd love and obey him the rest of my *life*? Mama had married Sewel hastily. I'd seen where that had led. And what sort of life would it be—the wife of a poor privateersman in wartime? As Asa faced daily peril at sea, I'd be alone for months or years, praying he made it home. Every wharf town in the world was filled with widows of mariners. I did not want to be one of them.

And I had to honor Mama's memory and live for more than she'd had.

I wouldn't let her down. No matter how much it hurt.

=★=

I returned to the main deck, my breath still ragged, an ache in my heart like spikes had been driven into it. The noise and commotion of the crew had ended and an uneasy silence hung over the ship. I slipped into the shady spot by the quarterdeck stairs and peered at a scene that seemed unreal.

The *Ambrosia*'s hands stood in a neat line. All sixty-some men, shoulder to shoulder. Their backs straight. Their eyes pinned to the massive warship looming beside us.

In all my years wrecking, I'd never seen anything half so grand. It rose like a mountain of shining black paint and gleaming gunports, its sails filling half the sky. A ramp ran from one of its middle decks to the *Ambrosia,* where Captain Jansen stood waiting with Hackett and Izra.

Marines came pounding across, two by two. Everything about them, from their bayonets to their crisp red coats and white cross belts, looked so sharp. Hewn from wood. Behind them followed men of a very different feather. Rough men in shoddy garments, carrying cudgels and ropes. Never had I seen a press-gang before, but I knew I was looking at one now.

I turned back to the *Ambrosia*'s men, my knees softening beneath me. They had piled into all their garments and wore shirts upon shirts and trousers upon trousers, sweating under the weight of all their earthly belongings. The fear in their eyes reminded me of stories Sewel had told me of the Royal Navy's harsh treatment and meager pay. Four hundred lashes for laziness. For stealing a biscuit, a thousand. *The rebels don't call us bloody-backs for nothing.*

I spotted Asa near the end of the line. He stared straight ahead, his dark hair curling out from beneath his knit cap. Nothing that had happened in the past fifteen minutes felt real. Had he really just asked me to marry him?

An officer crossed the ramp to the *Ambrosia* last. He was a short man, nearly as slight as me, his coat made of more gold epaulets and buttons than wool.

He spoke to Captain Jansen in hushed tones. Captain Jansen handed over the ship's logbook. The officer took it and passed it immediately to the marine beside him. In moments, I watched bright uniforms disappearing into the *Ambrosia*'s dim hatches as the marines began a search of the ship.

Suddenly, the lieutenant saw me by the stairs and walked over.

Without deciding to, I felt myself drifting out to meet him.

"Good day, Miss Coates," he said with a bow. "I am Lieutenant Vance of His Majesty's *Jason*." He had clever eyes, I noticed as

I curtsied. Black as a bird's. "Captain Jansen has just apprised me of your misfortune. I am exceeding sorry for your loss, madam. You have been in good care on the *Ambrosia,* I trust?"

"Miss Coates does not speak, sir," said Captain Jansen, "on account of the shock."

"I see." Vance's lips thinned like he'd tasted something bitter. "Well. A pleasure, madam." He turned back to Captain Jansen, no longer interested in me. "I assume all hands are present?"

"Aye, sir. But I must say, sir, if I may, that I am rather deprived of able sailors at the moment."

"Aren't we all," Lieutenant Vance said dismissively. Then he went to the beginning of the line and began to pace along it, taking each man's measure. Eyeing them up and down like livestock. Nearly a hundred men were out there, yet all I could hear was the knock of his heels and the quiet whistle of a hot breeze blowing through the rigging. "You." He stopped before Livingston. "What is your name, birthplace, and position on this ship?"

"Edward Livingston, sir. From Sussex. And I'm a gunner."

"Are you any good?"

"I try to hit my marks, sir."

"Better than do some. Will you volunteer for His Majesty's Royal Navy, Mr. Livingston? Or shall we encourage you?"

Livingston glanced at the press-gang, waiting like eager hounds. "I . . . I will, sir."

"You will what, Mr. Livingston?" Vance said with a cheerful lilt in his voice.

He enjoyed this, I realized.

"Volunteer, sir."

"Brilliant. Your king thanks you."

Livingston dropped his head and stumbled over his own feet as he left for the boarding ramp.

Lieutenant Vance moved down the line, pressing three more men into service. With every one, my fear and anger increased. I thought of Thomas Paine's arguments against tyranny and Asa's words about loyalty *not* depending on coercion.

This was coercion. *This* was wrong.

As Lieutenant Vance neared Asa, I held my breath. Asa looked relaxed, his gaze distant, like he was lost in a memory, but I could see the corded muscles in his neck.

Vance slowed down; then he caught his toe on the deck and stumbled. He frowned in annoyance at the planks and kept walking.

I gasped, relief flooding over me, and whispered a quick prayer of thanks to God for His mercy.

Vance rejoined Captain Jansen, but he was immediately distracted by Hackett beside him. "You look worse for the wear, sailor," Vance said, peering at the bruise on Hackett's face. In the days since his brawl with Asa, it had settled into a purple half-moon. "How came you by that most colorful eye?"

Oh no.

Hackett's scowl moved to Asa. He jerked his chin. "That pup there did it. He's a Yankee privateer."

Vance swiveled and strode back to Asa. "A rebel, are you?" He linked his hands behind his back. "Did you attack that man?"

There was no lilt of enjoyment in his voice anymore. Now it hummed like a quiet poison.

"Aye, sir. In my defense," Asa replied.

"But you provoked him?"

Even from where I stood, I could see the bone in Asa's neck bob as he swallowed. "Aye, sir. I did."

Silence stretched out, loud and thick.

"And who was the victor?" asked Vance.

"*Me,*" Hackett said. "*I* won."

Vance never looked away from Asa. "And you, lad? What say you?"

Asa glanced my way. Briefly, but I saw concern, apology, and so much more. "I say that I am still drawing breath," he replied.

Vance threw his head back and laughed, a brittle cackle that filled the cloudless sky. "You colonials are spirited, that I'll grant. Your name, lad. And your provenance."

"Asa Lane. Marblehead."

"Massachusetts? I ought to have known. Do you hate England so much, Mr. Lane, that you enjoy preying upon her ships?"

Please, Asa, I begged. Now was the time to shrink. To bend and cower and agree.

"Lieutenant Vance, if I may." Captain Jansen came forward. "Mr. Lane has been pardoned for his actions." He fumbled inside his coat. "Here are his release papers."

The papers.

Lieutenant Vance glared at them for a moment, then snatched them up. "It says here you pleaded habeas corpus, Mr. Lane." The sheets quivered as he read. "That you were pardoned because you were 'denied the rights of a true Englishman to due legal process.'" He pushed the papers back at Captain Jansen. "If you are so determined to be treated as a 'true Englishman,' I believe I may be of assistance. Providence has brought you the perfect opportunity to make amends for your perfidiousness. A way to honor your beloved Britannia."

I couldn't stand by anymore. I stepped forward.

Something latched onto my wrist.

"Don't move." Hackett's voice rumbled into my ear. "En't no stopping this, so don't try."

"Will you volunteer for your king's navy, Mr. Lane?" Vance asked.

Silence again, then Asa's answer knifing through it. "Nay, sir. I will not. For I have no king."

Murmurs of shock swept the deck.

"But you *do*, rebel," Vance said. "You *do*. And we are happy to help you remember him."

Vance gave no order to the press-gang, but the brutes surged forward. Two enormous men flung themselves at Asa, grabbing his arms. Asa struggled and pulled away. They pressed after him. In a flash, fists were swinging—Asa's and theirs—and the rest of the gang pounced. They tackled Asa to the deck, the sound of bone and muscle against wood thunderous. Asa kept struggling even as the men piled on him. Then two men slipped cudgels from their belts and swung them.

"*No!*" I shouted. My voice so high, so piercing amid the thick bruising sounds.

Heads spun to me. Miss Coates had finally spoken. But the men turned away just as quickly, far more gripped by the violence.

The press-gang kept beating Asa, every second an eternity.

My eyes blurred. My lips went numb.

"Steady, Little Salt," Hackett muttered. "It's almost over."

But it wasn't. It went on so long that men began to take turns on him, catching their breath like they were at some mundane task. Izra buried his face in the captain's side and began to cry. Some of the *Ambrosia*'s crew turned away. Stars speckled before my eyes and I felt myself swoon.

"Yield, you stubborn fool," Hackett hissed, his grip the only thing keeping me standing.

Finally, the press-gang stepped back.

Asa lay on the deck, unmoving. Blood poured through his lips and streamed from his nose. Both his eyes were sickly swollen. His shirt and jacket were torn away, and welts and gashes covered his arms and his chest.

The world tilted.

Was he dead?

He coughed—a muffled, pained sound. Tears of relief spilled down my cheeks.

Vance sauntered over to him. "I beg your pardon, Mr. Lane? Was that another objection?" He nudged Asa's shoulder with his shoe. "Mr. Lane? I guess not. Bring him."

The men in the press-gang heaved Asa up. Then they carried him off the *Ambrosia*—and out of my life.

CHAPTER 9

LADY

★

After Asa was taken, I couldn't get him out of my mind. I hated myself for standing by as he'd been beaten. I worried about him and prayed he'd recover, but I wasn't a fool. I knew men died from much less than he'd suffered. Nights were the hardest times as I'd lay awake for hours, wading through every moment we'd shared—our last conversation especially. Without him, the cabin felt too empty. Too dark. Asa had taken the stars with him.

My heartache was constant and agonizing, but I forced myself to continue with my plan. I kept to myself in the cabin, where I practiced walking and curtsying properly and eating every meal, bite by careful bite. I finished *The Odyssey* and kept reading through the captain's bookshelf, writing down phrases and words that were *lyrical* and *erudite* in Miss Coates's journal and then committing them to mind. My traumatic muteness had ended with one shouted word on the deck, but I still feared sounding *unsophisticated,* so I worked to become *eloquent.*

Day by day and hour by hour, I prepared for the test that awaited me in New York, but inside I found myself changing as well. Asa had challenged my thoughts about the war and about monarchy and what was fair and just. Because of him—and because of what I'd seen *done* to him—my eyes had been opened. I'd shed Sewel's beliefs and found my own.

Tyranny was wrong. Abuse was wrong. And power ought *never* be misused.

If it made me a rebel to think so, then a rebel I was—but only in secret. As strongly as I felt, I could never share the truth with anyone. Soon I'd be Miss Coates, and she was a Loyalist. My new political mind was just another part of me that would have to stay tucked away if I wanted a new and better life.

As the *Ambrosia* coasted closer and closer to New York, I started to understand that I wasn't only becoming someone else—I was *un*becoming Frannie. Miss Emmeline Coates would never dive for sunken treasure, nor float seven fathoms below, lost in her imaginings.

If my plan worked, my days spent wrapped in the sea would forever be behind me.

=★=

Five days after Asa was taken, on the day I turned sixteen, I stood at the bow as the *Ambrosia* cruised into New York Harbor. Asa had warned me that I was heading toward the very seat of the war. He had not been wrong.

Hundreds of ships were gathered, floating on every last spot of water, their masts crowding so thickly they resembled a forest scorched of its leaves. The *Ambrosia*'s hands shouted huzzahs and waved their hats as we slid past frigates and sloops, fireships and bomb ketches. Every last vessel proudly flying English colors.

As we sailed into the harbor, Lewis, one of the hands, named the landmarks for the rest of the crew. Staten Island, with its sprawling British military camp. The Neck, where the passage grew pinched. Tiny Governors Island. And New York itself—which looked like a jumble of jagged rooftops and church spires clustered at the very tip of York Island.

What a besieged place it was, so surrounded by its enemies. And I was going right into it.

As I stood, marveling at the display of naval might, anger welled in my gut. I had seen the cruel way the Royal Navy wielded its power. I touched the thin scar that ran through my eyebrow, thinking of Asa. Whatever I looked like on the surface, my heart was decidedly with the Americans.

"There you are, Little Salt." Hackett came over and propped his arms on the rail beside me. "Out of your hiding spot, I see. What do you think?" He tipped his thick jaw at New York. "You scared?"

"Yes." There was no point in lying. If the doctor spotted me for a fraud and I didn't pass as Miss Coates, I didn't know what I'd do. "Especially when I look at your face," I couldn't help but add. I knew he'd come over to remind me of his threat.

He snorted. "En't anybody ever teach you to watch your mouth?"

"Yes. Then I tried to kill him."

Hackett stared at me. "My, my, Little Salt. I think I believe you."

"I don't care what you believe." I looked away and drew a deep breath. Just mentioning that night with Sewel made me queasy.

"I en't blind, you know," Hackett said after a few moments. "I know you fancied Lane. Don't waste any worry over him, though. Soon as he's able, he'll escape."

I swallowed the lump in my throat. "How could *you* know that?"

"I know things."

"You know *nothing*, Tom Hackett. Not a thing."

"All right, I'll tell you. Firstly, 'cause you couldn't separate that boy from his beliefs with a hammer and a pick. Secondly, 'cause only men who volunteer can be tried as deserters. Lane didn't go willing. He *fought*. He took that beating 'cause he knew it was his only way of getting out clean when he sees a chance to run."

I blinked my welling eyes. It sounded like Asa to think ahead. "Well, maybe he shouldn't have done that. They almost killed him. Maybe they *did* kill him. You saw how badly he was—"

"Lane'll be fine. That lad's tougher than leather."

Days of fear and regret caught up to me, lighting like a torch. "Stop talking like you *liked* him! You *hated* him!"

"I hate everybody, Salty. With Lane it was just easier."

"You've got no right to make light of this! You're a coward and a hypocrite. You claim to love England, but when a chance came for you to fight for it—truly fight for it—you just stood there and did *nothing*. It should have been *you* pressed into service, Hackett. Not Asa. If you were a man of honor, you'd have gone in his place."

"A man of honor?" He shook his head. "No, no, no. You got me all wrong. A man like me's got no use for honor. I wake up every day thinking, 'How am I putting food in my belly today?' If I'm lucky, I get it done. Dinner's what I live for. And I know you understand, 'cause it's the same damn thing for you."

I opened my mouth to argue, but he was right. Every moment of my life had always been about simple survival. Since I'd left West End, it had only looked a little different.

I blinked at Hackett, seeing him with fresh eyes. "We're just a pair of thieves, Hackett. You, taking Miss Coates's jewels. Me, taking her life. We're scavengers, Hackett. That's all we are." Suddenly, I felt so weary. Would my future be the same, even as Miss Coates? I sighed, swatting at the sweat tickling my neck. "Don't you ever wish there was more?"

More. It was what Mama wanted for me. More than she'd had. A good life. A good husband. But I wanted more than *her* more. I wanted to do things that mattered. I wanted to sink my teeth deep into the world. I'd stood by as Asa had been beaten. I never again wanted to feel that way again—like *less*.

"Maybe a long time ago I wished for more," Hackett replied. He clasped his hands together. "Too late now."

I studied the lines carved into his cheeks and between his eyebrows. I wondered how hard his life had been, to stamp so much anger and pain on his face. "I don't think it's too late." I didn't think it was, for either of us.

His eyes slid over to me. "You forgetting you hate me or something?"

"No. I remember."

"Well." He sniffed. "What's a little brat like you know about anything, anyway?" he said, but his tone was light. Almost teasing. He straightened off the rail. "Good day to you, madam." He bowed and took three steps before turning back. "Oh, I almost forgot. I won't be requiring those jewels after all."

"You mean—?"

"Yes, Salty, that's what I mean. Keep 'em, and don't make a big fuss about it. You need 'em more than I do. Besides, I already got my dinner worked out tonight, and tomorrow's tomorrow."

He winked and swaggered off, swinging his bosun's club like the sun shone just for him.

I watched him go in silent astonishment. The old buzzard had a heart after all.

=★=

A few hours later, with the *Ambrosia* safely riding at anchor, Captain Jansen came to my cabin to escort me to New York. "The boat is ready for you, my dear," he said, with tears in his eyes. He had dressed in his finest for the occasion, a navy suit and bright white neck stock. "I shall be quite sad to see you go."

"You've been so kind, Captain," I said, and meant it. He'd helped me when I'd been at my lowest.

"I only wish I could've done more." Izra entered behind him with Miss Coates's jewel trunk, setting it on the table. Captain Jansen placed the key on top and smiled. "I thought you might wish to wear a pretty bauble to meet your new guardian. Take your time. I will be waiting right outside."

I bolted the door behind them and sat at the table. The trunk's silver hinges made not a squeak as I opened the lid. The jewels inside glowed in spite of the dimness of the cabin in the cloudy afternoon. I lifted the pieces out, one by one. There were velvet chokers with cameos. Grand necklaces of gold and silver and gemstone. Earrings and rings. Bracelets, broaches, and more. Instead of feeling relieved or happy at such a bounty, a sullenness came over me that I couldn't explain. What I needed, much more than fine gemstones, was to feel safe.

I picked up a strand of pearls. They were made of the sea, like me, but I wasn't half as beautiful and flawless. I reached into my pocket for the captain's watch. A gift, from that first day. It was the only thing in the world that felt *mine*. I fastened it round my neck by a blue ribbon, turning it into a necklace. A reminder of the day I'd decided to become someone else.

Ten minutes later, I sat beside the captain on a shore boat, watching the *Ambrosia* recede. It had been my home for only two weeks, but I knew I would never forget it. The crew had lined up along the rail to watch me go, but I didn't see Hackett until a whistle pulled my eyes up to the crow's nest. He pulled off his hat and waved it in the air. I raised my hand and waved back.

"It seems we're providing the afternoon's entertainment," Captain Jansen said. "We have quite an audience." The *Ambrosia*'s men weren't the only ones watching us. Men stood at the rails of every ship, staring down as we passed. "We are crossing a barrier very few others have managed to cross in weeks. New York has been blockaded, and the Americans have a Committee for Detecting and Defeating Conspiracies regulating entry, for fear of spies."

"*Spies?*" I whispered.

"Nothing to worry you, my dear. These are war matters. You shall be quite protected from them."

Asa appeared in my mind, beaten unconscious on the *Ambrosia*'s deck. I'd already been deeply hurt by "war matters." I knew better than to believe I'd be shielded from them.

As we drew closer to the dock, the city seemed to stretch back and never end. So much hard brick. So many sharp rooflines. New York looked like it could devour me in one bite.

"Is that your Dr. Holdridge?" asked the captain.

I followed his milky eyes toward the dock. It was empty—strangely so—except for the small group walking to the end. There were two ladies dressed in gowns wide as sails—one purple, the other yellow as an egg yolk—and a short gentleman in a burgundy coat and buckskin breeches. As he walked with the ladies, he watched our boat and raised a hand, signaling to us.

"Yes, Captain. That's him."

I felt light-headed as we glided up to the dock. I couldn't look up as the men tied off the boat, but I felt Dr. Holdridge staring down at me. I squeezed my hands into fists till my fingertips tingled.

Had I prepared enough?

But if he saw me for an impostor, none of my efforts would matter.

The captain handed me up to the dock. As soon as I shifted my weight onto solid ground, my legs folded beneath me.

"Steady, dear." Dr. Holdridge reached out and took my arm. I looked right into cheerful blue eyes, like glass in sunlight; then they widened with shock. "You are *not* the girl I remember." I jerked back, my heart dropping like a rock. "My *dear* Miss Coates," the doctor continued, "you've gone and grown up!" His soft cheeks plumped with a huge smile. "How *glad* I am to see you again. How very, very glad I am, in spite of the unfortunate circumstances that have brought us together again. Do you remember me? But how could you, you were so young then. Scarcely a child of three—and then, like now, you had suffered so much. I came to Antigua to see your father just after your dear mother passed to heaven, God rest her soul. History can be so cruel in its patterns, so unfair in doling out hardships."

He kept talking with eagerness and such kindness. Assuring *me* of our connection.

As I stood there, listening, I felt no relief at having succeeded. All I felt was a sagging awareness that I was now going to have to live completely in lies and fabrications. My gown, my petticoats, my name . . . it was all false. Even the blood in my veins, which *was* true, felt hot and unfamiliar. But this was my chance at a good life. Everything coarse and uncivilized about me had to stay in the past. From now on, everything was going to be perfect.

I sank into a deep curtsy.

Then I rose, a lady.

CHAPTER 10

DRAWN FROM MEMORY

★

New York City
August 1779

"What a day it was when you arrived, Emmie. Do you remember it? A bit over three years ago, was it not?" Dr. Holdridge—Uncle Henry for a long time now—smiled as he peered through the chariot window, the August sunlight turning his wig into a white cloud.

Outside, Water Street bustled with waterfront commerce. Carts filled with green goods rolled over the cobblestones. Hogsheads rumbled over the dock. Stevedores, hawkers, newsboys, and drunken soldiers weaved past one another, every last one of them calling out or laughing. New York had proved to be many things, but quiet wasn't one of them.

"Of course I remember, Uncle," I replied. "How could I forget? That was the day I found a perfect home with a wonderful uncle and aunt." I looked from him to Aunt Nora, the two of them snug as squirrels on the bench across me, then to Lucy at my side. "And the day I met a dear cousin and true friend of my heart."

The best lies were also truths. I *had* come to love them. The

Holdridges were devout, decent, and loving—they knew no other way but kindness. Before I met them, I'd never have believed such people existed.

Lucy reached over and took my gloved hand in hers. "It was a very good day when you came to us," she said, "but today will be *sublime*."

Her skin looked like buttermilk in the sunlight, her blond curls like silk. Lucy had terrified me at first. I couldn't imagine ever being like her. So delicate. So feminine. Now I was—but it hadn't been easy. For a year, I'd squirmed in heavy, hot gowns and knocked vases off tables with my full petticoats. I'd cried myself to sleep over my dancing stumbles and regretted a hundred artless comments that had popped out of my mouth. But I'd survived and learned a couple of things along the way: people believed what they *wanted* to believe, and wealth forgave just about anything. That first year, *I* didn't convince New York's elite that I belonged in their midst. Miss Coates's inheritance did.

"Are you happy, Emmie?" Lucy gave my hand a gentle squeeze. "You're finally going to *swim* again!"

Today, I turned twenty-two. In another week, I'd turn nineteen, my true age. As Miss Coates, I was always three years older than myself. To celebrate, the Holdridges were taking me, Lucy, and our friend, Charlotte Winters, who rode in the carriage behind us, to one of the bathing machines on the North River. It'd been Uncle Henry's idea. He had seen them advertised in Rivington's paper—little houses that allowed ladies to bathe in privacy. Emmeline Coates had loved wading in the sea as a girl in Antigua, so of course she'd adore the chance to swim again.

I squeezed Lucy's hand back. "Yes. I cannot wait. Thank you, Uncle, for such a thoughtful gift. It will be wonderful."

Smiles bloomed on every face. Aunt Nora patted her husband's hand.

I looked through the window and slowly let out my breath.

Swimming.

How I dreaded it.

=★=

Half an hour later, we stood on the shores of the North River as Uncle Henry and Charlotte's father, Mr. Winters, spoke with the proprietor of the bathing machines, ensuring that our modesty would be preserved and that an attendant would not leave our sides. For sixteen years, no one had cared where I went. Now, my every move was closely considered and chaperoned. Women were held to modesty as men were held to honor.

Six bathing machines were lined up along the river's edge. They looked like little white huts built atop wagons. We had traveled well outside the city, to where there was nothing but farmsteads and grassy fields alive with butterflies and croaking frogs. In the distance, where the river bent, I could see Mr. Harrison's brewhouse, a lone country establishment. The adults would wait there while we bathed.

"How quaint," Charlotte said, observing the bathing machines. She fanned herself, the ostrich feather in her hat fluttering. She'd dressed in her scarlet sack gown and pink pearls for the outing—what I'd wear to a fine assembly. "They're just as my cousin described in her letters from Wales. That woman there will probably be our dipper—that's what the attendants are called. She will help us undress and be in the water while we swim."

Charlotte Winters was almost nineteen, like me. Unlike me, she thought she knew everything.

"Are we in danger here?" Lucy studied the shoreline, a tiny crease of worry forming between her eyebrows. "I didn't expect them to be in such an exposed location." All three of her brothers had died in the French and Indian War, and conflict of any kind unnerved her.

"We're fine, Lucy," Charlotte said. "This is hardly the front line."

Perhaps not, but danger was still a possibility. Skirmishes often broke out near Manhattan, as it was the British head-quarters for the war. My eyes fell to a powder horn hidden in the tall grass a few feet away. The war was never very far. I moved so Lucy wouldn't see it.

"I wish there *was* a front line," Lucy said. "Or a barrier of some kind that no rebel could ever cross."

My heart had begun to thud. I'd found a life where I fit, but when the subject turned to politics it no longer felt that way.

Satisfied that we were in good hands, Uncle Henry gave me three tickets. "You are to see Maude. She will take care of any-thing you need. Enjoy yourself, dear Emmie."

"Thank you, Uncle." I searched his pale blue eyes. Never had I seen anything but warmth and trust in them.

Maude was a black woman who waited for us by the first bathing house. General Henry Clinton, the British commander, had offered freedom to people enslaved by American patriots, so New York had become a haven for free blacks. Much as I detested the English for their oppressive rule, this was one thing I felt they'd done right.

Maude explained that we would enter the bathing house by the rear door; then a horse would haul the contraption into the river. We would then be free to exit from the water-facing door and bathe in perfect privacy.

"You can take houses one, two, and four," Maude said, piping twice on *houses*. She had a gap between her teeth a little wider than mine that caused her to whistle as she spoke.

"Thank you, but we only need two," I said. Lucy still looked uncertain, and I knew she'd be more comfortable with me.

"But your papa already paid for three, miss," Maude said. People always assumed Uncle Henry was my father. "And the houses are cramped for two. You can't mean to share?"

I turned to Charlotte. "Miss Winters, sharing bathing machines is a common practice in Wales, isn't it?" Charlotte knew a lot, but I could *pretend* I did and that was even better.

Her fan froze in the air for an instant. "Yes, Miss Coates. It is indeed," she said, playing along. "My cousin says that anyone who is fashionable does it. And we won't need two. One will do."

Maude shrugged her broad shoulders. "As you wish, misses."

We climbed up the rear steps into the first hut and sat on the little bench that ran to one side, Charlotte's hoopskirt tilting crazily as we wedged together.

"Really, Char," I said, leaning away. "Panniers on a swim outing?"

"I could have asked you why *no* panniers on a swim outing, Emmie. But I didn't."

111

"What now? Do we undress?" Lucy asked.

With only one grimy window above us, the space was dark and soupy hot with the doors shut. It smelled like rotten wood and the perfume of a hundred strangers.

"Not yet." Charlotte rummaged inside her basket and pulled out a thick green bottle. "First, spirits. Cousin Lydia wrote that it's a necessity before bathing as it promotes a stronger constitution for taking fresh air and cold water. The glasses are buried, and I am too hot to search for them, so off we go." She unstopped the bottle and raised it. "To King George's health." She drank and winced, then passed the bottle to me. "No retreat."

"No surrender," I replied, taking it. The strong punch brought tears to my eyes and sent Lucy into a fit of high-pitched hiccups. Soon, we were powerless to stop our giggling.

"Walk, Amber," someone said outside. "Walk on."

There was a soft nicker; then the little hut gave a jerk and began moving.

"I feel like a highwayman in a wagon," Lucy said through hiccups. "Like we are *stealing* something and escaping into some *dangerous* and unknown—*hic!*—wilderness!"

"Heavens, Lucy." Charlotte took the bottle. "Are you foxed already?"

"Yes! Aren't *you*?"

I was. I felt loose-limbed and relaxed. In the back of my mind, I knew that wasn't good. Keeping up pretense required constant awareness. Constant filtering of what I *wanted* to say and what I *could* say. But I let myself enjoy the lightness in my heart. I loved my friends. I was safe with them. And, for just a little while, I wanted to feel free. "It would be something if there truly were

112

highwaymen nearby, wouldn't it?" I said. "Don't you wish we could have a *real* adventure?"

"Adventures are for novels, Em." Charlotte handed me the bottle. "Here, finish it. The world has gone aswirl."

We lurched to a stop as I finished the punch.

Maude knocked on the door. "Ready for you, misses!" she piped.

Stumbling and laughing, we helped each other shed our hats, gowns, petticoats, and finally our stays. By the time we stood in our shifts, not an inch of the floor could be seen.

I clambered over the mountains of fabric to the door. My earlier trepidation about swimming had made a dramatic reversal. Now I felt breathless. Desperate to do it.

"Emmie, wait. Your father's watch," Lucy said as I grabbed the handle.

Captain Jansen's broken pocket watch sat around my neck, where it had been for years. The Holdridges had assumed it was a memento of Miss Coates's beloved father. I'd never corrected them. "Thank you, Lucy." I pulled it over my head and tossed it into the basket.

Then I opened the door.

A small platform stretched out before me. Steps descended from the end and disappeared into pewter water that rippled all the way to the New Jersey shore. A canvas awning extended above me like a kind of mobcap, providing shade.

Maude stood below me in water above her waist, her swimming gown billowing around her. "Come, miss." She held one hand out. "Nothing to fear. I won't let you go."

Heat spread over me. Sudden. Blazing.

I sank into my legs and leapt clear over Maude's head.

As I sliced into the cool river, a feeling like a shout exploded through my body. I kicked hard, pulling my arms through the water, cutting through it like a knife. I had strength to burn, strength that was furious and neglected. With my breath wearing out, I stretched out my legs and arms as far as they'd go.

The water was murkier and colder than I wanted it to be. There were no swells, no bright fish darting past. There was no white, white sand beneath me. And yet I was *home*.

A laugh of sheer joy burst out of me, carrying the last of my breath away. I kicked up and popped through the surface, still laughing.

Charlotte stood on the steps of the bathing house, her mouth agape. "*Bravo,* Miss Coates!"

"You frightened me!" Lucy said, from the step behind her.

"Sorry." I swam to Maude and treaded water. It was shallow enough to stand, but I could stand *anytime*. What I couldn't do anytime was feel weightless.

Maude clucked her tongue, suspicion in narrowed eyes. "You're a fine swimmer, miss."

"Thank you." I leaned back in the water and stared at the sky. "I used to swim as a girl in Antigua. How I've missed it! It almost feels as though I'm there, in the brilliant blue sea, my toes grazing the soft white sand. And *the waves* . . . There's no better dance partner in this world than Neptune."

With people like Maude, a dose of truth was usually enough to mask the taste of the lies. Peering at her, I could see it'd worked.

Lucy's face had softened, too. "Of *course* you miss it."

Charlotte took Maude's hand and hurried into the water. "Teach me. Teach me to do what you just did."

I laughed. "Happy to. Lucy, are you coming in?"

"No, I don't think so." She came down a step and sat where the water met her shins. "I shall be very happy right here, though. Look at this front-row seat I have to cheer you both on."

That was just what she did as Charlotte and I splashed and frolicked in the water. Soon Maude grew tired of our antics and waded back to shore. Not long after, Charlotte grew cold and went up to join Lucy. I floated and watched the clouds scud across the sky as I listened to them talking.

"Liesje has all three days planned, morning till night," Charlotte said, wringing the water from her chestnut hair. "It will be the wedding of the year, you'll see. Liesje never does anything by halves."

Our friend's upcoming marriage was all we talked about lately, which was saying something. We weren't easily impressed. New York was the main garrison for the British, and we were used to great migrations of military forces. British regulars. Hessians— German mercenaries hired by King George to fight in the war. Loyalist militiamen. Camp followers. They were all constantly sweeping into the city in supply caravans or naval convoys, then sweeping out again to win or lose, live or die. But for us, little changed. We went nowhere. Day after day, we dressed in our finest gowns and danced and dined and socialized, moving from one spectacle to the next, even as the war plodded on.

Never had weddings been my favorite topic, but today I had less patience than usual. I didn't want any reminders of the responsibilities that awaited me. I wanted to keep swimming and reveling in the airiness I felt all the way to my soul.

I kicked away, my shift flowing about my legs, but it was too late. I was already seeing West End's sunny shores in my mind. Then Mama stirring the soup over the fire as she told me about the dangers of marriage and how I was to have more than she'd had. A better life.

A dull pain began to thud at my brow. I shut my eyes and Asa Lane's earnest blue eyes appeared.

Marry me. I dare you.

This was what I'd feared. *This* was why I hadn't wanted to swim. I'd cured myself of the past. I'd gone months without thinking about him, without remembering Mercy's laugh or Sewel's bleary red eyes and slurred threats.

I sucked in a breath and dove. I swam deeper. Farther. Farther still. Pushing myself past the point I could bear. There was no depth in the river, no way to plunge into the bliss of the seventh fathom, so I swam away from shore, leaving everything behind me. Fear, responsibility, lies, love, *everything*.

When my lungs began to seize in my chest, I pushed up and broke the surface. For an instant, I had no idea where I was nor how I'd gotten there. Then I saw Lucy and Charlotte on the steps of the bathing house, waving their arms at me and shouting for help. Maude churned toward me in the water, her arms windmilling in steady strokes.

I kicked in place, blinking hot tears. I didn't want to go back.

I didn't know *what* I wanted.

I waved to let them know I was fine.

Then I pointed myself back to shore and swam.

That night, the Holdridges' friend Judge Latimer hosted a birthday dinner for me at his great house on Golden Hill. Charlotte came with her parents, but Liesje Visser had wedding preparations to attend to. Already it felt like she was becoming someone different. Rebecca Novis, who completed our intimate group of friends, was at a harvest frolic in Albany.

"Miss Coates, when do you think the cake will stand trial?" the judge asked, leaning toward me. My eyes went to the pink patch of skin on his forehead shaped like a strawberry—a scar from when an angry mob of Americans had tried to tar and feather him. Around the time I'd arrived in New York, the persecution of wealthy Tories had been terrible. The judge had escaped before the humiliating act had been carried out, but he'd suffered a burn from the scalding-hot tar. As he always wore black velvet and either a snowy white wig or powder, the patch on his forehead was often the only spot of color on him.

"The cake has been exonerated, Judge," I replied. Earlier I'd joked with him that I spoke the Language of the Law. Now everything we said was the height of silliness—which delighted me, as the judge was one of the most urbane gentlemen I knew. "You may appeal the decision if you wish, but only after we have committed these nourishments to incarceration in Stomachshire."

"Bailiff, if you would," he said to his fork. Then he swept up a bit of rice and ate it.

We laughed, and the coil of tension inside me eased. My morning outing had left me jittery and uncertain, reminding me of when I'd first arrived in New York. In those days, I'd doubted *everything.* My natural expression. The volume of my speech. Even how often I blinked. I'd found my way by imitating Lucy and the other young ladies in our social group. And I'd been fortunate to come into a circle of good people, like the judge, who'd never suspected me.

Thanks to his help, I had inherited the entire Coates estate. That had been a feat, considering the laws designed to keep wealth in the hands of sons, but the judge had influence and saw the proper conveyance of the will to me, the sole surviving heir. Through the process, he'd become a good friend to the Holdridges—and to me.

The judge hadn't yet heard about my "swimming adventure," as Uncle Henry called it, so I described the event and blamed my drifting away from shore on a rip current. No one knew what those were, thank goodness, because I wasn't even certain rivers could have them. My tale drew mixed reactions of amusement and mild concern. Nathaniel Coates had drowned in a shipwreck and, though no one mentioned it, I knew the thought of him was on every mind.

As dinner ended, Lucy and Charlotte placed a little stack of presents in front of me, each wrapped in pretty paper. From the Winters, I received a drawstring purse made of blue silk from the East Indies. "You're always tucking things into your pockets," Charlotte said.

It was true; I loved finding things. Buttons. Flowers. A beautiful line of poetry. It was one wrecker instinct I couldn't rid myself of.

From the judge I received a rock clustered with bright gemstones. "Blue agate," he said. "All the way from the gem mines of Brazil. You can have it made into a necklace if you wish, but I rather like its rough, natural beauty."

I smiled. No wonder I liked him so. "I adore it, Judge."

Aunt Nora and Uncle Henry gave me *Evelina*, a novel I'd been wanting desperately. After months of reading novels to improve my speech and conversation, I'd made the shocking discovery that I enjoyed books. I seldom daydreamed anymore, but reading gave me a similar escape.

Charlotte pushed the next gift at me. "Open, open. Before I do it myself."

I didn't get far before a visitor was announced.

Major John André's entrance always seemed to have the same effect. The gentlemen grinned broadly. Charlotte kicked me under the table. Lucy sat up straighter, sucking on her lips to redden them. Mrs. Holdridge and Mrs. Winter shared a private smile.

André was the most elegant gentleman I knew. Everyone's favorite—including General Clinton, England's top war commander. He had a face like a Greek statue's, a trim build he showed off in perfectly tailored regimentals, and a charming personality only made better by hints of devilment. I knew quite a few young ladies who'd had their hearts broken by him. Some men were King Arthurs, my friend Rebecca liked to say, but André was a Lancelot.

He tucked his hat under his arm. "Friends, forgive me the interruption," he said, his English voice carrying such a fine, clear ring. "But I won't take more than a moment. I sent a message earlier, Judge. My aide-de-camp has arrived sooner than expected. He comes tomorrow. I trust you'll be ready for him?"

Housing in New York posed a real problem. Every day, Loyalist refugees and runaways poured in by the dozens in search of the Crown's protection. It didn't help that the Great Fire had burned down a third of the city's dwellings a few years ago. With a large home all to himself, the judge sometimes lodged British officers.

"Yes, I received your message and wrote back this morning," replied the judge. "I have a relative arriving this week, but there's room for them both. I shall be glad to host your aide, Major."

André frowned. "You wrote me? Do you see how desperate I am for good help? I thank you, Judge. I know Lieutenant Duncan is quite eager to be here." His gaze came to me.

"Of course he must be," the judge said, and smiled at me as well. A chill traced a cold finger down my spine. "Won't you join us, André? I've not yet finished all the cake."

"Cake? Have I interrupted a celebration?"

"Today is Miss Coates's birthday," Aunt Nora said. "Do join us, Major."

"If you insist, madam. But first I must make a delivery." He rounded the table and drew something from his coat pocket. "A very happy birthday to you, Miss Coates." He bowed and offered me a rolled paper tied with twine. "I always keep my ear to the ground."

I smiled and took it. "Of course you do." I untied the twine, expecting to find a few pretty words about friendship, which I felt we had after years of turning in the same social circles. Amongst his many talents, André was a poet—some of his poems were even printed in the newspapers. But instead, I discovered a drawing.

"I did it from memory," he said, "or it would be more exact."

It was rendered sparely, like he'd tried to capture me in as few lines as possible. My face was made by a few slashes framed by curls. The hint of a pocket watch chain disappeared into a squiggle of lace. He had even gotten the scar at my eyebrow, but it was the eyes that drew me in. They were fierce eyes. Bold. The eyes of a girl who hunted through sunken wrecks. Who, when she was pushed, pushed back.

"Expertly done, Major André," Charlotte said, leaning closer to see. "That is her exactly. Don't you think, Miss Coates?"

A shiver rolled through me. "I do. Thank you, Major. The likeness is truly breathtaking."

We left the table and moved to the parlor, where Lucy played the judge's grand Viennese piano and Charlotte sang. While I spent most of my mornings reading novels or poetry, my friends practiced their talents, and it showed. They accompanied each other perfectly. Usually I loved listening to them perform, but I couldn't sit still tonight.

I wandered to the window. Outside, it was dusk and raining heavily. A pair of Hessian grenadiers ran down the street, their footsteps sending up tiny explosions of water.

Swimming had proved to be the mistake I'd expected. My skin felt too sensitive; my stays and gown too tight. I felt pressure inside me, an ache to *open*. Turn outward like an anemone.

"Have you had a good birthday?"

I found a smile as Uncle Henry joined me. "I have, Uncle. Very much."

"I am happy to hear it," he replied.

His wig was slightly crooked, I noticed, and a pie crumb rested on his burgundy waistcoat. I never used to notice such things before. I hadn't cared a whit about appearances until I'd needed to. The higher the status, I'd come to learn, the fewer the crumbs. My inheritance put me above the Holdridges, but the line between us had blurred over the years. My arrival had brought a flood of comforts, like linens and silver imported from England, better foods and wines, additional household help when we needed it—all so I could continue in the lofty mode of living to which Emmeline Coates had been accustomed in Antigua. This had incidentally elevated the Holdridges, which pleased me greatly—and eased my conscience.

"Today is cause for celebration, to be sure," Uncle Henry continued, "but 'tis bittersweet for me. Your father's will provisioned for your guardianship until you reached the age of twenty-two. That means that, as of today, you are no longer my ward. I no longer provide you 'wing, protection, and cover,' in the eyes of the law."

"Oh?" I squeaked. I was going numb from the inside out. This had never been discussed with me. "You have been the very best guardian, Uncle."

"You have made it easy to be. However, I have not fulfilled my obligation to your father. He requested that I see you settled in a good marriage, to a young man equal in fortune and status. I believe I have found such a suitor. The gentleman coming to be Major André's aide has an estimable pedigree. The Duncans are distantly connected to your father, through ties of marriage, which only makes the match seem the more fitting."

I leaned against the window. "The match . . . ?"

"Miss Coates . . ." He took a half step closer and softened his tone. "Dear Emmeline . . . there is no need to be embarrassed. It has not slipped my notice that your romantic prospects have been disappointing. Perhaps I am partly to blame for that. You have a rather masculine intellect and I have not discouraged it, but many men are not so liberal-minded."

Now I *did* feel embarrassed. The only gentlemen who'd ever showed me interest were "socially incongruous," as Aunt Nora put it. Dislikable. Lecherous. Ancient. But I'd never picked up a talent, like signing or drawing. I was no beauty, like Lucy. I had no flair, like Charlotte. And I'd inherited Miss Coates's fortune *and* her tragic past. I knew that men wondered if I'd been damaged by the shipwreck. That others dismissed me simply because I'd survived what sixty men hadn't. I belonged to the Fairer Sex, after all. Not the heartier one. Then there'd been all the little mistakes in my early days. Young ladies didn't catch spiders with their bare hands. They didn't call shoes "stampers" and they *never* belly laughed. My foibles had been forgotten, but an air of the peculiar hung about me. My stolen fortune and family name may have hammered me firmly into society—but I hadn't been driven in flush.

"Situations like yours call for a little intervention," Uncle Henry continued. "Before the door closes, so to speak." He glanced at Lucy. She was twenty-two, *really* was, but hadn't yet drawn the interest of any men of quality. "To get ahead of any trouble, I have made some discreet enquiries and landed on a good solution indeed."

Trouble. Solution. I sounded like something broken. "So . . . he's going to be my *husband*?" I couldn't even remember the gentleman's name. "I have to marry him?"

Uncle Henry took my hands. His felt damp and cool, like raw meat. "I should very much like you to come to this at your own will. 'Tis the best thing for you. Tomorrow, you will meet him." He patted my hands. "This is a gift. Soon enough you will see it for yourself. Happy birthday."

CHAPTER 11

OWN WILL

★

I rose before the sun the next day, tired and tense from a sleepless night of feeling like I was drowning in my own bed.

Tonight, at a garden concert, I'd meet a stranger whom I was meant to marry.

At your own will, Uncle Henry had said. But *my own will* felt like it didn't matter at all.

Of course I'd always known I'd have to marry—it was expected of me and the promise I'd given Mama—but I hadn't lived in the darkness of a man's shadow for a long time and I had a terror of it happening again. All night, I'd dreamed that I'd found *Sewel* awaiting in a flowering garden, his grin like a shark's, full of jagged teeth.

I rubbed my eyes, pushing away the image, and pulled on my brown jacket and ocher quilted petticoat in the darkness. Then I hurried downstairs, quietly shutting the kitchen door as I stepped into the back courtyard.

The sky was purpling with the coming dawn, the stars just beginning to disappear. I drew a deep breath, smelling the tang of the garden herbs and the freshly cut oak stacked by the door. Soon life would settle again.

But not today.

Ducking under a few clotheslines, I crossed the courtyard and knocked on the cottage door. "Malcolm, are you up?" The door swung open as I was about to knock again.

"Good morning, Miss Em." Malcolm pulled a hat on over his red hair and picked up a crate. "You're up early."

"I couldn't sleep," I said, heading for the courtyard gate. Today was our weekly charity outing to the city prisons, and I couldn't wait to get going. This errand *was* at my own will.

Malcolm held the gate open, his gaze following me. He had the greenest eyes I'd ever seen. I imagined they were green as the grass in Cornwall, where he was born. "I am sorry to hear it."

"It couldn't be helped," I said lightly, though I felt the urge to tell him more. How it'd been weeks since my last nightmare of Sewel. How, in sleep, I could never escape him. At times I felt Malcolm alone might understand me. He was my age and had also been raised without wealth or education. He and his mother, Maggie Bowie, were redemptioners. They'd served out their indenture contract years ago, but the Holdridges had kept them on as free laborers. Uncle Henry was a kind master, which wasn't always the case, and the arrangement suited everyone. Malcolm made most of Uncle Henry's remedies in the cottage workshop, mixing elixirs and tonics from recipes. Maggie cleaned and cooked for us, and kept the house noisy with her cheerful voice.

The streets were empty at this hour and the cobblestones wet from overnight rain. The vials of medicine clinked softly in the crate on Malcolm's shoulder with his long strides. American prisoners of war were crammed all over the city, dying of disease and hunger. With Malcolm's help, I delivered medicines to them every Wednesday.

I'd never forgotten my conversation with Tom Hackett on the bow of the *Ambrosia* about having a purpose in life, nor had the political beliefs I'd discovered on that voyage lessened in intensity. Though I wished I could do much more for the cause of liberty, this was the only way I'd found to help that didn't call my loyalty to the Crown into question. Uncle Henry allowed me the errand because it was ungodly to let men suffer—even confounded rebels.

At the corner, I could hear stevedores down on Water Street shouting back and forth as they unloaded cargo. The morning guns from Fort George boomed, scattering pigeons into the sky. In New York, neither God nor the sun began the day—General Clinton did.

We reached the Commons, where Hessian grenadiers in tall furry hats drilled in neat formations, and finally came to Provost Prison, where I smelled the reek that used to make me want to vomit. Men crowded at the barred windows, their garments filthy, their faces grimy and gaunt. The British didn't think it necessary to adequately feed or care for American prisoners. No speaking was allowed, to them or by them, so they stared at me with agony shouting in their eyes.

This was the war I saw—these men. Not fighting. Not the battlefield heroics, nor the frantic retreats, but what came after. Defeat. Injury. Disease. The tragic and undignified deaths of men wasting away in prison. Yet another injustice done by British Parliament that left me livid.

"What have you got for me today, Miss Coates?" said the pox-scarred guard at the entrance, his gaze roaming to my chest and then to my hips.

Prayers for your rotten soul, I wanted to say. But I pretended I didn't hear.

Malcolm set the crate down and removed one of the glass vials, then pushed the crate to the guard.

"Skimming right before your mistress, are you?" said the man.

I instantly felt defensive; Malcolm was as upright as men came.

"No, sir," Malcolm replied, his back straightening with surprise. "Mr. Robert Townsend ordered this tonic. I am delivering it to him next."

"So you say. Put that back or—"

"I'll take it to Mr. Townsend, Malcolm." I snatched the bottle from his hand and stalked away in a fury. "*He* accuses *you* of pilfering?" I said as he caught up to me. "*He's* the one who's stealing."

Everyone knew the guards took anything they wanted from the prisoners. I'd long suspected many of our medicines were resold elsewhere for a profit. Maybe all of them.

"We don't know that for certain," Malcolm said.

"No, we don't. But what do you *think*?"

His eyes met mine. "I think we must trust he carries out his responsibilities with honor."

I sighed. That was Malcolm's flaw, right there. He always assumed the best in people. "That man is a *thief,* Malcolm."

"If he is, he's a thief invested with the king's authority."

There was nothing else I could say. Like everyone else in my life, Malcolm was a Loyalist who'd never speak a word against the Crown.

We parted ways at the corner of Smith and Wall Streets. Malcolm would go on to *Rivington's Gazette* to collect medicine orders that came in from the newspaper ads Uncle Henry ran, then meet me at Mr. Townsend's dry goods store a block away. For thirty steps, I got a tiny glimpse of independence.

Inside the store, Mr. Townsend was at the counter, predictably lost in a book.

"Good day, Mr. Townsend." I peered at the pages opened before him. "Whose brilliant words are you reading this morning?" Most men grew uncomfortable with my love of reading, but not Robert Townsend. Every week, I purchased a new book from him. Often, we also had a spirited discussion about Milton or Homer.

He looked up. "Ah, Miss Coates. I have just spent the past hour with Alexander Pope, who has taught me that"—he ran a finger down the text, angling his head to read through his eyeglasses—"'fools rush in where angels fear to tread.'"

"I suppose I'd better stop rushing places."

Townsend's smile broadened. He had one of the sweetest smiles I'd ever seen. Slow to spread, but complete—like a sail opening to the wind. "You could never make a misstep, Miss Coates." He closed the book and slid it aside. "I'm afraid I don't have your order."

"I know you don't. *Evelina* was given to me last night as a present."

"Ah, good. Mrs. Holdridge came by yesterday. She was keen

to surprise you. Happy birthday, Miss Coates." His gaze moved past me, to the street outside. "Is Malcolm with you today? I hate to trouble you, but a child is unwell and I had ordered a tonic from Dr. Holdridge. I would be most indebted if Malcolm could deliver it directly, as I'm stuck here until my clerk arrives."

"Of course he can."

"Thank you. The child is in my storeroom with the mother, who's fallen on hard times. 'Tis in this very building, but it must be accessed through the alley. Malcolm won't miss the door—the handle was installed improperly, at a slant. He will find Mrs. Burgin in the room at the top of the stairs."

As he spoke, the same wild feeling came over me as yesterday, swimming in the river. A pressure in me, like I wanted to break open. Release the tension inside.

"Consider it done," I said. "I'll give your instructions to Malcolm myself." I bid him goodbye and stepped outside, feeling the glass vial through the soft silk purse as I rounded the block quickly. It was improper for me to deliver it—Miss Coates should *never* shool about like this—but I wanted to do this small thing. And soon I'd be married; then perhaps my *every* step would be commanded by a husband.

I came to the alley behind the store and dove between the brick buildings, picking past puddles and street rubbish till I found the door with the slanted handle.

I opened it. Narrow steps led up. Gathering my petticoats, I scurried to the top.

The landing was cramped and dim, with only one door. A child's weak cries came from the other side. I nudged it open, my heart racing, and found a tiny, stuffy storeroom illuminated by a single window covered with newspapers. Crates were piled against the walls. At the center, a woman slept in a rocking chair as a baby whimpered in her arms. A girl sat by her feet. She held one of chair's spindles and rocked it in a slow rhythm. Beside her, a little boy played with a doll made of sticks and twine.

The girl saw me and froze. "Mama," she whispered.

The woman jerked awake. "Who are you?" she spat, fixing a vicious glare on me. She had jostled the baby in her arms in surprise and the child began to wail.

"I—I'm Emmeline—Emmeline Coates," I stammered. "A friend of Mr. Townsend's."

"A *friend* of Robert Townsend?" Mrs. Burgin scrutinized me from my Oriental silk shoes to the French hat perched on my head, her gaze so biting my hands came defensively to my stomach. "Forgive me, madam, but I hardly believe you."

It had been ages since anyone had spoken to me so coldly. I felt more awake for it. More alive. "Mrs. Burgin, may I come in please?" I reached into my purse. "I've brought something for your—"

"Stay where you are and never speak my name again."

"I have medicine." My eyes had adjusted, so I could see the poor child's sallow skin. "Please. Let me help."

As her severe expression melted away, I noticed the dark circles under her eyes and her gnawed fingernails. She looked like a woman who'd been holding the world together with her bare hands.

"Mama, please let her come in," said the girl. "Millie is sick."

"The lady only wants to help," added the little boy. "She won't tell the lobsterbacks where you are, will you, miss?"

"Hush, Elias!" Mrs. Burgin hissed, slapping the arm of the rocking chair. The boy jumped clear off the floor, then buried his face in her petticoats and began to sob. His older sister blinked twice and burst into tears as well.

As all three children wailed, Mrs. Burgin and I stared at each other. My heart thundered in my chest and the little boy's words echoed in my mind. I went over them, again and again. *Lobsterbacks.* It was an insulting term for regulars. But even more shocking was the part about staying hidden. This woman was *hiding* from the British military.

I swallowed. "What have you done?"

Her smile was grim. "Do you think I'm going to tell you?"

I didn't, but I *had* to know. Then I realized I already *did.* The British were fighting for control of an entire continent; they wouldn't trouble with prosecuting a woman for any small crime. I licked my dry lips. "Have you—have you committed *treason?*"

The daughter popped up from her mother's petticoats. "It isn't like that! All she does is help—"

"Shh, Kate. Hush, now." Mrs. Burgin stroked the girl's head as she began to cry again. "Don't fuss. All will be well."

"You're a patriot," I whispered. Mrs. Burgin looked up, her eyes going cold as granite. I held my breath, waiting for her to acknowledge it. She didn't, but the truth was plain enough in her silence.

"I am a widow, Miss Coates," she said at last. "If you go to the British, they will imprison me, and my children will have no one."

"I won't. I won't say a word to anyone—I promise you." I felt for her, in spite of her coldness toward me. She reminded me of

Mama when she'd been newly widowed, struggling to care for me after Papa had died. "Tell me what I can do," I said. My mind was on fire, burning to know more about her. Finally, someone with the same political beliefs as me. "Let me help you."

"Forget us. That is what you can do."

"I won't be able to."

"Your problem."

"Please, Mrs. Burgin. You can trust me. We are more alike than you realize. If you'll only—"

"Goodbye, Miss Coates. Close the door as you leave." She bent to her whimpering children, whispering soft comforts to them, clearly finished with me.

I took the vial from my purse and set it on the floor. Then I stepped out and shut the door behind me.

Malcolm stood at the bottom of the stairs, his green eyes wide.

I had no idea how much he had overheard.

CHAPTER 12

SWORD FOR SONNET

★

That evening, I sat in Ranelagh Gardens under a sky filled with clouds and pretended to listen to a string quartet.

My friends sipped tea and coffee. Our silk petticoats spilled colors down the length of our row like a wave at sunset. Lucy perched on the edge of her seat, listening with her entire body. Charlotte whispered with Liesje Visser about her wedding festivities, which would begin tomorrow. Rebecca hid my new copy of *Evelina* in the folds of her petticoat, squinting to read in the dim lantern light. It might've been any ordinary night, but it wasn't.

I felt light-headed, almost dizzy, my ribs pushing against my stays as I fought for more air. I ached to look around me.

Was my future husband here?

On top of that distraction was Mrs. Burgin.

A *patriot.*

I had *years* of political outrage built up inside me; had I finally found someone to whom I could voice my opinions? I desperately wanted to see her again. I needed to know more about her.

I wanted to help her in whatever trouble she was facing. I'd have to go back *tonight,* in secret, as tomorrow we were leaving for Liesje's wedding.

A thrill skittered through me at the thought, and I found myself lifting out of my chair. "I'm going to walk the garden path a bit," I told Lucy. I couldn't sit any longer—not when I felt like I wanted to take off and fly.

She looked up, her gaze dreamy. "Shall I come with you?"

"I could never take you away from your beloved Bach. I won't be long."

As I left the seating area, I noticed Uncle Henry and Judge Latimer talking with some other gentlemen by the tables of champagne and wine in the back. Older men in fine wigs and silver-buckled shoes that flashed in the darkness. I recognized them—displaced Tories from Virginia who'd come to New York, like so many others, for the protection of the British military. Several of them owned expansive tobacco plantations.

My mind shot back to Mercy and the time we dove, so eager to find a silver tea set, a gold coin, and instead found rusting manacles and chains spread over the seabed. So many scattered over the white sand, there'd seemed no end. Some with bones still attached. Mercy had cried for a week after that.

"Oh—pardon me," I said, bumping into one of the men on my way to the gardens. His champagne jumped out of his glass and drenched his waistcoat. I heard Uncle Henry sputter and apologize, but I kept going. "Monster," I whispered.

My mind had gone to Mercy, and there it stayed as I entered the path. I thought of the time she'd thrown fish guts at me and laughed herself to tears. Then me, chasing her across the sand to return the kindness. I had dear friends now. But none were like Mercy. I shoved the images away—my wistful feelings, too. Since I'd gone swimming in the North River, my past seemed to be hounding me.

Delving deeper into the path, I turned my mind back to Mrs. Burgin. How could I visit her—and move through the city streets unseen? If I was spotted out alone, after dark, my sanity and virtue would be questioned. Socially, it would be devastating. Mama had lost everything when her reputation had been ruined. She'd had to turn to *Sewel*. I couldn't let that happen to me.

"I beg your pardon, Miss Coates?" said a male voice behind me.

I froze, invisible pins pricking my entire body. Forcing my shoulders to relax, I turned.

A young officer strode up with his hat tucked under one arm and a hand steadying the saber at his side.

"Good evening, madam. My name is Lieutenant James Duncan and, um—" He glanced over his shoulder and frowned. "Major André was behind me a moment ago. I had asked him to make our introduction."

André stood at the path's entrance surrounded by fawning young ladies—a sight I'd seen a hundred times.

"We may have to get by without him," I said, my voice high and shaky.

"So it appears." He took a step forward. "Well, I am . . ."

"Still Lieutenant James Duncan?"

"Yes." He looked down at himself and laughed. "Yes, it's still me. I am Major André's new aide-de-camp—boarding at Judge Latimer's. I understand your family is close with the judge?"

"We are indeed. He is like an uncle to me." Words were somehow coming out of me without any involvement from my mind.

"I met him only today, but he seems a capital man," said Lieutenant Duncan. "He has been a very accommodating host. He has a terrific library, and his beds appear to be quite soft."

A laugh burst out of me.

He winced. "Oh no. Did I just mention his *beds*? Miss Coates, forgive me. That was indecorous and . . . disastrous. Believe it or not, I was trying to make this *less* awkward."

"You have not offended me, Lieutenant. And in a surprising turnabout, I think you have succeeded in your goal."

"Thank you. You are kind."

"On occasion."

A slow smile spread over his face.

I relaxed a little, my attention finally settling fully on him. Lieutenant Duncan had fine, straight features. A mouth that seemed to want to smile and eyes the same warm wheaten color of his hair, which he wore unpowdered and in a simple queue. I couldn't resist a look at his figure. He had an athletic build, with strong calves and thighs that gave shape to his fitted white breeches. By the way he stood, I could tell he felt comfortable in his body.

Suddenly I realized he was standing still, waiting for me to finish my perusal.

I turned away, my embarrassment sharp.

"Might I join you, Miss Coates?"

"You may, Lieutenant." We entered the rose garden path and walked in silence, our footsteps loud on the gravel. Was he observing *me,* too? What did he think?

"A fine night, is it not?" he asked after a little while. "I am glad the rain has held off."

"Very fine. And it was clever of the proprietor to create stars for us." I looked to the paper lanterns strung above us. "Since the clouds have not cooperated and cleared." I cringed. Small talk was the work of the devil.

"Indeed." He glanced up. " 'Doubt thou the stars are fire.' "

" 'Doubt that the sun doth move,' " I said, picking up the next line. " 'Doubt truth to be a liar.' "

" 'But never doubt I love.' " He smiled. "Have you seen *Hamlet,* Miss Coates?"

"I have only read it."

"I believe it will soon be staged at the theater," he offered. "But I may be wrong. Perhaps it's *Macbeth.*"

"Oh," I said witlessly. I stopped to admire a white rose bloom, unable to think of anything else to say. Courting was such a complicated riddle. I was supposed to be modest and agreeable, yet also lively and spirited. But not *too* spirited. I wasn't a horse, after all. And intelligent, but only mildly, as too much intelligence was undesirable in ladies. Inevitably, when I tried to banter, the expectations—and constraints—overwhelmed me.

A violin solo began in the concert area, the sound such a rich, plaintive wail it raised the hair on my arms.

Lieutenant Duncan tilted his head, listening. "Beautiful, isn't it?"

"Like grief, if grief were music." Just *once* could I say something soft and feminine?

He looked over sharply. "Miss Coates, you have put my *very* thought into words. That violin is undoubtedly in mourning. In moments like this I feel such devotion to my king and country— and such thankfulness not to be ruled by the nonsensical American Congress. Can you imagine a world without music? How can this glorious sound possibly contribute to depravity and idleness?"

"I thought it was only theater." We began walking again. "Was it music, too?" I'd heard Congress had prohibited theater performances, but it had never affected New York.

"The injunction was against any entertainment that diverts the mind away from the defense of the freedom. Have you ever heard such irony? 'Tis as though they are saying, 'We want rights, so we shall *take away* rights.' Forgive me—I did not mean to bore you with politics."

"Not at all. I was thinking how right you are." And how this conversation suddenly interested me. Officers were always talking about war and politics *near* me, but never *with* me. This was a refreshing change. "I wonder, Lieutenant, if the rebels have told themselves that the ends justify the means?"

"That is what I tell *myself* all the time. War is hypocrisy. We are fighting to restore peace, after all. And the right to attend theater."

"The sword for the sonnet?"

"Madam, you are brilliant. I must amend the Duncan arms. *In ferrum pro verbum.*"

"It *does* have a good steely ring. But do you mean to say that you have qualms about the war?"

"No indeed. No qualms here. Just earnest deliberation and respect for the complexity of the situation. I never want to be a man who makes easy with war—I hold my honor too high for that. But I shall never fail in duty to my king, nor do I fear walking difficult paths. One only becomes stronger through adversity." He stopped, so I did as well. "Miss Coates, is it normal for you to elicit private confessions from people you have just met or am I such an easily picked lock?"

"Perhaps I have a secret key, Lieutenant." Saints, what had I just said? Never had I sounded so dizzy and flirtatious. "How goes the work with Major André?" I asked, moving to safer ground.

"Excellent. He is an outstanding superior. He is loved by all and no one denies him anything. I am trying to learn his ways."

I laughed. "And how are you faring?"

"Not very well yet, but I am a good student and keep hope for the future. Which reminds me . . . will you be attending the Visser-Devoor wedding? I thought perhaps we might continue talking there? Not that we need stop talking now. The opposite, in fact, is what I was trying to say. Before I interrupted myself." He shook his head. "You know, for a moment, I thought I'd rescued it."

"You had, Lieutenant. For a moment."

"'Tis something, I suppose."

We stood, smiling at each other. Waiting as an elderly couple strolled past us.

He had enchanted me, I realized. Caught in his amber gaze, I felt warm and glowing. Like a lantern had been lit inside me.

Who *was* this handsome young gentleman with beautiful lips and intriguing conversation? Then I remembered—he'd been put up to courting me, and I now understood why.

Lieutenant Duncan likely had a good name and reputation but lacked wealth, which I could provide. We were problems and solutions, after all. Estates and family names to be protected and strengthened through marriage bonds. It stung, but this was how it needed to be. And if a fortune had drawn him to Miss Coates, how could I really fault him? It had drawn me to her, too.

Lieutenant Duncan shifted his weight. "Miss Coates, I have enjoyed your company tremendously." His voice deepened with sincerity. "Might I see you again tomorrow?"

"Yes," I said, and almost said it again.

I wanted to see him. I wanted more of this good ache humming through me, like I was a string played by a bow.

It'd been such a long time since I'd felt it.

Three whole years.

CHAPTER 13

ACROSS THE RIVER

★

A few hours later, just after midnight, I prepared to leave the house to return to Mrs. Burgin.

I stuffed twelve Spanish dollars into my new silk purse. Money, I well knew, rescued desperate situations better than any novel's hero. Grabbing my black velvet mantle, I blew out the candle and crept downstairs.

In the kitchen, I hurriedly packed cheese, apples, and bread in a basket for the Burgin children. My every movement sounded too loud and my fingers twitched. Lucy's tabby cat, Johann, watched me from his spot on top of the cupboard, his tail swishing. I'd just added a jackknife Maggie used for peeling to my purse when I heard footsteps crunching in the courtyard.

I spun to the door. Terror speared through me. Through the glass, I saw a face hovering in the darkness outside.

It wasn't Sewel—it *wasn't*—but it took me a few seconds to recover. I released a hissing breath and opened the door for Malcolm. My memories needed to quiet down again.

He stepped inside and pulled off his cap, brushing a hand

over his spiking red curls. "My turn not to be able to sleep this time." He wrung the black wool cap in his hands. "I heard what that woman said earlier, at Mr. Townsend's. I have been worrying that . . ." He glanced at the basket. "That you would go back."

"I *am* going back." I slid the basket onto my arm. "I have to help her."

"Let me go with you. It's dangerous out there, Miss Em. At night especially."

I knew it was. New York brimmed with soldiers and displaced men. Attacks on women were far too common. I wanted to point out that I had a jackknife and that my dark cloak would keep me hidden, but they seemed like ridiculous defenses now. "You would be dismissed if we were discovered. You and Maggie would be sent away."

"I will lose my honor if I do not go with you. That I cannot live without."

I shook my head. He had more dignity in one eyelash than most gentlemen I knew. But why shouldn't he come? We were only going a few blocks and we'd only be gone an hour. Two, at most. "Whatever happens tonight, you must *never* speak of it to anyone. Do you promise?"

"You have my word."

That was more than good enough for me.

We left through the courtyard gate and made our way into the streets. My legs felt shaky at first, but I soon found my stride. Walking with Malcolm felt familiar—it was everything else that seemed strange.

New York was a different place at night. Only weeks ago, General Clinton had issued a curfew at evening gunfire, but no one would ever know it. Laughter and music poured from taverns. Sailors and soldiers crashed through the streets, stumbling and stinking of rum and ale. Every second that passed, I felt better about having Malcolm with me.

In minutes, we arrived at the door with the slanted latch in the alley behind Townsend's store and took the narrow steps up. I felt light-headed as we reached the top.

The door to the little storeroom was open. Mrs. Burgin stood inside, fastening the ties of a mobcap under her chin. She stilled as she saw us, the lone candle burning on the windowsill painting her in silhouette.

"You're back," she said, without a trace of surprise. Her three children slept on the floor, piled together like kittens.

I licked my dry lips. "How is the baby?"

She finished tying her cap. "Asleep now. The tonic you left helped."

Never had thanks sounded so ungrateful.

"I am glad to hear it." I lifted the basket. "I've brought food for—"

"Thank you." She took the basket from me and set it down, then stepped out and shut the door behind her. I heard Malcolm bump into the wall as he stumbled back. "Why are you really here?" she asked. We were cramped on the landing now, face to face in the darkness.

"Because I want to know why you're hiding from the British. I need to know."

"Miss Coates, why are. *You. Here?*"

She said the last two words separately, filling them both with power. Suddenly I became aware of my own blindness to the

144

situation. No amount of explaining would put me—a highborn lady—in the position I was in now. To answer her question, I'd need to begin with the story of a girl who'd once been a wrecker in West End, who'd been living a lie for years and was now suffocating and utterly desperate to feel something *true*.

Mrs. Burgin sighed with impatience, her breath whispering past my cheek. "Go home, Miss Coates. Before you damage yourself beyond saving. You haven't the slightest idea what you're doing."

"I do, Mrs. Burgin," I insisted. "I've been waiting for this. I've been waiting for *you*." I felt pulled toward her strength. Intrigued by the mystery of her. Even her sharpness drew me in.

She looked past me. "And you? Are you here for answers, too?"

"I am here for Miss Coates," Malcolm said.

Her gaze returned to me. "You both ought to have a higher regard for your lives. Come. Follow me." She slipped between us and glided down the stairs, stopping at the bottom, where the light of the streetlamps found her. "You want answers, Miss Coates, but so do I—and I shall have mine first."

We followed her without a word, venturing back into the streets.

Though she was even shorter than me, she walked quicker than a sandpiper. She took us north on Water Street—then north and still farther north. With the city blocks disappearing behind us, anticipation buzzed inside me. My lungs opened. My stride lengthened. The night's sights, sounds, and smells sharpened. I felt like I was breathing through my own skin.

As we reached the outskirts of the city, we passed a field of makeshift shacks. Stray dogs pecked at dying cook fires. Men's arguing voices rumbled to my ears. Like the Holy Ground to the west of us, I knew these were brothels and molly houses—brothels catering to men who favored men. Places where the orphaned and destitute often ended up. Where I might've ended up, if not for Miss Coates.

Leaving the field behind, we crept past a pair of snoring Hessian sentinels guarding a shipyard, where hulls curved into the sky like giants' carcasses, and finally came to a ropewalk that stretched down to the East River.

A small boat rested on the muddy bank, two men standing by it. One chewed a piece of straw as he watched us. The other watched the river like he saw more than darkness and water.

"Mrs. Burgin, don't you think it's time you told us where we're going?" I asked. "You can't expect us to leave—"

"Stay here. I'll only be a moment." She walked away.

I let out a shaky, exasperated breath. This had already gone farther than I'd expected. At least an hour had passed since we'd left home.

"We shouldn't go out there." Malcolm stared at the river. "It's past curfew, and there are night patrols."

He was right—boats out after gunfire were in defiance of General Clinton's laws. There were plenty of other dangers, too. When Maggie laced my stays and curled my hair in the mornings, she sometimes told me about wealthy Tories being kidnapped and held for ransom. About women, lured from the city and ravished. *Best you know a little truth about the world,* she'd say.

I knew plenty of truth. If we went out on the river, we might not make it back.

"I cannot protect you out there, Miss Em."

"Go, then."

"Not without you."

I'd put Malcolm in a terrible position, but I couldn't turn back now. I was close to something important. Something valuable. Whatever awaited at the end of this journey was calling to me. "I have to see this through."

"Then so must I."

Mrs. Burgin returned. "They are ready for you," she said.

I knew better than to question her for more.

As we walked down to the waterside, my heart punched inside my chest.

Mrs. Burgin made quick introductions. The man with the straw in his mouth, Austin, handed Malcolm a scull. The black man with eyes as clear as water was Beckett. He offered an arm to help me aboard.

"Wait," I said as they pushed off the gravelly shore. Everything was happening so fast and Mrs. Burgin hadn't yet boarded. Then I saw how she stood on the river's edge—her arms crossed, her feet planted firmly—and realized she'd never meant to come with us.

"You will have your answers, Miss Coates," she called out. "For better or worse." Without another word, she hurried back to the trail by the ropewalk and disappeared into the darkness.

I settled on the thwart beside Malcolm. There was nothing to do now but continue.

As we glided away from shore, familiar sensations swamped me. The rock and sway of the waves. The trickle of oars moving through the water. The smell of brine and damp wood. All of it took me back to a time when I'd been someone else. The currents grew rougher as we moved farther out, swirling with eddies. I sensed the little boat's struggle and confusion, but the two men steered us ably and we moved deeper into the night.

"Starboard quarter," Austin said some time later, his voice a quiet rumble, the straw bobbing in his mouth. "London traders."

"What are London traders?" I whispered. I didn't see anything off the starboard.

"Smugglers," Beckett replied just as a whaleboat sliced from the darkness.

I gasped—it was so startlingly close I could've touched it. As it glided by, I saw a blur of eyes and dark caps. Blankets thrown over baskets and crates. Beckett raised a hand. One of the men in the whaleboat returned the gesture. Then it was gone.

For long moments after, my blood hummed from my head to my toes. I suddenly wanted to know everything about this strange and forbidden world. My body knew this—this feeling of daring and possibility. It felt new—and like coming home.

As the Brooklyn coast took shape, Austin and Beckett wrapped rags over the paddles to quiet them and plied on slowly, like they were stirring honey.

"There it is," Austin said soon after. "Wallabout Bay."

I'd heard of it before. The British had converted sugarhouses, warehouses, and even churches into prisons, but there still wasn't enough space to keep captured Americans, so they'd turned to using condemned ships. Wallabout Bay was where many of these floating prisons were moored. But knowing about it didn't prepare me for what I now saw.

Several gaunt ships were scattered over a wide bay silvered by moonlight. *Large* ships. Brigs. Ships of the line. Each had to hold hundreds of men, perhaps thousands, yet the entire bay was wrapped in an eerie, graveyard silence. A smell of human waste wafted our way, so foul I shuddered.

Malcolm coughed into his sleeve.

"You think that's bad?" Austin made a gruff sound. "Just wait."

They steered the boat into a narrow inlet north of the bay so covered with branches we had to duck to pass through. I stepped onto the silty shore and helped the men pull the boat between shrubs, sliding it into hiding.

I was in Brooklyn now. On shores that had always been across the river.

"Follow me," Austin said. "Only a little farther."

He led us through the woods, up an incline that kept crumbling beneath me. With every breath and stumble, more mud caked my gown and shoes. My hair came loose from its pins and fell down my back. I began to sweat and soon grew too hot to bear my mantle. I tucked it under my arm, wishing I'd left it and my purse in the boat.

We reached the top of the rise and knelt on the edge of a rocky drop. Wallabout spread below us, its moonlit waters streaked by dark patches of mudflats. The ships were much closer now, the stench so vile my stomach seized.

"Miss." A kerchief appeared before me.

"Thank you, Austin." I pressed it to my nose. Lavender essence flowed into my nostrils, bringing blessed relief.

"The one closest to us is the *Jersey*," said Beckett. "The men call it 'Hell Afloat.' It's prison to privateersmen mostly, but also some soldiers and militiamen. Some foreign captives."

Hell Afloat. A perfect name. What a tormented thing. The portholes and gunports were boarded over, the decks stripped of spars, rigging, rails. Only the main and foremast stood, both bare as flagpoles.

"In the mornings," Beckett continued, "the men are brought above decks. You see them and your heart weeps. They're filthy. Rags hanging on skeletons. Eyes with no hope. Some scarcely have the strength to stand. Every day there's some don't last the night. Ten. Twelve. Sometimes more—that's on every ship, not just the *Jersey*. Their bodies are put on carts and rowed ashore and buried. But they dig shallow graves and tidal flats are bad soil for it, as you can perhaps see."

I looked to where he pointed. "Do you mean those are—" Hot water pushed into my mouth as my eyes adjusted. "Those are limbs? They're *bodies*?"

"They are. God keep them."

It was a horror. Elbows, feet, heads. Half-buried. Rising from the earth like some terrible crop. Tears blurred my eyes. "There's so many."

Austin plucked the straw from his mouth, tossing it away angrily. "Thousands."

I knew no American soldiers. No militiamen. But I had known an American privateersman once. I couldn't even bear to imagine Asa Lane on one of those hellish ships. I swallowed, finding my voice. "Why did Mrs. Burgin want me to come here?"

Beckett and Austin exchanged a long look. Austin was the one to answer. "She told us if you made it out here, we were to give you the truth."

"I'm here. I am ready for it."

"Eliza's been helping some of those men escape. Thanks to her, some two hundred men have avoided the fate that awaited them on that shoreline."

Awe swept over me. "She freed *two hundred* prisoners?" She was a heroine!

"That she did, till she was betrayed. Some weeks ago, a man by the name of Higday was captured by the British on suspicion of spying. Higday's wife knew too much for her own good. She gave Eliza up to lessen her husband's sentence. The bloody-backs came pounding on Eliza's door, but she escaped and went into hiding. We've been trying to get her out of New York ever since."

"Will you be able to?"

Beckett looked toward New York. "Ought to be done by now."

Malcolm stirred beside me. "She left? She and her children?"

"She alone," said Austin. "Eliza launched right after we did, about a half mile north of the ropewalk." He lifted a pistol. "We were to sound the alert if we saw any patrols. Her children are in less danger. We'll get them out when we can."

"Who'll care for them until then?" I asked.

The two men shared an uncertain look. "We're still working that out."

"Here." I dug the Spanish dollars from my purse and pushed them at Beckett. "Take this. To buy food for them or hire a nursemaid—whatever they need, see they have it."

Beckett stared at the coins in his hand. "This is too much."

"No—it's not enough. I want to do more." This was my chance. I'd helped the cause of liberty how I'd been able, but I wanted to do more than deliver medicines to American prisoners. I needed to. I couldn't let this pass me by.

Austin's mouth tugged up. "Eliza thought you might say that. She said if you did, we were to tell you that only you know how you can help, and when you're ready, you're to see your friend."

I shook my head, absorbing his words. Elizabeth Burgin had known what I wanted from the beginning. This entire outing had been a test of my daring and commitment, I realized. I'd proved myself tonight. "She said to see my *friend*? What friend?" Even now, she was a frustrating puzzle. Then I remembered her harsh words earlier—*A friend? I hardly believe you*—and it came to me. The eyeglasses. The sweet, full smile that greeted me every Wednesday from behind the store counter.

Robert Townsend.

Of course he was involved. He'd given Mrs. Burgin shelter.

A strange mix of excitement and shock moved through me. I'd known Townsend since I arrived in New York three years ago. Now I realized I hadn't known the real man at all. He was part of this world. He was much more than the mild, bookish storekeeper he appeared to be.

"*Beckett.*" Austin suddenly whirled and raised his pistol.

I spun, searching the woods behind us. Through a shroud of branches and leaves, I saw the glint of weapons.

"You there!" shouted a voice. "Announce yourselves!"

"Loyalist militia," Austin said. "*Go!*"

Fear exploded through me; I leapt up and ran.

"This way!" Beckett shouted, leading us downhill.

The slope was steep, but I didn't dare slow down. Branches tore at my petticoats and slashed at my arms. My ankles twisted and jammed on the loose, pitted earth.

"Halt!" The shout was louder—so close.

A pistol fired, the sound thunderous. I stumbled, hit the ground, and went rolling, the world spinning, my cloak and purse flying from my hands. My hip slammed against a rock, stopping me.

Malcolm pounded up. He swept me to my feet. "Are you hurt?"

"No." Pain roared in my hip. He jogged over to my purse and cloak. I glanced downhill. I didn't see Beckett anymore. "Malcolm, leave them. We have to keep moving."

A figure shot from the darkness and rammed into Malcolm. He flew back and crashed into the dirt.

"Who are you?" demanded the man, pinning him. "Are you a spy?"

"No!"

A blade flashed and came to Malcolm's throat. "Care to change your answer?"

Instinct drove me. I pulled my pocket watch over my head and threw myself on the man's back. I slammed the hard silver into his ear as I came down. He yelled and rolled away, the knife falling from his hand.

I dove, scrabbling for it in the dirt, and shot to my feet. "Malcolm?"

"Here." Malcolm came to his feet. In the darkness, all I could see was the muted red of his hair, the whites of his eyes.

"Bitch!" shouted our attacker, a beetle-backed man with a face cratered by scars who stood much closer. He touched his ear and his hand came away dark with blood. "Look what you did!"

I strode up to him. He reeled back, and then froze when I brought the knife to his nose. The rage that flooded through my veins came from somewhere else. It came from years ago. *Never.* I'd never again stand by as someone I cared about was hurt. "Don't follow us," I said. I leaned closer and lowered my voice to a breath. "If we're caught, I will tell all your men that a girl made you cry out and bleed." I flicked the tip of the blade, slicing his nostril.

He screamed and grabbed his face, doubling over.

I spun and ran, Malcolm right beside me.

When we were safely back on the river, with Austin and Beckett rowing us home, I finally relaxed my fingers. The knife peeled away from my sweaty fist and dropped into black water, vanishing. Only then did my hands begin to tremble.

I folded them in my lap, like a young lady, and watched the sun lift over the horizon.

Beckett calmly plied the oars. "Once again we have failed to die," he mused.

"Aye," Austin replied. "Once again."

=★=

On the way home with Malcolm, I stopped at Mrs. Roberta Powers's milliner's shop and purchased a royal-blue ribbon. As it was morning now, my plan was to claim I'd gone out early to buy ribbon for Liesje's wedding. The excuse was thinner than a cat's whisker, but it was the only one I had. The Holdridges would either believe it, or I'd be ruined.

Pausing at the courtyard gate, I whispered a quick prayer. Malcolm stared straight ahead, avoiding my eyes. A small cut wept blood at his neck where the man had held the knife. Seeing it, my eyes blurred, the full scope of the danger we'd been in hitting me.

Inside the courtyard, Maggie Bowie was pinning bed linens to the clotheslines. She dropped her work and came over to us, anger sizzling in her gaze. She stared at her son for long moments. An eternity. Then she turned to me, taking in my muddy, torn gown. My mussed hair. "I made excuses. I told them I saw you this morning before you left on an errand."

I exhaled. "*Thank you*, Maggie. That fits perfectly with—"

"With respect, Miss Emmeline, I did not lie for *you*. Malcolm is all I have in this world. I'll thank you to not treat him as a toy that exists for your amusement. The Holdridges are away, but they'll return soon. I will be waiting in your room. Best hurry. We have much to do."

She disappeared into the house, leaving me to absorb the sting of her words.

Never had Maggie shown me anything but warmth. Every morning, she brought me tea just how I liked it, then helped me with my toilette, dressing me and curling my hair. Prattling on about who she'd seen at the fish market or in Hanover Square, somehow making the mundane lively and compelling. She loved talking as much as I loved listening to her. I hated that I had upset and disrespected her. I had wronged her just as I'd wronged Malcolm.

Suddenly the meaning of her words dawned on me. "Malcolm, she thinks you and I were—" My cheeks heated with embarrassment. "She thinks we snuck away to—" I couldn't even say it. Malcolm was strapping. Striking even, with his vibrant green eyes and red hair. I'd seen both men and women baldly ogle him. But even had he not been a servant, I'd always thought of him in a brotherly way. He was too pure. Too good. I only pretended to be.

"Yes. Of course it's what she assumes." Red patches bloomed up his neck and over his cheeks. "I will speak to her and see that your virtue is restored in her eyes."

"No—maybe it's better this way. The truth is . . . well, it's worse."

He stared at me. "Miss Em, this night should not have happened."

"I agree—I regret it terribly."

His eyes narrowed. "You do?"

"Yes! I risked everything over a little curiosity. That *man,* Malcolm! And your *neck.* I put you in that position, and it shames me. I hate myself for it. I'd be so grateful if you could forget it ever happened."

"Please—don't hate yourself. You couldn't have known what it's like out there. I should have stopped you. I should have *protected* you. Instead, I—" He looked down, hanging his head in shame.

"We survived. That's all that matters now. Let's never mention it again."

"Yes," he said eagerly. "Done." He reached into his pocket and handed me my watch. It had smears of dried blood on it. "A night forgotten."

We stood a moment longer listening to street noises. A newsboy's shouts. The rattle of wagon wheels on cobblestones. Then he left for the cottage workshop without a word.

This was exactly what I wanted. Whatever I did next, Malcolm would be no part of it.

He'd be safe.

CHAPTER 14

EVERY MINUTE AND EVERY MOMENT

★

Later that morning, I sat in a carriage heading toward Liesje Visser's country estate, absently listening to the Holdridges chatter about the coming festivities. I yawned behind my fan, the gentle rocking of the carriage lulling me. My ankles throbbed. I had nicks and cuts all over my arms. I was thirsty. Tired. Physically worn out. But my mind churned, going over every detail of my escapade. Coming back, again and again, to the message Mrs. Burgin had passed to me through Austin and Beckett.

Only you know how you can help.

I *did* know.

Some part of me had always known I'd make a perfect spy.

In a way, I had already been one. From the minute I put on Miss Coates's gown on the beach all that time ago, I had lived inside a secret. I'd been cautious of the things I said and watchful of others. What was more, I had daring and courage I hadn't been able to use in years. Cleverness that had only collected cobwebs. Best of all, I had opportunity.

Every night, I socialized with British officers. Men who under-estimated my intelligence and overestimated my virtuousness. Men who discussed the war around me like I was invisible.

How difficult would it be to take the information I heard to Robert Townsend?

My entire life had led me to this, I realized. Every minute and every moment. I hadn't been able to fight Sewel's abuse, but I could fight this abuse of power. I could fight for the thousands of men rotting in prisons across New York. I could fight now because I had failed to help Asa Lane. I could fight because I was more than a problem, or a fortune to be married into. And I could fight because I *wanted* to fight.

But not right now.

I smothered another enormous yawn. In the sluggish heat of the jostling carriage, the only fight was staying awake.

I leaned against Lucy's shoulder. She rested her head on mine and began humming her favorite minuet by Bach, her fingers key-ing the notes on her pink silk petticoat.

Aunt Nora smiled at us, her plump cheeks going rounder.

"My angelic girls," Uncle Henry said.

Not quite, I thought.

One of us had just decided to spy.

= ★ =

The Visser country home sat on rolling fields along the North River. It resembled a small village, with an impressive main house and smaller cottages scattered throughout the estate.

The festivities had already begun when we arrived. Gentlemen played cricket on the front green and ladies strolled in groups, hiding from the sun under parasols. Lucy and I joined Charlotte, sending our valises and trunks ahead with servants dressed in lavish crimson and white livery. In minutes, we were sipping lemonade under the shade of an oak tree, watching gentlemen competing in games.

This type of activity—being a spectator to others' fun—was my least favorite form of socializing. At least theater sparked the imagination. A concert, emotion. This turned me into a decoration, and I'd never much liked it. Till today.

Today, I felt a *purpose*. By the time I made my weekly visit to Robert Townsend next Wednesday, I'd have learned something valuable to share with him. I gazed across the sunny lawn, wondering which of the gentlemen present had power *and* a loose tongue. A familiar feeling of anticipation stirred in me. Three years later and here I was again, risking my life in search of bits of treasure.

"Emmie," Lucy whispered, "are you unwell? You seem unlike yourself."

"She isn't ill," Charlotte said, surveying the lawn as carefully as I'd been. "She is *expectant*. She is waiting for her gallant knight to arrive. I confess, I'm eagerly awaiting his arrival, too."

I'd barely mentioned my walk in the gardens with Lieutenant Duncan to them, but it appeared I'd said enough.

Charlotte looked at me and her smile disappeared. "Emmie, please, just for today, tuck that unattractive pocket watch into your stays. And straighten your—here, let me do it." She fussed with the flounces on my sleeves, tending to my appearance as always. Charlotte had curated my entire wardrobe, including the canary-yellow *robe à la polonaise* I now wore. Without her expert eye for fashion, I'd have looked like a theater curtain. "That's better. You must look your best when he sees you."

"Char, go gently," Lucy said. "You've made her anxious."

"Have I made you anxious, Emmie?"

"Well . . ." With all that had happened overnight, I hadn't had much chance to think about Lieutenant Duncan. Now I realized I *did* feel anxious about seeing him again. He'd been genuine and charming. A true surprise. But even Sewel had once seemed charming to Mama, and I couldn't let myself forget that I was a purse to be won by Lieutenant Duncan. A financial consideration, not a romantic one. I couldn't forget—or help resenting it.

Charlotte's eyes widened. "Oh, you *are* nervous! This is good. This is *very* good. We must find him immediately."

"I don't think he has arrived yet," Lucy said.

"Perfect. When he does, he must see our Miss Coates conversing with the most eligible gentlemen here. A man does not value a tree if its fruits are left untasted."

Lucy and I looked at each other. Charlotte didn't read, but she liked to sound as though she did and occasionally created her own questionable quotes.

I couldn't resist. "Am I the tree or am I the fruit, Char?"

"Never mind. Come. This is no time to shilly-shally."

She hooked her arms through mine and Lucy's, and we strolled toward the officers playing games in the sunshine. Charlotte fell into conversation with Benjamin Stone, a Loyalist refugee from South Carolina. Lucy chatted with Rebecca about *Evelina,* which

Rebecca had finished overnight and adored. I placed myself near the most prominent gentlemen. One in particular I knew to be an influential Loyalist.

The men were discussing the French impact on the war. A year ago, in great part because of Dr. Benjamin Franklin's diplomatic efforts, France had allied with America against England, their age-old enemy. The man who'd drawn me closer was Dr. Franklin's own son, but unlike his father, William Franklin was staunchly loyal to the king.

"With the French alliance," Mr. Franklin was saying, "this dispute between a nation and its unruly colony has turned into global chaos. Now our problems have spread like a pestilence. The Spaniards have entered as well—even as they continue to threaten Gibraltar—while the French have one foot securely in Senegal. Our Baltic shipping channels and West Indian interests are no longer secure. Even our home shores cannot be considered safe! We have the mightiest navy in the world, but we cannot *be* everywhere, holding sway over every corner of the globe."

"You have a point," said a man with olive skin and black hair. "'Tis unfortunate we've had to divide our naval might, but our southern strategy is sound and doesn't depend on marine assaults."

"On the contrary, it very much depends on the successful coming ashore of our troops. How we manage to do that while keeping a strong naval presence here, there, and everywhere mystifies me. Our protection of New York mustn't slacken. Washington will surely try for it again with the French. What's more, I have it that the French commander, d'Estaing, is devilish cunning and brave, too."

"A brave Frenchman?" said the olive-complexioned man. "Is such a thing possible?"

"There is the Marquis de Lafayette," said the stout man beside him with the extravagant wig.

"The marquis is an aberration; there is no other like him. And I am going to need another drink if you are going to try to convince me otherwise."

"I as well."

"In wine, wisdom."

"Indeed. Let us go become wiser."

They strolled off, leaving me standing there, breathless.

Some of what I'd heard had no apparent value. Of course General Washington would want to try for New York. It was the seat of British power in North America and Washington's army had been poking at the British lines around Manhattan for years. I imagined it also had to be personal for the general, as he had lost control of New York to the British shortly after I'd arrived. I remembered seeing him once at an assembly before he had fled. Tall. Dignified. Capable and proud. He did not strike me as a man who accepted defeat.

While that didn't help me, other pieces of information held more promise, like the bit about the French commander, d'Estaing, and the "southern strategy." The British had spent years fighting against the New England colonies to no material gain, and with the French entering the war, I knew their tactics would need to shift—surely this related to what I'd overheard. I stashed it away for later, feeling a thrill shoot all the way to my toes.

Saints, how I felt different. Powerful. Purposeful.

Awake.

I wanted more.

I spent the next hour roving the lawn and listening where I could. I overheard a group of officers bemoaning their inability to capture West Point from the Americans. Listening, I gathered that the military stronghold was strategically important because of its position on the North River, which ran between the northern and southern colonies.

"It is the key to everything; if we take West Point, we cut off the head of the snake," said one man. "The war would be ours."

My hands damp with sweat, I listened for useful information, like plans to attack it, but they only carried on with their lamentations.

Still, I knew it was just a matter of time before I uncovered gold.

=★=

With sunset approaching, the party moved to the lawns along the waterfront for the last sport of the day—a boat race on the North River. Many of the older guests had forgone the earlier games and were already there, enjoying the prospect of the river under the shade of a large tent. We congratulated Liesje, who looked radiant with her groom-to-be, and stunning in a blush-pink sack gown. Then we joined the Holdridges, the Winters, and Judge Latimer, accepting spiced wine that tasted deliciously of cinnamon and apple.

All the top men in the British army and navy were present. Nearby, General Clinton took wine from a white-gloved slave and handed it to his mistress. His proclamation granting freedom to slaves affected only those owned by American patriots—not slaves owned by Loyalists like Liesje's family and most everyone there. Giving preferential freedom seemed unjust to me—how could one person be valued over another? But I couldn't argue that the general's proclamation had bettered the lives of many.

I studied Clinton more closely—the most powerful man in North America. Thick dark eyebrows gave him a glowering appearance. Epaulets spilled from his shoulders in brilliant waterfalls. His coat buttons shone like gold coins in clear water. If only I could only spy on *him*.

"Look!" Lucy said. "There they are!"

Upriver, I saw four sloops, each flying flags of a different color. I squinted, seeing a dozen men on each boat. They stood at the rails, awaiting the starting signal.

My stomach tightened. How I ached to be out there with them.

David Henrickson, a friend of the groom's, stepped forward to offer a toast. "Casper Devoor," he declared, the river gleaming behind him, "you have a lovely bride in Miss Visser. She is much too good for you; I know not how you have come to deserve her. Truly—'tis a mystery." Laughs rumbled from the guests. Henrickson lifted his glass. "Mr. and Mrs. Devoor, allow me to be the first to wish you a lifetime of happiness together—or even longer. May your love last, as Shakespeare wrote, 'for ever and a day.'"

Hearty *hear-hears* sounded from the guests, and cups tilted back. Then Henrickson traded his wine for a ship's pistol, which he fired to begin the boat race. Across the steely water, anchors weighed, sails hoisted, and the sloops began to cruise to the cheers from the riverbank.

"Who's winning—can you tell?" Lucy bounced on her toes, her blond curls bobbing. "Since there is no white flag to pick, I am for the yellow—the yellow will win it!"

"I'm for the red," Charlotte said. "Obviously."

I smiled, seeing her apple-red gown out of the corner of my eye.

"The black flag will take it," I said, sure of it. The sloop had gotten a slow start, but now it was practically skipping across the river.

"Black flag?" Lucy wrinkled her nose. "Isn't that for pirates?"

"Yes, but those may be the least pirate-ish men to ever walk the earth," Charlotte said.

Most of the "pirates" were British officers in vivid red-and-white regimentals. Young men of vigorous health whose laughter and spirited voices carried across the water, growing louder as they approached the finish marker. As they stole the front spot from a sloop filled with British navy men and sailed to victory, they roared and waved their hats wildly.

Their celebration was irresistible. I was laughing as I recognized the pretty amber of Lieutenant Duncan's hair. Another young man's hearty hug had knocked his hat away and I watched him sweep it up and search the shoreline.

I suddenly had a strong feeling he was searching for *me*.

"And there he is," Charlotte said. "Our dashing lieutenant."

As the sloop drifted toward shore, several of the men shed their hats and coats and shoes and jumped into shallow water to cheers of delight from the onlookers. They looked ridiculous as they splashed the short distance to the shore, like boys without a care. Duncan was right in the middle of it. Then suddenly several of the men pounced on him.

"Grab him! Grab Duncan!" they yelled.

Duncan tried to slip away, but he was outnumbered. With playful shoves, his friends shepherded up the bank, toward . . .

"Oh dear," Lucy said. "Are they coming toward *us*?"

"They are," Charlotte whispered. "Emmie, take this with grace or you will only make it worse."

I had no idea what I was taking with grace.

By the time the rowdy young men delivered Duncan to me, his hair and regimentals disheveled and dripping, a small crowd had begun to form around us.

Duncan shook his head. "Miss Coates, I—" His cheeks were flushed and his eyes held a deadly sparkle. He looked like he was either going to laugh or tear his friends apart with his hands. "I cannot begin to apologize for—"

One of his mates shoved him. "Ask her, Duncan! Go on!"

My legs twitched, aching to escape. Never had I liked being the center of attention, but now I felt guilty. Exposed. Even Major André and General Clinton were watching from a distance.

"Come on, man!" encouraged a tall blond with another playful shove. "Ask!"

"Miss Coates," Duncan said, "please believe me when I say that I had no part in—"

"Duncan, if you don't—"

"Will you honor me with a dance at the wedding ball, Miss Coates?" Duncan blurted. "Now, you may refuse me. I deserve it." He waved at the grinning young men surrounding him. "*We* deserve it."

Liesje came over, her smile wide. "Oh, Miss Coates. You *must* agree!"

My mind had gone blank. All I wanted was for this to be over. "I accept, Lieutenant."

Huzzahs broke into the air. Duncan's friends spirited him away to loud congratulations.

"Goodness," Lucy said, her blue eyes blinking. "What did I just see?"

"Either a siege"—Charlotte smiled—"or a courtship."

=★=

"Are you pleased, Emmie?" Lucy whispered that night. As bridesmaids in Liesje's wedding party, we were staying in the main house and had been given a room Charlotte had christened "Our Little Cathedral" for its soaring ceilings. I lay in bed between my two friends, staring up. The sloped rafters rose so steeply that candlelight didn't reach the top, and the darkness up there unsettled me. "I worry you might have agreed to dance with him to spare him the embarrassment."

I shimmied away from Charlotte, who was snoring softly and crowding me. I envied her. Tired as I felt, I couldn't sleep. "I do want to dance with him, Lucy," I said. I couldn't wait for it, in fact. "It was all the attention."

"I thought so. I felt overwhelmed for you."

I hadn't expected to be so *seen* on the very day I'd decided to spy. The attention had lingered on me the rest of the afternoon, everyone asking me about "that dashing young rogue from the winning sloop." It had spoiled my quest for more information. Wherever I went, *I* became the topic of conversation.

After the sailing race, the bridal party had retreated to a private dinner with the women in Liesje's family. We'd spoken of easy topics, not the war, but I hadn't expected much else. We were meant to inspire men to noble deeds through our goodness and virtue—not to dabble in their affairs. Patriot women were bolder in their political involvement, I knew. Long before the fighting began, they'd stopped purchasing goods imported from England, even learning to spin their own cloth so they could make their own garments. Many of the gentlemen I knew mocked their involvement. They had good laughs over the spirit of American women.

"I am happy for you, Em," Charlotte croaked sleepily. "Lieutenant Duncan is one of the best bachelors here. I asked Mrs. Visser about him at dinner. He is respected by friends and peers, and his fortune overshadows ours both."

I glanced at Lucy. She wasn't on the same level as us, and it bothered me when Charlotte called attention to it. Then Charlotte's words sank in. "Did you say he has *wealth*?"

"Yes. A very snug fortune, in fact."

"But I thought . . . Uncle Henry was carrying on discussions with him. . . ."

"Duncan's not after your purse, Emmie," Charlotte said. "He doesn't need it. Just be sure he's not after something else."

"Charlotte!" Lucy said.

"What? We must share these things and protect each other. Duncan is a gentleman, not some obscure country rustic, but you must still be vigilant. You may dally with him a bit, if you wish, but only under the strictest pledge of secrecy."

"Charlotte, *please*. Emmie's not thinking about that!"

I hadn't been before, but now I was. Duncan had beautiful lips. They were pale pink and looked so soft. I had no idea when I'd began such a study of them.

"Well, she *should* be thinking about it," Charlotte said. "Better to know ahead of time whether there is hope for pleasure in their marriage. It isn't always so."

My mind suddenly took me back to the night I'd left West End. The wherry pitching and rolling in high waves. The horrible rain and wind. Sewel pinning me. Reaching under my shirt.

Tears flooded my eyes. It'd been such a long time since I'd remembered. I had no idea why it came to me *now*, but that was the thing about unwanted memories. They were surprise attackers. I drew a deep breath, willing it to go away.

"Do you think Liesje has chosen well with Devoor?" Lucy asked.

Charlotte sighed. "They are equally handsome and wealthy. He is from old Dutch stock like her. And she does seem quite in love now."

She didn't need to say the rest. We all knew things could change—and love wasn't what we expected from marriage or even hoped for, anyhow. We wanted a companion. Someone reliable and respectable, who could provide. Someone we wouldn't grow to loathe.

"To think tomorrow the die will be cast," Lucy said. "Her future, all her life's happiness, determined by the vow she'll make. It frightens me—but how I wish for it, too."

I felt a pinch in my throat. Kindhearted and pretty as Lucy was, she brought almost nothing to a marriage beyond herself. In our world, that wasn't enough.

"I wish I could marry you, Lucy," Charlotte said.

That gave us a good giggle, but it wasn't the first time I'd wondered what Charlotte truly wanted. She could marry at any time, yet she hadn't. She always seemed more interested in our lives than her own.

Lucy turned on her side. I could feel her stare on my face. "Tonight at dinner, Mrs. Sedgwick called marriage our 'dark leap' because we have no idea what awaits on the other side."

I thought of Mama. She'd taken two dark leaps. One had led her to heartbreak, widowhood, and disgrace. The other had led her to harsh treatment and loneliness. And to death, I believed. I missed her so much right then, my chest felt like it was caving in.

I cleared my throat, finding my voice. "My mother used to tell me marriage was the 'something more' I was meant to find in life. It was the last thing she ever said to me."

"Oh, Emmie," Lucy said. "You have never told us about your mother." She curled against my side.

To my surprise, so did Charlotte. "You have nothing to worry about, Emmie," she said. "Duncan is beautiful, charming, wealthy, and well loved."

"Is that all?" I joked, though it was true—he appeared to be all of that. He was everything Mama had wanted for me. I found myself smiling in the darkness. I'd never thought fulfilling my promise to her could be so in harmony with what I wanted.

"No, in fact," Charlotte said. "There's more. He has fabulous prospects as André's aide. He'll rub elbows with the top men in the army. Probably even with General Clinton himself."

I jolt shot through me. I had no idea how I'd missed it. Duncan had a direct line to the very highest sources of information in the British military. But spying was something committed against strangers. Distant acquaintances. Not *suitors*.

Was it?

Long after Lucy and Charlotte fell asleep, I lay awake and wrestled with my conscience. Spying was stealing from the enemy—but what if that enemy was someone decent? Someone with a charming personality, perfect lips, and eyes like pools of honey when they caught the sunlight?

But this was about the fates of *nations*. It was about freeing America from a tyrant who wielded power like a hammer. Abuse was wrong—and I wanted to fight it. To spy—to *truly* do it—there was no room for doubt. I had to march into the danger as boldly as a soldier, heedless of the pain I might cause.

I couldn't let anything stop me.

CHAPTER 15

FRIENDS AND FOES

★

The following afternoon, Liesje Visser took her dark leap at the North Dutch Church as rain fell steadily outside. When she and Casper Devoor exchanged vows, my eyes drifted across the church to Lieutenant Duncan, a few rows to my right.

He looked over sharply, as though I'd called his name.

I turned away and fought a smile, a velvety heat spreading through me. One thing I couldn't deny: my body knew exactly how it felt about Lieutenant Duncan.

After the ceremony, we returned to the Vissers' for the celebration assembly. I gazed across their grand parlor, feeling like a hunter as I scanned the room for Major André or Lieutenant Duncan. I loved it, this thrill of the search. The rush of a dive. I'd been asleep for three years. I'd been holding my breath. Now, *finally*, I was awake and breathing again.

As the wedding couple began the first minuet, Judge Latimer leaned down to my ear. "I understand I've been set aside for tonight. I hope your young lieutenant is worth the bruise to this old man's heart."

I smiled. "You could never be set aside." The judge was my usual dance partner. My first one, when I arrived in New York. I'd been so scared then. I'd tripped over both my feet and his, but he'd guided me through it, never questioning my gracelessness. For months, till I found my dancing feet, I had only partnered with him or Uncle Henry. "I'll save a dance for you."

"Will you? I shall try to wait patiently. Duncan seems a fine lad. Major André is certainly very high on him, and André is quite the rising star." There was something gritty in his voice, but just as I noticed it, his gaze was pulled to the dance floor. "Ah, look. Some fearsome brigands have arrived to spoil the party."

The "fearsome brigands" were actually the groomsmen, who flowed into the parlor wearing black breeches and cloaks with hoods pulled low over their faces. A few wore swords at their hips. They played their part comically, stalking and creeping toward Liesje and Devoor like bandits.

"Get her!" they shouted suddenly. "Steal the bride! Kidnap the bride!" They rushed the final steps to the dancing couple, then, with the courteousness of true gentlemen, offered Liesje an arm and shepherded her from the parlor.

The judge let out a weary sigh. "Youth."

"What *was* that?" Even now, there were customs I wasn't familiar with.

"Wedding games. Steal the Bride, in this case. Sometimes the groom pretends to run off before the ceremony as well and has to be hauled back, but I think young Devoor was too nervous for that with this rowdy lot. Typically the assembly chases after the bride to rescue her, as it were, but with the rain soaking the roads I'm told only the wedding party is going."

That was just what we did. Minutes later, Charlotte, Lucy, and I piled into waiting carriages with the rest of the bridesmaids and the groom.

"I told you Liesje would spare nothing," Charlotte said excitedly as she accepted wine from a servant. Through the open carriage door, I could see guests crowded in the glowing windows of the Vissers' grand home, smiling and waving at us.

Devoor climbed into our carriage and we were off, rollicking through the rainy night.

"How do we rescue her?" I asked. "Do we need muskets? *Spados?*" The Spanish word for "swords" slipped right through, like a hiccup from my mind. The entire thing was stoking the fires of my imagination and I was ready for an adventure.

"Goodness, no," Charlotte said. "We will simply drink champagne and toast the wedding couple—and hearty cheers to you, Devoor." She took a sip.

Liesje's new husband plucked the glass from her hand. "I thank you, Miss Winters. Cheers to myself." He tipped it back, draining the rest.

I wanted more than cheers. I wanted peril and daring deeds. *And* champagne.

Soon we arrived at a cozy tavern with a door left open to the rainy night. Chatter and music poured out and only grew louder as we entered.

Inside, we found the bride thieves surrounding Liesje, who sat smiling and talking happily under their doting attention. Some of the other wedding guests had come from the Vissers', crowding the little tavern, and I spotted Lieutenant Duncan right away. Just as earlier, his gaze hit me with a delicious warmth.

Casper Devoor strode right to Liesje, pulling her into a long embrace that raised a chorus of cheers.

"Oh my," Lucy said. "I think Liesje was just rescued."

Charlotte and I looked at each other and laughed.

We entered the fray holding our wineglasses high, my panniers squeezing and swinging in the tight press of bodies. Lucy and Charlotte stopped to talk with Rebecca, but I headed for Major André. By some miracle, a chair sat unclaimed beside him. I slid into it and found him in conversation with General Knyphausen, the Hessians' most elevated commander. Knyphausen reminded me of Captain Jansen, due to the way he held his head slightly turned to one side on account of having a blind eye. Three years ago, in gratitude for his efforts in helping seize New York from General Washington's army, the British had renamed Fort Washington after him. Another man was in the conversation as well—a civilian who was sweating terribly and whose jowls shook as he spoke.

"Ah, Miss Coates," André said, breaking away for a moment to greet me. "My muse."

"Here to inspire, Major."

"As ever." We spoke for a little while about the production of *Macbeth* he was staging at the Royal Theater; then he gracefully made his way back to the conversation he'd set aside for me.

The topic was the court martial trial against the American general Benedict Arnold, who'd been accused of using public items, like provision wagons, for his private gain. The trial had been all over the newspapers for weeks, though, so it hardly counted as secret knowledge. My attention shifted to Major André's aristocratic profile. For the first time, I saw him as an adversary, truly connected to the atrocity of Wallabout Bay and Asa Lane's impressment, the blockades, the unfair taxes. Connected to everything else that I believed unjust. And yet I was still fond of him.

Love thine enemy, the Bible taught. I'd never understood that till now.

"Be scarce, Grupe," Lieutenant Duncan said, tapping the man in the chair beside me on the shoulder. Like that, the man left and Duncan took his place.

"Miss Coates, I don't expect your forgiveness," he said immediately. "But if you would allow me to, I would like to explain yesterday's debacle by the river."

"Certainly," I said. With his brow furrowed in concentration and his posture straight, he looked very martial. Tense. "And good evening, Lieutenant."

"Yes—forgive me. I should've said that first."

"Fortunately, there's still time," I replied, my voice high. My breath had run away from me. Duncan's thigh was resting against mine, a solid and distracting presence.

"Is there?" A smile fought its way to his lips. "Good evening, Miss Coates. How do you do?"

"Quite well, sir. And improving by the moment. I am ready for your explanation."

"And now I don't want to give it."

"Alas, we have already entered into a contract."

"Have we? Very well." He hesitated, then bowed his head to mine, bringing his lips close to my ear. "Will you allow me this nearness? 'Tis very loud in here and I would prefer not to shout my apology."

I fought a shiver. His voice had melted half of me. I nodded.

"Thank you. . . . Now, where to begin?" he said, his tone losing its formality. "Some time ago, I was told of how you lost your father and became a ward of the doctor's."

I looked up. "You heard *gossip* about me?"

"No—certainly not. I'd never allow it. Major André shared your story with me, trusting in my character to be respectful of it and knowing of *my* past. You see, Miss Coates, I lost my father at sea as well.

"'Twas a year ago. He was on an East Indiaman bound for Bombay when it struck a rock and wrecked. His body was never recovered. Not as harrowing as what you experienced, I imagine, but it haunts me knowing he is out there. Never properly laid to rest. 'Tis a feeling no one can understand . . . unless they have been through it.

"So when your uncle began a discussion of possible . . . *possibilities,* my interest to meet you was piqued. I admit, I came to Ranelagh Gardens more out of curiosity than anything else. But after we talked, I became very eager to see you again, inheritances and sad stories aside. The mistake I made was in letting that slip. My friends were quick to want to help, and that is how the ordeal by the river came to be. So now that I have . . . that I've— I'm sorry, Miss Coates. Pardon me a moment." His eyes flicked up to the man standing behind me.

It was the sweaty-faced man who'd been with André and Knyphausen. Both of them had wandered off, and the sweaty man now spoke to an officer I didn't know. He reeked of drink and swayed so badly his hip kept bumping the back of my chair.

"He calls himself 'Monk,'" he snoached, in a high-pitched

voice like a trumpet. "Though God only knows why—he couldn't be farther from it!"

"Rattoon," Duncan interrupted. "Have some discretion, sir. This is hardly the place."

"Yes, Lieutenant," he replied, and hoisted his wine. "No need to worry."

Duncan turned back to me, but it was a moment before I felt his attention again. "So here we are, Miss Coates. I have burdened you with my tragedy, but I wanted you to know I never intended to create any awkwardness. I believe I fell victim to . . ."

"To what, Lieutenant?"

"To feeling a great deal of hope."

The room seemed to fall away. I felt exactly that myself. Hope. I noticed the depth in his eyes. He'd known pain—true pain. The orphan in me, the part of me that always felt alone, yearned to reach for him. I swallowed. "I am very sorry about your father, Lieutenant. I do understand how it feels to miss a beloved parent. I believe your father is very much resting in peace. How could he not be, having the love of such a devoted son? And I thank you for explaining the commotion yesterday, but I now feel it quite a worthwhile thing to have endured."

He said nothing for long seconds, just stared at me unblinking, but I felt our connection strengthening. "Have I still a chance, then?"

"A chance?"

"Of dancing with you."

"Oh, that." I smiled. "Yes. But it is only a *slight* chance."

He laughed. "I shan't lose it—but I hope it will keep for

another day. I must go to Fort George tonight. There's rebel action near Paulus Hook, and it appears I am useful enough to be needed.

"'Tis a bit dark in here, Miss Coates, but can that be disappointment I see?"

It was, absolutely, but I had *a little* pride. "Lieutenant, I daresay your departure will disappoint *everyone*. Our minuet has become quite an anticipated moment."

"That *is* a problem. I may be away a few days, but when I—" His smile vanished and his gaze flicked up.

I awoke from some spell I'd been under and found myself gazing at him like a smitten girl. Then I heard that shrill voice again, every word sailing into my ears like arrows.

"*Ten thousand* pounds, he's asking," said the sweating man behind me. "For that, he's got to offer Clinton something useful, else what good is—"

Duncan thrust to his feet and threw his arm around the man's neck. "Excuse me," he said to me tightly. Then he hauled the man away as one would a drunk friend—almost. There was veiled aggression in Duncan's movements. He strode powerfully, and even through his red coat I could see the rigid muscles in his arms. In a matter of seconds, he cut a path through the crowded tavern and pushed the man out into the rain.

I sat in a stupor for long seconds after they disappeared outside, the noise of laughter and celebration swirling around me.

I knew what I had to do.

Now.

I stood and crossed the crowded tavern to the door, my heart thundering. Cool air washed over me as I stepped outside. The rain had lessened to a drizzle, but water ran from the eaves and gurgled in a nearby creek, filling the night with sound. The chariot drivers awaited us by a barn in the distance, the smoke of their pipes rising into the darkness. Duncan's voice came from the other direction, around the tavern. Angry, but still controlled.

I crept closer, choosing my footsteps with care, till I was almost at the corner and could hear him perfectly.

"Why is it so difficult for you to comprehend 'confidential'?"

"I *was* being confidential!" replied the nasal man. "I called him 'Monk'! Who'll ever guess anything from that?"

"*Fool.*" There was a grunt. The sound of a body thudding against brick. "Speak another word about *any* of this and it won't be punishment you suffer, Rattoon. I'll have your *life*. Are we in understanding?"

A wheezing cough. "Yes! Bloody hell, Lieutenant. My *head!*"

"Your head is indeed a problem. Be gone—and never let me see you this drunk again."

I scurried back, hurrying for the tavern door.

Halfway there, I knew I'd cut it too close.

I whirled just as Duncan rounded the corner and stepped into view. He looked up, his eyes tight with fury, then wide with surprise. "Miss Coates. What are you doing out here?"

"You left without saying goodbye and I—I wanted to say goodbye." I looked up, wincing. "I didn't expect it to still be raining, though." I looked at my slippers. "Or so muddy."

Duncan rushed over and offered his arm, his gallantry instinctive, just as I'd hoped. He drew me under the eaves, and right in time as the rain picked up. "How long have you been out here?"

"Not as long as you. You're soaked."

"I had to deal with something." He looked toward where he'd been with Rattoon.

My hand was still on his arm. I tugged him toward me. "Your coat. You're getting wet."

"Shall we go inside?" he asked.

"Or just . . . come closer." I drew him in till he was only inches away. He looked down at my petticoats pooling around his legs. Then his eyes lifted to mine and I knew, without a shred of doubt, that I was now the sole object of his thoughts. "Must you really go soon?"

My entire body felt energized. Terrified by him. Drawn to him. The grittiness I'd just witnessed only made him more appealing. Less like every other pampered dandy.

"Not yet. When Major André summons." His gaze roamed my face and came to the scar on my eyebrow. "What happened there?"

"I fell when I was younger." Asa Lane had no place here now.

Duncan was silent a moment. "Would that I could go back in time and catch you."

I had no response to that. Such pretty words deserved their own space. So I held his arm and let myself wade deep into his warm eyes, where I remained until we had to say goodbye.

The British are concerned with keeping a strong naval force across the globe and how that will stress their ability to protect New York Harbor.

They suspect General George Washington will want to make an attempt on New York with the French navy.

The French naval commander is named Comte d'Estaing. He is thought to be very capable and clever.

The British have developed a southern strategy. Unclear on this, but it doesn't depend on naval actions once soldiers have been deployed. I will seek more information.

Someone is negotiating with the British and asking ten thousand pounds for intelligence. I believe it is a spy who uses the name Monk.

CHAPTER 16

TO BE WORTHY

★

With my discoveries written on a paper tucked inside my purse, I set off with Malcolm toward the Sugar House Prison. It felt like an ordinary Wednesday—the firing of the morning gun, the tinkling of the vials in the crate on Malcolm's shoulder—except today I was delivering my first spying report.

I glanced at Malcolm, wondering if he had the slightest idea, but he seemed deep in his own thoughts, even a little distant. Since our night in Wallabout Bay a week ago, a coolness had settled between us. Though it shouldn't have mattered to me, it did. Part of what I'd always enjoyed about Wednesdays was his company. Now I almost felt like he wasn't with me.

As we left the crate of medicines with the guard at the prison, my weekly charity seemed smaller than ever compared to Elizabeth Burgin's deeds. How many people could claim they'd saved *two hundred* lives? She had inspired me. Charged me, like Asa Lane had all those years ago. I'd done so much lying and deceiving for my own gain. Years and years of it—and for what? So I could wear silk slippers and eat chocolates imported from Europe? So

I could sit while Maggie curled my hair and then attend tea gatherings in the afternoons? I had a comfortable life, but it wasn't enough. I wanted to do something worthy.

As always, Malcolm and I parted at the corner of Smith and Wall Streets, and I rounded the block to Townsend's store. I found Townsend alone at the counter.

"Good morning," I said, a bit too cheerfully.

He looked up from his ledger. For the first time ever, he didn't seem pleased to see me. "Good day, Miss Coates. I have no new volumes for you today, madam. No shipments have come in."

"Actually, I'm here for paper today. A full quire, please."

Townsend peered over his eyeglasses at me. "Certainly." He brought a stack of paper down from a back shelf and slid it across the counter. "There you are."

I slipped my folded letter on top of the stack and held my breath. Why did this feel more dangerous than the act of spying itself? But he'd either see my scribblings as valuable—or as treason.

Townsend unfolded it and read, his face slowly draining of color. He looked up, his intelligent eyes regarding me like a stranger. Till then, I hadn't been positive he was a spy—but now I was. Townsend, who'd always seemed so bookish and gentle. A *spy*.

I could see similar thoughts running through his mind.

We both started as the door jangled, swinging open. A rush of customers entered, brushing the rain off their clothes. There were two black women with market baskets, two sailors speaking loudly in Dutch, and three Queen's Rangers with rifles as tall as they were. New York in all its variety.

"Would you step aside with me, Miss Coates?" Townsend said, already moving to the end of the counter.

I followed him. His partner, Henry Oakhum, appeared from a back room to help the new customers.

Townsend pulled a book off the shelf and set it on the counter before me. It was a blank book—a commonplace journal. "Perhaps this will be of interest to you. The leather is dyed in carmine and treated with a special oil to give it water repellence." He opened it. "The paper is Venetian. Very thick and soft, as you can see." He paused, glancing at the other customers, then asked very quietly, "Have you any idea the danger you're courting, Miss Coates?"

I'd prepared myself for his objections. "I do," I replied. "And I also know that I will not be stopped by any warnings you give me."

"But this is . . ." He leaned closer. "This is *beneath* you."

If only he knew the truth. Nothing was beneath me. "What I wrote—was it helpful?"

"It was not poor, but . . ." He sighed and glanced around the store again. More people had entered, seeking shelter from the rain. My pulse skipped as four Hessian grenadiers ducked inside. Unlike British regulars—who tended to be driven into the army out of poverty—Hessian soldiers were hired mercenaries. Dangerous men, easy with violence. Men who wouldn't hesitate to run a spy through with a bayonet.

Townsend held my gaze. Sweat beaded on his upper lip. He turned the leather book on the counter so it faced me. "The details are what make this exceptional. The quality of the paper, the strength of the binding. You can clearly see it was fashioned by a master who understands the value of precision. None of the materials used are ordinary."

I understood. He had accepted my decision and was telling me to be more exact with the information I brought him. "But the last part . . . that was useful, was it not?"

I knew I'd stumbled on something the night of Liesje's wedding. Someone who went by the name Monk was out there, selling valuable information to the British.

Townsend drummed his fingers nervously on the book. "How did you learn of it?"

"I overhead some officers talking," I said, feeling the urge to protect Duncan.

"The sum you wrote . . ." He shook his head slowly. "You must be mistaken. 'Tis *enormous*. An enormous payment."

"I'm not mistaken."

"Pray you are. I can only imagine what it would purchase. It could be devastating."

He doubted me, but I'd find proof. I'd discover Monk's identity and what he was scheming.

I picked up the book and smiled. "You have sold me on this, Mr. Townsend. Thank you. I will take it."

CHAPTER 17

SHOT AND SHELL

★

September 1779

"I wonder if Lieutenant Duncan will remember you, Emmie," Charlotte said as we stepped onto Whitehall Slip. "Perhaps he's forgotten you, totally and completely?" she teased.

Tonight, Judge Latimer had invited us to dine aboard one of the ships at the end of the dock. The entire Winters flock was present—all seven of Charlotte's siblings, her parents, and one nursemaid—and chaos already reigned.

"Say again, Char? Lieutenant who?" I said as I chased her little brother, Daniel. I caught him just before he ran into the water and swept him onto my hip. Daniel was the naughtiest of her siblings, and by far my favorite. "Was it Lieutenant Dorn—or Dorman? Or was it Dean?"

Though I was joking, I worried she might be right. More than a week had passed since I'd seen Lieutenant Duncan at Liesje's wedding. I'd attended the theater, a picnic, and two assemblies and learned that I'd been lucky in my early spying, which was turning out to be more challenging than I'd initially thought, and that Lieutenant Duncan could steal my attention even when he wasn't present.

"You won't fool me, Emmie," Charlotte said with a little smile. "I know you better than you know yourself. You are smitten, smited, smote!"

I said nothing. She might have had that right. My feelings had grown stronger over the past days, but so had my inner conflict. Being courted by Duncan felt right, but spying felt right, too. I was divided, simultaneously going in opposite directions. I couldn't worry about outcomes, though, or I'd go nowhere. As Tom Hackett had once said, "Tomorrow's tomorrow."

Charlotte picked up her sister, Clara, who'd tired of walking. "I have never dined on a ship before." With the little ones to shepherd, we'd fallen to the back of the party. In the low afternoon light, her parents' shadows as long as poles on the dock. "Will I get seasick?"

"I doubt it, Char. The water looks calm."

Judge Latimer's nephew, a Loyalist shipowner, had arrived in New York to conduct business. As the judge had no close relatives, he was eager to introduce us and had coordinated an evening on the harbor. It had turned into an odd assortment of guests: A small brigade of Winters children. Lieutenant Duncan and Major André. And me and Uncle Henry, as Lucy had stayed home with Aunt Nora, whose gout had flared up.

"Will this make you sad?" Charlotte asked. "Being on a ship?"

I smiled. She always turned a little sweeter when Lucy wasn't with us, like some balance had to be kept. "I don't think so. It was a very long time ago."

I held tighter to squirming Daniel as we approached the waiting ship, a pretty sloop lit up by festive lanterns with the name *Endurance* written on its freshly painted black hull. Duncan stood at the main deck rail, looking down. He raised one hand when he saw me, and a feeling tickled the skin on my arms like a feather.

"Boom!" Daniel shouted, shooting him with an imaginary musket. "Boom!"

"Daniel, no!" Charlotte grabbed his plump little hands. "Good Lord. What a little rebel."

My laugh came out sounding shrill. If she only knew.

We huffed up the boarding ramp to the *Endurance*'s main deck, where our party awaited us. Duncan stood with Major André and the judge. Also with them was a young man who bore a striking resemblance to Asa Lane. So incredibly striking that my heart stopped.

Then my breath stopped—and then my mind—and then time itself.

He didn't *resemble* Asa Lane. It was *him*.

He'd changed in a dozen ways—too many ways for me to absorb in a glimpse—but it was, unquestionably, *him*.

"Welcome to the *Endurance*!" the judge said cheerfully, spreading his arms. "Come, you must all meet my nephew!"

As Asa came forward with the others, my body threw a kind of a revolution. Suddenly, I had cannons booming in my chest. Fires blazing in my heart. Alarm shouting through me. As I waited for Asa to look my way, my vision smoked over. Only little Daniel, on my hip, kept me tethered to the present.

"Allow me to introduce my sister's son, Mr. Asa Latimer,"

the judge said. "Asa, these are my dearest friends, so do be your charming self and do not disappoint me."

More shock, rocking through me.

Asa *Latimer?* He was using the judge's surname?

"I shall do my best, Uncle," Asa said.

His deep, languid voice struck me. I felt like I'd heard it only yesterday. As the greetings unfolded, the realizations kept exploding in my mind.

Asa was here.

This was his ship.

He was the judge's nephew.

Time had polished him. He was dressed like a gentleman, in a dark blue coat and breeches cut close to his tall figure. The buckles on his shoes shone in the dusky light, as did the silver-headed cane he held idly at his side. In spite of such fine trappings, there was something toughened about him. Something darker and distant.

"And this is Miss Emmeline Coates," said the judge, arriving to me.

Asa looked at me, finally. No shred of recognition. "Your servant, Miss Coates," he said, and bowed deeply.

I curtsied, but couldn't find the words to reply. I'd fallen off a cliff and I had yet to land anywhere solid.

A hard tug at my neck startled me. Daniel had snapped the chain of my pocket watch. Before I could stop him, he hurled it to the deck.

Duncan shot over as it rolled away and scooped it up. "Who's this little mischief-maker?" he said, bringing the watch back to me.

"Daniel." Thankfully, I'd finally found my tongue. "Daniel Winters. But I'd keep a safe distance."

Duncan laughed. "Yes—I see he has spirit. Firing at officers. Theft of property. Vandalism." He tugged gently on Daniel's foot. "We shall have to reform you, little chap. Won't we?"

Daniel clapped his hands. "Chap, chap!" he said. Then he wriggled out of my arms and toddled after his siblings, who, like the rest of the party, were following a young ship's captain with a slight limp up to the quarterdeck.

"I feel as though I've not seen you in an age," Duncan said.

It had seemed a long time to me, too. But not nearly as long as three years.

= ★ =

Before we sat down to dinner, Mr. Asa *Latimer* gave us a tour of the *Endurance*.

As he led us through the various parts of the ship, his stride slightly uneven, his voice steady, I struggled to catch up.

Was he really a *Loyalist* shipowner now? How could such a passionate patriot be aligned with the British—*especially* after what they had done to him? And had he known all this time that I knew the judge? Surely not. This had to be a coincidence, or he'd have sent me a message.

Our tour brought us to the captain's cabin, where we gathered before the stern windows. Though it was smaller than the *Ambrosia*'s cabin, my mind raced back to long dinners and to longer nights talking, whispering, kissing. Then to the time Asa had said, "Marry me. I dare you."

"Pray tell, Mr. Latimer," Charlotte said. "Where have you sailed the *Endurance*?"

"To enough places that I will surely bore you if I name them."

"Oh, tell us, Mr. Latimer!" said Charlotte's brother, Albert. "Tell us, please!"

Asa smiled. "All right—but you must stop me when you've heard enough. I have seen many British ports, of course. Torquay, Madeira, Salvador." He paused, like he hoped that was enough, but the entire group was rapt. "Havana, Martinique, Nevis." His eyes came to me. "Grand Bahama."

"What did you think of Grand Bahama?" The question shot out of me, unbidden.

His gaze slid back to me. "In truth, it disappointed me."

A high-pitched ringing began in my ears and my face went numb. Everything suddenly seemed very distant and flat, like I was staring at a painting of a ship's cabin filled with friends and family.

As soon as I saw a chance, I slipped away and hurried outside.

Duncan followed behind me. "Miss Coates, are you all right?"

"Yes," I said. "I just need some air." I did need air; I felt faint. And I needed to get those words—*In truth, it disappointed me*—out of my head.

On the main deck, two long tables had been set up for our dinner. Servants—who appeared to be the ship's crewmen—lit candles and set out platters of fragrant food. Creating something beautiful right where I could imagine myself reading Miss Coates's journal, Tom Hackett swaggering by swinging his bosun's baton.

"Shall we walk?" Duncan said, offering his arm.

I took it eagerly. "Yes, thank you." We wandered past the dinner tables and climbed to the forecastle deck. A cool breeze swept off the river, cooling my overheated cheeks. Fort George glowed in the distance. Several large warships floated in the waters around it.

"Are those Royal Navy?" I asked. I desperately wanted to put Asa out of my mind. Instead, I found myself wondering how he had escaped after he'd been pressed into service.

Duncan peered into the distance. "Yes, they are." He turned toward me. "I worried this might strain you. The judge might've been more sensitive to your past when he decided to host a dinner here tonight."

"Thank you, but I am fine, Lieutenant. I would have declined the invitation had I been uncomfortable with it."

"Of course, I didn't mean—" He smiled. "Forgive me. I have gone through tonight a dozen times in my mind, thinking how to make it perfect."

"Perfect?" I smiled. "That is a high standard, sir. However were you going to achieve that?"

"Well, I thought I might compliment your beauty, cater to your every comfort, say charming things to entertain you, and seize upon any other opportunities to impress you. But now you know my strategy and I must abandon it and improvise."

"Oh dear. I daresay you're out of weapons. What's left—shot and shell?"

"I was thinking honesty." He placed his hand on top of mine, a comfortable heat seeping through my glove. "I am very happy to be with you again."

His earnestness disarmed me. It brought me back, putting me firmly inside my skin again.

We stood for a while watching the stars appear, one by one. With the shock of seeing Asa receding—and with the handsome young officer beside me—I remembered my objective for the night. This was a perfect chance. "Have you settled in at Judge Latimer's?"

Duncan nodded. Under the lanterns, his hair looked like gold. "I have, though I've not been there very much. There's been more to do this week than time to do it."

My instincts prickled. "Uncle Henry has sold out of many of his medicines. He said there have been fever outbreaks amongst the men on a ship that's newly arrived—I forget the name of it." I hadn't forgotten.

"The *Europa*? Yes—it was a bad stroke for us. A fresh reinforcement of men and they arrive deathly ill."

"How awful. Were many affected?" Uncle Henry had estimated five hundred.

"Too many. Some three thousand, flattened. Almost to a man, if you can believe it."

"That's awful. I hope you were not exposed?"

"No—do not worry for me. I'm quite apart from the rank and file. Most days, I'm surrounded by paper. André's post alone keeps me busy. He's quite in demand."

"So you're his penman?"

"Yes, I scribble for him, but he's been generous to involve me in matters of greater significance."

"Will you save these colonies for us, Lieutenant?"

He smiled. "Without a doubt."

My stomach muscles tightened. We would see about that.

His gaze moved past me. "Miss Coates, I have just made a shocking discovery. It appears other people exist in this world." Our party had returned from the tour and was settling at the dinner tables. From where we stood, I could hear Asa and Major André carrying on a conversation in French, their voices lively, like birds swooping in the sky. "I suppose we should join them. What do you think?"

"Lead on, Lieutenant," I said, though I didn't want to leave our spot. He'd said such pretty things to me. Such *useful* things, too. He'd given me the kind of detailed information Townsend wanted. And I wasn't exactly eager to see Asa *Latimer-Lane* again just yet.

Duncan held a chair for me as we joined the group, putting me immediately to Asa's left. Before Duncan had even seated himself to my left, I found myself leaning toward him like a flower searching for the sun.

"Will you be staying in New York long, Mr. Latimer?" Charlotte asked across the table.

Her parents and the judge were at the other table. The Winters children had been fed and now played chase somewhere in the maze beneath our feet.

"I hadn't planned on it," Asa replied. "I only came to make a delivery, but my uncle insists I stay longer."

He had the same heavy-lidded eyes I remembered. It was the coolness in his expression I didn't recognize. I noticed a bump on the bridge of his nose where it appeared to have been broken. I knew in my gut I'd been there when it'd happened. His limp, too, surely had resulted from that horrible day on the *Ambrosia*.

"I hope he is able to persuade you, Mr. Latimer," Charlotte replied.

"My uncle does not persuade as much as pass sentence, Miss Winters. I believe if I refused him, he'd have me thrown into irons."

Everyone laughed, but given where my mind had wandered, I suddenly saw him slumped on the deck, bleeding and motionless. I took a sip of my wine, forcing it past the claw in my throat.

"This is a fine little raft you have, Mr. Latimer," André said. "Seems a waste to use such a beauty for transporting furniture and wine. We ought to give you a letter of marque and turn you into a privateer."

"Nay, Major," Asa replied. "There is enough excitement on the high seas for me as it is. I don't mind hauling cargo—especially if it is good wine."

André raised his glass. *"C'est délicieux."*

I almost shook my head. Asa had been driven by ideals once. Not *profit.* Maybe that day on the *Ambrosia*'s deck, I'd seen the last of Asa Lane.

"I am fond of the name you've given her, Mr. Latimer," Charlotte said, smiling prettily. Was she *flirting* with him? "I hope she lives up to it."

"Not every ship does," Duncan said. "A Yankee privateer seized our *Fortune* last week near Boston—which strikes me as most *un*fortunate."

Charlotte laughed. "What was the privateer named? *Fortune Hunter?*"

"No, it was something else that now escapes me. I only remember it was one of the deadly sins."

"*Vainglory?*" Charlotte guessed. "*Greed?*"

"*Sloth?*" André offered, to laughs from all.

Asa's shoulders lifted with a slight shrug. "To be honest, I think *Wrath* would make a fine name for a privateer."

My silence would soon get me noticed, so I roused myself and said, "Was it called *Envy?*"

Duncan smiled. "Yes—that's it. *Envy* captured *Fortune.* Rather a predictable little story, isn't it?"

"More worrisome than predictable," Charlotte said. "Now I fear all our merchant ships will be captured by *Envy.*"

"Banish the concern from your mind, Miss Winters," André said. "We have it well in hand. Three of our best warships, in fact, sail this week to help secure the waters around Boston."

My fingertips began to tingle; I was close to something good. "I hope they're named *Courage, Resilience,* and *Fortitude,*" I said, casting for more.

"They are the *Romulus, Daphni,* and *Delaware,*" André replied, "but I assure you they will fare well in spite of their uninspired monikers."

I took a moment to commit the names to memory, amazed at how easy it'd been to come by them. It wasn't more on Monk, but it was something. I felt giddy as I imagined sharing the information with Townsend.

As coffee was served, Charlotte wanted to hear André describe the Meschianza, a grand festivity he'd organized in Philadelphia for General Howe's departure from America, before the British command was handed over to General Clinton. The three-day event had turned André into a legend amongst fashionable society.

"Miss Shippen—she was there, was she not?" Charlotte asked, though she already knew, as the Shippens were family friends of the Winters.

"She was indeed," André replied.

Charlotte sighed. "And now she's married to that American general who is always in the papers, Benedict Arnold. I grow embarrassed for her." She gave a tiny shudder. "She thought she was marrying a heroic figure. Now his honor is on the coals, and he is the favorite subject of every gossip in America."

As Charlotte went on, I became aware of Asa bowing his head to mine. "I am glad to see you well," he said quietly.

"*Are* you?" I said. He didn't look glad. He wasn't even looking at me. His eyes were still on Charlotte. "I'm glad to see you well, too. You know, I worried about you for years. For *years,* I worried you'd died."

His fingers tightened on the head of his cane. "Alas, I did not."

"Oh, good. Mystery solved." I tried to stop there, but I couldn't. "Did you know that I know your uncle? That all this time, he has been a dear friend to me? That you could've easily contacted me?"

Long seconds passed. Duncan said something that made André laugh into his napkin.

"Yes," Asa said at last. "I knew."

"You *knew.*" I felt a shattering deep inside my chest. "You *knew* and you didn't think to write? You didn't think to send a single word to tell me you'd survived?"

He looked at me, finally. "No." He shook his head. "I did not."

Suddenly, I saw how I'd put him on a throne in my mind. How I'd been thinking of him as the reason I believed in the worth of every human and their basic right to liberty. But those were *my* beliefs. All Asa had done was put a pamphlet in my hands.

"Will you walk with me?" His gaze moved over my face and came to the scar on my eyebrow. "There's more to say than can be said here."

"*Now* you want to talk?" My cheeks ignited. Three *years*. What a titanic waste of time! I'd been a fool to cherish his memory when he'd so easily left me in his past. "I'm sorry, Mr. Latimer, but I'm quite occupied." Asa's gaze slid past me to Duncan. "Perhaps we might find time to talk three years from now?" I picked up my wine. "Or perhaps in thirty?"

I turned to Duncan.

His smile vanished when he saw my face. "Is everything all right?"

I reached under the table and took his hand. "Perfect."

=★=

County Cork victualing ships having difficulty reaching New York. American privateers causing a great deal of disruption in supply lines. British command alarmed over impending food shortage.

British reinforcing waters around Boston with His Majesty's ships Delaware, Daphni, *and* Romulus, *all to arrive there week next.*

Many British and Hessian soldiers falling ill with yellow fever, in spite of quarantines of incoming ships.

Three thousand newly arrived men on the king's Europa *fleet devastated by illness.*

CHAPTER 18

355

★

October 1779

Three weeks after dinner on the *Endurance,* on a rare, rain-less morning in mid-September, Townsend met me at the corner where I usually parted ways with Malcolm.

"Miss Coates—just whom I'd hoped to see," he said, hurrying over. He nudged his eyeglasses higher on the bridge of his nose. "My supplier has arrived with the calico you requested. I am going to him now. The weather is fine for a change—would you care to join me?"

I had delivered three reports to him since the first one. "This is quite good," he'd said. Then, "This is very good." And then, "This is excellent."

I knew I was only getting better. Night after night, I had listened and watched. I had inquired and gently prodded at concerts. At dinners and assemblies. Pulling shiny bits of information from Duncan, André, and other officers, as easy as finding a silver spoon in a sunken hull.

Patterns were beginning to emerge. Names and places were becoming familiar. When I heard "Savannah, Georgia," I no longer thought *tobacco* and *humidity.* I thought of its significance in the southern strategy. This, I'd come to learn, was the British plan to shore up the support of Loyalists in Georgia, Virginia, and the Carolinas. For years, there'd been skirmishing between Loyalists and patriots in those states and the strategy sought to swing them decidedly to English rule. With these secured, British interests in the West Indian sugar islands could be strengthened, and supply chains and troop numbers could be bolstered for campaigns to win the North. Savannah, firmly in British control since January, played a crucial part in this quest, providing an anchor point, but the patriots had not given up on taking it away.

Though nearly everything I heard had to do with fighting in Georgia and the West Indies, Monk was always at the forefront of my spying—the real treasure I hoped to find.

"I'd be glad to join you, Mr. Townsend," I replied, keeping my voice smooth in spite of my surprise. I turned to Malcolm. "I will see my way home."

"Yes, Miss Em," he said. With a glance at Townsend, he strode away.

Regret pressed on my heart as I fell in step with Townsend. I missed the easy companionship Malcolm and I used to share. That night in Wallabout Bay had made me into a spy—and it had also drawn a hard line between us. We were mistress and servant now—the first time I'd ever felt that. The feeling was even stronger with Maggie, who'd become distant and formal.

Townsend led me two short blocks to the corner of Queen and King Streets. Barely far enough for me to set aside my Malcolm woes to wonder where he was taking me.

"Here we are," he said, stopping in front of Underhill's

boardinghouse. "You will know the man to whom you must speak. He's accompanied by a lady. It will be better if I wait here."

I stared at the bright red door. "Are you feeding me to the wolves, Mr. Townsend?"

"I prefer to think I'm bringing a wolf into the pack."

I drew an unsteady breath, only slightly reassured.

Inside, I found a warm public dining room with a fire snapping in the hearth in spite of the muggy morning. Four small tables were scattered around it, three of which were empty. On the far end, a man polished a glass behind a bar. As soon as I entered, he set it down and disappeared into a back room.

At the occupied table, a slight man shifted his dark eyes from me to the door and back. The woman seated with him was older than him by some ten years. She wore a lace-fringed mobcap and sat very erect, her hands folded in her lap. As I joined them, I could scarce catch my breath. I wasn't the only nervous one. The man's leg bounced under the table, making the floorboards hum beneath my feet.

"'Tis safer if we do not give you our names," he said.

"That's fine with me," I replied.

Under the woman's mobcap, I could see the graying hair at her temples. Her steady eyes, too, were a steely gray.

"'Tis unlikely we'll ever meet again, anyway," the man added.

"That is fine as well."

He frowned, like it surprised him that I spoke, then went on. "We must go over a few procedures to help reduce the risks. First, you must stop writing your reports. Letters that fall into the wrong hands are death sentences. From now on, you will deliver oral reports to Mr. Townsend."

I didn't know how I'd be able to do that discreetly—passing paper messages to Townsend had been hard enough—and I didn't care for the man's tone, either. But spying had become too important to me to quibble over it, so I nodded. I'd find a way.

"Second," he continued, "do not deviate from your weekly meetings. By being regular, you avoid suspicion."

"Fine." I'd already identified that as an advantage.

"Third, never speak a word of this to anyone—not a living soul—or you will endanger all our lives and risk our country's future."

This was the easiest one of all. Keep a secret? That was all I ever did. "Of course."

"Madam, I *do* mean that. Spies *hang*. Perhaps you, as a woman, might not, but you could be tortured, or violated, or—"

"I understand the risk, sir," I said, enunciating slowly. I turned to the woman. "Does he think my head is full of vapor?"

She turned to him. "I will pick it up from here," she said, in a quiet but firm tone.

"Will that be *fine* with you, Miss Coates?" he asked, with a wry lift of one eyebrow.

I smiled. "Very."

The woman waited till he had stepped outside before she said, "You must forgive my friend. We have been under intense pressure. Robert told us you saw the *Jersey*?"

Robert. Not Mr. Townsend. They were on familiar terms. "In Wallabout—yes." I recalled the ghostly prison ships on that eerie bay and almost shuddered.

She nodded, studying me closely. "I believe my husband is a political prisoner there, though I don't know for certain. I have

205

not heard from him in a very long time. Some days I scarcely even think of him, as other problems shout louder for my attention.

"For weeks, I have had two British officers boarded in my home. They drink their rum and there is fighting and brawling under my roof, dice and cards at all hours. They eat the food I grow, cut down my fence rails for firewood, allowing my cattle to stray, and hand their garments to me for washing. I can never be alone in the house with them—I think you can easily guess why. I have taken measures to ensure I am not, but I know women who are not as fortunate.

"A girl of barely twenty was got with child by a redcoat who breaks bread with her and her husband every night. Another has been told she will never bear children—she was savaged by five men, redcoats all. We have an evil in our midst, Miss Coates. Our husbands are imprisoned. Our sisters and daughters are raped. Our crops and livestock are taken and we are given no payment for them—nothing." She paused. "That is why *I* am here. Now, tell me . . . why are *you* here?"

Nothing she'd said was news to me but hearing it firsthand shook me. I drew a deep breath and thought about how to answer her. *Because I know what oppression is, too. Because I was subject to a tyrant once, and escaping him cost me three years, my home, my name— and the sea. Because I believe you. Because I desperately need to squeeze good from all the lies. Because I'm strong and I can help.*

I couldn't say any of it.

None of those reasons belonged to Miss Coates.

The woman leaned forward, resting her hand on the table. "Miss Coates, the man who just left does not think you witless at all. On the contrary. He has been impressed with what you have contributed. He was only trying to convey the perilousness of this work. Every letter that leaves York Island is read in Black Chambers. Every person is searched upon entry and again upon leaving. There are patrols in the rivers, day and night. Do not think yourself safe because you're a lady. The British suspect that there are women in Manhattan working against them. They have their own spies searching for *us*. Your lieutenant is a good source, but do not take him for a fool."

My blood iced. For the past three weeks, Duncan and I had seen each other as much as we could, which hadn't been nearly enough for me. We'd danced at an assembly at Mayor David Mathews's house—and I'd learned he was as graceful as Judge Latimer. We'd had dinner at Rebecca Novis's home—and I'd learned he could charm an entire table with stories of his boyhood in Surrey. We went to a picnic cut short by rain, then a horse race cut short by rain. With every passing day, I had grown fonder of him—even as I'd probed him for information. "You *know* about him?"

"'Tis our trade to know things, Miss Coates. I do hope you understand now. . . . Doing this could kill you."

"*No*, it *won't*." I said, tired of all the warnings. "I was *made* for this." I leaned back in my chair only to lean forward again. "This is *saving* me." It was a truth I hadn't admitted to myself until that very moment. Spying let me breathe again. It let the sunlight shine through the cracks, to reach the heart of me. The suffocating, hidden girl.

The revelation rocked me. It left me blinking away tears and furious at myself for looking weak when I'd never been surer of anything. But then, to my shock, I saw that *her* eyes glimmered with tears as well.

She reached across the table and clasped my hand and squeezed it. Fiercely, fiercely, fiercely. So tight. Like she was joining us bone to bone.

"I know," she said simply, and I felt her love and grace wash over me. With a final squeeze, she released my hand and bent to the leather satchel by her feet. She removed a folded length of black calico patterned with colorful pansies and pushed it across the table. "Have a look inside."

Unfolding the soft material, I discovered a paper. I leaned closer to read it.

"Abe was right," she said as my gaze drifted over writings unlike anything I'd ever seen. "The less you know, the less risk there is for all of us, but we must protect you and keep your information coming. Those are the codes we use to communicate. The numbers in the first column correspond to the names in the second."

My eye caught on the name *Culper*. There was a senior and a junior listed.

"We use the codes to encrypt our messages in the event our letters are intercepted. 'Tis but one of many safety measures we have in place. The letters also go through a series of transfers to ensure secrecy as they travel"—she pointed to a name—"to him."

I had already seen it. "Is that truly *him*?"

She nodded. "We serve at General Washington's request. I am told he calls us his intelligencers."

"I saw him once years ago, when the Continental Army was

still in possession of New York," I said, remembering. It'd been one of the first social events I'd attended—an assembly filled with the top American officers. In those days, crowds and noise had left me feeling panicked. Overwhelmed, I'd left the parlor in a rush and come through a door too quickly—slamming into a very tall, dignified man with the most piercing blue eyes I'd ever seen. I cringed, feeling the embarrassment all over again. "I may have spilled a bit of wine on his coat sleeve." I hadn't stayed around to see. Since then, General Washington had become a mythic figure. He was somehow holding the Continental army together—men he couldn't adequately pay, feed, or arm—against the greatest military power in the world.

She smiled. "Now you have the chance to make a better impression. Our intelligence helps steer his military decisions. You're in a powerful position."

Me, *powerful*? Never in my life had I thought I'd hear that.

She ran her finger down the list, stopping at 355. Beside it was the word *Lady*. "This is how we can refer to you." Her gray eyes lifted to mine. "But if you wish to have your true name listed instead, I can make a request."

My true name could never be listed there. I hadn't spoken it aloud in years. There were moments when I couldn't even remember it. "Where is your name?" I asked.

"Not here. My husband is a political prisoner. If I were caught spying, it could mean death for us both."

I looked at the paper again.

3

5

5

It was like the push and pull of a wave. A breath, rushing in and out.

This was me. It felt right. "This will do."

She smiled. "Very well. You and I will share this obscurity."

"Don't we all?"

"Yes. We do."

She knew as I did . . . glory wasn't for us.

Her attention was pulled to the door as Townsend and Abe stepped inside, both of them sending us pointed looks of impatience. Our time was ending and I didn't want it to. Right then, I wanted to spend the rest of my life talking with this brave and intelligent woman—whose name I didn't even know.

I reached into my purse and slid my letter on top of the code sheet. "I didn't have a chance to give it to Townsend. There's not much this week, aside from their preparations for the French fleet."

Of all the threads of information I pulled, this one was turning out to be the longest. The French, the French, the French. Where were they now? When would they try for New York? But this week something had changed. The British were preparing defenses, moving their warships, sinking old hulks to block passage into the harbor, and giving every sign that they believed General Washington and the French fleet would finally lay siege on Manhattan.

"Yes, we are well aware. Robert says the same." She pushed the code sheet toward me and folded the calico, putting it away. "Pray the French do come and end this once and for all." She rose from her chair, picking up her basket. "There's one last thing,

Miss Coates. We've not been properly introduced." She smiled. "My name is Anna Strong, and I am very honored to meet you."

=★=

The following night, I attended a performance of *Macbeth* at the Theater Royale. Judge Latimer had purchased tickets for us. I sat with Duncan, Charlotte, and Lucy. The judge, the Holdridges, the Winters, and Asa—Lane or Latimer, whoever he was—were seated in the row behind ours.

Though he'd been staying with his uncle, under the same roof as Duncan, I'd scarcely seen Asa since the *Endurance,* and that was more than fine with me.

He was different, but it no longer shocked or upset me. Now I was just curious.

I turned in my seat, pretending to search for Liesje, and found Asa in what sounded like a deep philosophical conversation with Charlotte's father. In a sea of red coats splashed with gold, bright silk gowns, and feathered coiffures, he held his own in an emerald-green coat over a fawn silk waistcoat, his silver-headed cane resting against his leg. He was twenty-one now, a shipowner. No longer the passionate privateersman I knew. No more torn shirts or scrapes from fights. But he still had the same air of self-reliance. And those eyes. They were the same, too. Somehow slightly sleepy *and* utterly absorbed.

His transformation into a Loyalist had shocked me at first, but not anymore. People reacted differently to hardship and abuse. Mama, I remembered, had grown softer under Sewel's violent temper. She'd fought his ire with gentleness, while I'd only ever wanted to be violent back. I had no idea what had happened to Asa over the past years, in truth. And who was *I* to question change? Regardless, I wasn't going to waste my time thinking about it. To me, he was nothing.

The murmur of the audience hushed as the curtains drew open. Duncan slipped his hand over mine furtively, sending me a smile that was quick but sultry.

Three officers—friends of his—took the stage costumed as witches. As they shambled to the center of the stage, their long straggly wigs and dirty robes dragged behind them, a ripple of laughter swept through the theater at the ridiculousness. Here were the finest examples of humankind portraying the worst. Even Lucy stifled a giggle. Only I found it insulting.

The witches warmed their hands over a fake campfire—crimson rolls of fabric shaken through a trapdoor by someone beneath them.

"Fair is foul," they declared in cracking, high-pitched voices. "Foul is fair."

Words fit for a spy's motto, I thought. Good could be done in the service of evil. Evil could be done in the service of good. So I told myself every time I tapped Duncan for information.

"Where is Major André?" I whispered to him after a little while. "I thought he was supposed to be in this?"

He leaned in, his shoulder pressing against mine. "Called to duty."

"But he was meant to play King Duncan, wasn't he?"

"Yes." He smiled, leaning even closer. "He was eager to make a monarch of me." His lips brushed my cheek, sending waves of heat down to my center. He had yet to kiss me. I was so desperate for it to happen, I'd begun to pray for him to be less genteel. "But some critical matter arose with General Clinton that he could not escape."

My gaze fell to his hand, which had moved to my knee.

A *critical matter*? What had happened that was so urgent? Were the French finally coming?

But I'd have to wait to know more. Plenty of outings were good for spying, but theater wasn't one of them.

Turning my attention back to the stage, I reached for my watch and ran my fingers over the cool silver. Last night as the household slept, I had unscrewed the back plate and pried out the tiny gears and springs with a hairpin. Then I had folded and refolded the code sheet Anna Strong had given me and pressed it inside the empty case. The fit had been perfect—and I could think of no safer place to keep it than always with me, right over my heart.

I smiled to myself, remembering my meeting with her. So brief, but our connection had been so powerful. I shut my eyes and the number appeared.

355

Lady

Anna. Me. Elizabeth Burgin.

How many more of us were there?

I felt like a true spy now—one with tools and a network of support. With rules I'd devised to stay safe: Trust no one. Expect the worst. Be prepared. Most important of all—choose patience over risk.

This last rule I struggled with most. I knew my findings were valuable, but I ached to uncover information that would pierce deep into the heart of the British effort.

I opened my eyes and forced my attention back to the drama onstage. The actor playing Banquo was warning Macbeth against evildoers who used truths to bring about the total destruction of their enemies.

"The instruments of darkness tell us truths," he said, opening his hands expansively. "Win us with honest trifles, to betray's in deepest consequence."

I was an instrument of darkness.

My heart hammered as my gaze fell once more to Duncan's hand on my knee.

Was he?

=★=

After the play, the judge had us over for dinner in his fine home. Duncan sat to my right again, like in the theater. It seemed to be understood by everyone that we were a pair.

"I had such high hopes for the judge's nephew," Charlotte whispered, on my left, as the others at the table discussed the play. "But I find his conversation so subdued and colorless. What's more, he is exceeding evasive. I have tried repeatedly to learn about his family and his home. I have even asked about his ship, the *Exuberance*."

"The *Endurance*?"

"Yes. When I inquired about it, he gave me only the tersest reply."

"Perhaps because you called it by the wrong name, Char."

She blinked. "Maybe. But my point holds. He's impossible to engage. I'm beginning to think he's one of those mechanical gentlemen from—what was it again, Emmie?"

My blood went warm. "Trumbull's *Progress of Dullness*." A week ago, she had asked me to read aloud from the book in my lap. The text had been a criticism of people who hid behind natty clothes and fumbled through polite conversation, pretending to be refined and well bred, when they were just trussed-up country clowns.

Charlotte had no idea. She was insulting Asa *and* me.

I took a sip of my wine, glancing down the table. Asa was deep in a discussion with Duncan about hamartias and tragic heroes. "Do you fancy him, Char?" I whispered.

"*Psh,* Emmie—what does it matter? He's a merchant; he's beneath us both. But he *is* handsome, to be sure. In a sharpish way, like a knife is handsome. I was thinking of him for Lucy. They'd make a pretty picture, don't you think? Dark and fair. Tall and delicate. Knife and—well, I was going to say a spoon, but Lucy's not a spoon. You know what I mean."

I nodded absently, still watching Asa. An ember of anger had begun to burn a hole in my stomach. Like a knife, Charlotte described him. He used to be. As quick. As sharp. Was any of that still there?

"Mr. Latimer," I heard myself say. "I have just realized you have been in New York several weeks and we still know so little about you. Are you such an unsolvable mystery, or have we failed to draw you out of your shell?"

All conversation broke off. Charlotte kicked me under the table for my forwardness. Asa calmly set his wine down and met my gaze.

"I rather like my shell, Miss Coates," he said, "but I would be happy to dispel any mystery that surrounds me."

The judge cleared his throat. "My nephew is exceeding easy to know. A good book and the open sea are all he needs. Isn't that so?"

"Yes, Uncle. I have just finished Sir Isaac Newton's *Principia*, as a matter of fact. Do you know it, Miss Coates?"

"No. Not at all."

Asa's eyebrows lifted. "Oh? I was told you are fond of books."

"Not of that one."

"I'm afraid I misunderstand. You dislike a book you've not read?"

"I have heard it explains forces in nature, Mr. Latimer. Forces I'd prefer to enjoy than try to understand."

"Leaving them unsolvable mysteries?"

The angry heat spread through me. How dare he twist my words?

"Mr. Latimer," Uncle Henry said, "it must be rather crowded at sea nowadays, with privateers and navies everywhere. Have you found that to be the case?"

Charlotte nudged my arm. *What are you up to?* her eyes asked, but I wasn't at all sure. Provoking Asa was the last thing I should be doing. He was the only person at the table who had knowledge that could destroy me.

"The war has certainly changed the world's oceans," Asa replied, "but there are a few corners where one might still find solitary water."

"Are you a solitary man, then?" Duncan asked. "No lockstep for you? Never thought of serving in the militia?"

I blinked at Duncan. Asa's limp was obvious and the question struck me as indelicate.

"I'm afraid that's an impossibility for me," Asa replied. "My ankle prevents me from pursuing the arts of soldiery."

"But not from pursuing personal riches on high seas." Duncan wiped his mouth with his napkin. "Which is fortunate for you indeed."

Throats cleared down the table. Asa's eyes held on Duncan, and there, finally, I saw what I'd sought. Sharpness. Steel. Duncan's mood, too, had darkened. He looked immovable—but also like he might explode across the table. This was the Duncan who'd roughly handled the man in the tavern at Liesje's wedding.

"Pray tell, Mr. Latimer," Lucy said quickly, ever the peacekeeper. "Does it ever grow tiresome being at sea?"

"Not to me, Miss Holdridge. I have never found the sea to be dull."

"How have you found it to be, Mr. Latimer?" I said. "As riveting as Newton's theories?" I didn't know what was driving me—I wanted to attack, defend, retreat. I wanted to scrape and scratch and claw till I broke through the ice that I just *knew* he was hiding behind.

Asa turned to me. *You know what I think of the sea,* his eyes said. *You know and you know and you* know. "I find the sea to be devastatingly powerful, enthrallingly beautiful, and fathomless in scope."

Silence filled the room. Then the sound of Duncan swallowing a laugh. "Mr. Latimer, you have a talent for embellishment, sir. Rather like a poet. I'm almost ready to resign my commission to become a navy swabbie, working for a day's grog and hardtack."

My mind went white with panic, and I found myself rising out of my chair. My slight had been rude, but Duncan's was a

217

cliff's edge. This banter had taken a dangerous turn that could easily end in a duel. "I think the rain has let up. Shall we take some air?" I asked Duncan.

"Excellent idea," he said, thank the Lord above. We excused ourselves, and I floated out of the dining room and up to the balcony.

"Still a bit damp out here." Duncan opened his hands to the falling mist.

A few British ships sailed up the East River. They looked like shadows drifting through fog.

"I don't mind." I lifted my face to the sky and let the moisture cool my overheated skin. I didn't understand my own frustration, nor why I'd made Asa my target.

Duncan pulled his cloak off and held it over us. "Better?" he said, his face inches from mine.

"Yes," I lied, and felt my pulse kick faster. "Why did you say those things just now?" I asked.

He was quiet a moment, his eyes searching mine. "I know you hold Judge Latimer in high esteem, but I have to admit, I agree with Miss Winters's opinion of his nephew."

My heart stopped. "Were you listening to us?"

"I overheard your conversation inadvertently. You were sitting right next to me. Regardless, she is right—he is insincere."

"You suspect him of something?"

"I do not suspect; I *know*. Latimer is an opportunist and a criminal. He imports illegal goods into New York for wealthy Loyalists. Men like his uncle."

"Asa's a Loyalist *smuggler*?" I shook my head, stunned. I had no idea *who* he was.

Duncan's eyebrows snapped together. "I confess I'd hoped to hear *my* Christian name pass your lips before *Latimer's.*"

No! What had I just said? "Heavens! It would be improper for me to address you so informally."

"And him?"

"I don't know why I said it, to be honest. After what you've just told me, perhaps my mind decided him unworthy of being styled a gentleman. I don't know," I said again. "It was thoughtless of me. Lord knows I'll never do it again."

I couldn't believe the things coming from my own mouth. When people told lies, they stammered. They avoided eye contact and invoked God and said things like "to be honest." I'd observed these markers over the years. I'd spent years weeding them out of my own speech—only to use them now, at the worst possible moment.

Duncan shifted closer. "Well, now you have me thinking . . ." He trailed off and panic feathered in my chest. I could feel the weight of his stare. Anna Strong's warning echoed in my mind. *Do not take him for a fool.* "You have me thinking that when we're alone, as now, perhaps you might call me James and I might call you Emmeline?" He let go of one corner of the cloak and took my hand, letting the wool fall over us like a shroud. "What do you think? Is that a yes? 'Tis rather dark under here and I cannot tell if you are smiling."

"Yes," I said, waiting for the relief to come.

"Emmeline," he said, like it was the most beautiful sound he'd ever heard.

"James." Though I tried my best, it came out sounding like a kind of currency. *Guineas, dollars, shillings . . . James.*

His lips curved up, a pale crescent. "I'm going to kiss you now, Emmeline. May I?"

"Yes."

He leaned in and did.

He was perfect. His kisses gentle, soft, warm. Desire struck me, and I stepped closer and clutched his arms. As I did, I felt my mind pull back, and back, and back—and then I saw waves. One after another, furling out into the distance.

A hundred waves. A thousand. A world's worth.

The sight devastating. Enthralling. Fathomless.

CHAPTER 19

BLOOD AND THUNDER

★

November 1779

"Well, I suppose that settles it. The French aren't coming to save us after all."

"I'm afraid not," Townsend replied. He paused, looking up from polishing the counter. He was so fastidious, I'd come to associate the smell of lemon and vinegar with him as much as I did with Maggie. "Not yet, anyhow. The priority was the south."

After weeks of bracing for an attack, the New York garrison had relaxed. Instead of attacking Manhattan, Comte d'Estaing had taken his thirty-some ships and four thousand men to lay siege on Savannah. Townsend had fresh intelligence, and we had his shop to ourselves, thanks to a heavy snowfall, so he was sharing it with me comfortably, no whispering. No fear of detection. We talked enemy movements as casually as we used to talk about books.

"And what of Savannah?" I asked. "Did we take it?" Outside, a black horse hitched to a cart swished its tail, puffs of breath rising from its nostrils.

"No. The siege was a disaster. We had every advantage. We

221

had the city surrounded and were poised to begin our assault, but the British used delay tactics. They rallied local Loyalist militia and strengthened their defenses. D'Estaing was forced to sit off the coast for weeks with his fleet, exposed to the battering of hurricanes. His ships sustained significant damage, and I'm told disease and scurvy struck as well, killing some forty men a day. They were half defeated even before they attempted the final siege—Pardon me." Townsend turned away and blew his nose into a kerchief.

I shook my head. Illness wasn't only a problem for the French. Poor Townsend had been red-nosed and bleary-eyed since last week. New York seemed to be cursed with bad weather. We had gone from constant rain in September and October to constant snow. Now the city streets were slushy in places and thick with muck in others. Such dismal weather caused epidemics to sweep through the city, keeping Uncle Henry and Malcolm busy day and night. Just this morning, Malcolm and I had taken the crate of tonics to Canvas Town instead of to a city prison. Thousands of poverty-stricken families lived there, in shacks built in the ruins of the Great Fire, and when disease struck, they suffered worst of all.

Townsend turned back to me, his eyes red and swollen behind his glasses. "I expect the French will make another attempt on New York in the New Year. In the meantime, the British will continue to shift south. General Clinton has ordered several regiments to South Carolina. They will make a move for Charles Town, I think. If they can secure it, they will be in a strong position to push for North Carolina."

222

I let out a slow breath. At times I wished I could just carry a musket and lead a charge.

"Miss Coates, I believe your lieutenant will be amongst those sent away."

My heart stopped. "Are you certain?"

"General Clinton and Major André are going. . . ." He shrugged lightly. "I cannot imagine he would not go with them. I apologize. Perhaps I shouldn't have said anything."

"No—thank you. I'm glad you did." Duncan was *leaving*. I didn't know how I felt about that. I wasn't even sure how I felt about *Duncan*. He was my perfect future. My perfect foe. But he couldn't be both forever. Or even for much longer. The more I cared for him, the more it hurt to betray him. Maybe that was why I felt shock, sorrow—but also *relief*? "You've outdone me with your findings today, Townsend," I teased, needing to turn away from my own thoughts.

He smiled. "'Tis not a contest. Our victories are shared."

We stood a moment, enjoying our unique companionship. I'd come to treasure our Wednesday mornings; they were outlets for the things I thought about all week. But then I felt a rising desperation. Without Duncan, André, and their circle of officers, who would I spy on? "My work will be harder when they leave."

"Yes. The flow of information will slow for us both."

I didn't want it to slow. I wanted more—a *real* victory. Something that would make a difference.

"I'm going to bring us a grand discovery next week." *Monk.* I'd push myself and find him before Duncan left and the door closed. "It'll be astonishing, Townsend. You'll see."

"Should you be able to enter into General Knyphausen's lair, you might find it easy to do so. The New York garrison will be left in his hands while General Clinton is away on campaign. General Clinton will transfer all of his important records to the Hessian commander in the next weeks."

I laughed, stunned by my luck. "I'll be at General Knyphausen's *tomorrow* for the queen's birthday!"

Townsend's dark eyebrows rose over the rim of his glasses. "I believe you're poised to outdo me with your findings, Miss Coates. But I beg you . . . be careful."

"I will be. I promise." An invisible brick settled on my chest as I spoke the words—and stayed there all the way home. Sometimes, even when I told the truth, I felt like I was lying.

=★=

The following night, I sat in General Knyphausen's grand parlor, listening to my friends discuss *Evelina*.

"She is the most darling creature," Lucy said. "So sweet and comical!"

"Yes!" Rebecca agreed, leaning across Charlotte in her excitement. "I have never read a novel featuring a character like us— someone we'd call a friend. What did you think of Lord Orville?"

"Orville!" Lucy beamed, her hand coming to the strand of pearls she'd borrowed from me. "He is the very soul of chivalry!"

Charlotte nudged Rebecca. "If you want me to read it, then don't spoil everything. I think I may already know more about it than novels I have actually read."

Tonight, Charlotte had insisted we all dress for the occasion and had chosen a "celestial theme" for us. Our gowns ranged in color from Lucy's soft periwinkle to my rich indigo. We'd spared nothing, wearing our best boned stays and widest hoops. Instead of having Maggie style my hair, I'd spent hours that morning with a coiffeur who had curled and piled it, adding scarlet ribbons and raven's feathers so black they looked blue in the candlelight. I seldom applied paint, but tonight I wore blanc and rouge, as well as vermilion lip stain. "We are à la mode tonight," Charlotte had said earlier. "We would rival the French court."

I'd expected to hate all the extra trappings, but I didn't.

I felt beautiful. Dangerous.

"Dearest Miss Winters, you know I adore you," Liesje said to Charlotte from across the table, "but you have never read a book in all your life."

"Nonsense, Mrs. Devoor. I read French fashion plates daily."

I laughed. "You *look* at them. They're *pictures*."

"There are a few words."

Asa, who sat beside Liesje, appeared to be listening to his uncle, but I had a feeling he was really listening to us, judging by the smile he was fighting.

I cast my gaze farther down the table. At the far end, Major André recited one of his poems, predictably holding everyone in thrall.

Everywhere I looked, there were powdered wigs, rich silks, satins, and brocades. Wrists and collars exploded with lace. Today, the men's fashions were as lavish as the women's. Every eye glimmered with candlelight and the parlor roared with happy conversation, but above it, I could hear the noises in the street outside. While we were here, wrapped in luxury, common folk paraded to the sound of flutes and the tattoo of kettledrums.

Though the queen's birthday was actually in the summer, like the king's, it was celebrated during a different season to give city inhabitants more occasion to rejoice in their royalism. The middling class, in particular, loved festooning themselves in high style for the day. All morning, I'd heard church bells ringing and cannons firing. Townsend had told me that very different celebrations happened elsewhere. In patriot cities, effigies of the king and queen were sometimes mutilated and burned in public. Unlike here, the toasts being given weren't for God to save the Queen.

I took a sip of my wine, eager for the dancing to begin. With such a large assembly, it would be easy to slip away in the commotion to search this elegant mansion for useful information. Patience, I reminded myself. My chance would come.

"Emmeline," Duncan said quietly, his hand settling on the back of my chair. "I have some news to share. Not good news, I fear. I must go south with my regiment in two days. I shall be away a few weeks, at least. Likely longer. Perhaps for months."

Though I already knew this, I didn't have to pretend to be disappointed. He was charming, beautiful, gallant. Informative. And over the past months, my life had molded to his. Like a young plant, I'd encircled him in delicate roots. It would hurt when he left. He'd leave a void.

"Will you miss me?" he whispered.

"Yes," I said, staring right into his eyes. "I will."

"It pleases me to know that." He smiled and traced a finger down my neck, toying with the chain that held my pocket watch. Fear washed over me—the code sheet was inside—followed by embarrassment as I began to feel like some sort of display.

"There's another thing I have to tell you. I have asked Dr. Holdridge for permission to carry on a private correspondence with you while I am away. He has assented."

"That's wonderful."

"Yes. It is."

I had nothing more to add. A private correspondence was a formal step forward for us—it would almost certainly lead to him proposing to me. Then to marriage. Which I wanted. Which would give me *everything* I could ever want.

I picked up my fork and pushed a piece of chocolate around my plate.

My hand was shaking.

I set the fork down.

The conversation had turned to the fine meal we'd enjoyed. Quantities of roasted meats and vegetables had been cleared away and replaced by platters heaped with jellies, syllabub cakes, and sweetmeats.

"What an exquisite table," Liesje said. "The way my servants talk, New York is always on the verge of starvation. They make it sound as if every last one of our victualing ships succumbs to rebel privateers. I imagine them like a pack of wolves, lying in wait."

Duncan smiled. "Take heart, Mrs. Devoor. We'll not starve. We have the overwhelming advantage at sea. Our prisons are filled with your wolves, as a matter of fact. We've captured so many, we hardly know where to put them."

I thought of the prison ships in Wallabout Bay and the men who were slowly dying on them. How could he sound so callous?

"That is a shame, Lieutenant," Asa said. "Would that there were prisons enough to lock them all away. You would make my life much easier."

"Yes, upright merchants such as yourself have suffered greatly at the hands of Yankee privateers," Duncan said. "Especially those who've turned a quick coin and have no true wealth with which to weather hard times. I find it most unfortunate when bounty falls to low men who have no idea how to manage it. One sees them peacocking in velvet and silk today and dining on bread and butter tomorrow."

I tensed. Asa wore a stunning blue velvet court coat embroidered with silk flowers in silver and gold. Bread and butter sat on the plate by his hand, left over from his meal. As I watched, his fingers slowly drew into a fist.

"It always saddens me to think of the prisoners in town," Lucy said. Her eyes were wide with alarm as they flicked to me. Even she'd registered Duncan's slight. "Rebels or not, their situation seems so wretched. I only wish I had Miss Coates's charity and generosity."

"Imprisonment is certainly a harsh fate," Duncan said, "but 'tis one they chose."

Asa shook his head slowly. "Surely you can't mean that men *choose* to be captured?"

"No, Mr. Latimer. What I mean is that harm is the objective of war, so those who *make* war must accept the possibility of meeting dark ends. 'Tis simple—rain clouds bring rain."

"Sometimes not, says this seasoned sailor, but your point is certainly made." Asa raised his glass. "I salute you, Lieutenant. Your unflinching mind-set is admirable."

Duncan raised his glass in turn. "As is your enviable under-standing of clouds."

Words flowed from my mouth before I had a chance to think. "I have delivered medicines to the prisons for years. I agree with Miss Holdridge. I find it tragic how the men are mistreated."

"Perhaps 'unfortunate' is a better word," Duncan said with a mild smile. "Regardless, 'tis a common soldier's fate. My concern is for our men, and our king and country."

By "our men" he meant gentlemen. He was well above the riffraff—which was the low-bred class into which I'd been born.

His eyes flicked past me. "What is truly tragic is that I'm being summoned to cards when I would prefer to dance with you." I followed his gaze to a group of officers waiting impatiently for him by the door. "But now that the subject has been broached, I spoke to your uncle recently and he agrees it's best you stop mak-ing your medicine deliveries. To have you aiding the enemy gives off a bad gloss—I'm sure you can see how it reflects unfavorably on me. Moreover, you are too refined and delicate to march all over town on an errand better handed to a servant. I'm sure your charity and generosity will make itself known in ways more befit-ting your worth."

Throughout his speech I felt a crumbling inside me, like a fire that finally surrendered and collapsed into a pile of embers and ash.

"Duncan!" one of the officers by the door called. "Before we grow old!"

"I must go," Duncan said. "But I shall come for you as soon as I can."

And with that, he took his leave.

Sometime later, I found myself in the grand parlor, with no memory of having left the dinner table and walked there. I watched the room swirl with pairs gliding through the allemande, trying to understand the hot feeling inside me.

Dismissed? Reprimanded? Diminished?

Or some blend of all three?

The parlor floor felt unsteady beneath me. Instead of perfume and candle wax, I smelled rum. Tobacco. Salt air. I pressed my eyes shut and felt blood trickling from the scar on my eyebrow. A bright coppery taste bloomed over my tongue.

You will yield to me.

You will obey.

Duncan wouldn't be like that; he'd be kinder. And it was a wife's duty to obey. *He for God and she for him,* Aunt Nora liked to say. That was the proper order of things. How I felt about it didn't matter.

"Emmie, what is it?" Lucy whispered.

I opened my eyes, disoriented. "Sorry?"

"She's thinking of Blood and Thunder," Charlotte said. She could only mean Duncan and Asa. "They're turning into quite a show. We must hope that Thunder will soon accept that he hasn't a chance." She glanced at me. "You look much too surprised. Have you truly not seen it?"

"I've seen it," said Liesje.

"Seen what?" Lucy said.

"Yes, what?" Rebecca's gaze swept the parlor. "What are we looking for?"

"Watch closely," Charlotte said. "Here comes Thunder now."

Asa and Judge Latimer were weaving through the crowd, coming toward us. Side by side, their resemblance was strikingly obvious. Their lean figures. Their poise, like they carried a kind of quiet with them.

"Miss Coates," Asa said. He swept a deep, formal bow. "Would you do me the honor of a dance?"

You'll see, Charlotte had said. I didn't. Asa couldn't have appeared more unenthused. He looked like he was staring right through me to the wallpaper behind me. Cold anger washed through me. Why ask me to dance if the idea was so disagreeable?

"I shan't even mind," the judge said genially. "This once, I will gladly step aside."

"Unfortunately, Mr. Latimer," Charlotte said, "Miss Coates has already agreed to dance with Lieutenant Duncan."

"I have indeed, Miss Winters," I said immediately, surprising myself, "but as the lieutenant is not yet here, I accept."

Asa handed his cane to his uncle and offered me his arm. I took it and felt instant regret. I didn't need social distractions. I had to take advantage of tonight and search General Knyphausen's home.

"You seem displeased," Asa said as we walked to join the line.

"On the contrary. This is so civil of you."

"Have I been uncivil?"

"You've been an unwelcome surprise." From the corner of my eye, I saw him wince. Lord, my veins sizzled. I wanted to push men into the sea, one by one, and it didn't matter who or why.

The violins and flutes struck up. I concentrated on the allemande, using the controlled movements to tame my frustration.

231

Asa made the dance quieter by staying grounded in steps that required hopping and by modifying it in other small ways. He was an elegant mover. Better than I remembered. Our *passés* and turns were graceful, but when we came together, our hands gripped hard and neither of us eased up. The dance continued, our feet gliding, our fingers biting.

"Coincidentally," he said after a while, "I have also been surprised. You're rather unlike who I remember."

I glared at him. "Says Mr. *Latimer,* the *Loyalist merchant.*"

"Yes. Says he. Well, this is good fun."

I ignored his dry tone and swept out in a wide turn.

"You still have that old watch," he said as we came together again.

My hand flew to where the watch rested at my breast. "I would thank you to be more gentlemanly, *sir.*"

"Would you? Very well, let me try. Shall I tell you how much it pleases me to see countless men condemned to prisons? Then deny you your good deeds? Then perhaps leave your side for a game of whist?"

"You're *jealous.*"

"Nay. He has nothing I want."

"Then you're ruder than I remember."

"Do you remember? That stuns me."

"What stuns *me* is your gall, but what else should I expect from a *smuggler?*" I hissed as our steps brought us close. Asa kept dancing, showing absolutely no reaction. "You're not even going to deny it?"

"Why bother?" Blue eyes cut to me. "You won't listen."

"When will you be leaving New York, Mr. Latimer?"

"Is that your way of saying you cannot wait to be rid of me?"

"It's my way of saying I don't know why you're here."

"It's simple. I came in search of Francisca Tasker—but I have yet to find her."

Shock pierced me, like a hook to the chest. I froze. Tears surged to my eyes.

Asa went ahead a few steps. He stopped and turned to me, the impassive look on his face finally falling away. "No. I didn't mean—"

"Ex-excuse me," I stammered. Then I fled.

=★=

The tears were coming. I wouldn't be able to stop them.

I hurried to the second floor, desperate to find a private place where I could let them go. The first room I tried was a game parlor, where men were seated at card tables. I darted back out; the last person I wanted to see was Duncan. The next room was filled with older couples listening to a young woman at a pianoforte. The next was a library filled with Hessian officers.

Frustrated, tears blurring my eyes, I hurried to the third-floor stairs—and came to an abrupt stop.

"Please, sir," I said to the Hessian soldier guarding them. "Please let me pass."

He glowered at me for a long moment, but then stepped aside as my tears finally fell. I gathered my petticoats and dashed up the stairs. On the landing, closed doors ran down a long hallway. I tried the first and glimpsed a man and woman tangled in the darkness.

I'd had enough. I flew to the last room and burst into it. Shutting the door, I fell back against it. Then I breathed and breathed and let the tears run.

Francisca Tasker.

It was *foreign* to my ears. The name of a perfect stranger.

But no stranger's name would make me ache this much, like I'd been hollowed out.

Asa had said he couldn't find her—and no wonder. I ran my hands over my gown. My beribboned and feather-adorned hair. I could barely remember her myself.

As my eyes adjusted to the moonlit room, I saw a confusion of furniture and boxes. A large desk sat at the center. A dark wardrobe loomed behind it. Chairs were stacked in the corner. Along the walls were random items like boxes, an octant, miter caps. A lap desk. It was orderly disorder—the stacks tidy, like they'd been placed temporarily, in the process of a reorganization.

I brushed at my wet cheeks and crept over to the desk, my instincts stirring.

Neat stacks of papers sat on top. Rolled charts. A quill and inkpot. A lamp. I grabbed a stack of papers and took them to the window to catch the moonlight.

They contained lists and lists of names. Muster rolls for Hessian troops.

I grabbed another stack. It was correspondence in German. No help to me. I hurried back for more. I had no idea how long I'd have to search, but I knew there had to be *something* here. I could feel it. The call of treasure, pulling me toward it.

I checked the desk drawers. More letters in German on the left, but the drawer on the right was locked. I knelt and rummaged through the boxes at the foot of the desk for a key, my hands moving on their own. I knew this searching. I had found thimbles on the seafloor once—a desk key was nothing to me. Easy.

As soon as I found the gilt snuffbox, I knew I had it. I opened the box carefully. A key rested inside on a little swatch of burlap. I took the key out and ran my fingers over it. It was hefty for such a small thing. Decorated with elaborate whorls and designs.

I felt for the lock in the drawer and tried the key. I heard the satisfying click and smiled.

Carefully pulling the drawer open, I discovered more paper—paper stuffed to the top. I took the first sheets and rushed to the window. More German. I grabbed another stack—every second I knew the risk increased. Finally, I found pages in English.

The first few sheets were field reports that I skimmed. Recommendations for courts-martial. Soldiers punished for things like theft or "war atrocities," such as the killing of enemy combatants who'd surrendered peaceably. At last I came to a letter written in a numeric code that resembled the paper hidden inside my watch.

A spy message! My heart roaring, I stared at the cipher, a senseless jumble of numbers except for the figure toward the bottom. Unlike the rest, it was a neat round number. Right there, plain as day, it read *10,000 pounds.*

A shiver rippled through me.

The message was dated at the top—only two weeks ago.

Recent.

My mind raced back to Liesje's wedding in August. General Knyphausen had been at the tavern that night with Duncan,

André, and the sweaty-faced man, Rattoon. Ten thousand was the sum Monk wanted for his information. This *couldn't* be a coincidence. This was proof of a high-level plot. Whatever Monk planned, top men were involved. Probably General Clinton himself. And it was still unfolding now, months after I'd first learned of it.

I had to know more. I bent to continue my search—and froze at the sound of footsteps in the hall. Quickly, I shoved the papers back into the drawer and pushed it shut, but I had no time to replace the key.

Two men were talking just outside. I was trapped—no way to leave the room. My head whipped to the window. I could leap through it—but that was certain death. I lunged for the wardrobe instead, throwing myself inside.

I'd just pulled the door shut when the room brightened with candlelight, a seam of it appearing where the wardrobe doors met. I cringed, seeing that I had shut them on my petticoats. My gown would be visible on the other side.

"Well, Lieutenant Blake. You've taken me away from the charms of the exquisite Miss Delaney. Tell me you have good reason for it."

I'd know that elegant English voice anywhere. Against all my better judgment, I leaned forward, my thighs shaking, and peered through the tiny gap. There he was, leaning one hip against the desk, his back to me. *Major André.*

"I believe I do, Major," replied a young officer. "I have news from Philadelphia." I had a poor angle on him, but I could see that he was tall. Even taller than Asa. "Very good news."

"Now I am awake." André set the candle down on the stacks of paper I had just rifled through and crossed his arms. "Go on."

I was seconds from being discovered. I still had the key in my hand. My hoops strained against the wardrobe doors, and the boxes I was perched on were slowly sliding out from beneath me.

"Earlier this week, we seized several reams of paper Congress uses to print their dollar. The *very* same paper, sir. And enough of it to draw blood. The particulars are here. I thought you might want to know sooner rather than later."

André took the letter from the officer and slipped it into his coat. "Well done, Lieutenant Blake. You were right to tell me. You may go now."

"Thank you, sir."

Lieutenant Blake left, shutting the door behind him.

For long moments, André remained in perfect stillness. Surely he heard my runaway breathing. My thundering heart. Any moment, he was going to come over and wrench open the wardrobe.

"Thank you, Lord," he said, and another long silence stretched out. Finally, he released a long, tired exhale and swept the candle up. "Weariness, thy name is war," he murmured, and pushed to his feet.

As soon as he shut the door behind him, I collapsed. Sweat tickled down my spine. My breath raced and raced; I was never going to be able to catch it. I couldn't believe what had almost happened. And I felt cruel, witnessing André in such a private and vulnerable moment.

Suddenly, I was spent, but I had to return the key to the snuff-box and hurry back downstairs. I'd been gone much too long.

I climbed out of the wardrobe, and froze when the door opened again.

A male figure stood at the threshold. For an instant, I thought it was André, returning. Then I saw the silhouette of a cane.

"What are you doing here?" Asa asked.

"It's no concern of yours," I snapped. I'd brought my hand to my stomach in my surprise—and the key was inside my fist. There'd be no replacing it now. "If you'll excuse me." I rounded the desk.

Asa stayed where he was, blocking the door.

"Let me pass," I said.

"What's in your hand?"

"What's in *yours*?" I shot back. I had no defense. Just fear.

Asa opened his hands in the darkness, showing me his empty palms. Then he brushed a finger over my eyebrow—a quick swipe down my scar.

I jerked back with a gasp. "Why did you do that?"

He watched me intently, his eyes piercing deep, like the answer to my own question was inside me. Like he was just waiting for me to find it.

"Go," he said, and stepped aside.

I went.

CHAPTER 20

THE KEY

★

November–December 1779

"And that's the key?" Townsend said the following Wednesday. He turned aside and coughed into a kerchief. The poor man. He looked worse than a week ago. "The very one?"

"Yes." I pushed the key toward him on the counter. It struck me as something from a fairy tale, all pretty swirled silver with a tiny diamond set at the crown. General Knyphausen had to be missing it by now. "The very one."

Townsend picked it up, studying it like it was a strange insect. "I must say, Miss Coates, you took an exorbitant risk."

"I know. I know I did."

"Alas. 'Tis done." He set the key down. "Do you think Mr. Latimer will go to his uncle with his suspicions?"

"No. I don't think so." It sounded so feeble. Truth was, I had no idea what Asa would do. Keeping quiet about my identity was one thing, but spying was treason. I could only hope he still had a scrap of regard for me that would keep him from turning me in. He held my life in his hands. Townsend's life. Our entire ring of spies. "I can't believe I took such a terrible risk—only to come away with information about stolen *paper*."

I'd decided not to tell Townsend about the clue I'd found regarding Monk. Not yet. I'd learned over the past months that I trusted instinct while Townsend trusted facts. I worried he'd call the connection I'd made thin and try to discourage me. When I brought Monk to him, I'd have evidence that was indisputable.

"Your discovery is far from trifling, Miss Coates. If the British have obtained reams of the very paper we use to print our own currency, they could flood us with counterfeit money, driving down the value. Our starved and disheartened soldiers will be paid in useless dollars—and when soldiers go unpaid, they mutiny. They abandon their posts and return to their families. Warfare by counterfeit *is* a real problem. We stand no chance on the battlefield if we have no soldiers. Your find was a good one. A very good one indeed."

I sighed. "Thank you for trying to find a bit of good in the mess I've made."

"Miss Coates, we all commit errors. Please try to forgive yourself and forge ahead. Wasn't it Virgil who said 'Come what may, all bad fortune is to be conquered by endurance'?"

My heart skipped at the mention of *endurance*. "Yes, but Virgil also said 'The descent into hell is easy.'"

Townsend coughed in surprise. I'd sounded coarse; a lady spoke reverently about heaven, not brusquely about hell. I needed to tighten my grip again.

Through the fogged store windows, I saw Malcolm waiting outside, his hands tucked under his arms against the cold. I couldn't remember the last day we'd had *without* snow. A group of redcoats strolled past, their regimentals bright against all the wintry white.

"You were right about Duncan," I said. "He left this morning." He had come over last night to say goodbye. Alone in the dim entryway, we had kissed. It'd felt like our mouths were discussing something complicated and trying to reach an understanding. After, he'd patted his coat pocket, where he'd tucked the portrait André had sketched of me, which Duncan had asked to take with him. Then he'd whispered sweet things into my ear, telling me he'd always wear it over his heart and that I was the most precious thing in the world to him.

"Miss Coates . . . ," Townsend said, pulling me back to the present. "What we do . . . it is very trying and difficult."

"You understand."

He nodded. "Yes. One grows weary of dissimulating and spinning lies."

I was more than weary. Being untrue, inauthentic, deceptive . . . it was closer to a slow suffocation. I'd thought spying would let me breathe—but lies were lies. Even when they were told for noble reasons. And yet, I wanted more. I *needed* more. Without the hunt, without *Duncan*, I had no idea how I'd manage.

The door opened with a burst of frigid air. A group of young gentlemen entered the store, carrying on a loud conversation. My time with Townsend was over till next week.

"Will you send that to Anna Strong for me?" I said, glancing at the key on the counter. It could never go back to General Knyphausen. "It's pretty enough to wear as a necklace."

"Of course." Townsend smiled. "I can think of no one better to have it."

Outside, I joined Malcolm and we began our trudge home through the snowy streets, leaning into a bitter wind. It was a colder November than anyone could remember. Streams all over Manhattan had frozen over, and the rivers were filling with ice.

"Do you think we'll get there this year?" I said. My thighs burned from wading through drifts.

"Perhaps after the spring thaw." Malcolm glanced at me. Beneath his hat, the lobes of his ears were red. "It might help to think of warm things, like a crackling fire."

I smiled. "Or steam rising from a cup of tea."

"A hot pie, fresh from the oven."

"The summer sun, shining through a window."

We kept going all the way home, talking as we used to before things had become awkward and distant between us. I never stopped smiling.

Sometimes little things could turn an entire day around.

= ★ =

Two weeks later, it was still snowing, and Charlotte Winters, my aptly named friend, couldn't have been happier about it. While most people huddled fireside and bemoaned the icy temperatures, she came to life.

"What a perfect wintry day!" she declared the afternoon of the annual sleigh race at her country farm in Turtle Bay. She stood before five hitched sleighs, stunning in her cardinal cloak. "Has everyone found their seats? Hurry, hurry! The race is about to start!"

We had arrived a short while ago in carriages and separated into two groups. The youngest and bravest had piled into sleigh teams, as instructed by Charlotte. The older set stood on the front porch with hot drinks and red cheeks, waiting to see us off. All except the judge, who had decided to join the youth and sat in the front seat of my sleigh.

"I am already regretting this," he said to Asa, who'd be driving for us. "Surely I'm meant to be by the fire with a glass of port."

I shifted under layers of blankets, already regretting this, too. I'd wanted to avoid Asa today, as I'd managed to do since the night at Knyphausen's. Instead, I was sitting directly behind him.

"You don't have to come, Uncle," Asa replied.

"*Psh!* Nonsense. How often can I adventure with you, *mon neveu?*"

"It's time, it's time!" Charlotte shouted. She climbed into the two-person sleigh she shared with Benjamin Stone and looked right at me, her eyes pleading with me to enjoy myself.

Like everyone, she thought I'd grown sullen over Duncan's departure. It wasn't *untrue*. Since he left, I'd felt aimless and low, but not for the reason she assumed. I hadn't missed him nearly as much as I'd missed how I felt being with him—daring and purposeful. I waved back at her, putting on what I hoped was a convincing smile.

She beamed. "Let's race!" she yelled, raising a kerchief in the air. "To the groundskeeper's cottage! On, set—*go!*"

Ben Stone snapped the reins. "*Walk!* Walk on!"

The four other drivers echoed the command. Our sleigh gave a lurch, my back pushed against the seat, and we glided forward to the jangle of sleigh bells. It was such a cheerful sound, and the countryside looked so pretty draped in white, that soon I felt my spirits lifting. I hadn't enjoyed myself—*truly* enjoyed myself—in months. Everywhere I'd gone since Liesje's wedding in August, I'd gone as a spy. But now, shooting through the wintry woods with bells ringing, there was nothing to do but sit back and *fly*.

"Conspiracy!" shouted William Keyes. "How have I ended up with the plow horse?" Rebecca laughed at his side.

"At least you've a horse! I think I got a cow!" Charles Van Pelt called back.

"Follow our tracks!" Ben Stone called. "See you around midnight!"

He and Charlotte took an early lead, but our horses—a pair of beautiful dapple grays—were fast, and Asa drove with daring. Lucy and I held on to each other, giggling from the sheer joy of the trees blurring past.

"My Lord, Asa. Slow *down!*" the judge cried.

"Faster!" Lucy yelled.

"*Much* faster!" I shouted. With the wind stinging my cheeks, I almost felt I was back at sea.

"Asa!" yelled the judge. "You will flip this sleigh! You will flip it and what will I tell the Holdridges?"

Asa laughed. "I have it, Uncle! I can win it!"

"Is it worth risking life and limb?"

Lucy and I looked at each other "Yes!" we yelled. "*Faster!*"

We shot into second but couldn't compete with Charlotte's best horse and rig. She and Ben Stone were the first to the groundskeeper's cottage. We coasted in moments after.

I vaulted from my seat before Asa could hand me down, and we tromped into the cottage's little parlor, brushing snow from our coats and hats. A warm fire and hot chocolate awaited us. We sipped it from clay mugs and stood around the hearth, thawing our frozen hands.

"What *fun* that was!" Liesje said.

"Fun?" Judge Latimer shook his head. "I have had fun before—that wasn't it."

Asa dropped a hand on his shoulder. "Sorry, Uncle. My competitive spirit got the better of me." His hair was coming away from its queue in damp curls, and his cheeks were flushed a healthy red. He looked very much like Asa *Lane* right then.

"You did nothing wrong, lad, except fail to win."

"The way back is mine."

Ben Stone's eyebrows shot up. "Care to make a wager, Mr. Latimer?"

"Now hold on," Charlotte said. "We're not going back yet. First we're going to the pond for a skate." She looked through the window. "And we must go now, or we'll lose the light!"

For this, the judge chose to stay behind. I expected Asa to stay with him, but he joined the group as we headed back outside and walked down a path to the frozen pond.

There, the groundskeeper had skates for anyone who wanted them, but only Ben Stone and two of his friends accepted them. For a little while, as we watched them speed past in races and attempt jumps and turns, I didn't feel the war at all. Not a scrap of it. It was just laughter and snowy beauty. A window of pure joy. I didn't see who threw the first snowball, but it didn't matter. In moments *everyone* was throwing them.

I ran behind a tree and plunged my gloves into soft powder, packing it into a tight ball. I knew who I wanted to make suffer; I'd been waiting a long time for this. I was going to put a ball of snow right between those deep blue eyes. I peered out, searching for Asa's black cloak and gray cap.

"That must be for me," he said behind me.

I threw as I spun. Asa ducked. The snowball struck the back of his head, exploding in a burst of white powder.

"Well thrown," he said, brushing the powder off his shoulders and scooping it away from his neck.

I laughed. "Thank you."

"My turn," he said.

"You'll have to catch me first."

After that, it was mayhem. Shrieks of laughter. Calls for alliances or for mercy. Everyone participated. Even the skaters came off the pond to join in.

I was digging ice out of my shoe when I heard a male voice holler in pain. I ran to see what had happened, fearing for Asa, but it was Ben Stone who had fallen near the pond.

"My foot!" he said, writhing on his back. "It's stuck!"

Asa knelt and scooped away the snow. "You broke through a thin layer of ice. Hold still." He used the blades of a skate to chip away the ice, finally freeing Ben's foot, but as soon as Ben stood, it was clear he'd injured his ankle. As we headed back to the cottage, his friends had to support him on either side.

Swept up in our antics, we'd lost track of time. The sun had sunk low on the horizon and snow had begun to fall in heavy, silent white waves. I was frozen through. My shoes and gloves soaked. My hair loose, dripping at the ends. I wanted to run to the cottage as fast as I could, but I found myself drifting to the back of the group and drawing even with Asa.

"I'm here under a white flag of truce," I said.

He looked over, his breath fogging in the dusk. "No need for it. I'm not your enemy."

I felt a squeezing in my breastbone, like an ache for breath. "Once, I was sure that. Now everything's changed."

"Not everything."

"But it has. Look at where we are." I waved at the wintry woods. "Look at *who* we are."

"Right. I'm Asa Latimer, the smuggler. That must be your beau's assessment of me."

I sucked on my chapped bottom lip. I stole information from Duncan and lied to him. But I also wanted to protect him.

"It's all right—he and I are not friends. And he's not wrong. I *am* a smuggler. But a poor one, as I've never turned a profit at it. My uncle abhors the pickled and jarred foods that come on the victualing fleets, so I send him fresh goods from time to time. Cabbages, corn, apples. Prime cuts of meat, when I'm feeling especially nefarious. As for 'Asa Latimer,' that is who I must be here in New York." He watched me, waiting for my reaction.

"Because . . . ?"

"Because the truth would not go over well."

My mind reeled as I understood. He was still a patriot. Still the Asa I'd known on the *Ambrosia*. I stared ahead, the snowy path blurring.

"I wanted to tell you this months ago. I tried to."

"And I didn't let you." I winced, remembering that first night on the *Endurance*. "I was awful to you."

"You were angry and had cause to be. What I said about disliking Grand Bahama . . . it was rude. I have regretted it very much."

"Why *did* you say it?" I swallowed. "To hurt me?"

247

"No. What I said was the truth. I did go there and it *did* disappoint me—because you were not there. But only when I saw your reaction did I realize how you'd perceived my words. Then it was too late." He glanced over, his eyes softening. "I resigned myself to waiting thirty years to clear the air."

"You're teasing me, Asa. But I can't laugh."

He smiled. "It was a rather wicked comeback. I quite respected it."

For reasons I didn't understand, that *did* make me laugh. Then I didn't know what else to say. I had too much to absorb. Too many feelings. We walked the rest of the way in silence.

At the groundskeeper's cottage, we discovered our party in a state of commotion. The sleighs were gone. All the carriages were lined up out front. The second leg of the race was called off, due to the threatening weather. Dinner at the Winterses' country home as well. Everyone would hurry back to the city before Bowery Road became impassable.

"Mr. Stone will come with us so that your uncle can tend to his injury," Aunt Nora said. "We will take him directly to the Stones. Lucy will go with Charlotte. The judge will see you home."

There was no time for discussion. Before I knew it, Asa was handing me into the Latimer carriage. Inside, Judge Latimer sat in the middle of the anterior seat, breathing heavily and tugging at his neck stock in obvious discomfort. I took the facing bench and moved to the end. Asa climbed in and settled beside me. The judge rapped on the roof to signal the driver and we sped off, racing against nature now.

Sitting still, I couldn't ignore the cold anymore. Shivers racked me and my teeth chattered. I couldn't help either.

"Poor Miss Coates." Judge Latimer frowned in concern. "What if you become ill?"

"I won't, Judge. I will be fine."

"But what if we get lost?" he said, looking through the fogged glass. "Who can see more than three feet in this weather?"

"We won't get lost, Uncle," Asa assured.

"But we might drive off the road and break a wheel."

"We won't, Uncle. But if we do, we'll unhitch the horses and ride back."

"What if one goes lame? What if both do?" As his panic increased, a red flush crept over his cheeks. "We could be kidnapped by Tory hunters this far outside of town. There are madmen out here. *Mon dieu.* Forgive me, Miss Coates. Asa, the laudanum. In the basket under the bench."

Asa was already getting it. He rummaged inside a wood box. In the unsteady light, I watched him remove a small vial like the ones Malcolm prepared in the workshop. He poured a dram and gave it to his uncle, who took it in one tilt.

"Thank you," the judge said, gasping. "Thank you."

"Here." Asa removed his cloak, laying it over his uncle's shoulders. "Lean your head and sleep."

"*Je suis désolé, mon neveu,*" said the judge.

"*Ne sois pas désolé, mon oncle. Tout ira bien.*"

They kept on in soft French for a little while, Asa kneeling close to his uncle and giving him his undivided attention. As I listened to the gentleness passing between them, I remembered Mama pulling her fingers through my hair, slowly untangling the salty knots as she whispered stories about her girlhood. Mama kissing my forehead. *Te amo muchísimo, mi vida,* she'd say into my ear. Nothing in life was more precious than having someone to whisper tendernesses to.

Soon, the judge's soft snore filled the carriage. Asa reached under the bench again and handed me a thick blanket.

"What about your uncle?"

"I gave him my cloak."

"What about you?"

"There is only this blanket. Take it. Please."

I was too cold to refuse. I pulled the blanket over me.

"I'm sorry you have to see him this way. He suffers from attacks on occasion. They started after the mob abused him. He becomes irrational with fear."

"That's awful.... I didn't know."

"My uncle hides much about himself. He has had to."

I thought I understood. The judge was wealthy, handsome, older—and unmarried. I'd never seen him observe or mention a woman in an amorous way. Like me, I suspected the judge hid his true self. "He's a wonderful man," I said.

"Aye. He is."

"You never mentioned him on the *Ambrosia*."

Asa's mouth tugged up on one side. "We had six days together. I believe I'd have gotten to my uncle on the seventh." He looked at the judge, who'd fallen into a deep slumber. "He's actually my mother's uncle—distantly connected to the Parisian Latimers, as he was born and educated in England. He has always been there for me when I needed him." Asa turned back to me, his eyes narrowing. "Frannie, you're still shaking. You're not going to freeze on me, are you?" He took my hands. "Your gloves are soaked."

"Are they? I can't feel my fingers to tell."

"That won't do." He tugged my gloves off carefully, then pressed his hands over mine, giving me his warmth. "Better?" He leaned down and blew a hot breath over my hands—but somehow I felt it all over me.

This wasn't right. *Duncan.* But Duncan wasn't here, and this was nothing more than staving off frostbite. "Getting better," I replied hoarsely.

"Good. Progress."

He wove his long fingers through mine and massaged my palm with his thumb. My heart began to beat with such force it nearly hurt and I soon felt molten deep in my core.

People often said that eyes showed a person's soul, but I'd always thought it was hands that spoke the truth. Hands hammered nails and gentled babies. They burst like happy fireworks or cowered in pockets. I couldn't put into words what Asa's hands were saying as they kneaded my cold ones back to life. But I wanted the whole world to be made of what I felt in them.

"Do you remember?" Asa whispered. "We were always burning up on the *Ambrosia.*"

"*Asa.*" I pulled my hands back and looked to the judge.

"He's out, Frannie. And I meant we were always hot because it was *summer.* What did you think I meant?"

"Nothing."

He laughed. "Definitely something. We *are* different now, aren't we? *You* chiding *me* for being improper?"

He was making light, but I was struggling with embarrassment, and even more so with memories of how we used to be. An intense sadness swept over me. *I came in search of Francisca Tasker,* he'd said at Knyphausen's. *But I have yet to find her.* "You prefer the girl you knew then, don't you?"

The humor in his eyes vanished. "I'd rather not answer."

"Why?"

"Because I'm determined not to be at odds with you anymore."

"But you might as well just say it, 'cause I already know, Asa. I *know* you prefer her."

"Frannie, why do you say 'her'? She is *you*. *You* are still *you*."

"But I'm not," I said, and felt tears rising. "Frannie's gone. She's no more alive than the real Miss Coates."

"No. That's not true." He turned, squaring his shoulders to me. "I *see* you. You're *here*."

An ache opened up in me that felt endless. "Am I?" I squeaked. I'd never wanted anything to be more true.

"Yes, Frannie. You're right here."

I hadn't a prayer of holding my tears back. I dove into Asa's shoulder and let go. I cried three years' worth of lies, letting them wash out of me. Fierce tears. Frannie's tears.

Mine.

Little by little, the pain eased and a pure, clean feeling replaced it. Freedom. Here, with Asa, I could say exactly what I wanted to say. As I surfaced from the hurt, I became aware of French words tumbling softly into my ear. I didn't understand them, but it didn't matter. The sound of his voice brought me all the way back.

I lifted my head. A handkerchief appeared before me. "Too late," I said, taking it anyway. "I've already ruined your coat."

"Nonsense. I like it much better now."

"Now that I've cried all over it?"

"Precisely."

I laughed, drying my eyes. I felt turned inside out, but so *light*. Like I'd drained an ocean. "What did you say just now?"

"Nothing you don't already know. Look." He brushed his thumb over my cheek. "Salt water. Proof you're still Frannie."

"Where've you been, Asa? Where've you been all this time?"

"You can't imagine how much I've wanted to tell you."

"Whoa," crooned the driver, and the carriage slowed.

Asa brushed his sleeve over the window. New York's wintry streets appeared on the other side. "We're here."

The carriage jostled to a halt and Judge Latimer blinked awake. "Asa, what—? Where—?"

"I'm walking Miss Coates to her door, Uncle. I'll be right back."

He climbed out and helped me down. I didn't let go of his arm as we walked to the door. Asa knocked on it and I silently prayed it would never open. That I could stand at his side in the middle of a blizzard forever.

"Frannie, I'm leaving New York."

I spun to him. *"Leaving?"*

"Yes." He reached into his coat and handed me a letter. "I came today to give you this before I go."

The lock rattled. Hurriedly, I slipped the letter under my cloak. The door swung open and Maggie gasped.

"Miss Emmeline, look at the state of you! Come in! Come in from this cold! Mr. Latimer, do come inside."

"Thank you, but I won't be staying. Your servant, Miss Coates." Asa bowed and returned to the carriage as I watched in a stupor.

All I wanted to do was break the letter's seal and read it, but I'd have to wait. Lucy had arrived only a short while before me and was still awake. We'd been sharing a bed to stay warmer and to conserve firewood. I quickly changed into a dry shift and climbed in beside her.

"Thank heavens you're here. I've never been so cold," she said, snuggling close, "but it was worth it, wasn't it? Today was the most fun I've had in months."

"In years," I said.

We whispered about the day's adventure for a while as we slowed thawed. When I was sure she'd drifted off to sleep, I slid out of bed and tiptoed to my cloak for the letter. Lighting a fresh candle, I opened it with unsteady hands and read.

=★=

Frannie,

In August, I arrived in New York with the intention of staying a few days. A week, perhaps.

I should have known better. I did know better, in fact. I will get to that in a moment.

The day I was forced off the Ambrosia was the worst day of my life. I feared I'd never walk again. Never sail again. Never heal from the pain of our parting. I understood why you refused me, but it did not lessen my suffering, nor the regret I have felt for spoiling our friendship.

The connection we share with my uncle is not the coincidence you might think. Captain Jansen needed a lawyer in New York to help with Miss Coates's will—I gave him the name of a judge I trust above all others.

I have written to my uncle over the years to inquire about Miss Coates, whom I knew on the Ambrosia, asking him to never mention me to you. I beg you not to think ill of him for this—he is the best man I know and was forced into the pretense by me.

You wanted to know why I did not contact you through him, but I was quite sunk by you that day, Frannie. And the answer, simply, is self-preservation.

And yet, when my uncle wrote that you were on the cusp of marriage, I had to come. Not to try to win you, nor to interfere with your happiness. I only wanted to see you once more. I came and I did see you. Then I needed to see you again, and then again, and in this way, five months were made to vanish.

Now the time has arrived for me to return to sea. My only hope is for us to have a better parting than the last. I should very much like to count you my friend again. We were good at it.

Adieu, Comet.

None but yours,
Asa

CHAPTER 21

THE HARD WINTER

★

January–February 1780

A fter Asa left, the snow fell and fell.

Day and night. Night and day. Never stopping. The flurries of white constant.

Numbing.

By Christmas week, the drifts lay five feet deep, making tunnels of the streets and keeping everyone indoors, but even indoors we found no reprieve from the cold. The rivers froze the traffic of ships, but the ice hadn't compacted enough for sleds to cross them with firewood. With no fuel to live or cook by, we had to turn to scavenging. One day, we warmed our hands by burning timber from old ships. The next, by burning fence pickets and barn siding. And we were the fortune ones. In some parts of the city, Maggie told us, people were even burning animal fat to stay warm.

But staying warm wasn't our only challenge. The city's storehouses were mere weeks from being emptied of food. With no victualing ships in sight, it appeared we'd soon freeze *and* starve. In such harsh conditions, even New York's unstoppable social scene suffered. No one wanted to venture out. With the heart of the British army in the south, my intelligence gathering came to an abrupt halt.

"The hardest winter," people began to call it. And we were nowhere near the end of it.

While Lucy and Aunt Nora spent the days darning stockings, shirts, and petticoats, I tucked Asa's letter between the pages of a book and read it. A dozen times. A hundred. I read it till I knew the curves and loops of every letter. Till I'd memorized each sentence. Till I found myself whispering *none but yours* to myself at breakfast. At church. At dinner. In bed.

It was a phrase for dreaming. A phrase that opened a door just wide enough for my imagination to slip through and escape. After years of plunging into thick volumes by Milton, Voltaire, Andrews, and Pope, I found myself leaping into the sea and cutting through water, Mercy right beside me. Pacing over white sand as waves clear as glass washed over my bare feet.

My imagination grew stronger by the day, till it was as colorful as the world was colorless. I traveled to Versailles and had long garden walks with Marie Antoinette. I stepped into the pages of *Evelina,* bringing my friends along so they could meet her. I became a pirate as wicked as Edward Teach. A pickpocket more cunning than Jenny Diver.

I knew such flights of fancy were dangerous. I had a family and friends. I had Duncan. Nothing good could come of imagining other possibilities. But I couldn't leave the house, nor could I spy. Nor could I ask Asa what he'd meant by *none but yours.*

So I allowed myself to dream.

"We are failing him," Townsend told me one Wednesday in late January.

Him was General Washington. Code number 711, according to the sheet Anna Strong had passed to me. For the past weeks, I'd had nothing to report. Not a thing. Even Townsend's information had slowed to a trickle, so we often found ourselves discussing what we already knew.

Indian tribes were fighting on both sides and trying to save their land, the fighting fiercest on the frontier. Blacks, too, were fighting on both sides, both as freemen and as slaves, but the British had been first to offer freedom in exchange for service, which swayed many. The French and Spanish navies were harassing everyone, from Europe to the sugar islands. Russia was toeing toward siding with the British, while the Dutch were edging toward the Americans.

"Our challenge now isn't only in finding new information," Townsend said after we finished going over old intelligence. "It's in *communicating* it. There's terrible inefficiency in how our correspondence travels. It goes through Long Island and then crosses the Sound into Connecticut before even beginning to head east."

I had suspected as much. Townsend was from Long Island. Anna Strong and Abe Woodhull, the prickly man that day at Underhill's whose surname I'd learned from the code sheet, were as well. The problem with going through Long Island was that General Washington's army was wintering in Morristown, New Jersey—the opposite direction. "So instead of taking a straight path west, we're going east, north, west, and then south to reach him?"

"Yes," Townsend said. "And what good is our information if it arrives late?"

"As good as a year-old newspaper."

Townsend sighed. "Precisely."

=★=

When I returned home, I found Aunt Nora stacking an assortment of trunks and valises in the entry.

"Make haste, Emmie," she said, shutting the door behind me to keep out the swirling flurries. "We're moving to Judge Latimer's. There's plenty of room for us all, and he's gotten hold of two cords of firewood, Lord knows how. Lucy and your uncle have already gone ahead. The judge's carriage will be back for us any moment."

I headed up to my room, uneasiness settling in my stomach. I hadn't seen the judge in weeks—not since the sleigh ride—and I wasn't eager to face such a blatant reminder of Asa.

Maggie was almost finished packing my things. My shifts, gowns, stays, and shoes all lay in neat, colorful bundles inside the valise on my bed.

"How will you keep warm?" I asked her. She and Malcolm would stay behind to care for the house and deter looters.

"We'll find a way."

I scooped eleven shillings from my purse. "Here . . . maybe this will help?"

She looked up from the valise. "We'll manage. But thank

you." Her eyes grew thoughtful as they held on me. I waited, sensing she had more to say. "I was young once, too," she said, after a moment. "I broke a few hearts in my time. I do understand youthful abandon."

Youthful abandon?

Then it dawned on me. This was about that morning she'd discovered Malcolm and me. Her words were an olive branch. I offered one back. "I've never been a mother, Maggie. But I do understand the strength of a mother's love. I still feel my mother is with me."

She smiled. "It pleases me to hear you say that. I know you lost her too soon." Her smile faded away. "I pray for you, Miss Em. Every night, I pray you find your place." She snapped the valise shut.

"I have a place. It's here," I replied. But by the time I said it, she was no longer in the room.

=★=

Half an hour later, I stepped into the judge's grand home on Golden Hill. A fire blazed in the parlor, roaring with heat. We made for it immediately, too cold to suffer through proper greetings.

"You are kind to take us in, Judge," said Aunt Nora.

"My pleasure, of course," he replied. "And at a most timely juncture, as it happens. Dr. Holdridge is upstairs ministering to my nephew. I'm afraid Asa is unwell."

"Asa?" I looked up from the flames. "But he left New York."

Judge Latimer fixed a long gaze on me, filled with the

unspoken. "He tried to go. He made several attempts to sail out of the harbor, but the ice prevented him. He'd planned to go overland to Boston this week, but then . . . this."

This.

This changed everything.

Suddenly, I couldn't catch my breath.

As Aunt Nora and Lucy saw to the unloading of our baggage, the judge stepped close and bowed his head to mine. "Miss Coates, my nephew has never said a word that would lead me to think he'd want you with him at this time, but—" One hand came to his mouth, his long fingers fluttering, then fell away. "He is very ill, Miss Coates. Very. And it would mean everything to me if you would go to him. I fear you may not have another chance."

I flew upstairs like I'd grown wings.

Instinct took me right to Asa's bedroom. He lay in bed, his eyes closed. His cheeks were bright crimson with fever—but the rest of him was so pale, so bloodless, he looked like he'd been dusted with chalk. His body trembled weakly. He looked like a young hero under some sort of evil spell. Like death had chosen him.

I felt myself swoon, old memories rushing back. "How is he?" I asked.

Uncle Henry looked up from a chair by Asa's bedside. "Better not answered," he replied evenly. "Morning may tell us more."

I stood, trying to understand what that meant. Trying to make it mean something different. Then I brought a chair from the corner of the room and sat beside Uncle Henry.

"Dear Emmie," he said, smiling. "There's no need to keep me company. This is what I do."

"Thank you, Uncle, but I'll stay." Nothing was going to make me leave. Nothing. I'd seen Asa at the brink before. This time, I wouldn't leave his side. "Is there anything I can do, Uncle? Can I—"

"Francisca," Asa breathed. His eyes opened—barely. "*Est-ce vous,* Comet?"

"Pay no mind to anything he says," Uncle Henry said. "'Tis from the fever. The delirium is setting in."

It wasn't delirium—it was the truth.

Asa had always seen me.

CHAPTER 22

FLOATING

★

February 1780

Asa's condition worsened in the night. He disappeared into fever dreams—true ones—one moment arguing in French, the next issuing rambling orders to a ship's crew.

I watched as Uncle Henry drew a lancet across his arm and let the blood pour into the bowl below. And let it pour and pour and pour.

"How much, Uncle?" I asked, my voice reedy.

"The draw is always in proportion to the strength of the patient and the violence of the disease."

The disease was violent indeed. "What ails him?"

"I don't yet know. He complained of a violent pain in his head a few days ago, then took to bed immediately. His laborious breathing leads me to suspect the inflammation began in his lungs." Uncle Henry looked at me. "You really ought to go, Emmie. He needs quiet and rest, and as few attendants as possible."

"Then I will be one of them," I said.

Uncle Henry conceded. Miss Coates's compassion toward the

infirm was well known—and there was nowhere else for me to go anyway. No dinners, no assemblies. We were totally snowbound.

I ran cool washcloths over Asa's feverish skin. I gave him a special tamarind liqueur when he was awake enough to drink. The rest of the time I read, prayed, or worried by candlelight.

After three days, the fever finally abated for good and I began to feel some hope. On the fourth, I was reading *Plutarch's Lives* when Asa stirred at last and looked almost like himself.

"How are the great Spartans of old?" he rasped.

"Alcibiades was rotten. He betrayed *everyone*." I rather related to him, in truth. I set the book aside. "How do you feel?"

Asa narrowed his eyes in thought. "I feel . . . electrified."

I laughed, but it made me ache to see how much he'd weakened. I helped him sit up, arranging the pillows behind him; then I swept the hair from his forehead, tucking it behind his ears. He'd gone even sharper around the cheekbones, having barely eaten for a week, but the keenness was back in his eyes and the veins in his arms were thick with returning health.

Suddenly, I became aware of his quiet stare on me. "Do you want to sleep?" I added a fresh log to the fire, hiding my embarrassment. I'd spent days as his nurse, his body my charge. It couldn't be so anymore. I returned to my chair. "Or I could read to you?"

Night would soon fall again. Lucy, Charlotte, and Liesje were braving the cold to go to dinner at Rebecca's house—now Mrs. Rebecca Keyes. I had decided I'd give myself this time with Asa. As much of it as I could have, I'd take it.

"No . . . no more sleep. Perhaps we can we talk?" He leaned against the bed frame. "And perhaps you can do most of it?"

"What shall I do most of the talking about?"

"Anything. Take my mind elsewhere. The aches of my aches have aches." He closed his eyes. "Tell me about the seventh fathom. What happens there now?"

"The seventh fathom! You *remember* that?"

Asa's eyes fluttered open. "I don't just remember it. I went."

"You didn't!"

"I did so."

"Asa, are you saying you went *diving*?"

"Yes. And do you know what I learned? It's *miserable* down there. Cold. Dark. Lonely. I nearly drowned. I had an earache for days after. I haven't got a clue why you like it."

I laughed. "You must've done it wrong."

"Oh, no. I did it right. I went three times—and never once did I see any castle."

"It's there, Asa. You missed it. Didn't you even see the forest?"

"A forest?" He shook his head. "Nay. I didn't see a single twig. You bamboozled me."

"Well, I can remedy that. Close your eyes and I'll take you there now."

"All right." He shut his eyes. "Take me."

Saints, it was like we hadn't skipped a day. "The forest," I began, "is on the south side of the castle, across a broad grassy field. We walk through it, our footsteps flattening a path. Then we reach the edge of the wood. There, we stop to admire black oaks and great firs so tall their tops stir in the wind, but where we are below, it's calm and quiet. The sort of quiet that steals time away. We delve inside, breathing in the loamy dampness. It's darker here, but there are ferns everywhere, bursting like green fireworks. As we go along, you start telling me stories of the places you've sailed to—the Azores, Salvador, Dublin . . . everywhere. Everywhere you've gone, you tell me about it, and it's just the rustling trees and your words. Words that shine and shine and shine in the foresty darkness."

Asa's mouth curved into a slow smile, but his eyes stayed shut. "Well, that all sounds fine, but where are we going in these woods?"

"That is *exactly* what you ask me. Then you stop and check your compass and tell me you think we're lost. I reply that we can't be, 'cause you are north and south, and I am east and west, and do you know what that means?" I was rising into the clouds of my own mind, spinning through them like a bird. "It means we're the point where the needle spins—the very point that balances the whole world—and *that* means that everything *else* is lost, and far, and forgotten, but not us, Asa. Not us."

"All right, but what if we want to go to the sea? I am partial to it, you know. What do we do then?"

"Simple. Simple as can be. We turn into birds and fly over the treetops and soar up into the sky, where we can see the sea."

"See the sea," he said sleepily, his head relaxing to the side. I knew soon he'd be asleep again—but recovering, thank the Lord. "What sorts of bird are we?"

"Terns, of course. So we can fly to the coast."

"And from there?"

"We fly over the dunes and then over the water, where our wings slap the waves. The ocean is a mirror beneath us, and the sun is the sun, and we soar on and on, chasing the edge of the world, and the start of the sky, and the place where the wind begins. 'But where *exactly* are we going?' you ask, 'cause you always have to ask something, and in answer, I say . . . I say . . ."

"Everywhere."

══ ★ ══

I stayed by his side the next night. And the next three after that.

There was too much to talk about, so many days and months to cover. I told him about the Holdridges and how they'd surprised me by being more than I could've hoped for. I didn't love them as I loved Mama—but I did love them. I told him how I adored books and theater. Fine assemblies with dancing. All the things he'd helped me learn, things that had felt so foreign to me in the past, I now enjoyed.

Asa told me all about the privateering he'd been doing. After escaping the Royal Navy, just as Tom Hackett had predicted he would, Asa had gone right back to seizing British ships for profit.

"They've been dangerous years, but good ones. This war turns on the sea. I've been fortunate to know what to do about it."

With no home nor family to care for, he'd poured his prize earnings into starting his own fleet. He now had the *Endurance* and two schooners, and was also part owner of two more schooners with his uncle.

The judge's secret political allegiance surprised me. How could a man who'd upheld England's laws support the American cause? A man who'd almost been tarred and feathered by a mob shouting for liberty? But Asa explained that his uncle wanted peace and justice above all and no longer had faith that England could deliver it.

While Asa had prospered in the war, his father had lost two

268

ships to foul weather, and another two to privateers. This had put him upside down with creditors and led to his ruin—which had severed clean his relationship with Asa.

"He blames me for his demise. My ships weren't the ones that seized his, but they easily could have been. To him, I am every American privateersman."

Though Asa claimed otherwise, I knew their estrangement still caused him pain. Some relationships just didn't end well. I knew that from Sewel—and from my parting with Asa years ago.

With our lost years taking shape, we started debating ideas just as we had on the *Ambrosia*.

" 'We can only love what we know,' " I read from the book on my lap. "That is Barbauld. I think it's wrong, as I love surprises and those are unknowns. What do you think?"

"I agree with you, and poems are my proof. Does one know them and love them, or does one feel them and love them?"

"I can't say without knowing a specific poem."

"Let me think." He squinted at the ceiling. I stared at his lips, remembering how they felt when we kissed. "I've got it. 'Stand and face me, my love, and scatter the grace in your eyes.' That is a fragment by Sappho."

I dropped my gaze to the book. Right then, I knew my eyes were scattering grace everywhere. "You're right. I don't understand that, but I do love it. You ought to write poetry."

"Nay, Comet. You're the one with the mind full of poems and dreams."

"I used to be."

"You are."

"With you."

"Because when I am with you, you are with you."

That was true as the sun was bright. He'd helped me become Miss Coates once; now he allowed me to escape her. With him, I felt my tongue loosen. Become "vulgar" again, as it once was. I began to laugh again. Truly *laugh,* with shaking shoulders and tears and everything. There was no point in pretending round him, nor in lying, so I didn't bother with either.

But that didn't mean I told him everything.

One week spilled into two. As Asa regained his strength, we left his room for the parlor. The library. The dining room. Taking our world with us wherever we went and never once bringing along his cane. When he leaned on anything, I made sure it was on me.

I left his side only once, to see Townsend briefly so we could repeat our grumblings about how our dispatches took too long to reach General Washington in New Jersey.

All I wanted to do was stay with Asa. We created our own little seventh fathom when we were alone.

Together, there was no rising. No sinking.

We just . . . floated.

=★=

A month after we moved into the judge's home, we returned to the Holdridge house and Asa began to fit out *Endurance* to leave New York. I spent the next week adrift, unable to concentrate on the simplest tasks.

The day before his departure, we piled into carriages and headed to the Winterses' country house. Charlotte's favorite spaniel had whelped a litter of puppies, and Charlotte was hosting a naming party. The winter had made everyone far too miserable, she'd decided. Our attendance was cordially demanded.

As we trundled along Bowery Road, the women in one carriage and the men in another, barren fields spread in every direction. Every tree, fence, and shrub had been sacrificed to our hearths over the past months. Deer that had frozen to death lay by the roadside, their thawing carcasses pecked at by crows. Making matters even more dismal, an insect plague had caused the spring growth to look sickly and wilting.

"This year's food rations will be worse than ever," Mrs. Winters said, staring out the window.

"*Worse?* How is that possible?" Charlotte drew the curtain closed with a snap, blotting out the landscape. "Sometimes I wish the rebels would win so we'd be done with this misery."

"*Charlotte.*"

"I am sorry, Mama, but I'm tired of this wretched war."

I wondered if she knew how close it was to ending. I'd seen Townsend only the day before. The situation for the American army in Morristown was dire, with soldiers on starvation rations and threatening to mutiny. There were even whispers that General Washington, ever stalwart, feared a total collapse.

I'd made a gain against British counterfeiting with my find that night at General Knyphausen's, but our economy was unraveling. Congress had no power to levy taxes. Years of printing money to pay war expenses had left the Continental dollar worthless—which in turn only made paying for our war expenses impossible.

Everyone had grown weary—not just Charlotte. According to Townsend, the spirit of liberty that had fueled our early years was fading. *We are fraying,* he'd said at our last meeting, *and I fear we'll not last the year.* The war had made enemies of families and neighbors. It had kept sons and fathers away from their loved ones and homes for much too long.

More and more it looked like the campaign that had taken Duncan to Charles Town would be the beginning of the final chapter in the war. If something didn't change, England would soon have its colonies back.

And I was powerless to help.

═ ★ ═

At the Winterses', puppies galloped all over the parlor, yipping and tugging at our petticoats. We sipped tea amid the furry chaos and named them one by one.

"I crown thee King Arthur," Charlotte said, tying a blue ribbon around a brown-and-white patched puppy. She lifted the puppy up in the air. "Good afternoon, Your Royal Majesty."

Through the window, I saw Asa with the other men. Mr. Winters was showing him a rifle. Asa rested his cane against his leg and took the weapon, sighting down the long barrel. He lowered it and said something that made Mr. Winters throw his head back and laugh.

"The big clumsy one with the sweet face looks like a Lancelot," Lucy said. "Don't you think, Emmie?"

I turned back to the puppies. "Yes. That must be Guinevere, then, running off with him."

"Which was a terrible *mistake,*" Charlotte said. "Wasn't it, Lucy?"

Lucy's blue eyes widened over her teacup. "Yes. Yes, it was."

Charlotte turned King Arthur to me. "Tell her, Your Majesty. Perhaps she will listen to a king."

I found a smile for my two dearest friends. Asa was the one lie I hadn't been able to put over on them. They had nothing to worry about, though. I'd given myself this time with him, but I'd always known it would end. Inside, I was already building up walls. Closing myself inside a fortress.

After a light repast of fresh bread and onion soup, Charlotte suggested a walk. We had barely started on the path when she leaned toward me and whispered, "Get it done, Emmie. Once and for all."

Then she hooked her arm through Lucy's and they sped off, shooting ahead to join the rest of our party.

"Are they trying to fly?" Asa asked.

I managed a smile. "Do you really have to leave?" I asked. "Isn't it dangerous with all the ice still in the harbor?"

"Yes to both."

"But why now, Asa? Couldn't you stay longer?" None of this was what I'd practiced saying.

His eyes brightened for a moment, then clouded over. "When do you wish me to leave? The day before Lieutenant Duncan returns?"

The words stung.

"I'm sorry, Frannie. This is—"

"No, don't be sorry." I was being selfish and unfair. I wanted him to stay longer purely for me. "Where will you go?" I asked, changing the subject.

"South. To Martinique."

"To clear waters and white sands."

"To naval battles and boarding actions, more like. But there will be water and sand."

I shut my eyes, imagining the sunny stretch where I'd learned to swim. Where Mercy and I had turned cartwheels and sprinted through shallow waves. "I wish I could see my beach just once more."

"I could send it to you." He smiled. "Next time I'm past there, I could collect some sand for you."

"Asa—will you really?"

"Of course. How much would you like? A few grains? The entire beach?"

"Just enough for me stand on with both feet."

"Done. You shall have your sand, Miss Tasker."

Up ahead, Charlotte and Lucy were disappearing behind a gentle slope step by step. On the other side was the Winterses' house. I stopped. "We're almost back. Aren't you going to ask me to leave with you?" I said.

Asa turned to me. "No. I'm not. But I do think I'm going to regret not asking you for a very long time."

"Well, it doesn't matter. I wouldn't have accepted."

"I know."

"Because this is my life now. I have a good life here. A life with friends and books and theater." He said nothing. I couldn't catch my breath, but I had to press on. He was the only person I could be honest with, who could truly know me, and I couldn't let this be like the last time we'd parted. This time, I wanted everything to be said. "I have Duncan," I continued, my voice quavering. "I'll marry him one day. When he asks me. And, till the war ends, I have—" Last chance. Last chance to say it. "I have spying."

My words hung in the air. Bare and awful. But I'd said them. There were no lies between us anymore. Only truth.

Asa nodded. "I understand," he said evenly.

"You *understand*?" How could he look *composed* when I felt like I was crumbling into pieces? "You're not supposed to *understand*."

"Frannie, you chose Duncan years ago when you decided to be Miss Coates. I cannot give you the life he can. And if you're putting your wit and bravery in service of a cause I believe in as well, what can I do but thank you and pray that you stay safe?"

That only made me hurt worse. "You're doing this all wrong, Asa. I thought you'd fight for me at least a *little* bit."

"Comet . . ." He swallowed, his blue eyes so intent. "Can you not see I *am* fighting for you? I'm certainly not fighting for myself."

"Well, this is terrible." I pushed away a tear. "I thought we'd at least kiss."

He looked down and stabbed at the dirt with his cane. "Have mercy on me, Frannie."

"No. I won't." I darted forward to kiss him, hopping to make up the difference in our height, but with nerves propelling me, instead of hopping, I *jumped*. I knocked his hat off and kicked his shin, my lips smacking somewhere above his mouth. Asa jerked back, catching my arms. His cane clattered to the dirt, joining his hat.

I stared into his shocked eyes. "I'm sorry," I blurted.

"You should be. How can I resist you now?" He wrapped me in his arms and kissed me. Deeply. Passionately. For blissful moments, we clung to each other like we'd only breathe again if we became one, but that was how he'd always made me feel. Together we made something whole. Something beautiful.

As we parted, I picked up his hat and cane for him. We walked back to the house holding hands until we couldn't any longer. And then we let go.

=★=

The next morning, I went to see Townsend. It was Tuesday, a day early, but I had to get back to spying again. I needed a way to escape my own mind and the pain in my heart.

As soon as I entered the store, Townsend rounded the counter and came to me. "Good day, Miss Coates. How good to see you. I was just walking to the Fly Market. Perhaps you'd care to join me? I'd be glad to see you home after."

His words tumbled out in an agitated rush.

"Certainly, Mr. Townsend," I replied, a bolt of fear spearing through me. He sent his clerk to alert Malcolm to go on without me, and we entered the bustle of New York's streets.

"Bloody news!" shouted a newsboy as he darted between us. He raised one arm, waving copies in the air. "Where are the damned rebels today?"

I glanced at Townsend, expecting to share a moment of wry amusement, being damned rebels ourselves, but his eyes darted restlessly from face to face, and I noticed that a patch of red had begun to creep up his neck. I'd never seen him so flustered. "Townsend, you're shook."

"Yes," he admitted. "I am. And I shall soon explain why."

We reached the market and stood a little distance from the stalls and hawkers, where several horse carts were parked.

Townsend removed a handkerchief from his coat pocket and dabbed the sweat on his forehead. "I thought I had a solution," he said with no preamble. "An answer to the trouble we've had sending dispatches in a timely manner. I asked my cousin to act as a courier, posing as a Tory, and sent him to New Jersey—directly across the North River." He grimaced. "It would've saved days had it worked. A week, perhaps. But the boy is young. Foolish. It seems he became impassioned in playing his role and tried to recruit other Tories to assist in the defense of the Crown. Only he didn't realize he was speaking to other patriots who were also masking themselves as Tories."

I needed a second to put it together. "*No* . . . He was deceiving our own allies? He was captured by—by *us?*"

"Yes. They suspected him of being a Tory spy. He was released, thank heaven. But only by the intervention of . . ." Another grimace—this one so contorted his eyeglasses slipped down his nose. "I can't bear to say it."

"You don't have to." It was obvious. General Washington. "I'm sorry." It was an embarrassment of the highest order. I understood his mortification too well. "You made a mistake. I've made mistakes too, as you know, but we've gone on, haven't we? Wasn't it Virgil who said, 'Fortune sides with him who dares'? You dared, and I am proud of you for it. Next time the outcome will be better."

"Miss Coates, there will be no next time. With the campaign shifted south and the winter we had, we've not been effective for too long. We have withered on the vine. There's no reason to go on. I have told them that I'm done."

"What do you mean, 'done'? You cannot stop."

"'Tis safer this way for both of us. We did some good, but this is the end."

It didn't make any sense. The war was still going on. It wasn't the end. "Not for me," I said. "I am not finished yet. I'm not giving up because of this. Monk is still out there."

"A monk?" he asked.

"*Monk*. That's the name he uses—the man I told you about. He's out there, Townsend. He's negotiating with the British—he has something they'll pay a fortune for. I'm positive he's connected to Knyphausen. Clinton. André." I couldn't say "Duncan."

Townsend's dark eyebrows drew together. "Yes. I remember now. Have you any firm information on the plan or on who this Monk is?"

"Not yet. But when Duncan returns I will."

"When he returns, this war might be over."

"Or it might not."

Townsend sighed. He took off his glasses and rubbed his eyes. "Miss Coates, it has been nearly a year since you first told me of this Monk. I must ask you, respectfully: If still you haven't learned anything useful, why should I believe that will change?"

"Because I don't give up. That's why you should believe it. Believe it if you believe *me*."

He turned to the market and watched the commotion for a while as I silently begged him to reconsider. I did my spying alone, but it was Townsend who made me a patriot. He was my connection to the rest of the spies. He made what I stole into something valuable. I trusted him. With the exception of Anna Strong, I didn't trust anyone else but him.

"I believe you're a true patriot, Miss Coates," he said finally.

"I believe you've made a difference. I shall always be grateful for your contributions and grateful to have shared in them. But my decision has been made. I simply cannot continue. You must try to see this as good news. You can live your life now. You no longer need be divided."

=★=

Divided.

I thought about that word for weeks.

I *was* divided. There were pieces of me scattered from West End all the way to heaven. Some pieces I'd left in the past. Others I guarded even from myself.

The more I thought about it, the more I realized I'd been divided since the day I had donned Miss Coates's gown.

I was two people living in one body.

And neither was whole.

April 23, 1780

My dear Emmeline,

I apologize for not writing more often. Our siege against Charles Town has begun and we are faring very well. The rebel commander has asked for quarter for his troops, but we have refused to give it. We will not give these liberty lovers any clemency; their defeat is imminent!

I confess my eagerness for this war's end grows daily, and not only from love of king and country. To be parted from you has only showed me the intensity of my feelings for you, feelings which I hope are present in your heart as well.

I am told you have been at Judge Latimer's house for some weeks. I hope it has been an agreeable stay with the judge, and his nephew, if he is still there, though I believe he was meant to sail in spring and must have done by now.

Major André is over my shoulder telling me that my insecurities are coming to light. Perhaps I do worry you forget me in my absence. Thankfully Major André has come to my aid like a true friend and made the enclosed drawing so you might have a remembrance of me as I have cherished the one I have of you.

Tell me my nose is not really so broad as he makes it? But you can see, I hope, that in my eyes are warmest thoughts of you.

With esteem and admiration,
Your most humble and obedient
James

=★=

May 5, 1780

~~Dear James,~~

Duncan,

The drawing is a good likeness of you, though André has shown you leaning away, and now I am remembering that you lean in and over, too. You are a human parasol and I don't know why I only now see that.

I was at Judge Latimer's for a time with Asa. He is gone now. But your insecurities were well founded.

Asa took my heart with him when he left. That part of me will never be yours.

The spying is not going well. Townsend is no longer helping. He had become a trusted friend and confidant. And you are not here.

Where you are, can you see the ocean? Is the water greener than it is blue? When you stand in it, is it clear enough to see your toes? I have never seen your toes, Duncan, but last night I dreamt you were missing three.

What's past is prologue. Shakespeare wrote that.

I do not think you will become like Sewel.

Will you?

My thoughts ramble. They don't stick anywhere anymore. I don't know what I've done. I don't know who I am. But things will be better when General Clinton returns, and André, and you, of course. For now, I can only wait. And wait.

You are only men, Duncan. You shouldn't turn the world,
and yet you do.

I must destroy this now and write you a real letter.

Your
Emmeline

=★=

May 15, 1780
My dear Emmeline,

We have taken Charles Town in a resounding victory. The rebels surrendered the city. We offered no parole and imprisoned some three thousand men—nearly the entirety of their southern army! What this means, my dearest, is that the South shall now be ours for the taking. We are close to ending this war once and for all.

I have news from New York that the thaw has come and travel is improving. Good timing, as I am returning, and very eager to be there, and would be displeased with any delay in seeing you. Unless I write to say otherwise, you may expect me in the first days of June.

Bright days lie ahead for us, and I cannot wait for each and every one.

Your humble and obedient
James

CHAPTER 23

HOMECOMING

June 1780

"*Finally*, Emmie! Lieutenant Duncan has come home at last!" Lucy said as she fell back on my bed, her golden curls spilling over the bedcover. "Your Lord Orville, returning triumphant! 'Tis as perfect a romance as in *Evelina*."

I turned to my reflection in the mirror on the toilette table and pressed my hands to my uneasy stomach. Duncan's return didn't feel "perfect." We had exchanged letters, but it had been six months since he'd left. I felt dread and anticipation. Heartburn.

Lucy propped herself up on an elbow. "Do you think he will propose tonight, as Father expects?"

"I don't know," I replied breathlessly. It wasn't just Uncle Henry who thought so—everyone did. Charlotte had been there all morning. She had chosen my pale-rose sack gown, bringing roses that matched it to pin into my hair, which she'd done herself. She'd even convinced me to trade my pocket watch for one of the lavish necklaces that usually sat collecting dust in my jewelry trunk. Soon the Holdridges would go to the Winterses' for dinner, leaving me home alone to reunite with Duncan in private—and possibly to accept his offer of marriage. "He will have traveled hard to get here. Maybe he'll be too tired?"

"Too tired? Good Lord, Emmie. I don't think so!" Lucy jumped off the bed and came to stand behind me, wrapping her arms around my shoulders. "Oh, I'm so delighted! He is so good. I couldn't dream of a better match for you."

Her face, beside mine in mirror, was so open, so genuinely cheerful and free of guile. "I wish it was you, Lucy. *You* deserve this happiness." I rested my head against hers, wishing my heart was half as pure as hers.

=★=

Once everyone left, the house felt especially empty after all the excitement of the morning. Even Maggie and Malcolm had retreated to the cottage.

I sat in the parlor with a book of Sappho's poems that Asa had left behind. Though the volume was in French, he'd penned the translations beneath each line. As the setting sun dove over my shoulder through the windowpanes, I stared at the lean, spare loops of his hand, reading the same words over and over.

In time one's mask becomes one's face.

I shut my eyes and thought back to the day I'd made a decision that had changed my life completely. I'd made Emmeline Coates's face my mask—had she become my face?

No. She hadn't.

With Asa, I'd felt *real*. I'd felt like *me*.

A rapping at the door made me jump. I set the book aside and stood. I smoothed my petticoats and drew a breath. Smoothed my petticoats again. I was ready for this. Ready to end my torment. There was nothing to decide or agonize over. I had to do what I had promised Mama, and what I wanted, and what was best.

I hurried into the entryway. The clock there read nine—later than I expected. I ran my hands over my hips one final time, brought a breath all the way down to my toes, and opened the door.

For an eternity, I stood still. Utterly frozen.

The whole world stood still.

It wasn't Duncan.

"Francisca," Sewel said. "How *fine* to see you again after all this time."

My body unlocked from the grip of terror and I jolted back like I'd been shot. "What—what are you doing here?"

"How kind of you to ask." His grin spread like oil. "En't you gonna invite me in so I can tell you?"

"No. You're not setting foot in this house."

"You gonna stop me?" He stepped through the door and filled the entryway, his rancid smell—rum, tobacco, sweat— striking me.

My stomach twisted. I staggered back another step. "Get out, Sewel."

"I don't think so." He looked bigger than I remembered, the seams on the shoulders of his coat separating, the buttons on his waistcoat straining, like some force inside him was begging for release. I had made him terrifying in my memories. But he was even more so in the flesh. Ragged. Enormous. Petrifying.

His eyes moved over my shoulder. "This en't no concern of yours."

I spun to see Maggie, rushing in.

"Miss Em, what—" She stopped suddenly, the confusion on her face transforming to fear. "Go! *Go*, you wretch, or you'll regret it!" Sewel didn't budge. Maggie's eyes darted to me. In them, I saw the horrible reality, one we both knew: we could not defend ourselves against such a monster without help. "I'll get Malcolm." She spun and ran back out.

"Leave, Sewel," I said desperately. "These are good people."

"You worried I'll hurt 'em, Francisca?" He shook his head in mock disapproval. "You always did think the worst of me. Look at you." His gaze swept over me, pausing at my waist, my breasts, my pearl collar. "You're all grown." The taste of blood poured over my tongue. Sewel's smile went wider. "You done well for yourself, Daughter."

"I'm not your—"

Suddenly, screams broke from back of the house. "*No! Help! Someone, help me!*"

It was Maggie. Maggie, screaming like she was being cut to pieces. My every hair stood on end. Sewel showed no surprise—none at all. He stared at me, waiting.

"No . . . Sewel, what have you done?" I looked at the dark red smears on his hands. On his forehead and waistcoat.

He shrugged. "I was just trying to come through the back door, Fran. How was I to know you got all these servants?" He looked behind him. People in the street were stopping as they heard Maggie's cries. "Guess this en't a good time to talk after all. I'll see you soon, Francisca."

He fixed a final, threatening stare on me. Then he strode into the street and disappeared into the darkness.

I bolted the door behind him and ran to the kitchen.

The back door was thrown wide. I sped through it, out into the courtyard.

Maggie crouched over Malcolm, who was lying in the dirt. She pressed her hands to his neck, trying to stop the blood that poured out of him. *So* much blood. It was everywhere.

"My son!" she screamed. "That thief killed my son!"

Malcolm's green eyes were open—but he was gone.

=★=

The next morning, Lucy and I sat in the parlor, holding hands as we waited for the police magistrate to arrive, our tea untouched and cooling on the table.

"I think I'm going to cry again," she whispered.

"Go ahead. I will cry with you."

We had been this way all night. She began our tears, or I did.

Hours ago, as our heads had lain on the same damp pillow, my room just beginning to brighten with the coming dawn, she'd admitted to me that she'd loved Malcolm.

"I know that's wrong," she'd confessed. "He was a servant, below me and out of reach, but . . . he was so kind. So decent."

Some spy I was. Missing something that had been under my nose for almost four years.

I'd told her she didn't need to explain. I understood—love obeyed no rules—and I couldn't bear to hear anymore. My guilt was strong enough. I hadn't drawn the knife across Malcolm's neck, but I was responsible for his death. If Miss Coates had stayed dead, he would still be alive.

In time one's mask becomes one's face.

288

And one's past becomes one's curse, I added silently.

Lord, how I wanted to shed myself like a skin. Disappear to a place where I would never hurt anyone again, and where I'd be safe from Sewel, but no such place existed.

He'd found me.

He'd killed Malcolm.

Nothing felt safe anymore.

"Thank God," Uncle Henry said by the front window, where he'd been all morning. He set his rifle down. "He's here." He pulled the front door open. "Come in, Duncan. Come in."

Lieutenant James Duncan stepped through the door and immediately looked at me in the parlor. In an instant, he stood before me. "Are you harmed?"

"No. I'm fine." He searched my face like he needed more proof. "I'm unharmed," I said. "Truly, I'm fine." I sank to the settee. Lucy and Uncle Henry disappeared from the parlor like mist.

Duncan drew the armchair closer and sat down.

His face was bronzed from the southern sun and tense with worry. His fingers twitched on his knee. "We were delayed on the roads. I came as soon as I heard."

This wasn't how I had pictured seeing him again. I'd been bracing myself for confusion and guilt, but all I felt was relief. He was safe—that was everything I needed for now.

I felt my bottom lip wobble.

"Oh, my darling . . ." His amber eyes were so warm, so filled with concern. "Tell me what to do."

"Nothing. I only need a moment."

"I will give you ten. A hundred."

I smiled shakily. "One was enough."

Duncan exhaled, the coil between his shoulders loosening. "Emmeline, it pains me to have to put you through this now, but acting quickly will give us an advantage in apprehending the murd—the man. I am going to ask you a few questions—I shall take the report in myself. Answer as best you can."

I nodded, suddenly scared. Sewel could *never* be caught. If he was, my entire life would collapse. He was still my stepfather. I stood no chance against him.

Suddenly, I saw how this was everything Mama had warned me against. In the eyes of the law and of society, the testimony of an unmarried woman held less sway than a man's—even a murderer like Sewel. With a few words, he could utterly ruin me.

"The man who came," Duncan continued, "was he trying to enter the house? Was he trying to—to attack you?"

"Both." The truth. For once.

"Can you describe his appearance? Had he any distinguishing marks or scars? Any disfigurements that might be useful in identifying him?"

I thought of the *M* on Sewel's hand. His bulky shoulders. His addiction to rum. His missing toes. "I don't remember. It happened so quickly."

"Did he say what he wanted?"

The questions went on. Duncan listened carefully to my replies, like he was committing every word to memory. When he was done, he came to sit beside me on the settee. For a moment, we said nothing. I was trying to remember how to be near him, how to share the same space. I suspected it was the same for him.

Gently, he took my hand. "Though it hurts me to see you in distress, I feel fortunate to be here now. Had this happened while

I was away, I might have torn down walls with my bare hands. I am glad I am here instead, taking yours. You're safe now. I promise you."

They were fine words. Good ones. "Thank you, Duncan."

"James . . . please."

I managed a smile. "The South did you good, James."

"Did it? I grew to like parts of it."

"The parts that weren't dug with trenches and redoubts?"

He smiled. "Yes. I did prefer the trenchless areas."

With that, we were off. Back to ourselves. Talking easily again.

As he told me about the siege of Charles Town, I realized this was how it'd always been between us. Duncan talked. I listened. We were like a river—flowing one way. Never had I minded it before. I imagined I'd even helped make it so, with all the questions I put to him in the course of spying, but today the spy in me felt very far away.

Soon, Charlotte, Liesje, and Rebecca arrived to offer their support. Liesje gave me beautiful yellow tulips. Rebecca, a book of collected poems by Alexander Pope. Charlotte handed me the drowsy puppy in her arms.

"Iseult," she said. "She's usually very alert and protective, but I guess now she's tired," she added with a little laugh.

My heart filled with love. "She's perfect."

With Iseult darting into the unlit hearth and tracking sooty paw prints everywhere, the mood grew more cheerful. Lucy and Uncle Henry joined us and we shared a lunch of ham, cheese, and jams, and it was almost as though Malcolm hadn't been murdered yesterday.

Almost.

As the party returned to the parlor, Duncan caught my hand and kept me in the dining room. "I'm loath to leave your side, but the French fleet is threatening again."

Even in my fog, my instincts prickled. "The French? They're coming to take New York?"

"It appears they mean to try. But don't let it add to your worries. We've had ample warning; we shall be ready for them. I'll return as soon as I can." He leaned down and brushed a kiss on my forehead. "I swear to you, Emmeline. I'll see the murderous scoundrel caught and destroyed. You will never have to worry about him again."

=★=

I slipped away to my room after Duncan left. Alone at last, I crawled into my bed and shed fresh tears for Malcolm—and for Maggie.

I'd thought being Miss Coates was the answer. But four years later, Sewel was still after me. I'd been a fool to think he'd ever forget me. All I'd done by escaping West End was fuel his anger. Along the way, I'd deceived good people and completely lost myself. One of the most honorable men I'd ever known was dead. And a mother had lost her beloved son.

I was finished with lies and deceptions. Finished with *all of it*—Duncan, spying, Miss Coates.

I wanted truth in my life again.

I wanted the freedom to be completely *me*.

But to have it, I'd need to confront Sewel first.

No running this time. No hiding. I'd face him head-on.

And I'd be ready.

CHAPTER 24

RETURN TO RANELAGH

★

July 1780

A week after Malcolm's death, Uncle Henry insisted we get on with our lives.

"The whiff of scandal has passed us by," he said, pacing the parlor, his arms linked behind his back. "We have had ample time to grieve and restore ourselves. Now we must return to society before we are forgotten and set aside. I have purchased tickets for Ranelagh tonight. The fresh air and music will do us all good. Lieutenant Duncan plans to be there also."

Beside me on the settee, Lucy smiled. "You must wear your blue brocade, Emmie."

"Yes, with something new," said Aunt Nora. She paused, waiting for our new day maid, Azubah, to set the tea tray down. Maggie had vanished. Two days after Malcolm's death, Aunt Nora entered the cottage and found it perfectly tidied. Vacant. I would never see her again. In the span of a week, two people who'd been part of my life for years had disappeared forever. "Let's go out this morning and find a pretty hat for you, or a new pair of gloves."

"Why not both?" Uncle Henry added cheerfully.

I knew what they were all thinking. I'd first met Duncan at Ranelagh—dressed in my blue gown. Tonight, they expected him to propose at last. I expected it, too.

"What a wonderful idea," I said, a lump rising in my throat.

I'd made them fall in love with a figment. A fabrication. Since I'd decided to leave my life with them, every word hurt. Somehow, after years of lying to them easily, I now couldn't.

Before leaving the house, I folded my pearl choker into a kerchief and stashed it in my purse along with a jackknife from the kitchen.

For the past week, I'd been thinking about how to rid myself of Sewel. He was hunting me. I *felt* him lurking in New York. I had to find a way to give myself the upper hand.

His greed was one thing I could always count on—I knew it was what had really brought him back to me. There had to be a way for me to buy my freedom. The pearl choker was only a taste of what I could give him if he agreed to disappear for good.

As we stepped outside, the streets struck me as noisier and more crowded than just a week ago. Duncan had returned from the campaign with thousands of British regulars and Hessians, and their triumph was evident, taverns and coffee houses overflowing, their laughter and music everywhere. It felt like England had won the war.

Uncle Henry hovered protectively as we walked to Mrs. Powers's shop. I found myself searching for Sewel in every face—but I knew him. He was murderous and evil but also a coward. He would wait to find me when I was unprotected and vulnerable.

As we neared the milliner's shop, I spotted Townsend crossing the street.

"Miss Coates," he called, jogging over. "Excuse the interruption, Doctor," he said to Uncle Henry, and expressed his regrets for the sad event that had befallen our house. As he spoke, I noticed the sweat on his upper lip and the rapid blinking of his eyes. "The book you ordered some time ago has finally come in," he told me. He handed me a packet wrapped in brown paper and twine. "'Tis the copy of *She Stoops to Conquer*."

"Thank you, Mr. Townsend. How kind of you to bring it to me. Have you a minute to talk about another order?"

"Certainly."

I turned to Uncle Henry. "I will meet you inside in a moment."

My voice held a firmness that wasn't Miss Coates's, but no one seemed to notice. The Holdridges stepped into the milliner's shop to look at pretty hats. Just like that, Townsend and I found ourselves alone and back to our old ways.

"I was contacted again," he said as we drew closer to the shop's brick exterior to avoid the street traffic.

I nodded. "Go on." It was General Washington who'd contacted him, of course. I could feel it. I could see it in his eyes.

"I was asked to discover what the British know of the coming French fleet. If they were to discover any information, such as landing points, gun and troop numbers, it would help them form a counterplan and rob us of the element of surprise." He paused to press a kerchief to his face and then returned it to his pocket. "Miss Coates, I have been able to discover that they have knowledge of *all* of it. Everything *we* know, *they* know as well. What's more, they obtained information almost as quickly as we got it. I can only think we are leaking intelligence at a very high level. I wanted you to know. What you've long suspected . . . you may have been right all along."

I knew I was. A traitor was working against us, giving up our information.

I remembered Duncan's mention of the French the night after Malcolm's death a week ago. He'd known of their coming then. He had even *said* the British had been given ample warning.

"Monk," I whispered.

I was getting close to him now. And I had an idea of just how to catch him.

=★=

"I believe you would like Maryland," Duncan said that evening as we walked the garden paths.

Instead of a balmy night, like we'd had a year ago, rain showers had been falling on and off, putting most of the lanterns out. Putting the musicians out, too. They'd stopped playing halfway through Handel's *Messiah* to run for shelter.

Most concert attendees had also given up on the gardens and gone in search of indoor entertainments. But a few, like us, had taken to the paths with the hopes the showers had ended for the night.

"'Tis a fine place," he continued, guiding me around a puddle. "The vegetation is very pretty. There are fine lodgings, noble estates in the surrounding areas, and the state itself is quite charming and free of the sordid types that infest New York."

"Sordid types? Do you the men in the city prisons?" I immediately wished I could unsay the words. It was becoming harder to hold back—and I needed to. Now more than ever.

Duncan stopped and gazed into my eyes. Like me, he'd made an effort with his appearance. His hair was braided into a pretty queue and fashioned with a ribbon the very same light caramel shade. A silver gorget shone at his neck, and his ceremonial sword flashed at his side. He looked thoroughly dashing. I'd thought so a year ago, and I *still* did, but the hum of desire I'd felt then was gone.

"Emmeline, your kindness impels me to want to be better. More compassionate and feeling. But on matters of war, there's precious little room for compassion or feeling. A certain coldness is required—'tis the unfortunate truth, but the truth nonetheless. I feel that if we are always going to disagree on the treatment of the American prisoners, perhaps it's best we set the subject aside for good."

"That seems wise," I said. "One cannot become sentimental about one's adversaries. I shall never mention the prisoners again."

"Thank you. You are all agreeableness."

"Is *that* so?"

"No. You are much more that." He drew closer, his hand drifting to my waist, a seductive smile spreading over his lips. "You are kindness and wit and virtue. You are elegance and gentility."

Wit, I'd claim, but the rest? It was all smoke. "And you, James, are a flatterer."

He laughed. "Guilty. 'Tis your effect on me."

We began to walk again. As the path took us through groves of apple and pear trees, he described good land in Maryland that had caught his eye. I knew exactly where the conversation was heading. "Weybridge has not felt much like home since my father's passing, and I've grown rather attached to America. There's great opportunity here. When things are settled again, after the war, I believe—"

"Duncan," Major André called behind us. "Excuse the interruption, Miss Coates," he said as he hurried up. "I must steal him for a few moments, but I promise he'll soon be yours again." His eyes darted to Duncan, flashing with mischief. "I daresay for as long as you'll have him."

"He is yours, sir," I replied with a smile. "Take your time. I'll just wander ahead a bit."

I left them and wandered deeper into the gardens, where the foliage grew thicker and wilder. I found myself staring into the deeper patches of darkness, my breath shallow and quick.

Was Sewel here?

The pearl choker was still wrapped in the kerchief inside my purse.

I was ready for him. Ready for marriage proposals. Ready for anything.

But not rain.

I stopped and looked up as I felt the first fat drops.

Suddenly, the hair on my arms lifted. I heard quick footsteps on the gravel. Saw a dark blur. Then iron arms struck me and wrapped me up.

I twisted wildly. "Let me *go*!"

Sewel's hand slammed over my mouth, smothering my cry. "Hush." He pulled me off the path, past thorny brambles. "Bloody hell, Francisca. *Shut up* and be *still!*"

I couldn't. I kicked and thrashed, my mind gone. He'd hurt me. He'd killed Malcolm. His smell, the feeling of him against me—they were from my nightmares.

"*Enough,* Fran!" He grabbed my hair and wrenched. My head cranked sharply to the side. "You done yet?"

I nodded as best I could with my ear against my shoulder. His hand came away from my mouth.

"Let go of me, Sewel." I gasped for air. My scalp burned. My neck pulsed with pain. "I won't run. I'm through running from you."

"Are you, now?" He let go. I straightened and spun away, but he held my wrist.

Through the scrim of leaves, I saw the scarlet of Duncan's coat. He was rounding the path and would soon come upon us. Reaching into my purse with my free hand, I grabbed the kerchief with the pearls inside and shoved it at Sewel's chest. "Take this. Use it to get a skiff and meet me at the ropewalk north of the ship yards tonight at three. I'll give you ten times more than what's in there if you leave me be. Now let go of me, Sewel. Let go before he sees."

"He?" Sewel frowned. Then his eyes found Duncan. He let go of my wrist.

I shot away and burst back onto the path. I had just enough time to sweep my gown and hat for leaves before Duncan rounded the bend.

He stopped sharply when he saw me, then rushed over. "I was growing worried. Where did you—" He tensed, reaching for the sword at his side. "Stand where you are, sir, and name yourself."

I turned, going numb from my scalp to toes.

Sewel ambled over like an old cur. His head low. His eyes menacing. Not smiling as much as showing his teeth. "My name's Sewel Tasker." He bowed, the gesture slightly mocking. "Your humble servant, Lieutenant. I was just remarking to Miss Coates how coincidentious it is to see her here."

Duncan spun to me. "You know this man?"

"I—yes. We met this winter at Judge Latimer's." It was the first thing that came to me—a terrible explanation. The judge would never brush elbows with the likes of Sewel.

"Right," Sewel said, his wicked grin spreading. "This winter at the judge's home."

"How do you know the judge?" Duncan asked, still having none of it.

Sewel's red eyes held on Duncan, unblinking.

"Mr. Tasker is actually connected with Asa Latimer," I rushed to say. "He's a ship's carpenter. He did some repairs on the *Endurance*. He came to the judge's house a few times over the winter to speak with Mr. Latimer, and that was how we met. As you know, we were living there for a few weeks."

The suspicion eased from Duncan's eyes.

"That's right," Sewel said. "I did some carpentering for Latimer. Made masts and spars for him and such." He waggled his thick fingers in the air like he was imagining ship's rigging. Then he leered at me, enjoying seeing me on a knife's edge. "Well, I best leave you to your walking. Terrible good to see you again, Miss Coates. Lieutenant." He bowed, and lumbered away.

I watched him go in stunned silence, trying to stop my legs from shaking.

Beside me, Duncan released a long breath. "I know you're fond of the judge, but his nephew is a scoundrel who I've long suspected of the darkest dealings. Now I see my instincts were correct." He looked at me. "I don't wish to alarm you, but that man was a criminal."

I gasped. "Are you certain?"

"I am. I saw a brand on his hand. You must never go near him again. Nor Asa Latimer."

"I won't! Not for anything!" An idea struck me suddenly. This chance meeting between Sewel and Duncan might be the best thing I could've hoped for. All I had to do was set a trap. "I can't believe it," I said. "Mr. Latimer always seemed a gentleman."

"My dear, you know little of the evils in this world. People are not always what they seem."

I widened my eyes in shock. Like I hadn't exploited that very truth for years. "Now all I feel is relief. Mr. Tasker said he's leaving for Long Island tonight. I'll sleep better knowing he's far away. But . . . how will he go? Won't it be curfew soon?"

If Duncan took the bait, I was free.

His eyes narrowed. "Yes. But men like him have ways to move about. Did he say anything else?"

I pretended to think. "No. Only that he's been working the ropewalk north of the shipyards. Does that help?"

"Yes." Duncan looked east, like he might see the river from where we stood. "I'll see that he leaves and never returns." His

301

eyes were still distant when he turned back to me. "There's a pavilion just up ahead. Shall we run for cover? I refuse to let that miscreant sour our night."

I took his arm, my mind reeling, going over all that had just been said. I'd set a plan in motion even as I'd been devising it. But it would work. I *knew* it would. Duncan would send men after Sewel and I'd see that Sewel's capture would lead to his demise. It was perfect. A perfect stroke of luck.

Under the pavilion, Duncan drew me to stand before the lone lantern that still burned. There was no roof, but a thick tapestry of rose vines kept the rain away. We were alone now, the empty footpaths weaving into the darkness.

"Do you remember a year ago?" he asked.

"Of course." He'd been so disarming. And I'd been so eager to be seen as more than a handsome fortune. I'd gotten what I'd wanted.

He took my hands. "I wanted to do this here, tonight, and to not rush through it, and to say all the right things, but I can't wait anymore. If you answer me as I pray you will, then you will hear from my bewitched heart every day henceforth, and as often as you wish. My dear Emmeline . . . will you marry me?"

This was the only way. All I had to do was survive this night. This moment. "James . . . I want so much to say yes, that I will marry you, but I *can't*. All winter long, when you were away on campaign, I worried every day I'd never see you again. It was almost unbearable. I have lost *everyone* in my family. I simply can't let my life's happiness depend on a husband who's away, and in mortal danger, for months at a time—no matter how noble the reasons. Tell me you understand?"

He stepped even closer, taking my arms. "I *do*. I *do* understand loss. We have always shared that connection. But I can assure you—you will *not* lose me."

I shook my head. "My father promised me the same."

"This is different. This is a *certainty*. There is no danger anymore. I will not go on campaign again. We have found an advantage so significant that our victory is all but sealed."

I was *so* close. All I had to do was push a little more. "We've been close to the end before—yet here we are. Four, five years in. And you've said yourself the rebels are tenacious and cunning. How many times have they slipped away when no one believed they could?"

"That is precisely why our plan is flawless. It was devised by one of their own. A man of very high influence in their army has given us the key to controlling the North River. Very soon, it will be securely in our possession. With our southern victories mounting, we'll have the upper hand everywhere. By Christmas, Emmeline, it will all be over."

There.

Finally.

Treasure.

A discovery that both thrilled and terrified me.

"What do you say then, my sweet?" he continued, his eyes shining brightly. "Will you be mine?"

I could do this. Just one more. Then I'd never tell another lie again. "Yes. I will."

CHAPTER 25

RECKONING

★

I
t was time.

At one in the morning, with the house finally settled, I lit a fresh taper and sat at my desk. It was time to finally end my life as Miss Coates.

After Duncan and I had shared our engagement with the Holdridges, we'd enjoyed an "impromptu" celebration that had included Aunt Nora's chocolate cake, a bottle of Uncle Henry's coveted champagne, and a spirited performance of "Heart of Oak," sung by Charlotte, with Lucy accompanying on the pianoforte. With everyone rejoicing, I'd never felt so poisonous. And now I had to sink the knife all the way.

In moments, I'd leave to meet Sewel by the ropewalk—and never return. To escape the lies I'd wrapped around myself, I had to make a clean break and let go of everything—and devastate the people I'd come to love.

I took a clean sheet of paper from a drawer. Pulling the pocket watch chain over my head, I turned the plate in the back and removed the cipher folded inside. I weighed the edges of the crimped page down with books to keep it flat and then, using the numbers as my guide, wrote a letter by mixing up the codes and reversing numbers. My goal was to make it *look* right but not *mean* anything.

In nonsensical code, I wrote to Sewel and told him that I loathed him. That he had destroyed so much of my life, and bruised so many things, but that he hadn't destroyed *me*—and that was going to be *his* undoing.

My fake spy message was my truth—and my battle cry.

The *real* spy message I had to deliver I didn't trust to paper. I'd share it with Townsend in person.

As the ink dried, I changed into my deep indigo gown. Then I folded the paper and stuffed it down to the bottom of a white stocking. Next, I swept every single jewel in my trunk into the stocking, tying a knot at the top, and there it was. Bait and trap in one. If my plan went right, this would bring Sewel down for good.

The fat stocking nearly didn't fit into my pouch purse, but I wedged it inside and still had a little room left to tuck in a jack-knife. I replaced the cipher inside my pocket watch; then I let out a long breath and gazed around my room one final time.

Four years. These walls had sheltered me well.

I slipped into the hall and stepped into Lucy's room. She had fallen asleep with puppy Iseult curled against her. Iseult made tiny whimpering sounds as she chased something in her sleep.

Eyes blurring, I dropped a soft kiss on them both and prayed they'd take care of each other. Then I crept downstairs, through the kitchen, and out to the courtyard.

I took one last look at the cottage. Then at the house that'd been my home.

"Thank you," I whispered, and drew my hood.

=★=

The streets were slick with mud from the earlier rain, but I moved swiftly over them, already feeling the pull of freedom. The clouds were parting, and a huge moon hung in the sky. I breathed in the cool night air. I felt alone and terrified but ready—so *ready* for whatever came next.

I arrived at the red door of Underhill's boardinghouse and knocked. I knew Townsend was staying here while he organized a new home and warehouse on the north edge of the city. I knocked again, impatiently.

I had precious little time before I met Sewel, but I had to see Townsend first. The promise of a new beginning tugged me on, but I was no fool. I knew there was a chance I might not live to see the sun. I had to tell Townsend what I knew *now*.

A few men stopped across the street.

"Lassie," called one. "You lost?"

I raised my fist to pound on the door again. The lock rattled. Townsend himself pulled the door open. In an instant he went from sleepy confusion to alarm. "What's happened?" he asked.

"Can you come with me? Please, Robert."

"Yes—of course." He disappeared for a few seconds and reappeared with his hat.

As we headed off together, the man across the street called out again.

"What's wrong with us, trollop? We got the same parts he's got!"

306

"I doubt it, you brainless pig!" I called back.

Townsend's head whipped to me, his eyes huge with shock, but I kept walking. I wasn't Miss Coates anymore. I didn't have to leash my vulgar tongue—nor apologize for its bite.

I retraced the path Mrs. Burgin had taken a year ago, Townsend a quiet and familiar presence beside me, my heart aching for Malcolm, who'd been with me the last time I'd made this journey. We passed the field with the shanties and came to the edge of the shipyard. There, with ships' timbers rising over us like Goliath's ribs, I told Townsend everything I'd learned from Duncan only hours earlier.

"They've found a way to control the *North River*?" He shook his head in disbelief. "Can it be West Point? If that is what's at stake, then *everything* is."

"Is it enough information?" I asked. "Enough for us to stop it from happening?"

"I do not know. Not knowing who Monk is, I will have to be exceeding careful with how I send the intelligence. If he's on the inside, then he could be within our circle of trust."

"But you will pass it on?"

"Oh yes. I will."

We stared at each other. At that moment, I felt we might've just done something great.

But there was no time to bask. "I need to take care of something alone, but I'll be back at Underhill's before sunup, and then I'll need your help," I said. "I can't go home. I have to leave New York. I thought I might go to Anna Strong's."

"I will help you any way I can, as I'm certain will Anna, but you have me worried."

307

"I have to go, Robert. But I'll see you soon. Trust me."

"I do."

"You didn't always."

His eyes sparkled behind his glasses. "You've worn me down."

I smiled. Then I snatched up my petticoats in one hand and my purse in the other and ran toward the shipyard. I didn't slow down until I reached the ropewalk.

Sewel was waiting at the river's edge with a skiff. He chipped at the gravel by his feet with an oar, like all of creation made him angry. Beyond him, a thick fog cloaked the river. Illuminated by moonlight, it looked strange. Almost glowing.

"Well, Francisca," Sewel said as I walked up. He propped the oar against the skiff and spread his arms. "Here I am. What devilment have you got planned for me?"

My knees felt soft. My heart like a rattle. But I had to see this through.

I pulled the white stocking from my purse. "See this?" I swallowed, searching for strength in my voice. "It's filled with jewels. This is what you want. Isn't it?"

He crossed his thick arms. "Perhaps."

"You get in that skiff and I'll toss it to you—but only if you promise you'll leave. You cross this river and never come after me again, Sewel. *Never.*"

"That really filled with jewels?"

"More than you could hope to see in your sorry life."

As the silence stretched, I sensed the greed rising in him. The mountains of rum and tobacco he was thinking could be his. "I take that and go away—that's your offer?"

"That's right."

"Hmm." He nodded. "I could do that. But what am I supposed to do with Asa Latimer's body?"

I bolted to the skiff, crashing against the gunwale. A figure lay in the well, covered in blankets. "No!"

Sewel rushed up behind me. Before I could react, he heaved me over, throwing me on top of the blankets, which gave way beneath me. I clawed at them, tearing the dark wool aside.

Straw.

Not Asa.

A sob broke from my lips.

The skiff jolted. I spun. Sewel had his shoulder bent to it as he drove it off the gravel and into the river—taking me with it.

He vaulted aboard agilely, like a man half his age, the skiff rocking with his weight.

I scurried back to the prow, stepping on my hem in my terror. "Where is he, Sewel?" I yelled. I dove for my purse and found the jackknife. "If you hurt him, I'll kill you!"

"Stop yelling, Francisca." His gaze fell to the knife. "And put that away. I got one of those too—only mine's bigger and I know how to use it."

Sick. I felt *sick* with rage. "You think you're the only one who can slit a throat?"

"Lord, Fran. Calm yourself. I don't know where Asa Latimer is. Never laid eyes on him."

I didn't understand. "You don't—you don't *know* him?"

"No." He grinned. "He served his purpose, though."

He'd *tricked* me. He'd used the one name I'd mentioned at the gardens. But I only felt relief—blessed, blessed relief that Asa was safe.

Sewel set the oars in their locks and dug the blades into the river, heaving his big body forward and then back. "Might as well put that down and settle yourself. You won't be going anywhere for a while."

I didn't put the knife down.

Sewel's big shoulders lifted. "Guess that's how this is gonna be." He stroked the oars again. Water trickled. Wood whined. In the fog, every sound seemed louder as I watched Manhattan's shores grow farther away.

My eyes fell to the stocking, which rested on the straw at the bottom of the well. I'd dropped it when Sewel threw me in. In the murky light, it looked pale as a fish belly in dark water.

This shouldn't have happened. Sewel was supposed to have taken it and left for Long Island on the skiff. He was supposed to have been caught by Duncan, or by gunboat patrols, and searched—then the false spy letter should've dealt the fatal blow.

I wasn't supposed to be here. I was supposed to be making my way back to see Townsend. When the sun rose tomorrow, I should've been starting my new life. A life of truth.

When only fog surrounded us, Sewel shipped the oars and gave the skiff to the river. "This is better, en't it?" I said nothing. "*I* think so." He rummaged in a leather satchel and uncorked a bottle. He tipped it back and drank, sighing loudly. "I didn't want to trick you, Francisca, but you'd never have come otherwise."

"What do you want, Sewel?"

"A bag of precious stones made a fine start, I must say. But I want more. I want *justice*." He drank deeply. "I want *revenge. Amends. Reparations.*" He tipped the bottle again and went on.

"I want *pain*. I want you, *weeping*. You, *begging*." Another deep tilt, and long sigh. "I think I want blood, Francisca. You sorry you asked?"

I *was* sorry. I couldn't even speak.

He finished the bottle and tossed it aside. Then he eased his head back and gazed at the sky, staring and staring, like he'd locked eyes with God. "It's time to put that knife away now," he said after a while, his voice dropping to a depth that put ice in my veins. "Toss it aside or I'll come get it."

Quickly, I hid the knife in the folds of my petticoat and pulled my pocket watch over my head, tossing that down instead.

It clunked against the planks.

"Thank you, Miss Coates." He wasn't slurring yet, but I knew soon he would be. I'd been in this situation a hundred times. "Remember our last time together?"

"You think I could forget?" I snapped. The fog was beginning to play with my mind, making me feel like I was *inside* the past, the blankness like a canvas for my memories to paint. I saw rain sizzling on surging seas. Lightning bolts slicing through thunderheads. Sewel's face hovering over me.

"You disappeared that night," he said now. "But I knew you didn't die. I knew you ran. I knew it in here." He thumped his heart. "I knew 'cause I taught you to be strong."

"You taught me nothing. All you did was hurt me and scare me."

He lifted his head, finding me with his eyes. "You tested me. You never learnt your place. That's why I had to be rough with you."

311

"*I* forgot my place? You're my *stepfather* and you—you—"
Hot spit flooded my mouth. I swallowed. Breathed. Pushed away
the feeling of his hands on me.

He sat up. "You want to talk right and wrong? How about the
time you tried to send me to a watery grave?"

Right then, I knew no amount of talking would ever change
anything. He was evil. We'd never understand each other. "I've
never known anyone with such a twisted mind as yours, Sewel."

"*Yours* is the twisted mind. But we'll remedy it right now." He
leaned down and plucked the stocking up. His knife flashed as he
sliced off the knot at the top. The stocking fell, jewels bursting
out as it struck the well. Sewel stared at the precious items strewn
over the hay. Necklaces and broaches. Bracelets and elaborate
hairpins. "My God . . . you weren't lyin'." He picked up a necklace. "Pretty little thing." In the whiteness of the fog, the rubies
looked red as holly berries. He held the necklace over the rail and
let go. It disappeared with a soft *plunk.* "Time to dive, Frannie."

A lifetime went by. Then I heard myself laugh. "You think I'm
afraid of going in there?"

"I don't care *how* you feel about it. Get in there."

I came to my knees at the gunwale, keeping the knife in my
left hand, hidden from him. Necklaces and rings crunched under
me as I leaned over the edge and stared down. The water looked
calmer than I'd ever seen it. Through wisps of fog, my reflection
stared back at me. I didn't look like Emmeline Coates or Francisca Tasker. I didn't know *whose* face was in the water.

"You know I won't be able to find it," I said, my voice trembling. I heard all the blunted edges in it again. All the fear and fury
of my past. "This gown will pull me under. Even if I could swim, I

won't be able to see anything in the dark and the current'll sweep me away."

"What a shame for you. Get in. I won't say it again."

This was a nightmare. Just another nightmare of Sewel. I firmed my grip on the knife. Then a sound tickled my ear.

A voice was calling in the distance. So faint, I thought I'd imagined it. Then I heard it again. Not just one man's voice—several.

"I gave you ample time," Sewel said, and the skiff rocked as he pushed himself up.

I had only one move now. I dove at him, aiming the knife at his neck. He lurched aside. The blade sank into his shoulder. He roared with pain and swung, his fist crashing into my temple.

I flew back and my head cracked against wood.

"Damn it, Francisca! You bring me to this!" he yelled. His face appeared over me. His hands closed on my throat, squeezing. "This is *your* doing!"

I fumbled through the wet straw for the knife I'd dropped. I couldn't get any air. I felt myself fading. Floating away into darkness.

Sewel's head snapped up. Dazed, I heard the voices in the fog again. He released me and moved away.

I rolled to my side and grabbed my throat. It felt broken. I couldn't swallow or draw breath. My lungs spasmed, starved for air, death a quiet grip on my body that refused to let go.

Sewel was frantically loading ball and shot into a pistol.

"What in the hell have you done?"

"Ahoy!" someone yelled. "Who's there? State your name!"

The gunboat sliced through the fog like a spear. So close I could see the buttons on the coats of the marines standing at the bow. There were three of them, and they raised muskets in perfect unison, as though in a drill.

"Bring to, or we will shoot!" yelled the one in the middle.

Sewel ducked behind the gunwale, curses spitting from his mouth.

"You're going to hang," I rasped.

"No, Fran. That I will not do." He peered over the gunwale and fired.

The sound of the discharge exploded in my ears. I slammed my hands over them and hunkered down. The marines fired back, raising a thunderous noise. Wood popped and shattered all around me. The skiff shuddered and shook. I curled into a ball and prayed for my life.

At last, silence returned. Gun smoke seeped into my eyes and my nose. Scratched in my throat. I'd gone numb everywhere else. I couldn't even tell if I'd been struck by a bullet.

Water. The river was pouring in through holes and soaking my petticoats.

"Stand down!" yelled a voice. "Or we'll blow you to pieces!"

I squinted, trying to see through wafting fog and smoke. Sewel was on his back, furiously reloading the pistol.

I dug through the well, my hands pushing aside wet straw as I searched for my pocket watch. Everything else I could blame on Sewel—the murderer, spy, kidnapper who'd brought me out here. But the code sheet in my watch could destroy me, Townsend, and our entire ring of spies. Possibly much more.

Instead of the watch, my fingers found the jackknife. The instant I grabbed it, boarding hooks bit into the wood beside me with sharp *thunks*.

"Haul!" someone yelled. Startlingly close. "Bring in the line!"

The skiff jerked as the lines went taut. Lantern light spilled through the splintered holes in the hull. Sewel sat up, resting his back against it, giving the destroyed wood only a passing glance.

"Throw your weapons over or we'll blow you out of the water!" yelled one of the marines, even as they hauled us in like a fish on a line.

"I don't much like either choice," Sewel said.

"It doesn't matter, Sewel. You're dead."

He looked at me. "I been dead longer than you've been alive." He heaved himself up and aimed the pistol.

Cracks exploded into the night. His body jerked back. His shoulder tore off. His hand disappeared in a bloody spray. Other pieces of him burst and broke.

The gunboat struck the skiff with a loud crunch. What was left of Sewel toppled into the river with a splash.

Men vaulted over me. Blurs. They landed in the skiff with explosions of water. I saw the flash of a musket stock coming at my head and reacted, burying the knife into the nearest limb. Then my head snapped back and darkness took me.

CHAPTER 26

SPY

★

The smell of sickness brought me back. I stirred awake and found myself on the floor of a ship's cabin, my face pressed to the dirty wool blanket that held the offending odor. Weak daylight floated in through a porthole. Two berths were fixed into the curve of the bulkhead.

Duncan sat on the lower one, elbows on his knees, my pocket watch dangling from his hands. He swung it back and forth as he watched me stir. Next to his black shoes, a lone candle burned a tall flame.

Inch by painful inch, I raised myself to sitting.

Nothing felt right. My head felt broken, my neck stiff. My pulse shrieked in my ears. I rubbed one hand over my aching throat. "Duncan?"

I didn't recognize the look on his face. Disgust? Fury? Or was it heartbreak?

He cleared his throat. "I'm sorry you were struck. It was dark and things happened quickly. The marines saw a threat to my life and reacted."

I didn't understand. A threat to his life? Then I noticed the bandage around his thigh. Blood had seeped through it, a scarlet bloom. "I'm sorry, I didn't . . ."

"You didn't what? Didn't intend to stab me? As far as I can tell, your only error was stabbing me in the leg instead of in the back. But you did that too, didn't you?"

I couldn't disagree. I *had* stabbed him in the back. I'd done it as I'd smiled at him and danced with him and kissed him.

"How long?" he asked.

"A while."

"Since the beginning?"

"Yes."

"I see." His eyes glossed with tears. "Was it always your plan?"

"No. When we first met, I wasn't thinking I'd . . ."

"Use me? Betray me?" He turned away, hiding his face in shadow.

I wanted to comfort him and apologize for the damage I'd done. It hurt me that I'd hurt him. But he'd said himself that a certain coldness was required in matters of war. And we were enemies now. True enemies. There was no confusion or murkiness anymore.

"I found this." He picked something up off the mattress. A paper. It was the message I'd hoped would frame Sewel as a spy. "I believe this is written in your hand."

Water had damaged it. Chunks were missing and the ink had smeared in places. But it was still a fine-looking spy letter—and it had done what I'd intended. Duncan thought it was real.

"I found the one hidden in this as well," he said, holding up my watch, "but it was already dissolving into pulp. I always wondered at your attachment to this, even being your father's. I suppose I should've wondered more."

He held the fake spy message to the candle, letting one corner catch. Then he dropped it on the planks between us and I watched the flame turn it into ashes and smoke.

I looked up, trying to understand.

"Tell me whom you're working with. Surely not that oaf on the river. Is it Latimer? Did he make you do this?"

"No."

"Give me a name, Emmeline. Give me anything that will help."

"No. I'm not going to help you."

He stood and stalked away, but there was nowhere to go. He turned back. "Can't you see I'm trying to protect you? We can survive this and still have a life together."

I stared at him. He still wanted to *marry* me? "Not a life I want."

"A life you—a life *you want*? What could you possibly want that I cannot give you?"

"Independence," I said, but it was even bigger than that. It was what *I* couldn't give *him*. I didn't love him.

"Are you serious? I don't know who you are anymore."

"You never did."

His eyes went stone cold. "Have you *any* idea what you're doing?"

"Yes." For the first time, in a *very* long time, I did. I'd chosen truth. I wasn't going back. "I've never felt surer."

Without another word, he left the cabin.

My eyes fell to the quivering candle flame. I watched it grow long and steady again; then I touched my head. I had a lump like a stone at my hairline. My vision blurred.

I'd swum with deadly sharks and stolen from deadlier men. I'd survived hurricanes, war, and even love—but I didn't know if I'd survive this.

I pulled myself off the floorboards, my legs shaking as I stood. The cabin spun around me. My hand shot to the bulwark, bracing. I breathed in. Smelled pine tar and bilgewater.

The door swung open and two redcoats hurried inside.

One carried shears; the other, a length of rope. They were big men, filling the cabin with their bright regimentals and shocked stares. They obviously hadn't expected to find a young lady in a tattered gown, bleeding from a head wound.

"We have orders to cut your hair," said the one with the rope. He cleared his throat and raised the rope higher. "If you resist, I shall be forced to use this."

I swallowed thickly against the fear clamping my throat. I had an idea what this meant. "I won't resist." I straightened off the bulwark and stepped forward, trying not to sway. "Go ahead. Cut it."

The man with the shears hesitated, then gathered my hair in a clumsy swipe and sliced. My long locks came away in his hand. He blinked like he was confused, then tossed them down and carried on hastily, cutting so close at times he nicked my scalp and left my eyes watering.

As my dark curls tumbled to the floor, years of dance assemblies and fine dinners flashed before my eyes. I shut them and imagined I was feeling Mama's gentle hands on me instead of this stranger's. Mama, singing in Spanish as she teased out my tangles with the patience of an entire ocean.

What would she think of this? I'd promised her I'd find a safe, respectable life—and done the exact opposite.

"Why?" whispered the man with the rope. I opened my eyes. The candle on the floor guttered and popped, making his shadow writhe behind him. He licked his lips. "Why are you here? Are you—are you *a spy?*"

"Shut up, Wilcox," said the other one. Then he glanced at me like he wanted to know, too.

"Tell me where I'm being sent and I'll answer." I already thought I knew, but I needed to be sure.

They shared a look.

"Go on, Wilcox," said the one with the shears. "Tell her."

"*You* tell her, Bradley."

Bradley lowered the shears and exhaled, his breath sour with the smell of tobacco. "There's whispers amongst the men you're going to the *Jersey* prison hulk."

My knees nearly crumpled beneath me. *Prison.* I'd guessed right. But even worse—the *Jersey.* Where men were sent to die. Where no women were sent at all. I'd be the first one. The only one.

"Your turn," Bradley said, impatient for my answer.

"No. I'm not a spy," I lied, though I could've told the truth. I'd been caught; the worst had already happened. But I didn't owe these men anything. Certainly not what I valued most. "This is all just a misunderstanding," I added, and in spite of everything, I felt a smile tug at my lips.

Bradley snorted.

Snip went the shears.

When he was done, I ran my hand over my scalp, learning a part of myself for the first time. I felt sharper. Honed. I could feel the air around me the same way I used to feel the ocean when I dove.

The marine with the rope—Wilcox—stepped outside and came back with a bundle of folded clothing.

"You're to change into these." He set the bundle on the berth, then turned away. Bradley went to stand beside him.

I stared at their backs for a moment, letting a wave of fear pass. Hands trembling, I unlaced my gown and petticoats and let them slip off. My stays were back lacing, though.

"I need help," I said.

"I'll go get—"

"No." I knew who they'd bring and I couldn't bear to see him again. I went to Bradley, turning my back to him. "Cut the laces."

"Lord forgive me," he muttered. Then he sliced a path up my spine.

The pressure of the stays gave way and my lungs eased fully open. I stepped away again and tossed my stays on the berth, then pulled my shift over my head. As it billowed to my feet, gooseflesh rippled over me and I had the strange realization this was my first time bare in the presence of a man. That it was *two* men and nothing at all how I'd hoped it would be.

I pulled on the shirt and trousers, the ozenbrig material rough as a cat's tongue. Such a part of my past—and now my future. There were leather shoes as well, dirty and worn, but a decent fit.

"I'm ready," I said. Another lie, but a strange calm had befallen me. I felt as quiet inside as winter. I was trapped—but freed from decisions. From calculation. All I could do now was continue.

The men turned.

Bradley shook his head. "There's no being ready for where you're going."

"Miss . . ." Wilcox's brow pinched with distress. "Whatever you may have done to find yourself here, surely it can be *un*-done?"

I thought of Townsend and the intelligence I'd given him. "I hope not."

I'd given up everything for it.

I had given my very life.

= ★ =

Ten minutes later, I sat next to Duncan on the tender that would take me to the *Jersey*. Six men faced us from the other end of the boat, pulling at oars in measured strokes. Across the river, the sun sank behind New York's rooflines.

A full day had passed without my knowing.

The Holdridges were probably distraught over my disappearance. They'd think I'd been kidnapped by the same man who'd murdered Malcolm, most likely. I doubted Duncan would tell them the truth—it would blacken his reputation and pull him down with me. Imagining the pain I'd inflicted on Lucy was unbearable.

And Duncan . . . I glanced at him, and my stomach clenched.

With every stroke of the oars, Wallabout Bay crept closer. It almost seemed fitting. My spying journey had begun there—and there it would end.

"Have you any idea where you're going?" Duncan's voice was like frost.

The men at the oars looked up and awaited my answer.

From the moment I stepped aboard, they'd been staring at my trousers and shirt. My shaved scalp, and the lump on my forehead.

"Yes," I rasped, my throat rough with thirst. "The *Jersey*."

"You know about the *Jersey*?"

I looked into his amber eyes, seeing the anguish I had put there. "I know a lot of things that would surprise you."

"So I'm learning." He bowed close to my ear. "You are a *lady*, Emmeline. You would be alone inside it, defenseless on a ship full of criminals and lechers. What do you think will happen when they discover your sex?"

"If you fear for me, then set me free."

"You're a threat to king and country." His forehead bumped mine as he shook his head. "I cannot do that."

"Then send me to my death."

"My God, Emmeline. Are you trying to destroy me? Can't you see that—" He stopped, finally noticing our audience. "If I see any of you looking this way again, I shall put stripes on your backs myself."

"Aye, aye, sir," the men replied sharply, and dropped their gazes.

Duncan turned to me again. "You'll regret this," he said quietly. "You'll cry for me when you are starving and terrified, but it will be too late."

I said nothing.

I knew he might be right.

As we neared the dock, the stench of sewage clogged my throat and bile rose up. The shallow waters around the massive hulk were thick with filth and buzzing flies. As I stepped off the tender, my stomach seized. I leaned over and retched emptily, my tears and saliva spotting the planks under my feet.

I straightened. Duncan offered me a kerchief. I took it, almost laughing. Almost crying. "Ever a gentleman."

"Unless forced otherwise."

We walked up a steep ramp to the main deck, no other sound but our footfalls. Night was falling, but I could see the black scum coating the *Jersey*'s hull and I sensed a kind of droning emanating from it, like it was alive. Suffering. At the top of the ramp, a pair of British sentinels came forward. One man held a lamp for the other, whose uniform had finer trimmings.

"How do this evening, Captain Sproat?" Duncan said.

"Splendid, Lieutenant, as always," said the older man. "What have we here?"

Duncan handed him a sheet of paper. Three letters appeared in my mind, penned in his fine hand.

S-p-y

Had he written them?

"What's the boy's name?" Sproat asked, handing the paper back.

"Judas."

Sproat smiled. "Aren't they all? You've gone to some trouble to bring him here yourself, Lieutenant."

"I had some time on my hands."

"Pity you had to spend it on a visit to us." Sproat looked at me.

I stood a little rounded on instinct, letting the billowing shirt cover me, but I felt my face burn.

"Very well, Lieutenant. He's our problem now." Sproat turned to a redcoat. "Take the boy below."

The man motioned with his bayonet. "This way, rebel."

My legs wouldn't move. I looked at Duncan. I had betrayed him and broken his heart, that I couldn't deny. But he was sending me to torture and death. He was *really* going to do it. Though I didn't want him to save me, it still stunned me.

The redcoat shoved me in the back. "Move." I stumbled forward, toward a hatch set into the decking. "Down you go." The man swung it open with a clang. "Welcome to the end of your life."

I stared down, waiting for my eyes to adjust. The top of a ladder dropped into darkness thick as coal. Trembling, I stepped into it.

Words I'd read in Virgil sprang to mind as my foot found the first rung.

The descent into hell is easy.

There was nothing below me; the bottom could be five feet away or a thousand. I climbed down another rung.

The descent into hell is easy.

"Hurry up." The redcoat jabbed his bayonet at me.

I jerked back, nearly losing my grip on the greasy bars. Toeing for the next rung, I climbed down again.

The descent into hell is easy.

This was something thicker than darkness, something that swallowed my own hands. The hot smell rising from below was worse than sewage. It was misery.

"Is there a problem, Lieutenant Duncan?"

I looked up. Duncan stood at the hatch, framed by a square of starry night. His eyes on me were frantic. *"Stop,"* he said. *"Please. Make this stop."*

I kept going.

Rung for rung.

Virgil for Virgil.

Finally, my foot touched something fleshy that let out a groan.

I jumped away and tripped over another body and landed on yet another, my chin smashing against sweaty muscle and bone.

"Watch yourself, boy!" said the hoarsest voice I'd ever heard. The heat of stinking breath pushed into my face. Invisible hands shoved me aside. I stumbled again, shoves and growls following me as I weaved blindly, desperately. The ladder had disappeared and there was nowhere to stand. Only bodies *everywhere.*

A nightmare.

My worst nightmare.

Finally, I found an open spot and let out a shaking breath. There, I lay down slowly and pulled my knees to my chest, tightening myself into a knot.

Breathe, I told myself. *Breathe.*

But the air was so thick with vile smells, I couldn't bear it. Cool wetness seeped through my trousers, dampening my thighs. The boards beneath me were gritty and covered in scum. I didn't want to know what it was.

My ears came awake to noises. Breathing and wheezing. Coughing and moaning.

Someone was weeping.

Someone else was rambling about a fire.

"We are *burning*. Can you not feel the flames?"

"Go to sleep, Fire Man," muttered a voice.

"*How?* How can I sleep when we are engulfed in flames?"

I didn't think I'd ever see anything in the darkness, but the line of a shoulder appeared before me. My face was inches from a man's back. Slowly, I came up on one elbow.

There were *hundreds* of men. I couldn't tell where they ended.

"We are all going to *burn*," Fire Man moaned. "It's so hot. Can you not feel the flames?"

I could feel them. Flames consuming me. This fear and stench would be the end of me.

I stood only one chance of escaping this torture.

I breathed in deep, pretending it was clean air. Then I imagined diving off the wherry and breaking into clear blue water. I imagined coolness washing over me. I pictured myself kicking. Stroking my arms forward and back, swimming down, down, down to one fathom.

Then two.

All I had to do was get to the seventh. There was no rising in the seventh. No falling. Just floating. Just freedom. Anything I wanted, I could have there. I could make it possible.

I kicked down to three and then four.

Five . . .

Six . . .

And finally, finally, *finally* . . .

What had I done?

CHAPTER 27

HELL AFLOAT

★

The light of dawn came through the *Jersey*'s barred portholes in a gauzy yellow haze.

I peered through my lashes, watching as men thin as skeletons woke and stretched and unfolded. Some began to form lines at the portholes. I didn't understand at first—there was nowhere to go. Then I realized they were taking turns breathing the fresh air.

I could see the entire deck now. There were a few hammocks here and there, but most of the men had slept on the floor. Only a few were still slumbering. Some talked in groups. Some stared vacantly. A few wept. The Fire Man still rambled.

He was an ancient creature. He appeared to be made of dead wood. Ashen skin. Branches for arms and legs. Long twists of matted gray hair fell to his shoulders.

"Fire, over there," he said as he paced and pointed. "You'll get that, won't you, Decker? And there's some embers there, Alex. Best put them out quickly."

There were men of every age, some barely old enough to grow

whiskers. Most white, but some black. They wore tatty garments that hung on their bony figures. Their skin was covered with grime; their eyes were sunken and wrinkled with suffering—even the younger ones.

There wasn't a single lady here—myself included. For as long as I could manage, I planned to stay a boy. It was time for my long-forgotten masculine ways to make a return.

"Boy." The man near me nudged my shoulder. "Wake up, boy. You need a meff."

"I need . . . *what?*" I squeaked.

Only a few teeth poked from the cave of his mouth and he'd fought a battle for every word.

"He means to say you need a *mess*," said the man beside him—so filthy he looked like a shadow with eyes. "A mess is a group of six men. That's how we eat, sleep, and suffer in here, and Barck's right: best you hasten and find one." All across the hold, I noticed, men were gathering in groups. "You miss out on day one and everyone'll think you got no will to live. Then you'll *never* find a mess, and that means a quick death—sorry to be blunt, but that is what it means. Go see Turtle over there with the humped back." He pointed a long, bony finger. "He lost a messmate yesterday. And hurry."

"Thank you, sir," I said.

"No *sir* in here, Greenie. Not even with the officers. We're all brothers."

"Thank you," I said again. Then I threaded my way toward the man named Turtle, deep in the back. Behind him, toward the stern, I saw what remained of a captain's cabin. The opening for the door had been widened and the stern windows boarded up. There wasn't a single piece of furniture inside. Only more men milling about.

"You can stop right there," said Turtle when he saw me coming. "I already got a new sixth."

"Well, then make me your seventh." I felt a dozen stares on me. "Or tell me who else can I ask," I added.

"How old are you, boy?"

I scratched my jaw, pretending to think. "Fifteen, I think? I don't know—what day's it?"

Just as I'd hoped, a discussion arose about the day. Was it July thirty-first? Or was it already August?

A few of the men were still watching me and I didn't know why—because I hadn't found a mess? Because they knew I was a girl? Panic shortened my breath. I turned to a black man wearing a kerchief as an arm sling. "Where can I find a mess that'll take me on?"

He lifted his unbound shoulder. "Might try asking the king of England. Anybody know where's King George?" he called out.

"Here! I am here, my faithful subjects!" someone piped in the dimness. Laughter rippled across the deck.

I forced myself to appear calm. If I didn't settle this now, I was finished. I needed allies or I wouldn't stand a chance. "You have to help me. I have to find a spot in a mess."

"I'll take you on, whelp," someone said behind me.

I whirled. A man came forward from the gloom of the stern cabin with an exaggerated stride. A swagger I recognized instantly.

Tom Hackett was no longer the barrel-chested boatswain I'd met on the *Ambrosia*. Like every other man here, he'd wasted away, his burliness worn down to big bones that had little to carry. Nevertheless, it was still him. He was still scowl-faced. Still had the mulish lift of his jaw and the look in his eyes like he'd steal your fingers if you shook his hand. Seeing him in prison didn't surprise me—but this was a prison for *patriots,* and that he had not been.

"I need a sixth," he said, looking me up and down. "I think you'll do."

"You can't take him, Hackett," said Turtle. "He's no officer."

Hackett moved toward him. "You got a point, Turtle. But we need a brat to fetch things for us and whatnot, and this scrap won't take up much space. Anyway, there en't time to debate it, so let's just call it settled."

That *did* settle it. Turtle muttered something and wandered off. To my relief, the last of my audience lost interest in me.

Hackett crossed his arms. "My, my, Little Salt. You seen better days."

"And you haven't?"

"Never. Never better days than these." His jaw ticked higher, his eyes flashing. I could see the surprise and the questions he was holding inside. "Well, Salty. Here you are, blest to be on the *Jersey* with the rest of us. It en't ideal conditions, as you can see, but you'll get used to it. Either that, or you'll die."

"I'm not dying."

"Is that right?"

I stared at him. He didn't know how strong I was, but I'd show him. I'd show myself. I had given up everything for a new beginning. I wasn't going to roll over now.

His eyes moved past me. Men were climbing the ladder, up

to the weather deck. A few were carried out by their messmates, limp and lifeless. The casualness with which they went about the task shook me.

"Expect that'll be you in about a month, Salty. Come on. Time to feast."

I followed Hackett up the ladder, feeling like I was rising from a swamp.

Outside, the air wasn't fresh, but it was worlds better than what I'd left behind. Marines and sentinels stood on the quarter-deck and on platforms built over the bulwarks. From these look-outs, they watched the sea of prisoners—a sea I was now part of.

Shaky as I felt and full of new fears, a kind of lightness came over me.

I wasn't Miss Coates anymore.

I could spit if I wanted to. I could sneeze as loud as a trumpet if I wanted to. Jump in circles on one foot, scratch my arse, *say* "arse" or any number of other coarse things and nobody'd think me vulgar. They wouldn't even notice. It wasn't a soaring kind of freedom, but it *was* something to be glad for.

I stayed close to Hackett as we lined up by mess number be-fore a large cauldron set over a barrel that smoked with a cook fire. Four other men came to stand with us.

"This is Little Salt," Hackett said, and tipped his head at me. "He's in our mess now." Then he introduced them one by one. Red had gingery scruff covering his jaw. The tall man wearing a shabby courtroom wig went by King George. Wilkins had an affliction that caused him to blink like he was trying to clear his eyes but never could. Finally there was Tim, who clutched mess three's pail to his chest like every man there was trying to steal it.

Not one of them spared me more than a glance. I suspected that, like Hackett, they expected me to die in a matter of weeks.

"Mess one!" shouted the immense black man behind the cauldron.

Six men stepped up to it, one holding a wood bucket. Squinting against the smoke wafting into his face, the cook ladled some kind of gruel into the bucket and passed out pieces of bread.

"Two!" he yelled.

Mess two went. Then it was three's turn.

As we walked up to the massive copper cauldron, I put myself right in front. I was shortest, smallest, and newest, but I wasn't about to be overlooked.

"Is that a greenie there, Hackett?" the cook asked as he ladled gray slop into the bucket Tim held out. The gruel was lumpy and thick, and pieces of the cauldron's corroding copper edges chipped off into it. I swallowed the sick taste in my mouth.

"Nay, Slushy," Hackett replied. "He was here yesterday. You just didn't see him 'cause he's small as a turd."

The cook snorted and handed us biscuits. "You're a lying scoundrel, Hackett."

"You been talking to my mother, Slushy?"

The cook laughed. "Get out of here."

As I followed my messmates to a bare spot on the deck, my fist closed protectively around the nourishment I desperately needed, I glanced at Hackett.

"Something on my face?" he asked, without looking over.

What I wanted to see on it was trustworthiness. "No," I said.

We sat in a half circle on filthy cracked planks, and Tim handed me the pail. "First day aboard, first one to eat."

Relief hit me, and I sighed in spite of myself. I stared into the pail, too hungry to care what the gruel looked or smelled like anymore.

"No spoons, Salty," Hackett said. "Use your bread."

I did as he said, spooning out a lump of meat and then tearing into it with my teeth. Something plump shot onto my tongue and began to *move*. I couldn't stop chewing in time. Whatever it was, I bit through it. A custardy liquid spilled out, hot and phlegmy. My stomach heaved, my throat closed. I doubled and spat, tears and snot pouring out of me.

"Oh, *hell*," I sputtered. Pieces of maggot splattered onto the deck.

Mess three laughed and laughed, King George losing his wig as he folded over his long legs. Other men were laughing, too, even some of the marines from their lookouts.

I looked at Hackett and found him watching me, his mouth tugging up on one side. "Don't worry, Little Salt. You'll get used to it. Either that, or you'll die."

I was *not* going to die on the *Jersey*.

I was going to escape it.

=★=

Over the coming weeks, I didn't get used to the gruel, but I did eat it. Every bit I could keep down. Bread filled with weevils. Meat from some unknown source, sometimes the texture of soap, slick and hard, other times like hemp, pulling apart in strings. No matter its appearance, it always tasted the same. Like corroded copper and sand, and so salty that a drink of seawater would've been refreshing in comparison.

I ate it anyway. I needed the strength to escape.

Still, I grew thin. Then thinner. Then, barely a month after arriving, I was a skeleton like all the rest. This had only one benefit to me: my breasts, small to begin with, disappeared. But I remained on constant watch, searching for signs someone suspected the truth about "Little Salt," as I came to be known.

Days, we spent wandering the decks. Round and round in circles under the open sky, or down below when it was raining. I studied the *Jersey*'s creaks and cracks, learning every inch of the ship that a prisoner could know. I spotted the marines lazy in their sentry duties. Observed the tides, the bay, the shoreline. I saw no way out. The ship was well sealed, the bay too marshy and shallow to swim, the coastline patrolled regularly.

The descent into hell had been easy. But rising from it wouldn't be.

Still, I didn't lose hope. Years earlier, Hackett had said we were both survivors by nature—and he'd been right. I had a fierce will to live, and I badly wanted a chance to do it right.

Nights were worse than days, as we were shut inside the hold, which grew hot and loud with misery. In the darkness, every madman's ramblings and every sick man's moans came right into my ears and tightened a fist around my heart.

Mess three had it easier than most, as our place in the officer's section gave us a little more room. There, I'd lie awake between Hackett and King George, both snoring like hounds, and I'd convince myself that I was safe. That if I stayed right between them, no one would try to touch me. Most nights, it took hours before I believed it. Then I'd slowly stretch my legs out and dive into the seventh fathom, where I could go anywhere I wished.

Floating in that peacefulness, I imagined Lucy and Charlotte at garden concerts or at lavish assemblies, their petticoats flaring as they turned and danced with Duncan and André. I imagined Robert Townsend in his shop, a quiet hero behind his gentle smile and eyeglasses, a book open on the counter. I imagined Aunt Nora and Uncle Henry. The judge. Liesje and Rebecca. Everyone but Asa.

A little hope kept me going, lighting my way. But I feared too much would blind me.

=★=

As the weeks passed, I came to know my messmates and their reasons for being on the *Jersey*. Red and Wilkins were privateersmen from Rhode Island, caught by the British off the East Florida coast. King George was a militiaman from Maryland, captured aboard a packet ship. Tom Hackett had come to the cause of liberty after seeing "a hotheaded but decent lad beaten to hell and all but murdered by a press-gang." He'd been caught privateering outside Boston. Tim's reason I never learned, as he was bayoneted through the gut for trying to filch a piece of bread a few days after I arrived.

They asked about my past too, but I dodged their questions. I wanted to disappear amongst them; telling them I was a captured spy wouldn't have helped. But my silence on the matter only increased their curiosity. Finally, after a few weeks of being pestered, I told them I was an urchin from Cuba who'd joined the crew of a privateer to free myself from poverty. But I wasn't satisfied with my story, so the next day I told them I was actually a prince from a tiny kingdom on the Baltic coast that'd been invaded, so I'd fled to the high seas, where I'd been captured by pirates who'd soon after fallen prey to the British navy, therefore landing me on the *Jersey*. The day after that, Red scratched his jaw and said, "Where're you from today, Little Salt?" and I'd let a tale spool out that was even better.

So it'd been since. My imagination offered the only freedom I could have on the *Jersey*. I didn't at all mind sharing it.

As fall crept closer, the trees along Brooklyn's shores turned amber, gold, and red. New prisoners came to replace the dead and the sick who were transferred to medical ships—always much too late to do them any good. Our food was poisoned by salt and copper. Our rations put us on the path to starvation; our filthy quarters fed diseases that ran like wildfire through the hold.

You'll get used to it. Either that, or you'll die, Hackett had said that first day.

I got used to it.

If the departed men had valuables, like knit caps or good shoes or blankets, those were passed on. No one had a pocket watch for me, but one day a fife made its way into Hackett's hands. Then, sometimes, amid the weeping and the wailing and Fire Man's nonsense, in the unbroken dark of that miserable hold, he played it quiet, quiet, quiet, so as not to be heard by the guards. And we listened and felt rich.

=★=

One thundery afternoon in late October, a victualing ship came to Wallabout and moored at the mouth of the bay. We gathered at the rail to watch the tenders rowing toward us with hogsheads and crates, relishing the break from the usual tedium.

"What do you think those hogsheads are full of?" I asked. "Rice?" Food was our favorite topic.

"Lemons. I've been dreaming of lemons," said Red.

"Apples." King George licked his cracked lips. "I'd give my right arm for an apple."

"I'd give both my arms for wine," said Wilkins. "A bottle of Madeira and I'd die happy."

"Pails," Fire Man said behind me. "I hope they've brought sturdy pails."

"Look at Sproat, boys," Hackett said, his voice low. Serious. "Something's happening."

The *Jersey*'s commander stood at the bottom of the ramp with a newspaper, reading aloud to several marines, who shook their heads in disbelief.

I itched at the rough wool cap I'd inherited a few days before. "What do you think it is? News of a battle?"

More than we wanted food, we wanted news of the war. If America won, freedom would be ours—and we'd live.

"Don't think so," Hackett said. "They en't celebrating."

"They're not wallowing, either," King George said. "They look *furious*."

He was right. One of the marines turned away from Sproat and smacked his hand against a wood piling. I could hear another uttering blasphemies. Both were offenses Sprout should've punished, but he did nothing.

Other prisoners around us took notice. By the time Sproat

and the marines came aboard, the deck was crowded with men wanting to know what had stirred such hot responses.

Sproat stopped at the top of the boarding ramp, his lips pressed into a hard line, and swept a look over us—hundreds of prisoners, all silent and waiting. "You Americans are all immoral beasts lacking in spine, decency, and honor. Never dare to think otherwise," he declared. He crumpled the newspaper into a ball and chucked it as he stalked to his quarters. It hit Hackett's chest and he caught it against himself.

"Who's an able reader?" he said.

"Me—I am," I said, already sweeping the paper from his hands. "It's the *Boston Gazette*. Dated October sixteenth." I skimmed lower—barely lower—and spots burst before my eyes. My balance teetered. The world had begun to rotate around me.

"Go on, Salty. Read it."

I drew a breath, forcing steadiness into my body, and then I read—even as I struggled to absorb the very news I was sharing.

Treason had been committed by the Continental Army's star general, Benedict Arnold, who had conspired to turn over the fort of West Point on the North River to the British. Arnold's deception had been uncovered before coming to fruition when Major John André, his coconspirator and adjutant general to the British army, was captured across enemy lines. Plans describing the West Point garrison and a letter from General Arnold were found on Major André's person. General Arnold managed to escape capture and fled to British lines. He was now a commander in the British army. Major André, however, had been tried as a spy by the Continental Army and sentenced to death by hanging, the right to an officer's death denied him. The execution, ordered by General Washington, had been carried out on October second, concluding the disgraceful affair.

The *Jersey* was silent as I finished. Then a din of voices swirled up as men shouted in outrage and cursed Benedict Arnold.

Arnold, whom I now *finally* knew was Monk.

"The rotten traitor!" they yelled. "The Judas!"

Their anger only increased. Every man there had given his life for what Arnold had nearly undone.

In the midst of the commotion, I felt a pair of eyes regarding me steadily.

"That's some look you got on your face, Little Salt," Hackett said. "You gonna tell me what's going on?"

I couldn't find the words. My mind had filled with memories: André giving me a portrait tied with string. André telling me about the sets he was designing himself for *Macbeth*. André sighing wearily in Knyphausen's study, no idea I was watching him.

Hackett leaned in. "Were you part of this?" he whispered. "Finding Arnold out?"

"I think so." I'd never know for certain, but I *felt* I had been.

"That's why you're here? For *spying*?"

I nodded.

"My, my, Salty." He shook his head. "My, my."

There was awe and pride in his eyes, but I couldn't share in it. Not now.

I shoved through the men, pushing my way to the starboard rail. There I looked across the river to New York and cried for my fallen enemy and friend, John André.

CHAPTER 28

FRANNIE

★

I proved Hackett wrong and survived a month, then topped it with a few more.

"'Cause I like to gloat," I told him. But in early November, I began to feel myself weaken. Not in my mind, nor in my will. It was something else. Something inside me.

A weight had settled in my lungs that made me tired all the time and short of breath even when I was lying down. If I stood any chance of escaping, it had to happen soon, before I became too ill.

After months of mulling it over, I'd determined there was only one possible way of doing it. I would have to take my own dark leap—scaling the rail and diving into the shallow waters surrounding the *Jersey*. And then, as the immediate shores were well patrolled, I'd have to swim out of the bay and come ashore someplace far downriver.

I didn't know how I'd manage it. I couldn't even walk without tiring anymore—how was I going to swim for an hour, keeping ahead of boats pursuing me? But I couldn't wait. Winter would soon freeze Wallabout's waters to ice, making a leap from the rail impossible, and I doubted I'd last long enough to see next year's thaw.

If I didn't make my attempt soon, I never would.

=★=

The morning after a hard night's rain, I knew it was time. The waters in the bay were gurgling and rising with the storm runoff, which would make my dive safer. If I waited until high tide at dusk, it would be safer still. That decided it. I'd take my leap just before the guards ordered us belowdecks for the night.

"Haven't heard much blathering from you today, Salty," Hackett said.

I lifted my head from his shoulder, where I'd taken to resting it. We were huddled together in the curve of the bulwark, which was only partly keeping us out of the passing showers, but there'd been a small epidemic of intestinal upset below. Like dozens of others, we'd chosen rain over howling men squatting over buckets. "Why's it sound like you mind?" I asked.

"It gets dull without your stories of derring-do and whatever else. You're shaking. You shouldn't be out in such weather."

"'Cause I might come down with something?"

He gave me a look like he didn't appreciate my back talk, which I knew meant he did. I leaned against him again, my head such a heavy thing to carry. "I used to hate you, you know."

"Yep. I miss those days."

I smiled. Me and Hackett were the same. A little rotten, but not *all* rotten. The fight for America's independence had drawn us both in, giving us a way to be better than we really were. That was the best thing about noble ideas like freedom—anybody could get behind them.

I dozed off. When I stirred, I was on my side and Hackett was leaning over me, blocking the rain. "Move, you old wolf," I said, pushing him away. "You're crowding me."

"How do you feel? Any better?"

"Shut up, will you? And back off before I catch your fleas."

"You sound better."

I didn't feel it, but I didn't say so. I'd slept the entire day. Night was falling and a new storm had come in. Raindrops exploded furiously against the planks. Only a couple dozen other prisoners were still out, most hovering near the marines who were rummaging through a delivery crate. As soon as they finished, I knew they'd call us below for the night.

I pulled my legs in close, my heartbeat speeding up. "Remember Asa Lane, Hackett?"

"Mm-hmm. I do." He turned to me. "I remember you going moony-face around him. Are you gonna tell me about the mistakes you wish you could go back and fix?"

"I guess I don't have to anymore. And better to be moony-faced than scowly-faced."

"I'll say. You know, my own mother used to shut her eyes when she kissed me?"

He was trying to make me laugh, but I was too tired, and a thick feeling had stuck in my throat that wasn't humor. "You're a good man, Hackett."

For a few seconds, I listened to the rain hammer on the deck.

"Didn't used to be."

"But you are now, and that makes it even better."

He sniffed. "Hush, now. You're scaring me with such talk." He must've been really scared, 'cause he curled over his pipe and played me a quiet song, risking trouble with the guards. I shut my eyes and listened to the flute and the thunder and the rain, all weaving around each other.

"Tasker? Francis Tasker!" I struggled up from a thick tiredness. "Anybody know a Francis Tasker?" asked one of the marines unloading supplies.

"Me." I convinced my body to stand. "That's me." I slipped through the circle of men, Hackett right behind me. "I'm Francis Tasker."

"Somebody sent you vittles, Tasker," said the smug-faced marine I knew as Nanton. Rain poured from the corners of his cocked hat in small waterfalls. He hoisted a linen sack from the crate and dropped it on the deck with a thump. He smirked. "Have a look at what we'll be enjoying on your behalf." He crouched and fumbled with the twine at the top, struggling to untie it in the rain and wind.

"Looks like oats," said one of the other marines.

"Beans," said another. "Everybody always sends beans."

Nanton lost patience and used his sword to slice off the top of the sack; then he peered into it. "Well, damn my eyes." He laughed and stood. "On second thought, Tasker, you can keep this generous gift yourself." He kicked the bag, which toppled over.

Sand spilled across the deck. Fine white sand.

Enough to stand on with both feet.

Asa.

I looked toward the river. With night falling and the sheets of rain, I couldn't see anything—not Manhattan's shores on the other side, nor any ships moored or cruising by—but he was out there. I knew it. He *had* to be.

"What is this?" Hackett stared at the sand. It was already washing away, disappearing into the deck's seams.

"A message," I said. "It's a message, Hackett."

His eyes went wide. "Well, well. Here we go."

He knew exactly what I meant to do.

"Play me something, will you? And make it loud."

"With pleasure, Little Salt." He bowed. "It has been my honor." He strode away and brought the flute to his lips, the first notes bursting into the air.

I didn't hesitate—I headed for the bow.

I passed two sentries, but neither of them spared me a glance. Their eyes were locked on Hackett. His flute was beginning to sound half drowned and warbly, but I recognized the song, "Yankee Doodle," and felt a bubble of laughter push up. I passed another sentry leaving his post, drawn by Hackett's antics, and finally reached the bow. I climbed onto the lookout platform that had just been abandoned and stood at the very nose of the *Jersey*.

The wind whipped up, and the swirling rain flew into my eyes. Far, far below, the bay's waters looked frothy with wind and chop.

It was time. It was *time*. But I couldn't resist a look back.

Hackett's flute had been all but overpowered by the rain. His piping was garbled, every third note flying, but he'd improvised and was dancing as he played, kicking his legs and elbows out like a fool. King George stood, gaping at him, his court wig pale in the stormy dark. Then he swept his gaze over the deck, spotted me, and broke into a mad, capering dance. Red jumped in without hesitation, then Wilkins, then Fire Man. Others came over in curiosity and were immediately swept up, till there were dozens of them, gamboling on their very graves. Singing their spirits out as the rain washed over them.

The British guards laughed and pointed, but I'd never seen anything more beautiful in all my life.

With a final glance at Hackett piping away in the middle of it all, I turned back to my escape. I shuffled to the edge of the platform. Peered down and felt my heart shoot into my throat. Never had I dove from so high. Not even close.

"*Halt!* You there—*stop!*"

Gathering every bit of my strength, I threw myself into the sky—and fell for miles and leagues and fathoms. An instant, a lifetime. Then I punched through the surface. Frigid water shot into my nostrils, my ears. Shocked my heart. But then it steadied me, slowed me, and I realized I had done it. I was still alive.

I kicked, spearing my arms above me, bringing myself back to the surface. I broke into the rainy night and pulled in air, pain flaring in my weakened lungs. Muskets cracked above me, marines firing from the platform where I'd just stood. Water exploded beside me—inches away.

I gulped in air and dove. Pushed my arms through dark water. Kicking. Kicking. Never stopping. Not to breathe. Not to think beyond leaving the bay and making it out to open water. As I swam, I sensed the bullets slicing around me, but I kept going, even when one found my calf and bit.

The water deepened beneath me. I could feel the space opening, widening like the sky. I kicked deeper—to one fathom.

Lord, I prayed. Please give me a chance to do this right.

And kicked harder, to two fathoms.

Then three. And there I saw Emmeline Coates, alive, beautiful. Thank you, I told her. Thank you for letting me borrow your life. I swam through her, past her, down to four fathoms. To Lucy and Charlotte. The Holdridges. I begged forgiveness for the hole I'd made in their lives.

The fifth fathom. *Malcolm.*

The sixth. *André.*

I swore I'd always keep them both inside my heart.

Then I reached it—the seventh—and the water released me. I relaxed my body and let myself float. West End appeared, its white beach stretching out before me. The water clearer than glass. And there, in the distance, a young man walked the shore in a patient, uneven stride.

Mama, I whispered. Mama, I have done it.

I've lived for something more, and it's you, and it's love, and liberty, and friendship, and hope—and all the other *mores* that can ever be.

And it's *me*, Mama.

Frannie.

CHAPTER 29

THE SEVENTH FATHOM

★

I broke the surface and treaded water as I caught my breath.

The *Jersey* was well away, but the boats that had been launched to chase me down were much closer. Lanterns swung this way and that as men searched the river.

I laughed. They'd never catch me.

My calf was bleeding. I was wheezing. Dying. But I still had a few breaths left.

There was no point deciding which direction to swim—all was darkness and rain and choppy waves—so I just followed the current.

With every kick, I felt a gathering within me. I had forgotten—Frannie was *strong*. Strong enough to swim around the world.

I lost myself in the strokes, entering a clearness of mind. A peacefulness I felt down to my soul. Then a voice filtered in.

I stopped and kicked in place, listening. Staring into the rainy night.

"Frannie!"

I turned to the sound and smiled. Then I put my head down and swam.

AUTHOR'S NOTE

"355" was real.

I learned about her when—hoping to fill some of the gaps in my education—I dove into the internet in search of "women I should know." There she was—an eighteenth-century spy. A woman who had found a way to insert herself into a pivotal moment in American history.

What do we know of 355 that's provable in the historical record? Not a whole lot. She was an active participant in the Culper spy network, which operated in New York City during the American Revolution. In the Culper code book, "355" corresponds to the word "lady," which suggests that she was of elevated social status. And we know that, at least in one instance, the Culper spies relied on 355 to "outwit them all."

Little as that is, when I learned these things, I was hooked.

In the eighteenth century, spying was dishonorable and unseemly—far from the stylishly appealing job portrayed in modern film and television. I began to wonder . . . what sort of lady would have risked her reputation to spy? And she didn't just defy king and country. At that time, politics was overwhelmingly the domain of wealthy white men—and yet 355 defied the norms of her sex to engage in this landscape in a bold, though secretive, way.

I couldn't resist the urge to know her better. Thus Francisca Tasker was born—over four years of research and writing.

Though it has been suggested that 355 played a role in uncovering Benedict Arnold's treachery, her involvement is not provable in the historical record. History does tell us, however, that Benedict Arnold scoured New York City for rebel spies after he turned coat and became a British general. A spy from Culper Ring, within which 355 operated, was among those who were captured and imprisoned. This upset Robert Townsend so deeply that he left New York for a time.

I like to think 355 *did* contribute to foiling Arnold's plan to turn over West Point. Had he pulled it off, the war might have had a very different outcome. Whatever impact 355 made, big or small, in my eyes she was a trailblazer and a heroine.

Frannie represents the imaginative leap I took from the facts available on 355, but many figures in *Rebel Spy* were real. George Washington, of course. Benedict Arnold, whose very name connotes treachery. For the English side, General Henry Clinton and Major John André, who conspired with Benedict Arnold and paid the ultimate price for it.

The Culper spy network had a handful of central figures, and Robert Townsend was one of them. A storeowner in British-occupied New York, Townsend was in a key position to obtain intelligence—and then funnel it through dead drops and furtive exchanges to the other Culper spies so that it ultimately ended up in General George Washington's hands. (Washington was quite a spymaster. Recognizing his steep disadvantage against the mightier British military, he sent out scouts and spy networks, using their information to help bridge the gap.) Anna Strong was also deeply involved with the Culper spies. Some even believe she was 355. Though not a Culper spy, Elizabeth Burgin was also real and received a pension from Washington himself for her efforts in freeing some two hundred men from the prison hulks in Wallabout Bay. (To date, no one has uncovered how she accomplished this.)

There were vast social disparities in America in 1776. The slave trade forced unimaginable horrors on hundreds of thousands for whom liberty was utterly out of reach. Native Americans were stripped of sacred lands and wrenched into a war that was not of their making. Experiences varied widely, depending on one's race, class, sex, location, and political paradigm. This book focuses on the highly privileged, wealthy white class. I chose to make Frannie an immigrant because the experience is close to me.

The histories of the American Revolution lean on the contributions of men: The Founding Fathers. The Sons of Liberty. Paul Revere's brave ride and Nathan Hale's brave words. But women also played important roles in the war. They held farmsteads and families together. They served as nurses, fund-raisers, political writers, spies, and much more. They filled the spaces that were allowed them—and a few found ways to go beyond. For more than any other reason, I wrote this story to help shed a little light on a great woman of the past in hopes that doing so will illuminate the path forward for many others.

Facts inspired and informed this story. The horrors of the prison hulks in Wallabout Bay, for example, have not been exaggerated. Historians estimate that as many as twelve thousand men died in them, more than twice the number of casualties suffered on the battlefield. I have endeavored to fit the fictional elements of this story into the realities of the time. On the occasions where the historical record varies, such as the date of celebration for the queen's birthday, I chose to use the information that best suited the narrative. Any allowances I made were as minor as I could keep them, and done in the service of telling a story of a young woman who was a true patriot.

ACKNOWLEDGMENTS

Rebel Spy is about a brave and intelligent young woman I greatly admire. I have been blessed to know many such women in my life, a few of whom were indispensable in the creation of this book.

Tina Dubois has been a constant champion of mine and Frannie's from day one. Tina, your compassion and support have made all the difference. The "pipe scene" was for you. I am so fortunate you're my agent; thank you for letting me daydream as I paced the shallows. Thanks also to Berni Barta and Tamara Kawar for your efforts on my behalf. I'm proud to be represented by an agency that attracts such good minds as yours. I'd be remiss if I didn't also mention Roxane Edouard; thank you, Roxane, for everything you have done for me behind the scenes.

Kate Sullivan provided passionate and thoughtful editorial guidance as I wrote *Rebel Spy*, not to mention an abundance of patience and encouragement. Thank you so much, Kate, for loving 355 and giving me a chance to tell her story. Effusive thanks are also due to Wendy Loggia, who brought a new energy and perspective to the manuscript, along with a fresh wave of support. My gratitude also goes to Beverly Horowitz for her belief in this book, and to Alexandra Hightower, Audrey Ingerson, and Alison Romig for their help along the way.

The stunning cover for *Rebel Spy* was designed by the ridiculously talented Ray Shappell, with art provided by the equally talented artist Ze Otavio. I'm in love with it. Cheers to you both.

Colleen Fellingham, Heather Lockwood Hughes, and Alison Kolani helped pull a raw manuscript into publishable shape. So much work goes into editing, designing, and marketing books. Thank you, and everyone who's been part of *Rebel Spy*'s journey at Delacorte, for your help.

Researching 355 and the American Revolution was an ongoing process that began in earnest nearly four years ago. Thank you, Tory Inloes, for your enthusiastic emails filled with references for me to explore. Thanks also to Nicole VanderMeer for your exhaustive and detailed research on my behalf; this story was informed and improved through your findings. JT Marcinkowski also helped me with organization and research; I'm rooting for you, JT!

A few years ago, I took a guided walking tour of Revolutionary-era New York with Karen Quinones. Three hours later, I had a new friend. Karen, it's wonderful to have someone to talk bathing machines and bundling with. Thank you for answering my questions, and for reading an early draft and providing your feedback. Kyle Dalton also read an early draft and provided valuable insight into the clothing, historical, and nautical details of the era. My cocked hat's off to you, Kyle. Mahalo to world-class free-diver Mandy Sumner for shedding light on diving and the zone of neutral buoyancy, aka Frannie's seventh fathom. Majelissa Sa Carvalho, Carolina Farfan Namen, and Valerie Congdon fielded my questions about Spain and France. *Gracias, merci,* and *thank you!*

My research took me to quite a few institutions. At the following ones in particular, I discovered rich historical collections and staff who went out of their way to help me: the New-York Historical Society, George Washington's Mount Vernon, the Smithsonian Museum of American History, Fraunces Tavern Museum, and Charleston Museum. Thanks also to the Historical Novel Society for providing a welcoming place for a first-time historical novelist to land.

I delved into primary source documents in my research as much as I could, but I also ended up reading more than sixty books on the American Revolution, covering everything from foods to fashions to social customs, not to mention the texts that focused on the war itself. A few of these books were especially helpful and never far from reach: *New York City During the War for Independence* by Oscar Theodore Barck, Jr., PhD; *Through Colonial Doorways* by Anne Hollingsworth Wharton; *Valiant Ambition* by Nathaniel Philbrick; *Revolution on the Hudson* by George C. Daughan; *Scars of Independence* by Holger Hoock; *Washington's Spies* by Alexander Rose; *George Washington's Secret Six* by Brian Kilmeade and Don Yaeger; *Narratives of the American Revolution*, edited by Hugh F. Rankin; *The Two Spies* by Morton Pennypacker; *To Be Useful to the World: Women in Revolutionary America 1740– 1790* by Joan R. Gundersen; *Revolutionary Mothers: Women in the Struggle for America's Independence* and *First Generations: Women in Colonial America*, both by Carol Berkin. Thank you to all the authors and historians above; your books provided the winds that filled this story's sails.

Only another writer can truly relate to a writer. Luckily for me, I have incredible writing friends with whom I could share the journey of creating this book. Kim Turrisi, Lorin Oberweger,

Katy Longshore, Talia Vance, Donna Cooner, Kristen Held, Beth Hull, Bret Ballou, Lucien Nanton, Kim Liggett, Tamara Ireland Stone, Lia Keyes, and Trish Doller: you kept me smiling when I was wandering and brought me back to the path. Susan Dennard, Kim Liggett, Martha Brokenbrough, and Jessica Spotswood, I am so honored to have your words of support for *Rebel Spy*.

Fritz and Phyllis Grupe, thank you for your boundless wisdom, kindness, and flexibility; I truly have *enjoyed the ride*. Mustafa Cochinwalla and Lisa Parris surprised me with a trip to "the room where it happened," and I'm forever grateful. Thank you also to the Society of Children's Book Writers and Illustrators for being such a pillar in my writing life, from the early days to now.

Friends have endured my absence at countless social gatherings, never once making me feel guilty for missing out because "I'm on deadline." Thank you for your understanding and forgiveness. There are so many of you I want to acknowledge, but I'd rather wrap this up so I can finally make it to those gatherings and thank you in person.

Finally, to my family, every bit of my love and gratitude. Thank you for being my Reason.

ABOUT THE AUTHOR

VERONICA ROSSI is the *New York Times* and *USA Today* best-selling author of the Under the Never Sky series. She was born in Rio de Janeiro, grew up in California, and graduated from UCLA. She lives in the San Francisco Bay Area with her husband and two sons, the youngest of whom just surpassed her in height.

veronicarossi.com